THE WAKE-UP CALL

BETH O'LEARY

QUERCUS

First published in Great Britain in 2023 by

QUERCUS

Quercus Editions Ltd
Carmelite House
50 Victoria Embankment
London EC4Y 0DZ

An Hachette UK company

A CIP catalogue record for this book is available
from the British Library

HB ISBN 978 1 52941 824 8
TPB ISBN 978 1 52941 825 5
EBOOK ISBN 978 1 52941 827 9

10 9 8 7 6 5 4 3 2 1

Text designed and typeset by CC Book Production
Printed and bound in Great Britain by Clays Ltd, Elcograf S.p.A.

Papers used by Quercus Editions Ltd are from well-managed forests
and other responsible sources.

For my readers.
I treasure every one of you.

December 2021

Dear Lucas,

I have a confession to make, and I'm kind of nervous about it, which is why you're getting it in your Christmas card. (Merry Christmas, by the way.)

Whenever we cross paths at the hotel, something strange happens. I get hot. Jittery. Say weird things like 'good morrow!', and forget what it is I'm chatting to a guest about, and look at you instead of looking at whichever of Barty's menu additions Arjun wants to disagree with today.

I'm not usually the sort of person to get infatuated. I'm more of the slow-burn, warm-and-cosy type. And I DON'T lose my head over a guy — I never have. But when I look at you, I get all . . . flustered.

And when you look at me, I wonder if you might feel the same thing. I've been waiting for you to say something, really. But my friend Jem pointed out that maybe you just think I'm not available, or maybe you're not big on sharing how you feel, or maybe I just need to woman up and make the first move.

So here I am. Putting my cosy warm heart on the line to say: I like you. A lot.

If you feel the same way, meet me under the mistletoe at 8 p.m. I'll be the one in the pink dress. And also the one who is Izzy the receptionist. I don't know why I said the pink dress thing.

I'm going to stop writing now, because . . . I've run out of space. And dignity. See you at 8?

Izzy xxx

Dear Izzy,

Merry Christmas and Happy New Year.

Regards,
Lucas

November 2022

Izzy

If Lucas is doing something, I have to be doing it too, but better.

This has generally been very good for my career over the last year, but it does mean that right now I am grappling with a fir-tree branch which measures at least twice my height and four times my width.

'Do you need help?' Lucas asks.

'Absolutely not. Do you?'

I swing my branch into position and narrowly avoid smashing one of the many vases around the lobby. I'm always dodging those things. Like much of the furniture at Forest Manor Hotel and Spa, the vases come from the Bartholomew family, who own the estate. Morris Bartholomew (Barty) and his wife, Uma Singh-Bartholomew (Mrs SB), have turned the grand house into a hotel, and they've repurposed as many of the old family furnishings as possible. I am all for an upcycle – it's kind of my thing – but there's something urn-like about some of these vases.

9

I can't shake the thought that one of them might contain an old Bartholomew.

'Is that whimsical?' Lucas asks me, pausing to examine my fir branch.

I'm tying it to the bottom of my side of the staircase. The Forest Manor staircase is famous – it's one of those gorgeous sweeping ones that splits in two midway and just begs you to walk down it slowly in a wedding dress, or maybe arrange your children up it for an adorable Von-Trapp-ish family photograph.

'Is that?' I ask, pointing to the potted tree Lucas has hauled in from the garden and placed at the bottom of *his* side of the staircase.

'Yes,' he says, with absolute confidence. 'It is an olive tree. Olives are very whimsical.'

We are dressing the lobby for tomorrow's wedding – the bride's theme is 'winter whimsy'. Lucas and I have decided that asymmetry is whimsical, so we are each doing one side of the staircase. The trouble is, if Lucas goes big, I have to go bigger, so now quite a lot of the garden is in the lobby.

'They're also Mediterranean.'

Lucas looks at me flatly, like, *Your point is?*

'We're in the New Forest. It's November.'

Lucas frowns. I give up.

'What about my silver fairy lights, then?' I ask, gesturing to the small, sparkling lights woven through the greenery that now runs up my bannister. 'Do you think we need some on your side too?'

'No. They're tacky.'

I narrow my eyes. Lucas finds everything about me tacky. He hates my clip-in highlights, my baby-pink trainers, my fondness for supernatural teen dramas. He doesn't get that life is too short for rules about what's cool and what's not cool; life's for living. In full HD. And baby-pink trainers.

'They're cute and twinkly!'

'They're so bright. Like little daggers. No.'

He unfolds his arms and places his hands on his hips instead. Lucas likes to take up as much space as possible. This is presumably why he is always at the gym, so that he can claim yet another inch of my airspace with his ever-broadening shoulders and his bulging biceps.

I take a deep, calming breath. Once this wedding is over, Lucas and I can go back to alternating shifts wherever possible. These days, things don't go well if we're at the front desk together for too long. Mrs SB says it 'doesn't seem to create quite the right atmosphere'. Arjun, the head chef, says 'when Izzy and Lucas are on shift at the same time the hotel is about as welcoming as my grandmother's house', and I've met Arjun's grandmother, so I can say with confidence that this was a very rude remark.

But Lucas and I are the most experienced front-of-house staff at the hotel, and we're the ones who manage weddings, which means that for the next two days, I have to endure nonstop Lucasness.

'Come up to the landing,' Lucas barks. 'See what I am seeing.'

He's always so *commanding*. When I first met Lucas, I thought his Brazilian accent was so sexy – I forgave his rudeness, called it a translation issue, decided he meant well but things didn't quite come out right. But over time, I have learned that Lucas has an excellent grasp of English – he is just an arse.

I traipse up to the central landing, where the staircase splits in two, and take it all in. Our lobby is huge, with a gigantic wooden front desk along the left-hand side, old-fashioned keys dangling on the wall behind it. There's a worn circular rug over the original brown and cream tiles, and a soft-seating area by the tall windows looking out at the lawn. It's gorgeous. And in the last eight years, it's become a home to me – maybe even more so than the little pastel-coloured flat I rent in Fordingbridge.

'This is a classy hotel,' Lucas says. 'The fairy lights look cheap.'

They *were* cheap. What does he expect? Our budget is – as always – non-existent.

'This is a *family* hotel,' I say, just as the Hedgers family walk into the lobby, right on cue. Three kids, all hand in hand, the littlest one toddling along in a snowsuit with his pudgy fingers tucked inside his sister's.

'Wow!' says the oldest, stopping in his tracks to stare at my sparkling bannister. The youngest almost takes a tumble; his sister yanks him upright. 'That looks so cool!'

I shine my smuggest smile in Lucas's direction. He continues to glower. The children look slightly disconcerted, and then intrigued.

I have noticed this phenomenon before. Lucas *should* be terrible with children – he's huge and scowly and doesn't know how to talk to them. But they always seem to find him fascinating. The other day I heard him greet Middle Hedgers (real name: Ruby Hedgers, age six, favourite hobbies include martial arts, ponies and climbing things that aren't safe) by saying, 'Good morning, how did you sleep? I hope well?' It is exactly what he says to adult guests, delivered in the exact same tone. But Ruby loved it. 'Oh, I slept *all* night,' she told him, with great importance. 'When it was seven on my clock, I got up and stood by Mummy and Daddy's bed until they woke up too, and Daddy didn't think I was there, so he screamed, and it was *so* funny.' To which Lucas nodded, quite serious, and said, 'That sounds like a horrible way to be woken,' and Ruby descended into fits of giggles.

Bizarre.

'The children like the fairy lights,' I tell Lucas, spreading my hands.

'The children also like shoes with wheels in them, and Haribo, and they will eat Arjun's ice-cream sundaes until they are sick,' Lucas says. 'Children cannot be trusted.'

I glance at the grown-up Hedgers to make sure they aren't offended by Lucas's comments, but they're ushering the kids into their room and don't seem to have heard. They're in Sweet Pea, because Mrs Hedgers is a wheelchair user – the lifts have been broken for over a month now, and it's been a nightmare with only five downstairs bedrooms.

'No fairy lights on my side. We should take those ones down, too.'

'Oh my God! Can't you just compromise and say, fine, let's use fairy lights but more sparingly, or something?'

'They hurt my eyes. It's a no.'

'When you work with someone you can't just say *it's a no* and leave it at that.'

'Why not?'

'You have to meet me halfway.'

'Why?'

'Because! It's reasonable!'

'Ah. Reasonable like reorganising the stationery every time you are on shift so that I can never find things?'

'That's not why I do it. I do it because your way is—'

'Reasonable?'

'Crap!' I say, belatedly glancing towards Sweet Pea to make sure the door has closed behind the Hedgers' children. 'Your way is crap. The drawer always gets jammed because you put the hole-puncher in on its side and the Post-its should be at the front because we use them all the time but they're right at the back, behind the with-compliments slips, which we never use, so excuse me for saving you time!'

'Is it reasonable to renumber the rooms without telling me?'

'That was Mrs SB's idea! I was just following orders!'

'Did she order you not to tell me?'

We're squared up now, and somehow I've ended up with my hands on my hips too, a posture I have only ever adopted when pretending to be a superhero (something you do surprisingly often when you work in a family-friendly hotel).

'I just forgot. I'm a human being. Sue me.'

'You didn't forget to tell Poor Mandy.'

Mandy is the other permanent member of the front-of-house team. She is not actually poor in the financial sense – she has just become known as 'Poor Mandy' here at Forest Manor Hotel and Spa because she's always stuck between me and Lucas when we're arguing about something. Poor Mandy doesn't care about the way the stationery drawer is arranged. She just wants some peace and quiet.

'Well, Poor Mandy didn't specifically tell me never to message her outside of working hours, so I probably WhatsApped her about it.'

'I did not say, don't message me outside of working hours. I just said that *bombarding* me with hotel administration at eleven at night on a Sunday is not—'

'Reasonable,' I say, through gritted teeth. 'Right, of course. Well, if you're so keen on *reasonable*, we'll stick to reasonable un-fairy-lit bannisters and we'll host a reasonably good wedding and Barty and Mrs SB will make the reasonable decision to close the hotel because it's no longer viable. Is that what you want?'

'Are you under the impression that you can save Forest Manor Hotel and Spa with large quantities of twinkly lights?'

'Yes!' I shout. 'No! I mean, it's not about the decorations per se, it's about going the extra mile. Forest Manor is *so* perfect for this time of year, and if this wedding goes well, then every single guest will go away thinking the hotel is gorgeous and they should minibreak here, or have their engagement party here, and that means we're that little bit closer to staying afloat in 2023.'

'Izzy, the hotel cannot be saved by a few minibreaks or engagement parties. We need investment.'

I don't respond to this. It's not because I agree with him, or because – God forbid – I'm letting Lucas have the last word. It's because the ceiling has just fallen in on our heads.

Lucas

One moment Izzy is glaring up at me, fierce and spiky, with her hands planted on her hips. And the next, she is on top of me, small and soft and smelling of cinnamon sugar, with half the ceiling on top of her.

I have no understanding of how we got from A to B here.

'Oh my God,' Izzy says, rolling off me in a cloud of plaster. 'Did I just save your life?'

'No,' I say. It is best to say no when Izzy asks you a question. 'What?'

'The ceiling fell in,' she says, pointing at the ceiling. Helpful, as ever. 'And I threw myself over you to save you.'

I lie there beside her. We are both on our backs on the landing. High above us, the ceiling gapes open. I can see the old wall lamps in the first-floor hallway.

This is not good.

I turn my head to look at Izzy. Her cheeks are flushed and

her pink-striped hair is all over the place, but she appears unharmed. There is a chunk of plaster behind her head, large enough to have killed one of us. I suddenly feel very cold.

'Thank you, then, I suppose,' I say.

Her expression sours and she stands, brushing her legs down.

'You're welcome,' she says. When Izzy says this to me, it translates as *go to hell, arsehole.* If she were speaking to anybody else, it would no doubt be entirely sincere. But when it comes to me, whatever Izzy's saying, the subtext is essentially always *vai à merda, cuzão.*

Nobody but me seems to notice this. Everyone else thinks Izzy is 'nice' and 'fun' and 'sweet'. Even Arjun treats her like a princess, and Arjun treats our customers in the way that a famous musician might treat his fans – with a sort of fond contempt. But then, Arjun didn't have Izzy yelling *You're not good enough for her anyway, you cold-hearted shiny-shoed robot-man!* at him across the hotel gardens last Christmas.

Izzy does appear to have just saved my life though, so I try to be polite.

'I am very grateful,' I say. 'And I apologise that I did not throw myself over you first. I had assumed you would be able to look after yourself.'

This doesn't go down well. She glowers at me. Izzy has a whole range of glowers and glares. She has big green eyes and very long eyelashes, and always draws little black flicks on the edges of her eyelids. When I think about Izzy, which is as rarely as possible, I see those eyes narrowed at me. Catlike and bright.

'I *can* look after myself,' she says.

'Yes,' I say. 'I know. That's why I didn't save you.'

'Hello?' someone calls from upstairs.

'Shit,' Izzy mutters, craning her neck to look up at the hole in the ceiling. 'Mrs Muller?'

For all her faults, Izzy has an exceptional memory for our guests. If you've stayed with us once, Izzy will know your son's name, your breakfast order and your star sign. Though even I remember Mrs Muller: she stays here often, always upsetting the cleaning team by getting splodges of paint everywhere while she works on her art. She's in her seventies, half German, half Jamaican, with an accent that I find frustratingly challenging, and a tendency to tip the hotel staff as though we're in America, which I don't mind at all.

'Call the fire brigade,' Izzy hisses at me, before returning her attention to Mrs Muller. 'Mrs Muller, please be very careful! There's been a – slight – umm—'

'Accident,' I suggest.

'Issue,' Izzy says. 'There's been a slight issue with the floor! But we're getting it sorted right away.'

We both try to peer through the hole. We need to do something before any of the other fifty guests currently staying at Forest Manor happen to step out of their bedrooms and risk falling down a storey or two.

'Mrs Muller, please step back!' I say, then head down the steps to the lobby – it is just as dangerous for us as it is for her. 'You should move too,' I tell Izzy over my shoulder.

She ignores me. Well, I tried. I eye the damage to the staircase and get my phone out to dial 190, then remember it's not that in the UK, it's . . .

'Nine nine nine,' Izzy says.

'I know that,' I snap. I'm already calling.

A shower of plaster comes cascading down from the hole, dousing Izzy in dust. She splutters, her long brown-and-pink hair now covered in white powder.

'Whoa,' says an excited voice from behind me. I turn to see Ruby Hedgers, the six-year-old, in the doorway of Sweet Pea. 'Is it snowing?'

'No,' I tell her, 'it is just structural damage. Hello, yes, fire brigade, please . . .'

The hotel is swarming with firefighters. Izzy is being unprofessionally flirtatious with one of the particularly handsome ones. I am in a very bad mood.

It has been a stressful morning. Understandably, the guests are a little disturbed by all this. Several of them did not take well to being posted out of windows and down ladders. One of the firefighters told us that the damage to the ceiling and staircase has 'no quick fix' and said 'this is going to be a big job', and in case that wasn't clear enough, he rubbed his forefinger and thumb together, a gesture that means the same in Brazil as it does here: money, money, money.

This is the root of all our problems at Forest Manor Hotel and Spa. As I understand it, the hotel was thriving before the pandemic, but business suffered badly during the Covid lockdowns, which coincided with the entire roof needing replacing. Now we are limping along, unable to give the hotel the renovation it needs. When I started here two years ago, Forest Manor was already looking tired; it has lost even more of its luxuriousness, and that, in turn, means prices have had to drop, even in our award-winning restaurant.

But the heart of this place remains the same. I truly believe there is no hotel in England quite as special as this one. I knew it the moment I first stepped into the lobby and saw the guests reading newspapers on the sofas in their hotel slippers, looking out at the children playing on the lawns. It was the picture of comfort. We treasure our guests here – the moment I hand them their key, they become part of our family.

'Lucas, right?' says a voice behind me, a hand clapping down on my shoulder.

I steel myself, placing my precious third coffee of the day on the lobby table. Of course, we don't always like *every* member of our family.

Louis Keele is staying in Wood Aster, one of the downstairs suites, for the next two months while he's in the area on business. It is our finest room, and Louis likes the finest things. *People don't appreciate quality any more*, he told a colleague the other day on their way through the lobby. I imagine it is much easier to 'appreciate' quality when your father made several million pounds on the property market in the 90s, but I wouldn't know.

'Yes, Mr Keele. The hotel is being evacuated,' I say.

He knows this, obviously. There are firefighters everywhere, and there is a cordon across the doorway that Louis has just ducked under. Also, a lot of the ceiling is on the staircase.

'I'm very sorry, but you'll need to vacate your room for a short time, just while we get all this sorted.'

He is looking at 'all this' with interest. I clench my fists. Louis puts me on edge. There is something hungry underneath his easy smile – something calculating. He was here last Christmas, and even then he was asking Mrs SB if she would consider selling to his father's company – or, as he calls it, 'the Keele family firm'. She had laughed and told him no, but the situation is so different now. We were in serious financial trouble *before* the ceiling caved in.

Louis whistles slowly, tucking his hands in his trouser pockets. 'This sort of damage, with the broader renovations needed here . . .' He grimaces in sympathy. 'Excuse the crude language, but you guys are in real deep shit, aren't you?'

'Louis!' Izzy trills, appearing from the dining room and shooting me a warning look that suggests my expression is not as obliging as it should be. 'Let me take you outside. We're having an impromptu winter picnic under the pergola, or the pergoda, or the pagoda, I have actually never known what the difference is between all of those, but you know what I mean.'

She has her hand on his arm. Izzy is very tactile for a Brit – with everyone except me.

'Mrs SB called,' Izzy says to me over her shoulder as she leads Louis away. 'Someone needs to phone the already-hysterical bride whose wedding just got cancelled. I told her how passionate you were about the set-up for tomorrow's wedding and said you'd be the perfect person to make the bride feel heard.'

I grit my teeth. Izzy knows I do not enjoy emotional

conversations. The only consolation is that I have already signed Izzy up to help Barty fill in a forty-four-page insurance document which he has definitely downloaded in the wrong format. It will be pure torture for her.

'And she wants to see us both in the office at five,' Izzy adds.

It is only as the front door creaks shut behind Izzy and Louis that I realise what this is likely to mean.

Even if it is safe to use the downstairs of the hotel, that leaves us with five bedrooms instead of twenty-five. They are five of the most expensive bedrooms, which is something, but still, it's a fraction of what we'd usually earn over the winter months, and doesn't exactly require a full front-of-house team. In the average week, Izzy and I would each share the desk with one of the agency receptionists Mrs SB employs, and endure our one overlap day (Monday. The gloomiest of days). Mandy would take most of the evening shifts, when only one receptionist is required.

If I were Mrs SB, I would be looking to cut a member of front-of-house staff. Given the short notice, she will probably have to pay the agency receptionists even if they don't come in, and Mandy is an old family friend of Barty's.

Which leaves . . . me and Izzy.

Izzy

It's five o'clock. I've got my pitch ready. I've had some useful feedback from Arjun, who said I was focusing a bit too much on why I was better at my job than Lucas, which doesn't make me sound like a team player. I disagree, obviously – if anyone isn't a team player, it's Lucas. He's always annoying housekeeping, and he once made Ollie cry when the dishwasher broke. But maybe I don't need the slide about how my booking book is better than his online booking system in literally every way.

Now that the two of us are standing side by side outside Opal Cottage – the old gate house where the Singh-Bartholomews live – I am finding myself feeling a teeny bit sorry for Lucas. He looks as anxious as I feel. It's a freezing cold day, and the grass is still wet from this morning's sleet, but he's rolled his shirt-sleeves up and keeps tugging at his collar as if he's too hot. He catches my eye, and I am *just* considering smiling at him when he says, 'By the way, I reorganised your box for you.'

All thoughts of smiling evaporate.

'My box o'bits?'

Lucas's expression shifts from 'tense and implacable' to a subtle 'I tire of your nonsense'.

'The box that you keep under our desk, filled with your belongings, yes.'

'You can't go through my box o'bits! That's been there for eight years!'

'That was obvious from the contents,' Lucas says. 'It was easy to condense it into a smaller, more sensible container when I removed all the out-of-date packets of sweets.'

'Sweets never go off! Tell me you did *not* throw anything away.'

He regards me flatly. 'I kick that box at least twice per day. I have asked you repeatedly to move it. Rationalising the contents seemed like a compromise. Aren't you always telling me to compromise?'

'Excuse me? You've been kicking my box? There are breakables in there, you know.' Well, my *Teen Wolf* mug. But that is *very* precious.

Mrs SB opens the door and we snap to attention. It's obvious that her day has been a lot more stressful than mine – and mine has been nonstop chaos. She's wearing a cardigan, but only has one arm in a sleeve. The other is just dangling down her back like a bright pink tail. She has a phone trapped between her shoulder and cheek, and her usually flamboyant eyeshadow is an ominously boring shade of taupe. She gestures us inside, cardigan arm flapping, and says into the phone, 'Absolutely, yes, that won't be a problem at all,' while pulling a face.

She flaps her hands at the armchairs in the entrance hall where she seems to have nested, judging by the half-eaten bowl of pasta, the hooded blanket draped over a chair arm, and the important-looking paperwork strewn everywhere. Barty waves at us from the kitchen without looking up – he is literally elbow-deep in ring-binder files, his spectacles balanced on the tip of his long, aristocratic nose.

Lucas sits down gingerly, as though all the chaos might be catching. I settle in with my laptop bag clutched to my chest, trying to remember my opening lines. *In the last eight years at Forest Manor, I have become an invaluable member of the team, coordinating everything from large-scale weddings to . . .*

'Hi,' Mrs SB says on an exhale once she's hung up the phone. 'You two are a sight for sore eyes. Is it still a crime scene over there?'

She waves her hands at the window that looks over the hotel. Lucas and I exchange a quick glance.

'There's a lot going on,' I say brightly. 'But things have calmed now that Barty's sorted everyone temporary accommodation, and I've got four builders coming around for quotes . . .'

'And I have contacted three structural engineers,' Lucas butts in. 'The work is far too extensive for a regular builder to manage.'

Mrs SB's eyes widen at *far too extensive*. I stay quiet. Sometimes Lucas scores my goals for me.

He doesn't know Mrs SB as well as I do. She and Barty opened this hotel as newlyweds, more than forty years ago – the building isn't just where they work, it's the child they never had. They love every inch of this place, from the quaint attic rooms to the big brass door knocker. Forest Manor was made for luxury and romance, for string quartets, slow dances and lavish candlelit dinners. I hate watching Mrs SB grapple with the fact that after all we've been through, they can't afford to keep this magical place from falling apart.

'We're staying open,' Mrs SB says, with resolution. 'The insurers have said we can, as long as the building work is "sufficiently cordoned-off", so I'm adding "buy cordons" to my to-do list. After "googling what cordons are". We've had to cancel all the winter weddings, but we've still got five good suites, and the kitchen is untouched, whatever Arjun says.'

Arjun is very concerned about plaster dust. I gave this short shrift this afternoon, but you do have to manage Arjun's ego quite carefully. I'll send someone around later to do some token dusting around the oven and tell him it's sorted.

'But closing all twenty upstairs rooms . . . and having builders and . . . *structural engineers* everywhere . . .' She rubs her forehead, pushing her glasses up on to her head. 'Will the Hedgers stay?'

I nod. 'Their home insurance is covering their stay – their house is flooded,' I tell her. 'They don't have anywhere else to go, to be honest.'

'Good,' Mrs SB says, then winces at herself. 'Sorry. You know what I mean. And we've got Mrs Muller, she's here until January. We'll need to prioritise the long-term guests, I think. The couple from New Orleans have cancelled and gone to The Pig, so we can upgrade Mrs Muller to their room. Louis Keele has made it clear he's keen to stick around . . .'

I glance at Lucas, curious. He made a little sound when Mrs SB mentioned Louis. A familiar, disgusted snort that generally happens after *I* say something, actually.

'Who else is here on a long stay?' Mrs SB asks.

'Mr Townsend and the Jacobs,' Lucas and I say simultaneously.

'The Jacobs are a young Belgian couple with a five-month-old,' I say. 'They love everything British, have their bacon well-done and are obsessed with *Fawlty Towers*.'

We all know Mr Townsend, so I don't bother sharing my facts about him. He's here every winter for at least three months, and these days he and I even exchange the odd email in the time he's away from the hotel – he's become a friend, as many return guests do. I know Barty and Mrs SB feel the same.

'Well, liking *Fawlty Towers* is a good sign,' Mrs SB says with a grimace. 'Right. And they're . . .'

'Keen to stay,' I say promptly. 'I've already checked.'

'Good. Well done, Izzy. As for the rest of them . . .' Mrs SB says, staring at the laptop open on her knees. 'I'll deal with them. Somehow.'

She looks up at us with a distressed smile. Mrs SB is the world's nicest boss, and she can't bear to let anybody down, so if she's upset, that almost certainly means bad things for us.

'Now. On to you two,' she says.

Oh, God.

'I must be honest with you both. From the new year, I just can't guarantee anything. We may well . . .' She swallows. 'We're out of money, quite frankly. These next few weeks will be make or break. But I know how important it is for each of you to be working at the hotel this winter.'

I feel rather than see Lucas stiffen at that. For the first time, I wonder exactly why Lucas is working for the whole of November and December, rather than going back to see his family in Brazil like he did last year. And then I immediately stop thinking about this, because any thoughts that involve last Christmas and Lucas are strictly forbidden by order of my friend Jem.

'With only five rooms in use . . . I just can't justify employing you both to work on the desk alongside an agency receptionist.'

There it is. I fiddle with the strap on my bag and feel my pitch drying up in my throat. What was it I wanted to say? Something about being invaluable? I've worked at the hotel for eight years? The stationery drawer is much better when I'm here?

'Mrs SB,' Lucas says, 'I understand your difficulty. May I remind you of the superior digital booking system I introduced when I—'

'Personal notes!' I shout. They both turn to look at me. 'It was my idea to have the personal welcome notes in the rooms, and so many of our good reviews mention those.'

'They mention your terrible handwriting,' Lucas says.

I flush. People are so mean on the internet.

'I am extremely economical,' Lucas tells Mrs SB, who looks wearier by the minute. 'When we need new printer paper, I always order—'

'The fancy overpriced stuff,' I finish for him.

'The quality paper that requires less ink,' Lucas ploughs on. 'Unlike Izzy, I think carefully about cost implications.'

'Unlike Izzy? Excuse me? Who was complaining about my

budget fairy lights this morning? If you had your way, we'd make everything in this hotel out of solid gold.'

'That is ridiculous,' Lucas says, without even bothering to look at me. 'My solution is not solid-gold fairy lights, clearly. My solution is no fairy lights.'

'What next?' I say, my voice rising. 'No sofas? No beds?'

'Stop it, please,' Mrs SB says, holding up both hands in surrender. 'There's no need to battle it out, I'm keeping you both on until the new year. The agency director has kindly released us from our contract, in the circumstances, and will just provide a skeleton staff for front-of-house on Tuesdays and Wednesdays, if the two of you are willing to work five days?'

'Yes,' we both say, so loudly that Mrs SB startles slightly.

Usually, our fifth day is a split shift, so one of us covers the evening for Mandy to have her night off. I won't miss that, though – evening shifts are less fun. All the kids at the hotel have gone to bed, for starters.

'Well. Good. Thank you, both of you. I need responsible, experienced staff here – I can trust you two and Mandy with anything. I know you'll muck in wherever you're needed. I'll be letting half the waiting staff go, and even more of the housekeeping team, and Arjun will have to cope with just Ollie in the kitchen.'

'You're only leaving him the kitchen porter?' I say, unable to help myself. Arjun is not going to take that well.

'Raw talent,' Mrs SB says briskly. 'He can mould the boy in his own image. Now . . .' She sniffs, reaching her hands out. I take one first; Lucas hesitates before gripping her other hand in his own. 'That's enough business talk,' she says. 'May I remind you that we are a family here. Whatever happens, that won't change. If Forest Manor has to close, I will do whatever I can to help you. *Whatever* I can. Please know that the two of you will always be very dear to me.'

I'm tearing up. Mrs SB knows exactly how hard it is for me to have a conversation like this, and she squeezes my hand tightly. For a second I actually let myself think about it: drinking my last coffee-spiked hot chocolate with Arjun; packing my box o'bits into my car; hugging goodbye to Barty and Mrs SB, the people who made me feel at home when that mattered more than anything.

'Absolutely,' I say. My voice is a bit squeaky. 'And I'm here for you for as long as you can have me. Just name a job, and I'm on it.'

Lucas nods once. 'Whatever you need.'

'Wonderful. Well,' Mrs SB gives us a small, tired smile and releases our hands, 'we're selling as much as we can. That's step one.'

I widen my eyes. 'And Barty's . . .'

'Very upset about it,' Mrs SB says, lowering her voice and glancing towards the kitchen. 'But if we can't raise funds, we will lose the hotel. So some of those old Bartholomew pieces have to go. Can I put you two in charge of the lost-property room?'

'In charge, as in, of *selling* it all?' I say. The lost-property room started out as a lost-property box, but over the years it grew, and now there are hundreds – if not thousands – of items in there. We're not big on throwing things away here at Forest Manor. 'Can we even do that?'

'I've had a look, and the law is a bit vague, but I think as long as we took steps to return the items – which we always do when something new lands in there – and a reasonable amount of time has passed, then we're entitled to call it ours. And if it's ours . . . then I don't see why it can't raise us some money. It's a bit of a mess in there, but you never know, there might be some gems. Can I count on you two to get it all sold off? I'm sure Poor Mandy will help.'

'Absolutely,' Lucas says. 'I look forward to it.'

My eyebrow twitches. Lucas hates the lost-property room. He calls it 'the bin'.

Mrs SB sits back with a long sigh, then notices she only has her cardigan half on and says, 'Oh, bother. What a day. I'm going to need you two to really step up, now. I hope you've realised this means you'll be working shifts together five days a week.' She brings her glasses back down on to the bridge of her nose and adopts her sternest expression. 'Can you both do that?'

Neither of us makes eye contact with the other.

'Of course,' I say brightly.

'Yes,' Lucas says. 'Yes, I can work with Izzy. No problem at all.'

The next day, I realise what Mrs SB means when she says *mucking in*. We're in the kitchen: I'm suddenly a sous-chef and Lucas has just been enlisted to wait on tables at lunch. There is a gold-trimmed notice on the front desk that reads, *Please ring for assistance and we will be with you in a jiffy!* in Barty's curling cursive. I suspect that note is going to be on the desk a lot in the next few weeks.

'It will not fit,' Lucas says, voice muffled from inside the polo shirt he's trying to pull on. The issue is that Lucas is enormous, and the waiting uniforms are not designed for people who tower over everyone and have those weird extra muscles joining their neck and their shoulders.

Arjun shoots me a gleeful glance over the pot he is currently stirring. Looking gleeful while slowly stirring a pot does make you look a bit witchy, so I try to stay poker-faced on the other hob. Arjun's making his black dal, which has to be prepared in an extremely precise way. He's already yelled at me five times and apologised seven times.

Arjun is a sweetheart, he just *acts* like a dragon. If Forest Manor is my family, Arjun's my overbearing older brother. He always thinks he's right, and annoyingly he often is – he was the first person to tell me Drew wasn't a good friend to me. But he's softer than he seems. Every year, he makes me a special batch of brownies on the date of my dad's birthday, because I once told him brownies were Dad's favourite, and if he clocks I'm having a rough day, he always slips a teaspoon of sugar into my tea.

'You're almost there,' Arjun says to Lucas. This is clearly cheering Arjun up, which is good, because he's been in a terrible mood ever since Mrs SB told him about the cuts to the kitchen staff. 'Just tug it a bit more,' he says.

'It . . . won't . . .' Lucas's head pops out. He clocks our expressions and his face darkens. 'You are laughing at me.'

'Never,' I say. 'Arjun, is it time to add the cream?'

'No! God! No! Do *not* upon pain of *death* add the cream yet!'

'Right,' I say cheerily. 'Not cream time. Got it. Lucas, are you just going to wear that as a scarf, or . . .'

Lucas looks down at the polo shirt currently dangling from his neck. He's wearing a T-shirt underneath, which isn't helping the polo shirt fit, and is doing a relatively poor job of hiding the endless ridges of muscle that make up Lucas's torso. I turn away and start tidying off-cuts of vegetables into the compost bin. Nobody needs to be seeing all those abs.

'We have no other polo shirts?'

'None,' I say, though I haven't actually checked.

Lucas gives me a look that suggests he may have guessed as much. With a weary sigh, he begins the arduous task of trying to squeeze an arm in, just as Louis Keele walks through the swinging double doors, casual as you like, as though guests pop into the kitchen all the time.

'Wow,' he says. 'It smells great in here. Isn't that a bit small for you, Lucas?'

Lucas's irritation radiates from him like the heat from the hobs. I stifle a grin. Louis is a bit entitled, but it doesn't particularly bother me – he's a guest, and I figure if it makes him happy to get involved behind the scenes, then what's the harm? Plus . . . he's cute.

'You shouldn't be back here,' Lucas says.

His tone is borderline rude. Lucas has never been great at the sunny-and-obliging-demeanour thing. I watch him realise he's been inappropriately blunt and reach for something more positive to say.

'Perhaps you would like to go for a swim in the spa, Mr Keele, if you're looking for entertainment?' he says, as he finally yanks the polo shirt down over his torso. It stops just below his belly button, a good three inches of black T-shirt showing out of the bottom.

Louis gives me a conspiratorial smile. He's one of those good-looking guys who can actually pull off a wink: a bit *EastEnders*, a bit cheeky. He wears his mousey-brown hair swept back from his forehead and has very white teeth; he's often in a suit with no jacket or tie. Our vibe has always been a little flirty, which Lucas clearly regards as *deeply* unprofessional on my part. This may or may not provide an incentive to smile back at Louis right now.

'I'll go for a swim if you'll join me?' he says to me. He glances at Arjun. 'She must be due a break soon, surely . . .'

'No breaks for the wicked,' I tell him. 'Arjun has me stirring that pot every two minutes and forty seconds.'

'This is the recipe that the *Observer* food reviewer said brought ground-breaking flavours to a sleepy corner of the forest, am I right?' Louis says, looking over Arjun's shoulder. 'Your trademark black dal?'

Arjun straightens slightly. 'Yes, actually.'

'Amazing, wow,' Louis says, clapping him on the shoulder. 'It smells fantastic. Incredible what you can do in this space.'

'Does anyone have *anything* I can take to table five?' Ollie says, bursting in through the doors to the restaurant.

As the only remaining permanent member of Arjun's team, Ollie should really be the one stirring this dal, but I took pity on him and let him fill the waiter job instead. Arjun already looked like he was about to start breathing fire, and Ollie – bless him – would definitely drive him over the edge.

'Bread? Olives? Something poisonous?' Ollie goes on. 'The bloke says it's not his fault you mugs let the ceiling fall in, and he doesn't see why it should be holding up his lunch, and I did say we don't usually serve lunch until twelve but he said this is supposed to be a boutique luxury hotel and he should be able to have lunch whenever he – God, Lucas, what are you wearing? You look like a right twat! Oh,' Ollie says, turning scarlet. 'Sorry sir, I didn't realise a guest was . . .'

'Just leaving,' Louis says, with another easy smile. 'Izzy – rain check on that swim?'

'Sure, looking forward to it!' I say, smiling back and checking the clock. 'Time to stir, Arjun?'

'You're not already stirring?' he says with absolute horror, as Ollie disappears into the restaurant with a bread basket and Louis slips out of the other door.

After the chaos of yesterday, today is eerily quiet.

You can really feel all those empty rooms. We put everyone in a bay window for breakfast, looking out over the lawns and the woodland beyond, but it's still too subdued for my liking. Mr Townsend stays hunched over his copy of *The Times*; Louis and Mrs Muller don't make it to breakfast; the Jacobs are grey with exhaustion, their baby asleep at last in the pram beside their table. It's the Hedgers who bring all the energy, but there's only so much that even three kids under ten can do to brighten up the atmosphere. As I return to the lobby, I vow to figure something out for tomorrow. Background music, maybe? Or will that come across as too corporate?

'Oh, Mrs Hedgers!' I call, as she wheels in with a pile of shopping bags on her lap. 'Let me help you with those.'

She waves me away, gaze landing on my latest innovation: the debris nativity on the staircase landing.

'That's . . . quite something,' she says.

I feel myself going pink. 'I just figured, even if the ceiling has fallen in, until the builders get here, we can still make the most of the space, right?' I say.

'Yes. Yes, I can see that,' Mrs Hedgers says.

I've built a nativity into the rubble of the fallen ceiling. Baby Jesus is lying in a cradle between two chunks of ceiling plaster, and I've spread artificial snow around the scene, even dusting the shoulders of the wise men (three old statues of previous Bartholomew family members from the gardens). My personal favourite element is the sheep, which I created out of an old white footstool and a lot of cotton wool balls. I know it's a bit tacky and over-the-top, but I think it's cheerful – and the hotel desperately needs some cheer right now.

'You're a very creative young woman,' Mrs Hedgers says, turning her steady gaze my way.

For someone with such energetic children, Mrs Hedgers is surprisingly calm. She wears her dark brown hair in a chignon, smooth and neat, and there's never a speck of mud on the wheels of her chair when she heads out of the door. On her check-in notes, she listed her profession as 'life and career-change coach', which is probably why she seems to be so impressively *together*. I guess you can't tell other people how to live their lives if yours is a bit of a state.

'Oh, thank you!'

'Is it hard work, staying switched on all the time?' she asks, tilting her head.

'Sorry?'

Mrs Hedgers smiles slightly. 'Creative people tend to need their downtime.' She looks at the nativity. 'You like to add a little sparkle to everyone else's day, am I right?'

'That's actually why I love working in hospitality,' I say, twisting my fingers together. Mrs Hedgers is making me nervous. She has a headteacherly sort of energy, as if at any moment she'll tell me I'm not allowed to wear clip-in highlights at school. 'I'm a total people-person.'

'And how do you switch off?'

'Umm. Hanging out with friends?'

'Hmm,' says Mrs Hedgers.

'I do yoga too, sometimes,' I find myself saying. I think I last did yoga in the first lockdown, when everyone got excited about working out in our living rooms, as if the lockdown rules were the reason we weren't all bounding out into the woods for fifteen-mile runs every morning.

Mrs Hedgers waits. I can come up with no other down-time activities except 'watching television', which sounds like something Ruby Hedgers would put forward in answer to this question, so I just get gradually pinker and wait in silence.

'Well,' Mrs Hedgers says, hands on her chair's wheels again. 'Perhaps something to think about. It's so important for us to nourish ourselves so that we can continue to nourish those around us.'

'Right! Totally. Oh, sorry!' I say, hopping out of her way. 'Actually, while I have you, I've been meaning to ask – we still need a card for any costs that your insurer won't be covering for your stay. Would you . . .'

'They'll cover it all,' Mrs Hedgers says, and there's steel in her smile. 'Just send the bill their way.'

'Oh, OK,' I say, as she pushes open the door to her suite and manoeuvres herself through.

As the door closes behind her, I stare at it for a while. Nothing about that conversation should have made me feel especially uncomfortable, but I'm all discombobulated. Maybe it's because she didn't really like my nativity scene. Is that why? *Something* has got under my skin, and now I feel as though I've made a mistake, but I can't figure out where.

I whip out my phone and message Jem. She's in the States, but I do some quick maths and decide that even though I can never remember whether it's five hours ahead or five hours behind, as long as it's five *something* I'm not waking her in the middle of the night.

Is this lame? I say, attaching a photo of the nativity.

Umm, no?!! she replies instantly. *It is in fact the best thing I have ever seen!*

I smile down at my phone as she peppers me with stars and Christmas tree emojis. There is nobody in the world with a heart as pure as Jem Young.

Why the self-doubt? she asks. *Are you OK, little pigeon?*

Oh sorry, I'm totally fine! Just 'having a silly moment', as your mum would say. Maybe time for a sugar fix . . .

It's always time for a sugar fix. And please do not quote my mother at me at this hour!!

But Mrs Young has so many excellent one-liners! What about that time she told me I was an abject failure, dragging her daughter to the dogs?

Or the time she told me I was 'a disappointment, fundamentally speaking'?

I press my hand to my heart. We joke about these moments now, but I know how badly they wounded Jem. Even if these days she has *fundamentally speaking* literally tattooed on her arse.

You have never disappointed me, not even when you chose Team Jacob over Team Edward, I type, with a string of hearts.

She writes back, *Love you. Rehearsals now – got to go. Missing you so much x*

I tap out a heartfelt *Miss you more* before sliding my phone back into my pocket. Winter is my Jem time – her being gone has left me feeling a little unsteady. We only do Christmas together every other year – I'm on rotation between Jem and Grigg and Sameera – but even if I'm not actually with her on Christmas Day, we always spend September onwards sending each other fantastically bad new Christmas songs and meeting up for mulled wine after work.

But this year she's so busy that bothering her with the new festive album from a washed-up noughties band feels kind of stupid. Jem's always wanted to be a performer – musical theatre is the dream – and this year she finally got a spot in the ensemble of a brand-new American musical. It's the perfect breakout role for her, after years slogging away in part-time jobs.

It just also means spending six months in Washington DC, where her parents live. Which couldn't be *less* perfect. Jem spent half her childhood living on my street in Surrey, and half in DC – her family moved back and forth twice. When her parents finally settled in the US for good, Jem stayed here. Nice and close to me, nice and far away from them.

Fate, she'd said gloomily to me as we'd drunk cheap wine on my floor and mourned the fact that her dream had come true in her nightmare location. *Or Karma. Or something. Basically, the universe has decided I can't escape my mother.*

I grab a bag of candy kittens from the shelf under my computer screen and let the sugar rush hit as I flick through the booking book. My phone buzzes with a notification: it's from Google, reminding me of a photo from this time last year. I wince. Google is missing some serious subtext: it's a picture of me with Drew, my old flatmate, who I emphatically do *not* want to remember, especially at this time of year. I swipe the notification away and ram in a few more candy kittens.

'Lost property time,' says a familiar voice behind me.

I slam the book closed on the desk and steel myself for an interaction with Lucas. As I turn, I see him regarding the booking book with his usual disdain. One of my favourite activities is to make Lucas say 'the booking book' as many times as possible during a shift, because he hates my cutesy names for things. The trick is to trap him when a guest is there so he can't be a dickhead – or at least not out loud.

'Is it?' I say testily.

I glance at the clock mounted behind the desk. It's another relic from the Bartholomew family. It needs rewinding every morning, and by the end of Poor Mandy's shift, it's always running nineteen minutes behind. Checking the time on the lobby clock involves a combination of maths and guesswork: it's around midday, so the clock is probably already at least five minutes slow, so that means . . .

'It's twelve on the dot,' Lucas says, already sounding exasperated with me. 'I don't know why you even look at that clock. Don't you have a watch?'

I do have a watch. It is mint green and fabulously chunky, and I remember to put it on maybe two mornings out of ten. Today was not one of those mornings.

'I don't need a watch,' I say sweetly. 'I have you here to yell the time at me.'

I do one last sweep of the lobby to check it's all in order and then grab the key to the lost-property room. It's directly behind us – the door is just to the right of the old Bartholomew clock – but I've not been in there for months. The lost-property room was a staffroom, once, with a coffee machine and two comfy armchairs. Now it's just . . .

'Chaos,' Lucas says, as I unlock the door and step into the small amount of available floor space on the other side.

Boxes and boxes of *stuff*. A rocking horse. A collection of broken teacups, once used for afternoon teas here. An old projector. An absolute plethora of umbrellas.

So yes, it's kind of a state. But it's also kind of a treasure trove.

My heart lifts as I cast my eye over it all. If I fixed up that old rocking horse, we could definitely sell it for at least eighty quid. Mending the teacups won't take long, and people will go crazy for that cutesy 1950s pattern on them. We might be able to raise some real money from all this. Mrs SB is a genius.

'We should decide how and where we want to sell each category of item,' Lucas says, rubbing his mouth as he scans over the contents of the room. 'I'll start a spreadsheet.'

I ignore him and dive in. The first box is labelled 'tatty books' and the second 'coats left behind in 2019'.

I hear Lucas mutter something in Portuguese behind me, and choose to believe it is an expression of delight and excitement.

Lucas

After two days of Izzy making everything as difficult as possible, we establish ourselves on various online stores for second-hand goods, and life is suddenly filled with boxes, envelopes and trips to the post office. Mandy volunteers to head up sales via social media, which Izzy and I are very happy about, since sorting the hotel's Instagram presence has been on both our to-do lists for as long as I've been here. Izzy tries to insist on a hand-drawn table to keep track of items, but then she spills her gingerbread latte on it, and has to come crawling back to my Excel spreadsheet.

My days off pass in a blur of studying, and suddenly it's Thursday. I pull my collar up against the wind and step closer to the manor wall as I lift the phone to my ear. Thursday means I ring my uncle. I don't know why I do this. Nobody asks me to, and it always puts me in a bad mood afterwards, but I've discovered that if I *don't* call him at least once a week, I feel even worse.

'Hello? Lucas?' Uncle Antônio answers in Portuguese.

'Hi, Uncle.'

'I'm just heading back into the office after hours of meetings – this week has been relentless,' my uncle says irritably.

I grimace. By the end of this call, I will feel stupid for ringing at all, and this is the first hit: the suggestion that he's too busy to talk to me. He's not *said* that, so of course if I mention feeling this way, he will say I'm being difficult.

My sister Ana and I have always been aware that we are a burden upon Uncle Antônio. Our father died shortly after I was born, but his brother Antônio supported our mother in the time when she was off work, and insisted on having a role in our lives after that. I am grateful to him, of course. Endlessly, repeatedly. It sometimes seems there is no end to the gratitude that is required.

'Is now a bad time?' I ask.

'Now is fine. Tell me how your course is going. Are you running that place yet?'

'I'm less than a year into the course, Uncle, and I'm doing it part-time.'

'There's no room for part-timers in this world, Lucas,' Antônio begins.

I cut him off before he gets into full flow. 'I mean, I'm doing it while working at the hotel. I need the practical experience as well as the degree.'

'Hmm, well. I hope they know you'll be their boss one day soon.'

My stomach tightens anxiously. I'm not doing the course out of a desire to take over Forest Manor. But as soon as Antônio says it, that old impulse kicks in: I need to work harder, I need to be pushing for a promotion, I need to do more, do better . . .

'Listen, Lucas, I think you should come home at Christmas.'

I clench my teeth. 'I can't afford it. The flights are too expensive. I've booked to come back in February.'

'February is the worst time to come home. Carnival, all the tourists . . .'

'I've made my decision,' I say again. It's best to be strong with my uncle – if you're anything but assertive, you've already lost. 'I have to go. Speak soon.'

After ending the call, I pull up my banking app, and then I shut it again very quickly, because the only thing guaranteed to make my mood worse is seeing quite how large that minus number has grown in the last few weeks. I'm still throbbing with all those old feelings, sweating them out beneath my thick coat. I can't feel the cold wind now. A phone call with my uncle: the perfect way to warm up in an English winter.

I head back to the hotel entrance, with its rounded privet hedges and its big stone steps. As I walk into the lobby, I eye Izzy's ridiculous rubble nativity scene. For an unpleasant moment, I'm reminded of last year's Christmas party – Izzy had set up a nativity for that, too. I remember walking past it with Drew, just a few moments after she'd introduced herself. *God, could that be more Izzy?* she'd said. *Who else would make the camels pink?* The memory makes me wince.

I approach the front desk. Mrs SB is there with Izzy, their heads bent close together, inspecting something. I am immediately suspicious.

'These could be worth a lot!' Mrs SB says.

Izzy looks up, her hand flying to the thin gold chain she's wearing around her throat.

'You want us to sell *these*?'

'Of course. Why not?' Mrs SB says.

'Mrs SB, I get it, I know how important the money is, but . . . These aren't just pieces of jewellery. They're *wedding* rings. *Engagement* rings,' Izzy says, her voice rising. 'These are little love stories, right here in this box.'

I look over their shoulders. There are five rings lying haphazardly on a folded piece of yellowing kitchen paper inside a Tupperware box. One of them is diamond studded; another sports a giant emerald at its centre, framed by two pink stones. Each one has a tiny sticker looped around it with a date printed in different handwriting.

'What is all this?' I ask.

'They're from the swimming-pool lost property,' Izzy says to me. 'I want to return them.'

'*Return* them? Aren't we supposed to be making money, not giving it away?' I ask, and then I catch Izzy's expression.

She's really upset about this. Her eyes are swimming. She blinks fast and looks away again.

'Losing a wedding ring isn't like losing an umbrella,' she says. 'I know the law says you have to keep items for a reasonable length of time – but what's reasonable when it's something with such sentimental value?'

At the mention of the law, Mrs SB looks a little distressed.

'Oh, well . . .'

'Just give me one week. Please, Mrs SB. We're doing brilliantly at selling off the other items already. But do we really want to be the sort of hotel that pawns off someone's *wedding* ring?'

'Yes?' I say.

'No,' Mrs SB says, with a heavy sigh. 'No, I suppose we don't. Thank you, Izzy.' She squeezes her shoulder. 'Our resident angel. You mustn't let us lose our heart here, all right, dear?'

I stare between them, and then back at the rings. What has heart got to do with it? These are just expensive items of jewellery. Who's to say they're more sentimentally valuable to people than their favourite umbrella?

'You can't be serious,' I begin, but Mrs SB is already striding off towards Barty, who has just appeared in the doorway, wearing a panicked expression and holding two laptops at once.

'One week!' she calls over her shoulder at Izzy, who immediately starts checking the dates on each ring. 'And then our duty is done!'

'There is no duty here,' I say. 'These are just the same as all the rest of the junk in there.'

Izzy brandishes an old booking book at me. There was a digital system before I arrived at Forest Manor, though a very bad one – and yet Izzy still insisted on writing things in that book as well as putting them on the computer. She continues this practice now, even with our superior new online system. It is one of the many ridiculous things she does.

'What's the date on that one?' she asks, pointing to the gold wedding ring I've picked up between thumb and forefinger.

'The first of November, 2018,' I say. 'Do you honestly think you can find the owner of a ring that was lost here four years ago?'

She flicks through the book and stabs a finger at the page. 'Ha!' she says. 'Five pool bookings that day, six spa sessions. All noted down in the . . .'

I raise an eyebrow at her.

'Sorry, I just can't quite . . . what's the word . . .' She taps her bottom lip, eyes wicked.

'Izzy. You are such a child.'

She grins at me, and there it is – a traitorous flicker of sensation in my gut. This happens sometimes. Ninety-nine per cent of the time, I think Izzy is the most annoying woman I have ever met, but very occasionally I can't help noticing how beautiful she is.

'This is ridiculous,' I say, looking back down at the rings.

'Tiffany Moore,' Izzy announces, flicking back to check the guest's original booking. 'And here's her landline number.'

'Izzy, this is a waste of your time.'

'OK, well, as you say: *my* time, so . . .' She motions at me to be quiet as the phone rings.

For one childish second, I am inclined to reach over and hang up the phone. I have no reason for this other than the satisfaction of knowing that she will find it deeply irritating. I don't understand how she does this to me, but something about Izzy Jenkins makes me want to behave very badly.

I don't even move – don't even twitch – but Izzy reaches a hand out and clamps it over mine on the desk. There is another twinge in my stomach, a sensation like cool seawater hitting sun-baked skin.

'Don't even think about it, Mister da Silva,' she whispers, and then slides her hand from mine. 'Oh, hello! Is Tiffany there, please?' she says into the phone, all sugar and sweetness again. As though I can't still feel the imprint of her nails tingling on the back of my hand.

I leave her to this ridiculous task and manage at least two hours of jobs before the next crisis hits. You can tell we are at one-sixth of our usual capacity. Generally, at Forest Manor, the crises come at least every fifteen minutes.

I am in Bluebell, the room where Mrs Muller is currently staying. Behind me, Dinah – our head of housekeeping – enters the room carrying a Hoover in one hand and a large bag of cleaning products in the other.

'There is nothing that will get that off. Nothing,' Dinah says immediately, dropping the Hoover with a thump. 'White spirit, maybe, but how will you avoid taking off the paint underneath?'

The wall is splattered in oil paint – red, green, and blue. The apparatus of Mrs Muller's latest form of artistic expression is still lying on a token dustsheet beneath her easel. It looks like a cross between a catapult and a leaf-blower.

'I apologise – when the muses strike, they strike, you see. I'll be needing another room, of course,' Mrs Muller says. 'I can't very well work in all this mess.'

Dinah begins vacuuming behind us. Leave Dinah anywhere for any amount of time and she'll start aggressively vacuum cleaning something. This helpfully masks the sound of me growling under my breath.

'Mrs Muller,' I say, 'you know we only have five rooms at present.'

She stares up at me from the armchair in the corner. I notice a splodge of blue paint on its fabric and am once again grateful for the sound of Dinah's Hoover. Mrs Muller is a regular at the hotel – she is an important guest. She is also a demanding one, but I understand that. I suspect I would be a demanding guest too.

'I will see what I can do, Mrs Muller. Leave it with me.'

'Well?' I ask Izzy when I return to the lobby.

'Well what?' she says, distracted as she sorts through a box of paperback books. 'Could we take some of this to a car boot sale, maybe? Use your car? My boot is teeny.'

I stare at her in horror. 'You want me to put all of this rubbish in my car?'

'It's not rubbish! These paperbacks will make a pound each. Every little helps.'

'We need tens of thousands of pounds of investment, so one pound does not particularly help.'

She dims a little and says something about the quantity of items still to be sold. I watch her counting out books on the floor behind the desk and feel an unexpected twinge of guilt for making her shoulders sag that way. Our endless back-and-forth is built into the rhythm of my day here: I had expected a sharp retort. Perhaps she will take revenge later – she likes to do that sometimes. I will probably find something sticky 'accidentally' spilled on my keyboard again this afternoon.

'So was it Tiffany Moore's wedding ring?' I find myself asking.

Izzy looks up at me, surprised, and then smug. 'Look who's already getting on board with The Ring Thing!'

Of course this mad plan now has a rhyming name.

'I'm not on board. I was just making conversation.'

'Gosh, I wasn't aware you knew how to do that. Well, it wasn't hers,' Izzy says, returning to the paperbacks. 'She said her wedding ring is still firmly on her finger. I've tried a couple more people but I'm hitting the rest of the list after this box. Unless you want to help, and give someone a call now?'

'I'm not getting involved in your childish plan,' I say as I return to my lost-property spreadsheet.

'Oh, of course not,' Izzy says, in an infuriating singsong voice. 'Understanding the concept of sentimental value requires some capacity for human emotion, I suppose.'

I ignore her as she busies herself around me. She's so *energetic*. I would expect her to be exhausted at the end of a shift, but from what I've seen, she always has evening plans with someone – she seems to have huge quantities of friends. They're always dropping in, hugging her over the desk, vowing never to go so long without seeing her again.

I've not noticed a boyfriend around recently, though. Last year there was usually one of those loitering about too, but since we've been working shifts together again, I've not come upon a man in too-tight trousers with a guitar on his back waiting in the lobby, so I'd have to guess that Izzy is currently single.

51

'Hello, is that Kelly?' Izzy says into the phone, catching it between her shoulder and ear as she sticks together an old teacup with both hands.

I listen as she explains the situation to the woman on the other end of the phone.

'Not mine,' the woman barks.

I can hear every word from where I'm sitting. It is incredibly distracting to have to listen to Izzy's phone conversations in this way. I have long suspected her of turning up the volume on that phone for this precise reason.

'Was I even at your hotel in 2018?' Kelly says. 'Seems unlikely. New Forest isn't really my scene. Not much to do. Too many trees. Very samey.'

I can't help bristling. I love the New Forest, and there are at least fifteen leaflets under this desk that will demonstrate exactly how much there is to do here. This place has become home to me. I'd defend it in the same way I'd defend Niterói, the city where I grew up. It has its faults, but it's mine.

'You came for a long weekend with your husband,' Izzy says.

'Oh, *that* husband,' Kelly says. 'Yeah, no, we're not married any more. But it can't be my ring. I keep my old wedding rings in the loft.'

Izzy snorts out a surprised laugh. 'Right. OK. Well, thank you for your help, Kelly.'

'You really go the extra mile, don't you?' Kelly says.

Izzy lifts her chin. 'Well, yes, I think it's—'

'Listen, a little life lesson for free, from me to you. Don't fucking bother. Nobody gives a shit and you'll just wear yourself out. Bye-bye!'

Izzy stares at the phone for a moment after Kelly hangs up. I can't help laughing. She shoots me a filthy glare and clicks the phone back into the receiver, returning to her boxes. She's made progress since I last looked. Or, at least, things are now in different piles.

'Is there a system here?' I ask.

She rolls her eyes. 'Of course. Unsorted; unsellable; for upcycling; for Mandy's little putting-pics-on-Twitter scheme; for the car boots; for Etsy; for Gumtree; for washing; for the bin.'

She points at each pile so quickly I'm lost by 'for upcycling', a word I don't understand anyway. I stare at it all, unwilling to ask her to repeat herself.

After a moment, she starts again, more slowly. 'Unsorted. Unsellable. Upcycling – so like, stuff I think I can glam up. This is stuff for Poor Mandy to take pretty pictures of. And this is for the car boot, Etsy, Gumtree . . . Then these need washing, and that's for the rubbish bin.'

I follow this time. I hate it when the language barrier slows me down – it's rare now, though it happened all the time when I first moved to the UK three years ago. Nowadays I even think in English most of the time. My *vô* would have been horrified to hear that – my grandfather believed no language is more beautiful than Brazilian Portuguese. But I like English, for all its awkwardness. It is usually worth taking the time to learn something difficult, I find.

I watch Izzy as she taps away at the keyboard, making an

irritated noise when the system takes a moment to load. I can still see the woman I thought she was last year. Independent, stubborn, but kind and funny too.

And then I remember her screaming at me across the hotel lawn last December. The countless times she screwed me over in the last year, the petty point-scoring, the way her humour turns barbed the moment it's turned on me.

I look away to sort the next box. Not *everything* difficult is worth the time.

Izzy

The next few days are a blur of restaurant service, odd jobs and building dust. Lucas and I come to a rare and begrudging agreement on one thing: if we must share shifts, we should be as far away from each other as possible. So one of us gets on with some of the four billion things that need doing around here, and the other covers the desk, even if that just means keeping an ear out from the kitchen and sprinting when the phone rings.

Slowly, items from around the hotel begin to disappear. An antique wooden dresser; several paintings of old men whose importance was long ago forgotten, which they would probably have found very upsetting; and the vases. I never thought I would miss those vases, but every time someone comes to collect another one, I feel a teeny twinge in my chest.

Meanwhile, I am making rubbish progress with The Ring Thing. It's actually a lot harder than I thought it would be, though of course Lucas is under the impression that I'm seconds away from returning every single one. I do get one promising email about the diamond engagement ring from an address that's a garbled string of letters and numbers. It says, *Hold fire, I'll call upon return to UK.* No name, nothing. All a bit weird. But nobody rings, so I forget about it, lost in a flurry of lost-property items, rain and social obligations.

When the phone call comes, I am talking through a new lunch menu with Arjun, who now has a very limited number of people with whom to discuss these things (Ollie suggested we should serve Doritos with Arjun's forty-eight-hour chilli and has been banned from having opinions).

'The bitterness needs offsetting,' Arjun is saying.

'Right, totally,' I say, bubble-wrapping a vintage snow globe that just sold to someone in Northumberland for a satisfying £85. It's a great price, but I hate selling this stuff – especially the festive decorations. I want the hotel to look like it did on my first Christmas here: glowing, gorgeous, its mantlepieces laden with thick fir branches and golden lights.

'I'm thinking salt-crusted parsnip?'

'Salt-crusted,' I say, tearing the Sellotape with my teeth. 'Perfect.'

'Are you humouring me?' Arjun asks, eyes appearing from behind the menu, which is held about two inches from his face. He's so overdue a visit to the optician that I have considered booking one for him and luring him there by pretending I've found a fantastic new deli.

'I'm giving you what you need,' I say, 'which is a sounding board and some validation.'

The menu drops further. 'Will you swap jobs with Ollie?' Arjun asks. 'Please?'

'Ollie's great. He's just new, and you never like new things. You thought I was annoying for at *least* a year.'

'You have always been my favourite!' Arjun says, outraged at the very suggestion. He has a selective memory for his own bad-temperedness.

'Give Ollie a chance.'

'Puh,' Arjun says, as he nabs my pen to scribble down a note about parsnips. 'You give Lucas a chance, then.'

He looks up and laughs at my expression. Arjun is usually the last person to suggest going easy on anyone. I remember the first time Drew popped in to see me while I was at work – she'd been hoping for a free lunch. Arjun had eyed her through the kitchen door and said, *That's the flatmate you're always bending over backwards for? I say cut her loose. She's ordered three sides, Izzy. That is a woman who takes what she can get.*

The phone rings before I can respond to Arjun.

'Forest Manor Hotel and Spa, this is Izzy speaking! How can I help you?'

'Hello,' says a gravelly male voice. 'Full name, please?'

'Umm. Izzy Jenkins? Isabelle Jenkins?'

'And can I ask you to confirm the address of your place of work?'

I blink. 'Am I, like, going through security for something here?'

There is a slight pause. 'I got an email,' the man says. 'And I need to confirm that I'm speaking to the correct person.'

'Was the email about a wedding or engagement ring?' I say hopefully.

'Affirmative,' the man says.

Ooh, I love that. I am going to start saying *affirmative*. When Jem next messages me asking if I'm all caught up on *Strictly*, that is exactly what I'm going to say back.

'I responded to say I would be in touch when I returned to the UK. I'm back now, and I'd like to request a follow-up email with an image of the engagement ring in question,' he says.

'I can do that for you, no problem!'

'I'll be in touch once that has been safely received,' he says. 'Goodbye.'

'The Ring Thing?' Arjun asks as I click the phone back into the receiver, slightly dazed.

'Yeah. Crap. That was all so weird I didn't even take his name. Though I'm pretty sure I know who it was.' I look up at Arjun. 'Am I being ridiculous about these rings, like Lucas says?'

Arjun tilts his head, tapping the pen on the menu. 'You're being an optimist,' he says eventually. 'And a romantic.'

'So . . . Ridiculous?'

'No.' He gives me his full attention – a rare thing from Arjun. 'You're being Izzy, and it's excellent,' he says, as though it's as simple as that. 'Now, excuse me. I have some parsnips to salt.'

I watch him go with a lump in my throat. I have seen Arjun almost every day for eight years. At first we didn't click, but slowly, week by week, we've become more than colleagues, more even than friends. I've cried on him several times, and he cried on me after his awful, toxic divorce. We might never have been mates outside of this place, but now we rely on each other – he's part of my life. For Lucas, losing this job would probably be an inconvenience. For me, it would be like losing a family all over again.

And I just *can't*.

On the last Monday of November, when I am two days away from having to sell that curious Tupperware of rings, a straight-backed man in a razor-sharp suit comes marching into the lobby. Poor Mandy is setting up, gamely creating herself a space amongst all the lost-property boxes, and I'm already on my way out the door – I've got drinks with a couple of temps I used to work with when I first started at Forest Manor.

'Eric Matterson,' the man announces when he reaches the desk. 'I'm here about a ring.'

Mandy's eyes find mine. I dash over.

Eric looks about sixty – he is greying at the temples and has a deep frown-line between his eyebrows. This is *exactly* how I imagined the guy on the phone. He has the carefully pressed look of a military type, and an intimidating air of steeliness.

'A French nineteenth-century rose-cut diamond,' he is saying, 'set into a claw in a D-shaped gold ring of approximately three millimetres in width.'

'Hi,' I say.

He looks at me. 'Hello,' he says, as if humouring me. 'Cushion-cut diamonds around the central stone.'

I already know the one he means – I emailed him the picture

two days ago. It's a beautiful ring. Obviously antique, even to an amateur like me. My stomach flutters with excitement.

'Does it belong to you?' I ask.

He stares at me. 'Yes. Obviously.'

A young man darts through the door behind him, shaking out his coat in a shower of drops like a dog out of water. Poor Mandy heads over to take his umbrella, unexpectedly dousing her own shoes as she pulls it closed. She looks down at her feet, crestfallen, before returning to the desk with the air of a woman who fully expects the universe to give her wet shoes.

'Dad, can you stop doing that?' the young man says, trying to rearrange his hair in the large mirror hanging on the lobby wall. Mrs SB was measuring that up this morning – I doubt it'll be here much longer.

'Doing what?' Eric asks.

'*Slipping off,*' his son says with exasperation. 'Dad was a spy in the Cold War,' he explains to us, joining his father at the desk. 'Some habits can't be shaken off, apparently. I've only just about persuaded him to communicate over an encrypted messenger app instead of using those super hardcore ones that all the terrorists are on, you know?'

'Charlie,' Eric says, face set in an expression of fixed patience, 'please will you stop telling strangers that I was a spy in the Cold War?' His eyes flick towards me, then Mandy, face barely moving. 'I wasn't a spy,' he says.

'No, of course not,' says Mandy, just as Lucas appears behind her, as if from nowhere, Lucifer-style.

For such a big man, he can be surprisingly stealthy. He's still in his uniform, but he's wearing the wrong shoes – trainers instead of his usual shining black brogues – as if he started getting changed and then thought better of it. I don't know what he's doing lurking here. We all know he thinks The Ring Thing is stupid and sentimental. I hope he's not planning to sabotage this in revenge for the pin cushion from lost property that I inadvertently left on his chair yesterday.

'Proof,' Eric says, reaching into his pocket and laying a photograph on the desk between us.

It's old and faded, A5, just like the ones in my parents' photo albums. The man in the image is unmistakably Eric – as straight-backed as he is today – and the woman showing the camera her ring beside him looks just as serious.

'My wife,' Eric says, and for the first time, I catch a hint of emotion from him.

'Thank you,' I say. It hadn't occurred to me to ask for proof, so I'm glad he offered. 'Here, it's yours. I'm so pleased it's found you again.'

Eric clears his throat as I click open the Tupperware and I make a mental note to move these rings into something less conspicuously shabby. This box does not scream 'we have taken great care of your possessions'. The trouble is, Lucas has been needling me about keeping valuable items in a Tupperware, so now if I switch them into something else, I look like I'm conceding.

'Give it to my son,' Eric says, when I hold the ring out. He averts his eyes. 'It's yours now, Charlie, all right?'

Charlie's mouth forms an almost perfect O. He looks between

each of us, even Lucas, who is just standing in a looming sort of way and not bothering to introduce himself to anybody.

'You . . . Do you mean that?' Charlie says to his father.

'Do you need me to say it twice?'

'No, I . . . But as in . . . You understand that if I have Mum's ring, I'm going to . . .'

'Use it to propose to that young man of yours, yes,' Eric says, tone clipped. He looks up at the ceiling. 'Quite right. You've made him wait long enough.'

'*I've* made . . .' Charlie snaps his mouth closed. 'Wow.'

I *knew* this ring mattered. I could just feel it when it first glimmered up at me on that piece of kitchen paper. I let my gaze slide to Lucas. It's generally hard to read his expression – he defaults to a pretty unchanging 'implacable' – but his gaze is very fixed as he watches Charlie tear up in front of us.

'Mum would have wanted that,' Charlie says to his father. 'I really . . . Thank you.'

'Yes, well,' Eric says. 'I may have been a bit . . . picky for you. Hiro isn't *too* bad. I just want you to be happy.'

This last part looks like news to Charlie. He takes it with a slight wobble of his bottom lip.

'There'll be a reward,' Eric says, turning back to us abruptly and pulling out his phone. 'Let me look into the numbers.'

'Sorry?' I say. 'A . . .'

'Financial reward. This ring is worth a large sum. I appreciate the lengths you went to in order to return it to us. It is . . . greatly significant to my family.'

I watch Eric's Adam's apple bob as he swallows, and despite

myself I feel my eyes brim up. My dad was nothing like Eric – he was warm, open, ready to laugh. But I can't help thinking of Dad. The ring he gave me for my twenty-first birthday, now lying at the bottom of the sea after a *stupid* drunk swim in Brighton on my twenty-second birthday. I touch my necklace, the gold chain Mum gave me for my twenty-first – *something different from each of us, you know what we're like, can't agree on anything!*

'That's incredibly kind of you, sir,' Lucas says, when I fail to answer. He shoots me an odd look before returning his attention to Eric. 'Can we invite you to stay for a drink with your son?'

I shake myself. 'Yes! And actually . . .' I look at Charlie as he steps forward and takes the ring reverently from my palm. 'If you're looking for a gorgeous location to propose, you've found the perfect place.'

He looks around the hotel as if noticing where he is for the first time.

'Huh,' he says. 'That would be cute, wouldn't it? Given Mum's ring was here all this time.'

'We can meet to talk about that now, if you wish,' Lucas says, smelling profit, no doubt. 'I'm available.'

'As am I!' I say, already mentally composing a message cancelling my evening plans. I suspect Charlie is going to do his proposal in a big way, and that disposable income is not a problem for his family, which means that right now, I am Charlie's number-one fan.

'Perfect,' Eric says, making his way towards the bar. 'Charlie! A drink before our meeting.'

Charlie follows after his father in a daze.

'You're not getting the credit for this, if that's your plan, muscling in with your "meeting",' I say to Lucas. 'The Ring Thing was *my* idea.'

'You hardly expected this to happen,' Lucas scoffs.

That grates on me, so I smile. I know this smile winds Lucas up. It's my most obliging, most engaging one – the one that always makes guests calm down when they're angry. It has the opposite effect on Lucas. I suspect he knows that when I smile like this, really I'm thinking, *You're an idiot, and I'm going to be so nice to you, you won't even notice that I'm getting my way and you're not getting yours.*

'If you think you can swan in now, and then tell Mrs SB and Barty that *you* got this reward for the hotel . . .'

Lucas pulls his chin back slightly, eyes flaring. 'Is that what you think I'd do?'

I pause. His acts of sabotage aren't generally that dishonourable, admittedly. But if he's not planning to take the credit, why is he helping?

'I care about this place too, you know,' Lucas says.

I tilt my head, like, *Really though?* I know Lucas likes this job, but I'm not sure the man has it in him to really *love* something the way I love Forest Manor.

'Whatever,' I say. 'I need to get changed back into uniform if we're doing this meeting.'

I'm in a white knitted jumper that hangs down to my knees over washed-out jeans and my baby-pink trainers – I love this outfit, but it's not very professional. I hike my bag on to my shoulder and head for the lost-property room. There's space in there now that we've cleared it out a bit – or, as Lucas put it earlier, 'moved the contents of this terrible room into the lobby where everyone can see them'.

I slip out of my jumper and trainers and then bend to yank my uniform back out of my bag. I like the Forest Manor uniform – it's just a simple white shirt and black trousers, with the hotel logo on the left breast, but I feel good when I'm wearing it. It's like slipping into the person I am at work. At the hotel, I'm not overstretched, I'm not exhausted; I'm nobody's tragic anecdote. I'm the one who . . . what did Mrs Hedgers say? The one who brings the sparkle.

'Oh, Izzy, I wanted to ask about this box of – oops!' says Poor Mandy, barging through the door behind me and then clocking that I'm in nothing but my jeans and bra.

I turn. Lucas is standing on the other side of the desk behind Mandy, and for the briefest of moments, before Mandy shuts the door, we lock eyes.

These days, Lucas tends to look at me with a sort of flat, weary regard, as though he's just waiting for me to annoy him. It's grown harder and harder to believe that I ever saw anything more than that in Lucas's gaze when he looked at me. But right now, as our eyes meet, something shifts. He's not completely in control of himself, and what I see makes my skin tingle. For the first time since that humiliating screaming match on the hotel lawns, Lucas da Silva is looking at me like he wants me.

The door slams shut and the moment's gone, but my skin still glows from his gaze.

God. I hand the man my heart, tell him to meet me under the

mistletoe, then turn up there to find him kissing my flatmate. I call him out for being a thoughtless dickhead and he tells me I'm *making drama*. He spends all year making this job as hard as possible for me, refusing to compromise on anything, even after what he did last Christmas.

And *still* he can turn me hot with one single glance.

Lucas

'Explain it to me,' Pedro says in Portuguese, coffee machine whirring behind him. 'You hate her because . . .'

'It's complicated,' I say, eyeing the coffee as it streams out of the machine into my favourite mug, the tall grey one with just the right-sized handle.

I've been frequenting Smooth Pedro's Coffee and Smoothie Bar for almost two years now. Pedro and I met at the gym – I heard his accent across the weights zone, and it was like breathing in and suddenly smelling home. He's from Teresópolis and has been in the UK for a few years longer than me. He gives terrible advice but makes excellent coffee.

'I can do complicated,' he says, and then, at my dubious expression: 'Go on, try me. Allow me to surprise you. Wasn't I right about putting avocado in your smoothie?'

This feels slightly different, but I humour him. 'Last year, we were flirtatious, but she was always seeing someone, and it never really came to anything. Then at the hotel Christmas party, I kissed this woman who turned out to be her flatmate. It was under the mistletoe, not even a real thing. But Izzy got so protective. She dragged me out on to the lawn and yelled that I had behaved like a pig, and that, hang on . . .'

I wrap my hands around the mug of coffee as I try to remember her exact wording.

'*You're not good enough for her anyway, you cold-hearted shiny-shoed robot-man.*'

'Whew. I am seeing some warning signs here,' says Pedro.

'I know.'

'Do you think she was jealous?'

'Izzy? No. And that would be crazy, anyway. We weren't together, we'd never even kissed . . .'

'Hmm,' Pedro says, unimpressed. 'So she just didn't think you were good enough for her friend?'

'Exactly.'

I swallow. I have enough self-insight to know that *not good enough* is something I struggle with. But it's more than that. I liked Izzy. I respected her opinion. Knowing that she thought Drew shouldn't be kissing a man like me had done more than just hit an old nerve – it had reminded me that wherever I am in the world, women always see me the same way. *You don't have a heart, so don't tell me I broke it*, my ex had said on her way out of the door. When she had first confessed to cheating on me, Camila had seemed genuinely surprised to see me crying. *I honestly didn't know you had it in you*, she'd said.

I close my eyes, sipping my coffee as Pedro gets the smoothie bar ready for opening. I'm off today and tomorrow, but I will be working here in my favourite seat at the window – my laptop is already packed in the bag at my feet. I am behind on my course, with an essay due on Friday, and on top of that, Izzy talked Charlie into proposing to his boyfriend on Thursday, and promised all sorts of bespoke elements that we now have to organise on a tight budget. I need to stay focused.

And I absolutely *must* stop thinking about Izzy Jenkins in nothing but jeans and a pink bra.

'I need Izzy,' Mrs SB says distractedly, as she powers towards me across the lobby with several ring binders tucked awkwardly under one arm.

It's Thursday morning. My essay is almost done, and Charlie's proposal is as arranged as I could make it without coming into the hotel or coordinating with Izzy outside of working hours. I watch as Mrs SB dodges a couple departing from the restaurant and gives them a wide, *it's all under control* smile before dropping a file on to the tiles and saying, 'Oh, bugger.'

'Izzy is—'

'Right here!' Izzy sings, sailing into the lobby from the restaurant.

She looks disarmingly pretty in waiting uniform, two strands of silky hair falling out of her ponytail. I try and fail not to think about the pink bra.

'Ah, good,' Mrs SB says, before glancing towards the corridor that leads to Sweet Violet. She lowers her voice. 'Mr Townsend is very upset about the builders.'

As one, we look at the builders, who are currently debating something at the top of a scaffolding tower by the staircase. They are incredibly intrusive. I have asked them to be quiet on multiple occasions, but the only effect has been that they have stopped greeting me when I arrive in the mornings.

Mr Townsend is a particularly special guest here. He's been coming for decades, I believe, at first with his wife and then, when she passed away, he would stay on his own for the winter. I don't usually have personal conversations with guests, but even I feel fond of the man. Every fortnight or so, I give him a lift to the shops, and we have started having a coffee together afterwards. He reminds me of my vô, with his spindly reading glasses and slow, thoughtful smile. He has Parkinson's, and every year he struggles a little more with his symptoms, but he is very stoic about it.

'Hmm,' Izzy says, tapping her bottom lip. 'OK. Leave it with me.'

Mrs SB smiles, already on her way again. 'My favourite sentence. Thank you, dear!'

I watch Izzy as she settles Mr Townsend on the sofa by the window, sitting on her haunches in front of him as they talk. How carefully she listens, how gently she explains the situation, how warmly he regards her. They end up discussing The Ring Thing – it seems to be all anyone talks about around here, much to my irritation. *I know why this project matters to you so much, Izzy,* he says, which makes me move a little closer to hear better. But he goes on to talk about his own wife. *I think it's lovely. My Maisie treasured her ring until the day she was taken from me,* he says, settling back into his seat as the rain comes down against the glass behind them. *When we were first stepping out together . . .*

I look away. I understand why Mrs SB wanted Izzy for this job. People love her without her even having to try. They don't see the Izzy I see all day – they don't know how cutting and uncompromising she can be.

To everyone but me, it seems, Izzy is absolutely perfect.

Charlie's plans for his proposal escalate as the day goes on. By the evening, our one remaining gardener is setting up fireworks at the end of the lawns, Arjun is searching the county for a very specific type of champagne, and several members of the Matterson and Tanaka families are gathering in the bar for a surprise celebration after Charlie and Hiro's private dinner out here under the pergola.

I am grateful to be outside for a few moments. I wouldn't say it's peaceful – Izzy is with me. But this afternoon's rain glimmers on the trees around us, and the air is soft and fresh as nightfall presses in.

When I moved here, I never expected to love the forest so much. I thought it would be picturesque, perhaps, but I didn't realise how something so old and so beautiful would make me feel. It is easy to find calm in a place that outdates you by about a millennium.

'I feel like it's not saying *proposal*. We need to dial up the sparkliness,' says Izzy, stepping back to survey the pergola with a critical tilt of her head.

I breathe out through my nose. Izzy offsets all calming

properties of the New Forest. My blood pressure is already climbing.

'Why does a proposal require sparkle, exactly?'

The pergola looks classy – there are candles, tasteful floral decorations and a light sprinkling of fairy lights hanging in loops between the eight oak pillars.

'It's a huge moment! It needs to feel epic,' Izzy says, and then, catching my eye-roll, she says, 'Oh, let me guess, you hate proposals? And joy? And love?'

'I do not hate joy and love. Or proposals. Put those fairy lights down,' I say, exasperated. 'You'll ruin it. We already have lights.'

What is it with this woman and those things? If she had her way, we'd all wander around the hotel draped in them.

'Not *enough* lights,' Izzy says, already mounting the ladder to hang the next set. 'And I don't believe you. I literally cannot imagine you proposing. You'd be like . . .' She trails off. 'OK, I'm not going to attempt a Brazilian accent. But you'd say something really factual. Like, *Why don't we get married, here are all the reasons I think this is a good idea.*'

'Do it in the accent,' I say, moving to stand under her ladder. No doubt if she fell and broke a bone it would be my fault, somehow. 'Then I might tell you how I would propose.'

That catches her by surprise – her hands falter on the fairy lights and she looks down at me. I meet her gaze after a day of avoiding eye contact by every possible means. She has surprising eyes. From her colouring you'd expect hazel or brown, but they're the green of palmeira leaves, and almond-shaped, with decadent long lashes. Izzy is 'cute', that's what men would say – she's petite, with round cheeks and a button nose. Cute, not sexy. Until you meet her eyes, and then you change your mind.

'I'm not doing the accent,' she says after a moment, returning her attention to the string of lights.

'OK.'

'I'm not doing it – it'll be offensively bad.'

'Fine.'

She waits. I wait.

'Oh, for God's sake, fine: *Why don't we get married*,' she tries, and then, when I start laughing, 'That was good! I thought it was good!'

'It started Spanish,' I say, straightening up and sniffing as I compose myself again. 'And then became Australian.'

Even in the half-light I can see that she's red with embarrassment, and I grin, mood greatly improved.

'Shut up, Lucas. Go on, then – how would you propose?' she asks as she climbs down the ladder and shifts it to the next pillar.

'Not like this,' I say.

With all the outdoor heaters set up and the table beautifully dressed, this is technically an ideal spot for a proposal. But there is something tense about it.

'This is too . . .'

'Spontaneous? Romantic?' she says, climbing up the rungs again as the colour subsides in her cheeks.

'I was going to say showy. What if Hiro says no? Half of his family is waiting in the bar.'

'Do you just *enjoy* sucking the fun out of everything? We're helping to create something magical here, and you're standing there talking about Hiro breaking Charlie's heart.'

I ignore this, taking comfort – as I will many times – from remembering Izzy trying to sound Brazilian. She is wilfully naïve about this sort of thing. I am just being realistic.

'Anyway, asking someone to marry you is a question,' she says over her shoulder, standing on one foot to loop the lights a little further along the beam. 'So there's always the possibility the other person will say no.'

'If there's the possibility she will say no, then I wouldn't be asking,' I say. This strikes me as a given, but Izzy pauses as she comes down the ladder, staring at me.

'You would already know she'd say yes? Where's the excitement in that?'

'A proposal is an agreement,' I say. 'It's a lifelong commitment. You don't do it on a whim.'

'Well, that makes sense, at least,' Izzy says dryly. 'I've never seen you do anything on a whim. Turn them on, would you?'

I flick on the lights, a bad mood blooming in my stomach. What's so good about whims? Isn't it just another word for not thinking things through?

'What would you want, then?' I ask her, as we step back to admire the overall effect. 'You would prefer to be blindsided?'

'No, of course not, I'd just want it to be romantic, not some sort of pre-agreed contrived thing, you know? Ooh, they're here!' she hisses, checking the nearest outdoor heater is working with one hand and lighting the candle at the centre of the table with the other.

We've instructed Ollie to come out and wait on the table no more than fifteen minutes after Charlie and Hiro are seated. Charlie wants to propose at the start of the meal, so that he can enjoy his dinner. Or – I can't help thinking – so that he has time for a quick getaway if Hiro says no.

'Go! Go! Go!' Izzy whispers.

She runs off into the woods. I stare in the direction of her flying hair and the white bottoms of her trainers before walking after her. Running is entirely unnecessary. Also, she's going in a completely random direction. I hesitate when I hit the path that will take me back to the hotel, and the evening I had planned for myself: drive home, heat up a portion of *feijoada* from the freezer, and eat it in front of *A Grande Família*. It is what I always do on Thursdays. Every two months I batch cook a huge *feijoada* specifically for this reason.

It is safe and comfortable. A small joy in a stressful week.

If I follow Izzy somewhere into the New Forest, I suspect I will not have a safe and comfortable night. I hesitate, listening to the sounds of Charlie and Hiro settling into their seats: Hiro's murmur of delight, Charlie's nervous laugh.

I step off the path.

Izzy

I'm up a tree by the time I realise Lucas has followed me. He really is surprisingly stealthy.

'Izzy. Are you in a tree?'

His tone is as dry and expressionless as ever. I shift on my branch to get a better view, ignoring the dampness soaking into my clothes. Between the trees, the pergola is lit up in yellow gold, and if Lucas would shut up, I'd be able to hear every word Hiro and Charlie are saying.

This place is so gorgeous at night. If the New Forest seems like a fairy-tale wood in the daytime, in the dark it's all goblins and witchcraft. No matter how wet or cold it is, there's magic in the air. I once saw a white owl drop between the trees right in front of me on my walk home, its pale face turned to mine in wide-eyed surprise. And the night sky here is stunning: reams of stars, as thick and bright as spilled glitter.

'Izzy. I heard something up this tree. Is it you? Or a cat?'

I snort.

'It is you. What are you doing?'

'Will you shush? I'm trying to watch!'

'Did you climb a tree so you could spy on Charlie's proposal?'

'Yes, obviously.'

'This is a private moment for two people you don't know.'

'Oh, please. It's not like I'm livestreaming. Aww, that is *adorable*.'

'What is adorable?'

'He's – oh, oh my God, this is too cute.'

'What is too cute?'

'Will you either shut up or get up?'

'I am not climbing this tree.'

There is a brief, wonderful silence. Between the branches, the light hits Hiro's face as he lifts his hands to his mouth in shock and delight, and I feel myself tearing up. Lucas is such a cynic. This proposal is exactly what Hiro wanted, and they're absolutely going to live happily ever after.

'Tell me what is happening,' Lucas says.

'Are you kidding?'

'Do you actually want me in your tree?'

It is a pretty small tree.

'Fine. He said yes. They're – aww . . .'

'You are terrible at this.'

'What do you want, like, a football commentary?'

'That would be perfect.'

'And he's leaning in, the ring's on Hiro's finger, I don't believe it, Charlie's done it! He's really done it! Charlie Matterson has proposed to Hiro Tanaka, and Hiro has accepted. Here today at Forest Manor Hotel and Spa, Charlie's shown the world what he's made of, and – oh – he's leaning in for a kiss! And it's another winner!'

'Please stop.'

I've given myself the giggles. I wriggle off my tree branch to the one below and then hop down to ground level with a little less grace than I'd like; I stumble and have to grab on to something, which turns out to be Lucas's arm, though it's hard to tell the difference between that and a tree trunk, to be fair.

He pulls away from me in the darkness as if I've scalded him.

'What!' I say, before I can stop myself. 'I'm not contagious.'

It's hard to read his expression – down here the lights from the pergola are blocked by the trees, and he's shadowy, edged in dark gold.

'What did I do wrong this time?' Lucas says, without particular rancour.

The forest floor is wet, its moss soaked through from today's rain. We begin to walk back to the hotel, skirting the clearing with the pergola to give Charlie and Hiro their privacy. Our work is officially done – it's over to Arjun, Ollie and the waiting staff now.

'Do you honestly find me so repellent? Seriously?'

I glance across at Lucas's profile, the hard jut of his brow and jaw, the precise lines of his haircut.

'You once expressed a desire never to come within two metres of me, "pandemic or no pandemic",' he says. 'I am just respecting your wishes.'

I wince. I did say that. It sounds harsh rather than funny when he quotes it back to me. I remind myself that this man read the Christmas card in which I confessed my feelings for him and *laughed*. I do not need to feel bad for offending him.

'That was right after you told Mrs SB on me when I'd broken lockdown rules for that wedding. I was pissed off,' I say, looking down at the path. We're lit by little inset lights – they glow against Lucas's ridiculously well-polished shoes with each step.

'I did not "tell on you". I raised a concern, because if you continued risking the health of everyone at the hotel in order to please a handful of guests, you could have got us closed down.'

'It was their wedding day,' I say, and here's the rising tide of frustration that always comes after prolonged exposure to Lucas. 'They wanted their whole family there and all I did was find an innovative solution to how to get more than fifteen people celebrating *without* technically all being at the same—'

'It's done,' he says, breaking in as we step on to the lawns. 'We have already agreed to disagree on whether it was right.'

I grit my teeth. We're almost at the hotel car park. Almost time to slam the door on my beautiful sky-blue Smart car, get Harper Armwright's Christmas album playing and drive away from Lucas at speed.

My phone buzzes in my hand, lighting up, and we both look down at the screen. An email from Mrs SB. Subject line: *£15,000 reward from Eric Matterson?!?!*

'Holy shit,' I whisper, coming to a halt and flicking the email open.

New plan, it reads. *Return every ring. Even just one more reward like that would make this worth every bit of effort. Wow. You're an absolute star, Izzy – WELL DONE!! X*

'Well,' Lucas says stiffly, setting off towards the car park again. 'You certainly got the credit.'

'Yeah,' I say. 'It was me who did it, so . . .' I have to double-step to keep up with him. 'Don't be jealous. This is a hotel mission now. You're officially part of The Ring Thing.'

He waits a long moment before responding. 'That *is* a significant reward.'

'I'm sorry, was that an admission that The Ring Thing was an excellent idea and from now on you're going to help me?'

'You didn't do this in the hope of a reward.'

'I did it because it felt right, and putting good stuff out into the universe gets you good stuff back.' I spread my arms as we step between the hedges and into the car park. 'Isn't that kind of the same?'

He stares at me flatly. 'I hope you don't actually think that's how the world works.'

I do, absolutely, so I roll my eyes at him. He slows, and I glance at his car. It's one of those sleek, dark ones with blackout windows, the sort of car a supervillain would drive. Figures.

'To answer your questions, yes, I will join you in working on this ring . . . business,' he says. 'Since Mrs SB wants it done. And no. I don't find you repellent.'

I raise my eyebrows in surprise. Lucas's head is turned away from me, towards the hotel, with its beautiful eighteenth-century windows glowing gold. I take the opportunity to really look at him. His eyebrows are hard slashes, drawn together in his habitual frown, but his lips are surprisingly full. He has the sort of soft, wide mouth you'd describe as *expressive* on someone who had more than one expression.

'It is one of the many things about you that annoys me,' he says.

I intend to snort a laugh and take my moment to walk away when he's conceded something. But I'm still looking at the light and shadow playing across his face, and instead, on impulse, I find myself saying, 'Vice versa, Lucas da Silva. You are offensively handsome.'

It clearly catches him by surprise, which surprises *me* – I mean, he knows I used to fancy him. Plus he's so objectively gorgeous, it didn't feel like a particularly revealing thing to say – it was like telling him he's tall or bad-tempered. He jangles his car keys in his hand, and I get the sense he's lost for words, which makes me a little giddy. All of a sudden I feel like doing something risky. I've not felt that particular zip of daring go through me for a while, and I'd forgotten how *fun* it feels.

'If you're helping with The Ring Thing,' I say, 'do you want to make it a bit more interesting?'

'Interesting . . . how?' Lucas says, keys still jangling.

I reach for my own keys in my pocket, Smartie's lights blinking in the dark car park as I hit unlock. This is a conversation that feels like it might need a fast exit.

'A bet. Whoever returns the next ring wins.'

The wind blusters through the car park, ruffling the hedges, sending a lone plastic bottle skittering under the cars.

'Wins what?' Lucas asks.

'Well . . . what would you like?'

The keys stop jangling. He is suddenly very still.

'What would I like?'

'Mm.'

It seems colder now, the breeze sharper. Lucas's stillness reminds me of a big cat waiting to pounce.

'I want one day,' he says. 'One day in which you do things my way. I am in charge. What I say goes.'

'You'd love that, wouldn't you?' I say derisively, but my breath quickens.

He looks at me with dark, glinting eyes. 'If you win, you can have the same.'

Lucas at my beck and call, agreeing with everything I say, doing as he's told? It is almost too good to imagine. And I'm confident I can return a ring before he can. This sort of challenge is made for me – Lucas will try to use statistics and spreadsheets, but this is about understanding *people*. I lift my chin, shucking off the strange, hot-cold feeling that's come over me in the face of his steady stare.

'Deal,' I say, and hold out my hand to shake his.

Our palms connect hard. The feeling of his fingers gripping my hand makes my heart quicken, like the moment at the start of a race – you're not running yet, but you know you will be.

Lucas

I arrive at the hotel the next morning to find that Izzy is already here, and has spread a great number of socks across the desk. After a moment, I conclude that this is part of an effort to sort them into pairs, which strikes me as an enormous waste of time – but then, Izzy loves to do what she calls 'going the extra mile'.

'I've sorted your Mrs Muller problem,' she says to me, not bothering with a hello.

One of the builders calls, 'Hey, Izz!' as he strolls in, still vaping, and she gives him a big smile and a wave, all of which irritates me. Despite the two hours I've just spent in the gym, I'm on edge – I have been all week. The stress of working shifts with Izzy Jenkins, no doubt.

'It's not *my* Mrs Muller problem,' I say, very deliberately shifting the clothes heaped on my chair to the already teetering pile on hers. 'Any problem Mrs Muller is having concerns all of us.'

A note from Poor Mandy says that Louis Keele requested a wake-up call for eight fifteen today, so I ring him, hang up as quickly as possible – he is still mid sleepy grunt – and then wait for Izzy to tell me what she's done. She just continues sorting socks, humming Ed Sheeran's 'Bad Habits'. She has stuck a note to my keyboard – something about paint in the store cupboard, but as usual her handwriting is totally unreadable. She has also moved the pen pot to her side of the desk, even though it should live right in the middle. I am disproportionately annoyed by both these things. Maybe I need to go back to the gym after work, too.

'Well?' I say.

'Well what?'

'What did you do about Mrs Muller?'

She smiles in satisfaction and brings out her phone, pulling up a photo of the paint splattering the wall of Mrs Muller's suite. I stare at it, trying to get the point, until she leans forward and zooms in on the bottom corner of the mess. Her hair falls forward, striped in green and blue today, and I make the mistake of inhaling. She smells of cinnamon again.

'See it?' she says.

I lean closer, my head just inches from hers. There is a small sign stuck to the wall. *When the Muses Strike, by M. Muller*, it reads. *December 2022*. It is just like the cards you see next to artworks in a museum.

'She was thrilled,' Izzy says. 'Honoured, she said. She's going to stay in "her room" at the hotel every year from now on.'

'So we have to keep that mess there?'

'It's art!' she says.

A message pops up on the top of her screen. *Sameera says . . . Will you just angry-shag him in a spare hotel room already?* it reads.

She turns the screen black and steps away from me instantly. 'Umm,' she says.

I sit down, directing my attention firmly towards the computer, but my heart is pounding. Who does this Sameera think Izzy should angry-shag? I don't know of anyone at the hotel Izzy is angry with other than . . . me.

'I assume you saw that,' Izzy says, sorting socks with too much enthusiasm – one goes flying over the edge of the desk on to the lobby rug. 'The message.'

'Yes,' I say, scrolling through the hotel's inbox, and then scrolling back up through the unread emails again, because I don't think I absorbed a single subject line.

'It's not . . . My friend Grigg's wife is just super inappropriate. I'm not going to shag anyone. Definitely not in an angry way. Having sex when you're angry is never a good idea. Not that it's any of your business.'

'I didn't ask,' I point out, keeping my voice as dry as possible. I will my heart rate to slow. The message probably referred to someone from outside the hotel. Just because it mentioned a hotel room doesn't necessarily mean it was about one of Izzy's colleagues.

'Morning Izzy. Lucas.'

Louis Keele. I offer him a polite smile and then return my gaze firmly to my inbox. Izzy can deal with him. He wants Izzy anyway. I type out a few emails to possible ring owners just as the rest of the builders traipse in, trailing wet mud across the lobby floor behind Louis. I reach for the phone to call house-keeping, but Dinah appears, as if conjured by inconsiderateness, and scowls after them, mop already in hand.

I like Dinah. She never goes the extra mile – she goes just far enough, and I have a lot of respect for that.

'I wanted to give you a heads up,' Louis says.

I glance up again. Louis is not a large man, or a particularly impressive one, but he is just the sort of guy who would put me on edge if I weren't there already. He's self-assured, and has a warm charm that makes conversation easy. In other words, he is very unlike me.

'Mr Townsend, the sweet guy with the tremor? As I left my room, I heard him muttering about this "miserable place" and how this will be "some Christmas".' Louis pulls a sympathetic face. He is always a lot nicer when Izzy is around. 'Sorry, I just thought you'd want prior warning . . .'

We all turn as Mr Townsend appears. He is visibly upset, his head bowed, his movements jerky. I look away – I suspect Mr Townsend would rather not have everybody in the lobby staring at him – and see Louis' phone, which rests between his hands on the desk. There's a photo of the lobby up on his screen. I frown.

'Oh, God,' Izzy mutters, stepping around the desk. 'Thank you, Louis. I really appreciate that. Mr Townsend? How are you today?'

'She's good,' Louis says, watching Izzy soothe Mr Townsend. He leans on the desk and starts to toss the socks in front of him

into a pile. This will annoy Izzy, so I leave him to it. 'A natural.'
He side-eyes me. 'Cute, too.'

The bad temper brewing in my chest begins to pick up
momentum.

'I'm thinking of investing, you know,' Louis says before I can
answer. 'In Forest Manor.'

'Oh. That's great news.' Perhaps that's why he's taking photographs. I should be pleased that he's considering investing,
but I can't help wondering what he would do to this hotel if he
had a say in how it's run.

'Mm. I think it has potential,' he says, still watching Izzy
as she leads Mr Townsend into an armchair, head ducked, listening. 'My dad loves buildings like this, old places, you know,
with history.'

'It's a very special hotel,' I say stiffly. I can't help noticing that
Louis seems more interested in looking down Izzy's shirt than
contemplating his future investment.

'Yeah, absolutely. The building has tons of development
potential. Hmm. Great figure, too, hasn't she?' he adds, tilting
his head to the side.

The building has tons of development potential? I bite down on my
cheek so hard it hurts. That sounds like something you'd say
if you were buying a manor house, not investing in a hotel. Is
that Louis' game? And might the Singh-Bartholomews sell, now
that things have become so desperate?

I look at what I have typed on the draft email to a potential
wedding client in front of me. *Hiog[rwJIPR;Wkgk.* Yes. If there
were a word for this feeling, it would probably look something

like that. Louis sees no reason why Izzy would not want his attention, just as he sees no reason why he shouldn't get to do as he likes with this beautiful hotel, and it makes my blood boil.

'Better shoot. Good chat,' he says, firing me a wink as he saunters off.

He dodges Mr and Mrs Hedgers, who are heading through to their room with the kids behind them, muttering furiously to one another. Izzy would try to figure out what's wrong. I watch them go, thinking they look like they'd rather be left alone.

I look back at my screen as my pulse slows. There's one new email. I click through.

OMG! it says. *That is totally my wedding ring! Can I come in on Monday to pick it up? Hubby will be so pleased!*

'*Porra!*' I mutter, already typing back.

Izzy

I lie back on my bed, pull the laptop on to my knees and reach for my tea. It's a spiced loose leaf tea blend – it's a total faff to make, but I love it, and lately it's become a bit of a ritual for my rare, precious evenings to myself. I open Netflix, looking for something new, even though I already know I'll be rewatching *Charmed*, and then I make the mistake of checking my phone. Sixty-eight unread messages from seven chats.

I am a people person. I've always had a whole gaggle of friends, and that's exactly how I like it, but lately I've started to feel like I'm keeping up with my WhatsApps for the sake of it. Replying just to get rid of the unread messages, not because I really want to hear how my old colleagues' kids are, or how a mate from school is getting on with her new job.

An ex-boyfriend once said that I collect people and don't let them go, and the comment has really stayed with me. At the time I told him you can never have too many friends, and that there's nothing wrong with being loyal, but when everything happened with Drew last year, it made me see things a little differently.

From the moment I met her, I knew we'd get along. She walked into my flat for a viewing with this big, cheeky smile and fabulous square glasses and I was smitten. I was on furlough and needed the extra money, and I knew that whoever moved in to my box room would be spending a lot of time with me – the perils of flatsharing in a lockdown. But she seemed so fun, I instantly relaxed.

And Drew could be really fun when she wanted to. Say, when she was trying to get a room in your flat. But once she was installed there with a twelve-month contract, she was a different person altogether. I tried so hard to rediscover that side of her. I coaxed her into a more positive outlook as she whinged on my sofa about being bored; I bowed to her requests to change my flat's decor because it was 'too childish' and 'too pink' in the background of her video calls. Basically, I was so determined to be friends with my flatmate that I put up with almost twelve months of absolute nonsense. And then she kissed the man she *knew* I liked, and I realised that I was making all this effort for someone who gave zero shits about me.

My outlook has started to shift in the year post Drew. Maybe I don't need to keep people in my life at all costs. Maybe I don't need to be surrounded in the way I did back when my parents died. There are a few people who will always bring me joy – Jem, Grigg, Sameera. But as I scroll through my recent conversations, I ask myself who I am looking forward to catching up with from this list, and the answer is kind of shocking. There's pretty much nobody I actually want to see.

The phone rings in my hand and I let out a yip of surprise, spilling tea on my duvet cover.

'Shit,' I say, dabbing as I answer the video call.

'Hello,' Grigg says, unfazed at being greeted with a swear word.

Not much fazes Grigg: he is the exhausted father of a seven-month-old who wakes up five times a night, and still he remains unflappable. We met when we both spent a summer waiting tables at The Jolly Farmer pub on the edge of the Forest, and, even aged sixteen, he'd had the air of a mild-mannered old man. I remember watching him drop a tray of full pints: he stood there for a moment, looking thoughtfully at the carnage on the floor around him, and then said, *You know, Izzy, I am just not sure I have found my calling, here.* He's an accountant these days, and likes it much better.

His wife Sameera bobs into view in the background, giving me a wave with a slice of pizza in her mouth.

'Hey, sweetness!' she calls through her mouthful.

'How's my favourite godson?' I ask.

'Sleeping! At bedtime!'

'Amazing!'

'I know, right? Did Sexy Scowly Receptionist really see Grigg's message?' asks Sameera, giggling already.

'Not my message,' Grigg says. 'I was merely relaying a message from you, darling wife. I have never said *angry-shag* in my life before.'

'Don't laugh, Sam!' I say, but I'm giggling along with Sameera, who is doubled over behind Grigg. 'It was so awkward!'

'Did he know it was about him, do you think?' Sameera calls, disappearing off-screen.

'I don't know,' I say, reaching for the spare pillow to bury my face in it. 'I obviously tried to make it sound like it wasn't. I don't even want to shag him! That's *you* talking, not me! But now he's going to think I want him.'

'Don't you?' Grigg says. He's gnawing on a pizza crust. In the rare windows of time when baby Rupe is asleep, they tend to do everything at once – I'm pretty sure Sameera is putting on a wash in the background. 'Didn't you write him that love letter last Christmas?'

From somewhere off-screen, Sameera throws a handful of dirty laundry at Grigg. He barely flinches.

'Grigg!'

'It was not a love letter,' I say, 'it was a Christmas card, and yes, I had a crush on him once, but all I said in that message to you was that there was a bit of a *vibe* at the mo – that doesn't mean I want him. We still hate each other.'

'You don't need to like someone to fancy them,' Sameera says.

'Don't you?' Grigg asks mildly.

'I don't fancy him,' I say, but the moment I say it, I know I'm lying. I know, deep down, that I didn't want to cover myself up when Lucas caught me half-dressed through the lost-property-room door, and that if I weren't still attracted to him, I'd have squealed and dashed out of view as quick as a rat. 'Oh, shit,' I say, re-burying my face in the pillow.

'I think this is good!' Sameera says. 'You always go for such . . .'

'Wet-arse men,' Grigg finishes for her.

'Excuse me?'

'Lost causes, guys who live in dimly-lit basements, men with big dreams they're going to get started on some time next summer.' Grigg takes a large bite of his pizza.

'Hey!' I say, though actually this is painfully pitch-perfect. I think about Tristan's flat above his parents' garage, and Dean's start-up plans, and I grimace.

'Grigg's right,' Sameera says excitedly. 'Sexy Scowly has drive and ambition! That's way more you! Didn't you say he lost the job he came here for because the place shut down, and then he got the job at your hotel, like, *days* before his visa was due to expire?'

'Yeah, he did,' I say, chewing my lip.

It's one of the very rare pieces of personal information I've gleaned from Lucas – it came up in a conversation about lock-down rules. Thank God those days are gone. We argued worse than ever when the government guidelines kept changing every few weeks.

'He's driven, sure. He's also a massive knob,' I remind them.

'Does he!' Sameera crows, bounding back into view again with a bunch of laundry bundled to her chest.

'*Is* a massive knob, Sam,' I say, and then laugh at the disappointment on her face. 'I promise you, I'm not interested in Lucas any more, not after what happened last Christmas.' I hold up a hand when they both open their mouths to speak. 'I *will* acknowledge that I still find him attractive.'

'What's wrong with a bit of flirtation, then? You don't need to worry about leading him on or hurting his feelings, given that he hates you as much as you hate him. And if the flirting leads to angry sex, hurray!' Sameera throws a hand up, sending a pair of knickers flying with it. 'If you decide you don't want to sleep with him, then you've wound him up for weeks on end – also hurray!'

'Well,' I say, sipping my tea, 'when you put it like that . . .'

'Hey, what address should we post your Christmas present to?' Grigg asks, turning the camera back to him again. 'I keep meaning to ask – where's Jem living right now?'

'Just post it here,' I say, shifting my pillow behind me. 'I'll take it with me when I go. I can't believe you guys have the headspace for shopping this early, with Rupe still up half the night. You're doing so well.'

'Cried on the sofa for a full forty minutes this morning, sweetness!' Sameera calls. I hear the slam of what I assume is the washing-machine door.

'Oh, Sam . . . Is there anything I can do?' For about the millionth time, I wish they'd not made the move to Edinburgh. If they were still down here in the New Forest, I could be the one putting on that wash, making them dinner, settling Rupe.

'Have a torrid love affair and then tell me all about it?' Sameera suggests, finally flopping down next to Grigg on the sofa. He pulls her in close and kisses her head.

'I love you,' I tell her, 'but not enough for torrid. Torrid sounds messy.'

94

'Torrid sounds *exciting*,' Sameera corrects me. 'You need a bit of that.'

'My life is nonstop excitement,' I say. 'Right, I'll leave you to the million things you've stockpiled to get done while the baby's down. Bye, loves. I hope Rupe sleeps through.'

'Me too,' Sameera says, with feeling.

I drop my phone on the duvet and settle back in with *Charmed*, sipping my tea and ignoring my WhatsApps. Trying not to mind that when I said my life is nonstop excitement, Grigg and Sameera both laughed.

Usually, winter is a whirlwind at the hotel. Work Christmas lunches, girly spa trips, cosy couples' minibreaks and lavish winter weddings. It feels horribly quiet now. On an average day here, I always play a hundred different roles (public relations manager, kids' entertainer, window un-jammer, whatever the crisis needs) but the roles I'm playing at the moment aren't nearly as fun as usual. Today, for instance, I am spending my Monday deep-cleaning the carpet and sorting umbrellas from the lost-property room. *All* the umbrellas are black. Black reminds me of funerals – I own zero black clothes, and my current umbrella is polka-dot pale blue, though I lose them so frequently it's hard to keep track.

The Ring Thing is keeping me going at the moment. After we phoned the same people within minutes of each other on Saturday morning (awkward), Lucas and I decided we'll each focus on a ring of our own, to minimise the risk of strangling one another in frustration. Lucas's ring is a fancy diamond-studded band – of course he picked that one – whereas I went for the gold wedding ring, battered and well-loved. The other two – the beautiful emerald engagement ring and the stylish hammered-silver wedding band – will have to wait until I've beaten Lucas at this bet.

He seems to be having even worse luck than I am. Yesterday I heard someone yelling at him on the phone for 'bothering them about a wedding ring five days after they'd been jilted'. Oops. I know I should want him to find his ring's owner for the sake of the hotel, and I *do*, of course I do, I just . . . don't want him to find them *yet*.

I smile as I walk back in from my lunch break (leftovers in the kitchen with Arjun) and spot Mr Townsend in the armchair by the lobby window. Now *there's* a success story. It took me a couple of attempts to figure out what Mr Townsend needed from his stay here. At first, I tried to give him a spa session, thinking he wanted peace and quiet – but now I've nailed it.

People come to a hotel at this time of year for all sorts of reasons, and I realised Mr Townsend's reason was exactly the same as mine: because he didn't want to spend Christmas alone.

So I've set him up right here in the middle of things. I've encouraged him to see the builders not as a disruption to hotel activity, but as *part* of it. Now that he knows the tall one hates the one with the ponytail, and the guy in charge is definitely in love with the one woman on the team, he's quite content to sit here in the lobby and watch their antics – and ours.

'Any luck with your ring?' Mr Townsend calls.

'Getting there!' I call back. 'Can I fetch you anything? A tea? A new book?'

'I'm all set, thank you. You missed a call,' he says, nodding towards the desk, 'but they left a voicemail.'

'We're going to have to put you on the payroll,' I tell him, just as Louis strolls into the lobby.

'Hey, Izzy,' he says. 'Up for that swim tonight?'

He's wearing jeans and a wool jumper, his hands tucked in his pockets. I get the sense there's more to Louis than the boyish cheekiness – a bit of an edge, maybe. It makes me curious. He's different from the usual men I go for, and after my chat with Grigg and Sameera, I'm thinking that's definitely a good thing. Maybe I should give this a go.

I try to imagine what my mum would have said about him. She and Dad always told me I should choose someone kind and attentive – 'a man who smiles easily, that's what you need', Mum once said.

That thought swings it.

'Why not?' I say, just as Lucas marches out of the restaurant, looking furious about something.

Louis smiles. 'Excellent. See you when your shift ends – five, is it?'

'Perfect.' I turn my attention to the glowering Lucas. 'What?' I ask.

The two of us have been avoiding each other more than ever since our interaction in the car park. Every time I see him, that conversation leaps into my mind – his intensity, the way he'd looked at me when I'd called him *offensively handsome*.

'You volunteered me to wait on the hen party for lunch?'

I press my lips together, trying very hard not to smile. I forgot I did that.

'Can you not do it?' I ask.

'I can,' he says, with deliberation. 'But I don't want to. You know I hate waiting on the big groups. Especially drunk ones. *Especially* hens.'

'But you always go down so well with the hens!'

'If anyone attempts to undress me, it will be you I'm suing,' Lucas says darkly.

'Well, I'm going to be spending the time sorting coins from the lost-property room and taking them to the post office. You could swap, if you like.'

I gesture to the jars of loose change lining the edge of the front desk. Lucas stares at them.

'Does that actually need to be done?'

'It's money,' I point out. 'Are you suggesting I throw it in the bin?'

He growls under his breath and stalks off towards the restaurant. Then he pauses, turning with his hand on the door.

'How is your hunt for your wedding ring's owner going?'

'Brilliantly!' I say. 'I'm down to my final five contenders.'

Five, seventeen – what's the difference, really?

'Good for you,' Lucas says.

I narrow my eyes. His tone is far too . . . nice.

'How's yours going?' I ask.

'A woman is dropping in to collect her lost ring at three

o'clock,' he says, pushing through the restaurant door and letting it swing shut behind him.

Shit.

I glance at the clock. Two minutes to three. Lucas's ring owner is due any second. Would it be wrong of me to run some intervention? Lock the hotel doors, just for ten minutes or so? Send Lucas off to do something urgent and then tell his visitor that the ring has already been claimed by somebody else?

It would be wrong, definitely. However . . .

'Don't even try,' Lucas says, not looking up from where he's cleaning silver candlesticks at the other end of the front desk.

'I didn't do anything!'

'You are . . . *tramando*.'

'I don't know what that means.'

'Scheming. Plotting.'

'Would I ever?' I say as he turns to look at me. I arrange my expression into the picture of innocence.

'That face doesn't work on me,' Lucas says.

His eyes hold mine, dark and knowing. Something flutters in my stomach. Then his gaze snaps to the door as a woman steps into the lobby, bringing in a blast of freezing air.

'Hello!' Lucas calls, with more enthusiasm than I've seen from him since someone suggested updating the restaurant table booking system. 'Are you Ruth?'

'Yes, hi, that's me!' the woman says, pasting on a large smile.

I am immediately suspicious. Obviously I have skin in the game here, but I meet a lot of members of the public in this job, and I've developed a bit of an eye for the ones who are going to cause trouble. The people who won't pay their bar tab, who will take things from the hotel that aren't strictly toiletries, who will print out the same Groupon voucher twice. And this Ruth has troublemaker written all over her, from her pristine ponytail to the toes of her trying-to-look-expensive boots.

I do not believe that Lucas's ring belongs to this woman. That ring is stunning, but it's not showy: the diamonds are tiny and the design is really subtle. I'd say a woman with a counterfeit designer handbag probably wants a wedding ring that shouts about how pricey it was, not something small and pretty.

'Thanks so much for coming in,' I say, standing up with my best smile. 'As I'm sure you'll understand, we'll have to check a few things to make sure we're giving the ring to the right person.'

To her credit, her expression doesn't change. 'Sure,' she says, pulling her handbag closer against her side. 'What do you need? Some ID?'

'Do you have a receipt for the ring?' I ask.

'Perhaps you could just describe it,' Lucas says, glancing side-ways at me.

I look back at him, raising my eyebrows. *Really?* my face says. *You're so concerned about winning our bet that you're prepared to give a valuable piece of jewellery to a potential fraud? What if it causes problems for the hotel?*

I watch his face darken as he comes to the same conclusion.

'I bought it in a jeweller's,' the woman says, patting at her hair. 'So there's no digital receipt. It was years ago! But I can tell you it's a thin gold ring studded with diamonds.'

I shoot another look at Lucas. His grim expression tells me that he said that much in his initial email.

'You'll see what a conundrum we're in,' I say, smile still in place. 'Is there any way you can prove it's your ring?'

'Can you prove it's not?' she asks. There's a sharpness in her tone now.

'Perhaps you could tell us when you stayed here?' Lucas asks.

Her gaze shifts from me to Lucas and back again. She swallows.

'2020,' she says.

'Oh dear. Not quite,' I say.

'2018?' she tries, confidence visibly evaporating.

'I know!' I turn to Lucas. 'We could ask if she knows about the chipped diamond. Oh, crap,' I say, covering my mouth.

'Yes!' she says, relieved. 'One of the diamonds was chipped! How could I forget that? There you go. There can't be many rings that fit that description, can there? And . . .' She waggles her bare hand at us. 'I've definitely lost my wedding ring.'

Well, this is awkward. I turn to Lucas, who is blinking rapidly, his expression fixed.

'Over to you?' I say sweetly, sitting down again. Mentioning the chip was an absolute masterstroke, if I do say so myself. There was – of course – no chip.

This has been super helpful. I've realised what an advantage I have over Lucas in this particular race, because my ring has an engraving on the inside. So even if I have a long list to work through, once I find my owner, I'll know they're the one – and just like that, I'll be the winner, glory shall be mine, and Lucas will have to abide by my every wish.

And, oh, I'm going to make him suffer.

Lucas

I started late today, so I am staying late too. That is only reasonable. And the seating areas dotted around the pool badly need tidying. There are magazines here from a time when all the UK had to worry about was whether a man named Jeremy Clarkson had or had not punched someone.

That is why I'm here: tidying. It's nothing to do with the fact that Louis Keele is currently powering up and down the swimming pool, waiting for Izzy to arrive for their ... plans. Their arrangement. Their date?

'Fetch me a beer, would you, Lucas?' Louis calls from the pool, twisting to float on his back.

Fetch me a beer. Like I'm a dog. I turn around, ready to snarl, but then Izzy appears in the doorway of the women's changing room and I lose my train of thought entirely.

'Lucas,' she says, surprised. She's wearing a dressing gown hanging open over her bikini. 'What are you doing here?'

I recognise that bikini: it lives in the box she keeps under the desk. I noticed it when I tidied her box, an act I knew would irritate her enormously, and which ended up feeling slightly sordid, partly because of that bikini. You can't see a bikini without imagining the person in it.

And it is very small. Turquoise green with thin straps. Right now, I can only see a few inches of it between the two sides of her dressing gown, along with a shocking flash of smooth, pale skin, but the sight makes my breath catch in my throat. My imagination did not do her justice.

She looks so different. She's barefoot, with her hair unstriped and pulled up in a bun. There's something vulnerable about her like this, and I feel a stab of an emotion that in another context I might call fear. But it's not that, it can't be – there's nothing to be afraid of.

'Hello,' I say, hating how stiff I sound. 'I started late. So I'm staying late.'

Her eyes narrow slightly. We're in a glass building that links the main house to the spa, which was formerly the stables – the space is lit only by a series of low-energy bulbs above the water, so it's shadowy in here. Behind me I hear the slick splash of Louis moving methodically through the pool.

'You're staying late . . . in the swimming pool area?'

'I am tidying the spa, yes.'

'Tonight?'

'Yes.'

Her eyes get narrower. 'What game are you playing, Lucas da Silva?' she asks.

'No game. I'm working.'

'Hmm.'

I'm sweating. I don't know what game I am playing, that's the truthful answer. Now that I'm standing between Izzy and the pool, I can't ignore how reluctant I am to step aside and let her pass. I don't want Izzy to spend her evening in a bikini with Louis Keele. I don't trust that man with the future of this hotel, and I definitely don't trust him with Izzy.

Which is ridiculous. I swallow and move aside, returning my attention to the dog-eared magazines in wicker baskets by the chairs. When I glance back at her, she's dropping the dressing gown on to a sunlounger.

Fuck. I look away sharply, heart pounding in my throat, suddenly very aware that I shouldn't be here. She's not wearing that bikini for me. I wasn't supposed to see that smooth sweep of naked waist, her long, bare legs, the tiny tattoo at the point where her bikini top is tied. Seeing her in such a different context is making it harder to remember that this is the infuriating Izzy Jenkins, and without that, she is just a dangerously beautiful woman in swimwear.

'That beer, Lucas, mate?' Louis calls.

I know why he's asking. It's not because he particularly wants a beer. It's because he wants Izzy to see me fetch him one.

'No drinks in the spa,' I snap.

'Damn. Can't you make an exception?' says Louis.

'No exceptions, Louis, not even for you!' Izzy calls as she slides into the pool. 'Race you!'

Louis looks at Izzy with blatant appreciation. I feel another stab of that strange, new fear. As they launch into their race, I watch him gaining on her, his form cutting through the water, and then I turn away, heading into the main spa, because what else can I do? In the same way that the bikini wasn't for me, I don't get to feel anxious when Izzy's on a date.

And I hate her, I remind myself. I hate her and she hates me.

After an hour of scrubbing the spa hall floor, I strip down to the vest top I'm wearing under my shirt. I've been in and out – I've needed various bits of equipment from the main hotel, and you have to walk through the pool to get there. But this time, as I move through to return the bag of cleaning supplies to their usual cupboard, Izzy is climbing out of the pool, and I have to slow down to let her reach for her towel.

'How was your date?' I ask in a low voice as she pulls it around herself, tucking it under her arm.

Louis has just stepped through to the men's changing room. I relax a little as the door shuts behind him.

'You've been here pretty much the whole time,' Izzy says. 'You tell me.'

'You won every race,' I say, setting down the bag and folding my arms across my chest. 'So I'd say he's no match for you.'

'Maybe I'm not looking for a guy who tries to outperform me,' she says, widening her eyes slightly as she tucks the towel tighter. Our voices echo in here, the water lapping quietly beside us.

'Oh, he was trying.' I smirk. 'I know his type. Pushy. Likes to win. Compensating for something, no doubt. He just wasn't fast enough.'

'Really?' She tilts her head. 'He seemed like the perfect gentleman to me.'

'You think that's what you need?'

She raises her eyebrows, incredulous. 'You think I need something else?'

'I think you're getting bored of men who will roll over for you on your command,' I say, lifting one shoulder in a shrug. 'I've seen your boyfriends, hanging around, waiting for you to tell them what to do next, chauffeuring you home in their beaten-up cars ...'

Her eyes flare with real irritation. 'That'll be your first job,' she says. 'When I win the bet. Chauffeuring me home in your beaten-up car.'

'My car is spotless.'

'Actually,' she says, 'it got a little scratched this evening. Someone in a Smart car is no good at manoeuvres.'

'You wouldn't,' I growl. 'That is ...'

'Seriously extra,' she says, and she's laughing now. 'No, I wouldn't. But it's got you raging, hasn't it?'

It's true. I am tense; heat is pounding through me.

'Big muscles, fancy car ... You sure *you're* not compensating for something?' she calls as she walks off into the changing room.

On Thursday afternoon, as I settle back at the front desk after a frantic day sorting lost property, my sister messages me on the family WhatsApp group. *Lucas, saudade! Está gostando do clima de Natal britânico?*

She wants to know if I'm enjoying my English Christmas. Messaging me via the family group is an unsubtle reminder that I've been too quiet, and probably a sign that my mother is worrying.

Uncle Antônio isn't in the family WhatsApp group. I occasionally feel guilty about this, but I can't quite bring myself to set up another space in which Ana and I will inevitably feel inadequate.

I flinch suddenly as something lands on my head, and spin around to find Izzy behind me. I catch the reindeer antlers she just tried to put on me.

'No,' I say.

'It's not festive enough around here!' she complains, adjusting her own antlers. Her hair is pulled back in a bun again, like it was that night at the pool. 'It's December now, and the builders won't let me decorate the bannisters yet, and my nativity is gone . . .'

'What about that?' I say, pointing to the enormous Christmas tree occupying much of the lobby.

It took Izzy half a day to decorate that tree. At one point she suggested abseiling down from the scaffolding to get the star on the top, and I don't think she was joking. I stayed out of it, which means that the whole thing is completely overdone, but I am trying to learn when to pick my battles. I can live with too many baubles on the tree.

Though it does annoy me. All the time. A lot.

'Everyone has a Christmas tree,' Izzy says, waving a hand. 'We need to step it up a gear. We may not have a full house, but the restaurant is booked to capacity most nights up to

Christmas – and all the diners will be walking through this lobby, wondering if maybe they should come for a weekend when the renovations are done . . .'

She's right. Despite the building work, we need to be a good advertisement for the hotel at the moment. I look around at all the mess and wince.

'Tidying all this lost property would be a start.'

'Most of this is waiting for buyer collection. Which, by the way, was *all* organised by me. What have you sold lately?'

I scowl. 'Today, I took a whole box of items to auction. I raised almost a thousand pounds. All you do is fiddle around pairing socks and trying to match sets of earrings.'

'Yeah, well, you keep bagsying all the high-value items!' Izzy says, then answers the phone as it rings. 'Oh, hi! Thanks for calling back! Yes, I'd love to speak to Hans about the ring.' She swivels in her chair to direct the full strength of her smugness in my direction. 'Fantastic. Whenever's good for him.'

Merda. I haven't got any further with mine since Ruth's attempted fraud, which was all extremely uncomfortable. There are still four contenders who haven't replied to my calls or follow-up emails. I mentally bump everything else on my to-do list. This is my new priority.

'Ooh, antlers!' coos Poor Mandy as she staggers into the lobby under the weight of her two giant Sainsbury's bags. She untangles them from around her shoulders and they land on the lobby rug with a thud as she digs out her phone – case flap dangling – and starts snapping photographs of us. 'Lucas, dear, put yours on too! This will be wonderful on the Facebook.'

Izzy clicks the phone back in its cradle with great deliberateness and then turns to me.

'Antlers on, Lucas!' she says. 'Do it for the Facebook!'

I glare at her, but put on the antlers. I must check what Poor Mandy is doing to the Forest Manor social media pages – this is one of the many things on my to-do list, just underneath creating a woodland play area and persuading someone other than me to deep-clean the fryer.

'Oh, that's a lovely one. I've sent it to you both too,' Poor Mandy says, tapping away at her phone. She has a habit of moving her lips or muttering as she types, so even before my phone pings, I could guess that she has written, *Fab photo of you two, lots of love, Mandy.*

I look down at the photo for a moment. Izzy has leapt in beside me – she's beaming, her antlers already sliding through her hair. She's wearing some sort of pale-pink sheen on her cheekbones today, and the lights of the Christmas tree make her glitter.

After a moment I crop the photo down so it's just me, wearing antlers, glancing off to the side. I send it on the family WhatsApp, telling them I'm getting in the Christmas spirit already.

'Guys, guys, guys,' Ollie says, power walking over from the kitchen. Ollie has been told repeatedly not to run through the hotel, so now he does an odd fast walk that involves a lot of arm movement.

The kitchen door swings behind him, almost whacking Arjun in the face as he follows behind Ollie. The chef's expression is so thunderous I want to laugh.

'Mrs SB is—'

'Crying,' Arjun says over Ollie. 'Ollie, there are five pans on the hob, what are you doing out here? It's dangerous.'

I watch Ollie hover for one tortured moment, deciding whether or not to point out that Arjun is *also* out here, rather than attending to the hob, and that he actually walked out second. Ollie makes the wise choice for his career and dashes back to the kitchen again.

'What? Where?' Izzy says, leaning across the desk as Arjun points towards the window.

Mrs SB passes outside, holding a tissue to her cheek. Izzy is already on her way out. I follow her, just catching the hotel's heavy wooden door in time to stop it slamming in my face. Presumably she got that idea from Ollie.

It's freezing outside, and darkness is setting in across the gardens. Mrs SB steps beyond the beam of the lights on either side of the hotel's entrance, disappearing down the path that leads to Opal Cottage.

'Mrs SB, are you OK?' Izzy calls, quickening her pace.

'Fine, dear!'

Her voice is muffled. Not very convincing.

'Talk to us,' Izzy says as we approach. 'Maybe we can help.'

Mrs SB turns her face aside so Izzy can't see her tears, but I'm on the other side of her. 'Oh, bother,' she says, coming to a standstill between us.

We're in the middle of the rose garden now, lit by the small lights along the borders. The glow catches each puff of Mrs SB's breath as she tries to pull herself together, tissue held to her eyes.

'It's just . . . a little . . . much,' she manages. 'At the moment.'

'Of course.' Izzy rubs her arm soothingly.

'I'm so sorry, both of you. I feel I've let you down horribly.'

'You've not let anybody down!' Izzy says. 'You've kept this hotel running through years of lockdowns and a cost-of-living crisis. That's incredible. It's no wonder the place is struggling – how could it not be?'

I stand, arms folded, feeling painfully awkward. I want to hug Mrs SB, but Izzy's already there, so all I can do is try to project quite how deeply I care – something I know I've never been especially good at showing even when the hugging option is available.

'You take so much on yourself,' Izzy says. 'Can we help more? With the management and administration, maybe? Lucas is really good at this sort of thing – spreadsheets and organisation and stuff.'

I stare at her in surprise. Her cheeks go faintly pink. I open my mouth to say something similar in return – I've long thought that Izzy could be put to better use at the hotel. She should be managing these renovations, in my opinion. She has a good eye for what makes a space work, and she's excellent at coordinating large numbers of people. But Mrs SB is speaking again before I can find the right thing to say.

'Oh, I'm embarrassed to show you the accounts, honestly. I know Barty will feel the same.'

'Don't be embarrassed.' My voice is gruffer than I'd like it to be. I clear my throat. 'I would love to help. I want the same things you and Barty want. I want this place to thrive, and for

our . . . the family we have built here to . . .' Why is this so difficult to say? 'I'm happy to help,' I finish abruptly.

Izzy is staring at me like I've just announced that in future
I'd rather we deliver all internal communications by carrier
pigeon. I avert my eyes, looking up at the sky. The stars are
just beginning to blink into life between grey smudges of cloud.

I should be searching for other jobs. This place will almost
certainly go under before the year is out. But standing here,
breathing in the forest air, with the hotel's grand old bulk
behind me . . . I just cannot imagine myself feeling this sense
of belonging anywhere else.

I know why Izzy's so surprised to hear me talking about the
hotel as a family: she thinks I don't care. That I'm heartless. But
if I am, then why does my chest hurt at the thought of letting
this part of my life go?

'I suppose I could just send you the accounts. Perhaps you
can look for places we can be more efficient.' Mrs SB sniffs,
pulling back from Izzy's arms. 'I find it a bit overwhelming, if
I'm truthful. I've never been good with numbers.'

My fingers flex at the thought of having access to the sums
behind the hotel's decisions. I'll get to see how Forest Manor
really works. All the moving parts. I can do more than just
raising a few hundred pounds with old lost-property rubbish – I
can *help*.

'I like numbers,' I tell her, the ache in my chest subsiding.
'Just send it all my way.'

'Thank you. Thank you.' She squeezes both our arms and
heads off towards Opal Cottage.

We watch her go.

'I appreciate what you said,' I tell Izzy eventually. 'About spreadsheets. When I have the opportunity, I would like to tell Mrs SB that you too deserve a chance to expand your skills here at the hotel.'

'What?'

'I mean . . . There's a lot more you could be doing here too.'

She bristles. 'I'm doing plenty, thanks. And you're welcome. Just . . . Go gently when you get back to her on the figures, OK? Some of us are humans, not robots.'

She walks away through the rose bushes, towards the hotel. The word *robot* stings like a slap. *I'm human too*, I want to say. *When you're unkind to me, it hurts.*

My phone flashes up a reply from Ana as I follow Izzy back inside. Ana has sent my photo back with a large red circle around the tiny portion of Izzy's shoulder that is visible in the photograph.

Quem é essa pessoa???

Oh, *porra*. She wants to know who it is.

É uma mulher?? says my mother.

Merda. Now they've clocked it's a woman. But how? It's about three millimetres of white shirt and . . . oh. A telltale strand of long pink hair. Damn.

I hesitate, wondering how to play this. My mother and sister are convinced I need a girlfriend, despite the fact that I have functioned happily for several years without one. And when I *did* have one, I was mostly quite miserable.

??! LUCAS?!

That's from Ana. I rub my eyes with my thumb and forefinger.

É só uma colega de trabalho, I type. *Just a colleague.*

Ela é bonita? Ana asks.

My thumb hovers. If I say yes, she's pretty, then they will not be satisfied until Izzy is flying over to Brazil for a large family wedding. So the obvious thing to do is to say no, she's not pretty. I glance across at Izzy as we step back into the lobby, watching as she tucks her hair behind her ear with a small, impatient hand, her gold hoop earring swinging as she walks.

I write, *She is very difficult to work with. We don't get along*, in Portuguese, and then wait to see if I get away with sidestepping the question.

Então ela é linda! Ana writes. *So she's beautiful, then!*

I click away from the chat. I can't have this conversation right now. I'm meant to be working.

Izzy

I'm just starting to think that my big fat gold ring is a big fat dead end when I *finally* get a hit on Friday.

Hi Izzy,

Thanks very much for your email. It reminded me how nice your hotel is – I'll definitely be booking another stay soon!

I smile to myself. If you put good stuff out into the universe . . .

I'm almost certain that ring belongs to my wife. She's actually bought a new one since we lost it, but we'd still love to have it back. I've attached a photo of the ring on my wife's hand, and the engraving. Does it match?

Yours,

Graham

It absolutely *does* match. I lean back in my desk chair, soaking in the feeling as I gaze up at the staircase behind the scaffolding. Winning is the best.

I snap another photo of the ring, then hit reply on Graham's email. I frown – the address he's responded to me from is slightly different from the one I used for him. Just to be safe, I put the other one in the cc line too.

Hi Graham!

Fantastic news! Please do drop in as soon as possible to claim your wife's ring back! I'm so happy it's found its way back to you. And what a lovely picture of the two of you on your wedding day! Here's another snap of the ring itself so you can see that the engraving matches 😀

All the best,

Izzy

After hitting send, I belatedly wonder if that might have been one too many exclamation marks. I've always been partial to an exclamation mark. Full stops just seem so . . . grown-up. When I stop wanting pick-and-mix for dinner, that's when I'll start using full stops. That's real adulthood.

'Golly,' Poor Mandy says, marching in and hefting her bag down into a space between lost-property boxes.

I love how Mandy has taken our lost-property project in her stride and not once complained about the mess – if only Lucas could be more Mandy.

'I just ran into that Mrs Hedgers the career coach outside. She's very . . .' Mandy flaps a hand in front of her face as if to cool herself down, though it's two degrees outside, and not much warmer in here – we're trying to skimp on the heating as much as we can without pissing off the guests. 'She's a lot, isn't she?'

I remember what Mrs Hedgers said to me about switching off and I wince. Last night, after going for drinks with my school friends, I spent two hours trying to work out the logistics of getting to a hen-do in January, concluded it would cost me £380, agonised about whether I could bail on these grounds, and then fell asleep on the sofa in front of the latest series of *Married at First Sight: Australia*, which I'd promised Jem I'd watch so that we can recreate our old MAFSA nights when we next Zoom.

I'm not sure that counts as switching off.

'What did she say to you?' I ask, diving into the next lost-property box. This one is pens. Even I think we probably shouldn't have kept all these.

'She asked if I had trouble asserting myself,' Poor Mandy says. 'I said, I'm not sure, but I don't think so? And then she told me all sorts of information about the value of strong boundaries and now I feel a bit . . .' she plonks herself down in her chair, 'funny.'

I bite my lip, giving Mrs Hedgers a smile and a wave as she passes on her way to Sweet Pea. Mandy *definitely* has trouble asserting herself. She's ridiculously amenable. Does that mean Mrs Hedgers was right about me, too?

When I'm at work, I'm always giving a little extra, going a little further, being a little nicer. But I wouldn't want to be any other way – I *like* being brilliant at my job. I like being the person who brings that sparkle. That's how everyone sees me and that's who I want to be.

If I'm completely honest, though, I do sometimes wish I could dial it down a notch and spend the day with unwashed hair and a bad attitude. Just *sometimes*. And it's not like I really get much of a chance to do that outside of work, either – I'm always with people, and lately, since Jem, Grigg and Sameera have moved away, those people aren't *my* people. They're not the people I can completely switch off with. I have to be nice, bouncy people-person Izzy all the time.

Except with Lucas, obviously.

Mandy leans across to answer the phone. 'Hello, Forest Manor Hotel and Spa.' She glances at me. 'No, Lucas isn't here right now, but I can take a message?'

Poor Mandy writes something down in her usual, painstakingly slow fashion. Is this how people achieve neat handwriting? Not worth it, I say.

I bob up to read over her shoulder.

Call back about wedding ring. Urgent. And then a phone number.

Shit, shit, shit.

'I'll take that to Lucas,' I say, swiping the note off the desk.

'Oh, thank you, dear!' calls Poor, innocent Mandy as I walk away.

All's fair in love, war and petty workplace feuding, right?

I tap the number Poor Mandy wrote into my phone and then crumple the note in my hand. I seem to have ended up in the spa. I was heading in the direction of the restaurant bin, but chucking the note away felt just a bit too unscrupulous. However, if it were to happen to get wet, and the number were to be lost until, say, I had managed to return *my* ring first . . . After all, I'm so close. Graham will drop in any moment now to claim his wife's lost ring.

I sidle towards the swimming pool, note in hand. The water slops and echoes in the still, thick air.

'What's that?'

I spin around and my foot slips on the wet floor. For an awful, teetering moment, I think I'm in danger of falling on my arse on the tiles in front of Lucas da Silva, as if the universe has decided I have not humiliated myself enough in front of this man. I right myself just in time. He folds his arms and a smile tugs at his lips.

I'm still clutching the note.

'It's just . . . a thing,' I say, then pull a face at myself. 'It's a thing Mandy gave me,' I go on, rallying. 'Not important.'

'Is that why you were holding it over the swimming pool?'

I look at his face – all smugness and chiselled jaw – and I narrow my eyes.

'I wasn't.'

'You were. Almost.' He holds his hand out. 'Mandy said you had a note for me.'

'Ugh. Fine. But I wasn't going to drop it in the pool.' I hand it to him, then, without much grace, I add: 'Probably.'

'Playing dirty,' Lucas says. 'Isn't that what that's called?'

I flush. 'It's called playing to win,' I say, marching past him.

His broad shoulders take up so much *space*. I circle by on the pool side, and then, because I'm angry and in a bad mood, and maybe – just a little bit – because I want to see what he'll do if we touch, I pass too close. But he moves at the same moment, leaning ever so slightly my way, as though he had the same idea. And I go glancing off him and . . .

'Shit!' I splutter.

. . . right into the pool. The shock of the fall leaves me gasping. I gulp for air, treading water, mascara stinging in my eyes.

'You arsehole!' I shout. 'You just pushed me in the pool!'

'I did not,' he says, crouching down and reaching a hand to help me out. He tucks the note into his back pocket with his other hand, and as anger surges through me, as my sodden clothes drag at my limbs, I have an idea.

There's more than one way to get that note wet.

I lunge for Lucas's hand and pull hard. He's squatting, balanced on the polished toes of his shoes – I overbalance him.

He descends into the water like a giant rock. Just tumbles in, slow motion, still curled up with his knees to his chest. Despite the anger swirling in my belly, I find myself laughing – more at the surprise of it than anything. I can't believe I actually just pulled him into the pool.

He bursts up through the surface and his eyes find mine immediately. They're *sparkling* with anger. I let out a nervous *eep*. He's actually pissed off now. I've seen Lucas annoyed more times than I can count, but I've hardly ever seen him really raging. It's kind of . . . God. Is it bad that it's kind of sexy?

He says something long and presumably very insulting in Portuguese. I swim backwards to try to create a bit of distance between us, but he's a lot bigger than me, and it only takes one swipe for him to grab my leg.

'You,' he says, voice low and furious, 'are not going anywhere.'

He actually lets go of my leg the moment I kick it, but I don't swim away again, I just bob there, trying not to grin. The rush of anger has gone as quickly as it came; now I am having to work very hard not to nervous-giggle.

'You push me, I push you,' I say. My shirt snags at my skin as I move – it is *not* comfortable swimming in clothes. 'If you're going to do something, Lucas, you need to live with the consequences.'

'I did not push you.'

'Well, OK, technically I didn't push you either,' I say, and I know my grin is winding him up, which just makes it even harder not to smile.

'You are so *childish*,' he spits, swiping at his eyes and advancing on me.

'What are you going to do, dunk me?'

'Something like that, yes,' he says, and then, with both hands, he sends a huge wave splashing down over my head.

I splutter, gasping. 'Oh my God!'

I splash him too. He splashes me back. We're soaking and the water's churning and my back has hit the edge of the pool now, my shirt slick as silk against my body. When the water settles, Lucas is right in front of me, arms braced on either side of mine, hands gripping the ledge. His chest is heaving. His eyes still have that spark in them, but as we face each other, dripping, his cheek twitches ever so slightly.

'You can smile,' I tell him, leaning my elbows back on the pool's edge, my soaked shirt pulling taut. 'It's not dangerous.'

He smiles. I take that back. This wet, dark-eyed Lucas is a different beast from the uniformed man who stands beside me at the front desk. With his white shirt clinging to the muscles of his chest and droplets gleaming on the skin of his neck, he's not just offensively handsome, he's *hot*.

'I'm going to win our bet,' he promises me, his voice low. We're so close I can see the flecks and tones in his brown eyes. 'You know I am. That's why you do things like pull me into swimming pools and try to destroy phone numbers.'

'I didn't . . .'

I stop talking. His gaze has dipped, eyes moving over me. I feel a droplet of water chase another over my collarbone, down to my sodden shirt, and I watch him catch that tiny movement, pupils flaring.

'Yes?' he prompts.

He looks at my lips. And for a wild, daring moment, I think I might kiss him – snake my arms over his shoulders, pull our wet bodies flush . . .

I take an uneven breath.

'I saved the number in my phone. You know I'd never do something that might actually harm the hotel. Not even to piss you off.'

Lucas studies me, unreadable. 'Why are we like this?' he says, after a moment. 'You and me?'

'Like what?'

The chlorine has made my throat ache; I swallow. His eyes are on mine now.

'Always fighting.'

He pauses, taking a small breath, as if he's hesitating over what to say. His eyes slide away from me, and I breathe out, as if he's let me go.

'Well,' he says. 'Since last Christmas.'

And there it is. I turn my head aside. I don't want to look at him now, not while we're talking about this.

'I think you just answered your own question,' I say. 'You know why I hate you.'

He flinches slightly when I say *hate*, and I almost wish I could take it back, though I don't know why – he knows it, I know it. I take another breath, steadier now, and meet his eyes again.

'I've always figured you hate me because I'm everything you don't like all wrapped up in one human being,' I go on. 'And you know you were a dick last Christmas and don't like that I'm right about it. How'd I do? Is that it?'

Lucas lifts a hand off the side of the pool to wipe his eyes. That tension between us is sluicing away, replaced by something much more familiar.

'You think you are everything I don't like? All wrapped up . . . in one human being?'

'Aren't I?'

He looks back at me. 'No,' he says eventually. 'Not at all.'

I shift, discomposed. 'You find me strange, though.'

'A little.'

That hurts more than it should. I thought I was past Lucas's insults getting to me – but then, I did just hand him the very one that could do the most damage.

Lucas shifts to the side so he can rest his back against the pool. 'Is strange that bad?' he asks.

Clearly that whole thought played out right across my face, then.

'No. I'm proud of being a bit strange now.'

'Now?'

'Let's just say, at school I was the weird kid.' I shrug, swallowing. 'It wasn't that great. Kids weren't always super nice to me. Strange isn't cool when you're thirteen.'

'You were bullied?' he asks.

I stare out at the gardens, fogged and hazy through the pool windows. I thought I could tell him about this without feeling pathetic – to justify why I'd reacted that way when he called me strange, so he knows it's not really him that's got to me, it's old stuff. But this is harder than I thought it would be, especially when my body is still tingling. I'm on edge, exposed; I hate this feeling. I hope he didn't realise how close I came to kissing him.

'A bit, yeah,' I say, kicking my legs slowly through the water. 'It probably sounds stupid to you, but these things do stay with you.'

'Did anyone help? Your parents? Teachers?'

I shake my head. 'They didn't know.'

'Not even your parents?'

'Nope. I'm very good at looking cheerful when I feel like crap.' I've not got the tone quite right – he side-glances me, and I'm too afraid to look at him in case I see pity on his face.

'It doesn't sound stupid,' he says quietly. 'Do they know now? Your parents?'

125

Ugh. Not this conversation too. I'm starting to feel worryingly emotional – this has been a lot.

'My parents both died when I was twenty-one, so, no! We didn't get the chance to have that chat,' I say as I drag myself up on my arms and out of the pool.

'Your parents died?' Lucas says.

'Yep.' I'm swinging my legs around, yanking off my dark, soaked trainers and peeling off my socks. I want to get out of here. The pool room is too warm, and my wet clothes feel suffocating.

'I'm very sorry.'

He sounds so formal. I wish I'd not told him. People always change when they know. If he starts being nice to me just because I'm an orphan, I will *not* be able to handle it.

'How did they die?'

I blink.

'I'm sorry. That was a bit . . .'

'Yeah. It was,' I say, shooting him a look over my shoulder as I tuck my wet socks into my equally wet shoes.

The pool water slops and slooshes. I'm just getting up to leave when he says, 'My dad died when I was still too small to remember him. My mum didn't tell me what happened to him until I was a teenager. So I always used to make up how he died. Tiger bite. Skydive gone wrong. Or – if I was feeling anxious – then I'd imagine it was some hereditary disease, and my mum knew I had it too, and that's why she wouldn't tell me.'

I turn my head slowly to look at him. There's not a hint of how he's feeling in his posture – he sounds as emotionless as he would if he were discussing the hotel restaurant. But what he's just told me . . . I may not like Lucas, but that makes my heart *ache* for the little boy he was.

'I'm so sorry, Lucas, that's awful.'

'It was a workplace accident, actually. He was a labourer. But yes. I'm sorry I asked about yours. It's just . . . habit.'

After a moment's hesitation, I settle cross-legged on the tiles, squeezing the pool water out of the bottom of my trousers.

'My parents were always into sailing – these madcap adventures all around the world,' I say. My voice barely carries above the sounds of the water. 'It was never my thing, really, but after I left home, they bought a new boat and took it all over the place. America, the Caribbean, Norway. And one day . . . their boat sank.'

I watch Lucas; he's still expressionless. I wonder if that one was on his list. It's just the sort of death a kid might imagine for the parent he doesn't remember. To me, though, it had seemed absolutely impossible. My parents were such experienced sailors – I never considered their adventures dangerous. It was just what they always did.

'It was so sudden,' I say. 'People act like that's better, but I don't know. It was like the world fundamentally changed into a horrible place in a split second and I was completely unequipped to handle it.' I can hear how odd my voice sounds as I try to keep it breezy. 'Anyway, now you know why I'm so "childish", as you put it. Life is so short! You can be gone just like that.' I click my fingers as I stand, looking down at the gigantic puddle I've left on the tiles beneath me. 'You've got to live every moment and enjoy it.'

Lucas tilts his head, saying nothing. I head for the towels, then pause as he says, 'No, you don't.'

'Pardon?'

'You don't have to enjoy every moment. Nobody can do that. It would be . . . exhausting.'

I'm thrown. I don't think I needed to worry about Lucas being more tactful with me on account of my dead parents.

'Well, I do,' I say, a little defensively. 'That's how I live my life.'

'No,' Lucas says.

He turns to look back at me, droplets sliding along the hard line of his jaw.

'You don't,' he says. 'You have bad days too. Everyone has bad days. As you so often like to remind me – you're a human.'

'You know what? Most people do not use the news of my parents' death as a chance to tell me I'm not living my life right,' I snap. But it's hard to muster my usual frustration – I can't forget his steady, low voice saying *I always used to make up how he died.*

'I'm not saying that,' Lucas says. 'I'm saying, you're not being honest.'

He pulls himself up on to the side of the pool, and even in the midst of this conversation I can't help but suck in a breath as the water paints his shirt to his skin. I can see every steely muscle, every contour. After a moment it makes me wonder what *he* can see, and I look down at myself to notice that my own shirt is clinging to my bra as if I'm in some sort of noughties frat-boy comedy film. Shit. I spin and reach for a towel from the basket by the wall.

'You are very positive, especially given what you've been through in your life,' Lucas says behind me. 'But you are still a real person. You swear when you drop things, and you think certain guests are idiots. You play dirty to win a bet.'

'Well, yeah, but . . .' *Only with you*, I almost say. Nobody else in this hotel would ever say that I swear or think badly of guests. If you asked Ollie whether I'd play dirty to win a bet, he'd go, *Izzy Jenkins? No way. She's a total sweetheart.*

I pull the towel around me, but all it does is bring the cold, soaked clothes closer to my skin – I need to strip off and get in a hot shower. I'm starting to shake, and I'm filled with the mess of emotions Lucas always seems to stir up in me: frustration, uncertainty, and the shadowy hurt that's been lurking there since last winter.

'So neither of us is perfect, then,' I say.

'Precisely,' Lucas says with satisfaction. He strolls off towards the men's changing room – not bothering with a towel, shirt clinging to the muscles of his back. I am left with the irritating sense that somehow, I've just managed to prove his point.

The ink didn't smudge. Poor Mandy must have used some kind of magical Team-Lucas pen. On Saturday morning, I listen morosely as Lucas conducts a second conversation with the owner of his diamond-studded wedding ring. I'm trying to work out exactly what the complexity is here – because there's definitely *something* complicated.

'Ah, I see,' says Lucas. 'Today will not be possible, but . . .'

He glances at me. I make sure to look extremely busy.

'Yes,' he says. 'I'll be there.'

After he hangs up, I don't ask. I continue not asking for as long as it is humanly possible to do so, and then I give up, because we've been coexisting in frosty silence ever since I arrived this morning and I am just not a person who can handle silence.

'Well?' I say.

'I will be returning the ring to its rightful owner tomorrow.'

'Returning it to them? As in, leaving the hotel?'

'Why not? This is hotel work. Top priority.'

I suppose it is, technically. I frown.

'And you're sure it's her ring?' I ask.

'No,' he concedes. 'But I will find out tomorrow.'

'Then I'm coming too,' I say, pushing my chair back from the computer and spinning to face him. 'I don't trust you.'

He raises his eyebrows slowly, still sorting through old receipts. 'Who will manage the front desk?'

'Ollie will do it. He owes me a favour.'

'Arjun will kill you if you take Ollie from him for a day.'

'Let me handle Arjun. I'm coming. I want to see the ring reunion anyway – this isn't *just* about the bet, remember?' I say, though I have definitely forgotten this myself of late. 'Whereabouts is this woman based?'

'London,' he says. 'Little Venice. I'll be booking an advance for the . . .' He checks his computer screen. 'Nine thirty-three.'

'OK, great,' I say. 'See you on the platform.'

'Great,' he says dryly, carefully stapling a collection of receipts together. *Click*, goes the stapler. As precise and meticulous and inexplicably irritating as ever.

Lucas

Mrs SB has forwarded me the last five years of accounts, and I've spent four hours poring over them.

I cannot remember the last time I felt this happy.

Everything I've learned on my course is coming to life now that I am looking at a real hotel's numbers – it is completely different from the test cases we've studied. This isn't theoretical. This is a place I truly care about, and as I sift through all our expenditures, noting areas where we could economise, I realise how powerless I've felt sitting here at the front desk while the hotel falls apart around me.

'All right, Lucas?' says Louis Keele, dinging the bell a few times, despite the fact that I am right here.

Well, there goes my good mood.

'Izzy about?'

'I don't know.'

That sounded rude. I look up and try to seem polite and

professional, but Louis hasn't noticed my bad manners. He's looking at a printout in front of me.

'Are those the hotel accounts?' he says.

I cover them with an arm, trying to make it look as though I'm just reaching for my mouse. I'm not sure what to do. Do potential investors see all these numbers? Or should I keep them hidden? I didn't need four hours to discover that they are not very favourable. If Mrs SB hasn't shared this information, I certainly don't want to.

'Why did you need Izzy?' I ask. As much as I don't want to talk to Louis about Izzy, some distraction is required.

'I'm thinking of asking her to dinner,' Louis says, eyes still on the paperwork.

Maybe I should show him the accounts.

'Actually,' Louis says, finally looking up at me. 'You might be quite useful. You know her better than I do. What's my best angle? Red roses? Impromptu picnic? Funny limerick?' His face turns a little sly. 'What would *you* do if you were trying to date her?'

Despite myself, I think about it. Izzy likes things that other people don't look at twice. Cheap second-hand jewellery; those awful teen dramas nobody else admits to watching; cocktails with silly names. I once caught her googling whether you could keep a wild rat as a pet. She will not want red roses. She would prefer a bouquet of interesting weeds.

Impromptu picnic is slightly better. She likes surprises. But it's freezing weather and she does feel the cold – when she leaves the hotel in the evening, she's always wrapped up as if she is heading out to the Antarctic.

A funny limerick could go either way. She's quick to laugh, but she is very funny, too, and I am not convinced Louis can match her sense of humour.

I should give him an answer along these lines. There's no reason not to help him. But then I see the calculating look in Louis' eye – the same expression he wore when he first saw the damage to the hotel ceiling all those weeks ago. And there it is again: the sensation I felt when Izzy slipped into the swimming pool with him.

'I would go for a classic date,' I find myself saying. 'Red roses and champagne at an expensive restaurant.'

'Yeah?' Louis says, frowning slightly. 'She doesn't seem that traditional to me.'

'Deep down she is highly conventional,' I say, returning my attention to my computer screen.

'Right, well, thanks, mate,' Louis says, and even though I'm not looking, I can still sense that charming, easy smile which has no doubt got him very far in life.

I look down at my phone as he walks away and see a new message from Uncle Antônio. He has sent me a link to an article with no message accompanying it. The article is called *Ten Signs You're Not Fulfilling Your Potential (Even If You Think You Are)*.

I turn my phone over and take a deep breath, trying to remember what really matters to me. My mother, my sister. Their happiness, and – increasingly – my own. All the small ways in which I make a difference to people's lives here.

But with Louis' expensive cologne still in the air, it's harder than ever to remember that the life I've built here is more than good enough for me.

On Sunday morning, it is so cold my breath is snatched from my throat. The forecast predicts heavy snow, though the British forecast is always promising extreme weather which usually ends up as drizzle, so I'm not too alarmed.

Izzy is at Brockenhurst station before me, dressed in fur-lined boots and a hooded, padded coat that reminds me of a sleeping bag. She is video-calling someone – no doubt one of her countless friends. As I approach, I recognise this one: Jem, a tall, smiling woman with box braids, multiple face piercings and a small, yappy dog. She used to live nearby and visited the hotel regularly, carrying the dog under an arm. The last time I saw her was a couple of months ago, when she came to say goodbye before she moved away. She and Izzy had hugged for so long that I'd wondered if the dog was still breathing in there.

'Have Grigg and Sameera got a big Scottish Christmas planned?' Jem is saying.

'Yeah!' Izzy says. Her voice is a bit too bright. 'Yeah, can't wait. And you're going to have a . . . have a . . .'

Jem starts laughing. 'Even Izzy Jenkins cannot put a positive spin on Christmas with my family. I am fucked.'

'You're going to have a . . . Christmas!' Izzy says, laughing too. 'And then it will be done, box ticked, and next year you'll spend it here with me.'

'Yeah,' Jem says, smiling. I glance at her over Izzy's shoulder. She is wearing a furry hat that I'm sure I've previously seen on

Izzy, her eyebrow piercings glittering beneath it. 'That's more like it. I'll be so jel of you getting buzzed with your buddies all Christmas.'

Izzy catches sight of me behind her. 'Got to go! Give Piddles a cuddle from me. Love you so much!'

'Love you too, little pigeon,' Jem says, blowing a kiss at the screen before she disappears.

I come to stand beside Izzy.

'Piddles?'

'The dog. Yappy and nasty. Unless you're Jem, in which case, adorable and misunderstood.'

'And little pigeon?'

'It's an inside joke. An affectionate nickname. You wouldn't understand.'

I just raise my eyebrows at that. There is something scrappy about a pigeon that suits the version of Izzy I have come to see this winter – perhaps I understand better than she thinks.

We join the nearest queue as the train pulls in. I pre-booked my seat, but Izzy didn't, and after I tut about this, she looks very smug to find an available seat directly opposite mine.

I plan to spend the train journey working on a draft budget for Mrs SB, but it's hard to concentrate. Izzy has removed her many layers and is playing solitaire with a set of battered playing cards, wearing a baby-blue top with no straps.

'Want to play something?' Izzy says.

I've been staring at her cards in an effort not to stare at the smooth white skin above that blue top. I think for a moment.

'Poker?' I say.

'With just two of us?'

'It can be done. Texas Hold 'em? Though . . .' I suddenly wish I'd not suggested it. 'I don't want to play for money,' I add, embarrassed.

'Of course not,' Izzy says, like the very thought is ridiculous. 'Though we're on a train, so strip poker is out.'

The idea that strip poker might otherwise be in throws me. She digs around in her rucksack and produces a small box of raisins, the sort you might give to a child as a snack.

'Chips,' she says, opening the box. 'Whoever's up by Waterloo gets to choose how we decorate the lobby?'

'I don't want to decorate the lobby any more than it is decorated right now,' I say, frowning.

'Exactly. Whereas I think we are seriously lacking in tinsel.' She smiles at me and I swallow.

'You up for a challenge?' she asks.

'Of course,' I say, reaching for the cards.

I try to be magnanimous for the journey from Waterloo to Little Venice. I knew Izzy would be terrible at poker. Everything is always written all over her face. She takes losing extremely badly, just as I would expect, and sulks the entire way to Shannon's flat.

The woman who greets us when we arrive is wearing a large hat that reads, *Thank u, next*. I look beyond her to the open-plan living area to find that everyone inside is wearing the same. The music is pounding already, though it's only lunchtime.

'I don't know you,' says the woman in the doorway. 'Did he send you? If so, tell him Shannon has every fucking right to—'

'Nobody sent us,' Izzy says quickly. 'Shannon invited us. We're here about a ring?'

'Oh!' The woman's face lights up. 'Come on in, she's in the kitchen working on the cake.'

Izzy's sulking expression has been replaced with the bright, fascinated look she wears when she's truly enjoying herself. She is a bad loser, but she is also very easily distracted.

Shannon is a tall blonde woman wearing a sequinned dress with an apron over the top. My first impression on entering the pristine kitchen is that she looks like a housewife from an American TV show. However, the cake she is icing is shaped like a penis, which does throw this image out a little.

'Hello,' she says, putting down her icing pen and wiping her hands on her apron. 'You must be Lucas! Did you bring your girlfriend?'

'Not girlfriend,' we say in unison.

'Even better,' Shannon says.

'I'm Izzy,' Izzy says, holding out her hand. 'Congratulations!'

It seems this is the correct thing to say, because Shannon gives her a wide smile.

'Thanks so much! I've been so excited for today. I wanted to give it as much energy as my wedding day. Isn't it amazing that they all took annual leave? We're going for a long weekend in Madeira for my unhoneymoon.' She gestures towards the people in the living area. 'You know what I did for my actual honeymoon? Hiked in the Alps. Did I like hiking? Did I like snow? Did I fuck! You know what I do like, though?'

She has the icing pen back in her hand, and is pointing it at us.

'Sunshine and cocktails with people who have stood by me.'

'*That* is my sort of holiday,' Izzy says. 'I love this. Can I have a hat?'

'Oh, hats are obligatory,' Shannon says, pointing to a stack of them on the kitchen counter.

Izzy looks at me. 'Perfect! Lucas *loves* novelty headgear.'

'I've brought the ring,' I say to Shannon. Someone needs to get this conversation on track. Though I can't help thinking that we aren't as likely to get a fifteen-thousand-pound reward for a ring representing a marriage that's ended. 'We will need some way to confirm that it's yours – that is, if you still want it.'

'One step ahead of you,' says Shannon, still icing as she pulls her phone out with her other hand. 'Here, my wedding photos.'

I glance from the screen to Shannon's face.

'Don't worry,' she says. 'They don't make me sad any more. I'm where I want to be right now. It doesn't matter how I got here.'

'God, that is such an amazing mentality,' Izzy says, mouth already full of a cupcake she's picked up from somewhere.

With her *Thank u, next* hat on, Izzy looks like everyone else at the party – already quite at home. I was so surprised when she told me that she had been bullied at school. Everybody loves Izzy. But I can see it now – the way she just fits in. I suspect that is a skill she picked up because she needed it.

'Are you sure that's your ring?' she asks Shannon. 'Could it be . . . a similar ring?'

Shannon looks at her in surprise. Izzy pulls an apologetic face, cupcake pouched in one cheek.

'Sorry. We have a bet,' she explains, swallowing. 'If it's your ring, I lose.'

'Ah. Well, sorry,' Shannon says. She spreads her hands. 'But if it's any consolation, every loss can be a win, right?'

Izzy absorbs this, then turns to me.

'Can I have a word?' she asks, tugging me into the corner by the drinks trolley. 'She hasn't *proven* it's hers,' she whispers.

'This is very undignified, Izzy,' I say, enjoying myself immensely. 'Perhaps you should learn to lose with grace.'

'She could have just ordered the same ring from the same jeweller!'

'And stayed at the hotel at the same time as someone else with that ring, who also lost it?'

'Yes!'

I fold my arms and look down at her. Her hair is mussed beneath her ridiculous hat, and for a moment, her relentless competitiveness doesn't seem irritating – it seems charming. She just cares *so much*.

Then her shoulders sag. 'Shit,' she says.

She looks genuinely gutted. I look away. Winning doesn't feel quite as good as I thought it would.

'Today is about fresh starts,' Shannon says, as we return to her side. 'Wiping that slate clean. If that means anything to you two, you're welcome to stay for the party.'

I check the time on the clock above the kitchen door. We

should be getting back. Ollie is on his own at the desk, and technically our work here is done.

'We should go,' Izzy and I say to each other in unison.

There is a pause. And then I find myself saying, 'Perhaps we could stay for a short while. An hour or so.'

Izzy stares at me, mouth slightly open. I feel a small flash of triumph at having surprised her.

'You want to stay at the party?'

'We can leave if you would prefer,' I say, as Shannon puts the finishing touches on her cake.

'No. I want to stay. Ollie's expecting to cover the whole day anyway,' Izzy says, and then stands on tiptoe to plonk a hat on my head. 'I need cheering up. And I'm pretty sure anyone we work with would say that you and I could do with a fresh start.'

I now see why Shannon was so keen to get the ring back today. We are gathered around a man wearing goggles and heavy-duty gloves, setting up mysterious pieces of equipment on the floor of Shannon's living room. In the centre is a large slab, on which rests the wedding ring.

'Shannon, if you would like to say a few words first,' the man says, gesturing for her to take his spot.

'Thank you,' she says, stepping forward in a pair of Perspex goggles. 'We are gathered here today to celebrate a union, not of two people, but of a whole community.' She smiles. 'You have all been here for me for every step of the last five miserable years. You are the ones who told me that it's not failing to give up on a love that isn't healthy – because that's not love. Without you all, I wouldn't be standing here today.'

Everyone claps. A small, curly-haired woman beside me wipes away a tear with the back of her hand. There are couples here too, and they seem just as moved as everybody else.

What a strange event. I don't know how I feel about this. I want to believe that marriage is for ever. When I choose to marry, that's what it'll be.

But there is something undeniably special about this, too, and as I glance at Izzy, I see how completely this has captured her. By nature, she is much more open-minded than I am. Usually that tendency strikes me as over idealistic, but right now I feel a little envious of the way she meets new things.

I look back at Shannon and try to see her the way Izzy would: without judgement. I try to imagine what that ring means to Shannon now, and I can see that there is something beautiful in what she's saying. We are all misled and misdirected from time to time. Perhaps there really is no shame in that, as long as we wake up to it before it's too late to change.

'Today, I want to let go of the past,' Shannon announces. 'I want to always remember the fact that if you burn a diamond . . . it only gets tougher.'

With that, she kneels and blasts the blowtorch at the wedding ring resting on the slab.

The gold melts fast – faster than I would have expected. With some careful support from the man in the goggles, Shannon splits the ring down into a heap of diamonds and a small ball of gold.

Everyone is whooping and cheering. I glance back at Izzy, who is deep in conversation with two strangers; she's laughing behind her hand. Lately, looking at Izzy has made me feel such a tangle of things. Fearful, lustful, wary, possessive. But watching her now through the anonymity of the crowd, I see a bright, bold young woman whose parents would be very proud of her, and the thought makes my chest feel tight.

She finds me in the spare bedroom some time later. I'm on my laptop in an armchair, going back over Mrs SB's spreadsheet. Izzy stops short, a champagne glass in hand, her bare shoulders now dotted with red and gold glitter. Through the window beside her the snow is coming down in thick, feathery flakes.

'Oh my God,' Izzy says. 'No way are you working.'

I am instantly defensive. 'We are *both* meant to be working.'

'Oh, please! You were the one who said we should stay. Besides, there is literally no work I can do remotely. Come dance. They're playing noughties tunes with eye-wateringly misogynistic lyrics. Half the room's raving, the other half is deconstructing the problematic songs. Basically, this is a fantastic party.'

She's reaching a hand towards me. I've never held Izzy's hand before – except when she pulled me into the pool.

'Fresh start?' she says, voice dropping a little. 'We could try it? Just for a few minutes, until we go home?'

I meet her eyes. I can see mischief glimmering there – just like when she met my eyes through the lost-property-room door in her pink bra. Just like when her back was pressed to the side of the swimming pool.

I am a careful man by nature. But Izzy makes me feel reckless.

There is a physical attraction between us, that is becoming increasingly obvious. But she doesn't respect me. There's nothing to stop her taking what she wants from me and leaving it at that.

Which should be fine. It *would* be fine if I hated her as much as she hates me. We would be on the same level, and there would be no danger of anyone hurting anybody's feelings.

Very suddenly, I see the problem. I don't hate Izzy Jenkins at all.

'I'm Izzy,' she says, when I don't answer. 'Pleased to meet you.'

I stretch my hand out slowly and shake hers. It's cool and small in mine. My heart beats harder, too hard.

'Lucas da Silva,' I say. 'Pleased to meet you too.'

We dance. There's distance between us at first – as there would be, I suppose, if we really were the strangers we're pretending to be. But the gap closes slowly from song to song, until my hips are bumping hers and her hair paints a trail across my arm each time she tosses her head. The music is bad American pop, but I don't care. I want to dance with Izzy. I want to give in to the thump-thump of desire that courses through me when I see her. I want to ignore real life for once and just pretend that I'm a guy, at a party, dancing with a beautiful girl.

'You're good,' she says, raising her voice over the music. 'You can dance!'

'So can you.'

'Well, yeah,' she says, as if this should have been obvious. 'But I thought the whole thing about Brazilians all being great dancers was a cliché.'

'It is a cliché. We are not all great dancers,' I tell her, thinking of my sister, who often cheerfully proclaims that she's about as good at keeping time as she is at keeping boyfriends.

'But if any Brazilian was going to be bad at dancing,' Izzy says, 'I feel like it would be you.'

I glare at her. She laughs.

'And how do you know I'm Brazilian?'

She pulls a face at the break from character. 'I mean, ah, where are you from?' she asks.

'Niterói,' I tell her. The song shifts and I watch her body shift too, finding the new beat. 'It's in Rio de Janeiro, Brazil.'

'Brazil! What's it like there at this time of year?'

'Hot,' I say, holding her gaze. I take a sip of my beer.

That thump-thump of desire gets louder. She's closer, looking up at me, the glitter on her shoulders sparkling under the light of Shannon's chandelier.

'How about you? Where are you from?'

'Surrey,' she says, her leg brushing mine as she dances. 'Way less exciting. Though I loved growing up there.'

Something passes over her face – a memory of her parents, perhaps.

'And what do you do?' I ask, to bring her back to me.

She stumbles slightly as someone moves past us and I steady her with a hand on her waist. Somehow it feels right for the hand to stay there, and now we're not just dancing, we're dancing *together*. Her hands come to rest lightly on my shoulders and her hips twist in time with mine.

'I work at a hotel.'

I try to imagine what I would say next if I didn't stand beside her at the front desk every morning. It's getting hard to concentrate. Her body moves with mine and there's just the soft fabric of her baby-blue top between my palm and her skin. She's warm and a little breathless. I can smell her cinnamon scent every time I inhale.

I settle for the question I often get asked. 'Are people always checking in under fake names to have affairs?'

She gives me a small, knowing smile. 'That or turning up naked under trench coats. Yeah. Nonstop.'

I let out an *ah* of recognition as the song changes to Anitta's 'Envolver'. Izzy clocks it and lifts her gaze to mine. We're body to body: her arms aren't just resting lightly on my shoulders now, they're wound around my neck, and my hand is at the small of her back, keeping our shifting hips in sync.

'Can you translate this song for me? What's it actually about?' she asks me.

'Well, it's in Spanish, so . . .'

'Oh.' She blushes. 'Sorry. I thought it was in Portuguese.'

For once, I'm not interested in embarrassing her.

'My Spanish isn't bad, so I can try . . . But, uh, the song is a little rude.'

'We just danced to "212",' she says, tilting her head back far enough that her hair tickles my hand on her waist as she looks up at me. 'I think I can handle some sexual undertones.'

I take a swig of my beer. 'She's saying something like . . . Tell me what we're supposed to do when we want each other this much. She's saying, if we go to bed together . . . you won't last five minutes.'

Izzy laughs at that, still dancing. 'What else?'

'She's saying that she won't let this guy get involved with her. Whatever happens there stays there.'

I think we're dancing close until Izzy closes those tiny centimetres between us and I realise what *close* actually feels like. Her stomach pressed to my hips, her breasts against my chest. The contact sends desire snapping through me. I'm hard, and she must be able to tell, but she just keeps dancing.

'What an interesting idea,' she says, looking me right in the eyes.

I feel her phone buzz in the same moment she does. That's how close my hand is to the back pocket of her jeans. She looks down and pulls away as she tugs the phone out.

'It's Ollie,' she says, and just like that, we're back. Standing in the middle of a makeshift dance floor in a stranger's living room when we ought to be at work. The room seems smaller, the music wincingly loud.

I can't hear the phone conversation, but I follow her off the dance floor and watch her body language. The way she stiffens and pulls her hair up in a one-handed ponytail, then lets it drop again as she talks.

When she hangs up, she turns and finds me immediately.

'We have to go back,' she says.

'What's happened?'

'It's . . .' She tugs her bottom lip between her teeth. 'Graham's wife has arrived at the hotel.'

'Your ring owner?'

'No-o,' Izzy says. 'Graham's *other* wife.'

147

Izzy

It seems that Graham has two different-but-similar email addresses for a reason. Because he has two different-but-similar lives.

And when I copied the other address into my email exchange . . . I gave Wife 1 access to a thread about a wedding ring that belonged to Wife 2, creating some understandable drama. Wife 1 turned up in our lobby, screaming and shouting, demanding answers from poor Ollie, who had absolutely no idea what she was talking about. Apparently, she is now refusing to leave the premises until she 'gets some answers from whoever sent that email'.

'We can get as far as Woking.'

Lucas is pacing back and forth along Shannon's upstairs corridor, oblivious to the people popping up to use the bathroom and having to dodge past him like he's the Big Bad Boss in an old GameBoy game. He is staring fixedly at his phone, National

Rail app open on the screen. I can't believe that half an hour ago I was grinding up against this man on the dance floor. The thought is completely surreal.

'Right, great,' I say, chewing my thumbnail.

I've really messed up here. Well, Graham did most of the messing up. But I've brought this whole bigamy drama into the hotel, and now I'm not even there to sort it out – I'm here, sexy-dancing with Lucas. What am I *doing*?

'Maybe from Woking there will be a bus,' Lucas says, furiously tapping away at his phone.

I look out of the window over the staircase. The snow is coming fast, caught up in itself, whirling and swooping like one of those Van Gogh paintings of the stars.

'UK roads can't really do snowstorms,' I tell him, leaning back against the wall as someone emerges from the bathroom and hesitates, then dashes past in the moment before Lucas pivots on his heels to pace back again. 'I think the odds of buses running in a couple of hours' time are pretty low.'

'It is a bit of snow! It is a little bit cold!' Lucas snaps.

'Well, OK, I'm not the bloody transport secretary, am I?' I snap back, nettled.

He's behaving like all that dancing never happened. Gone is the loose-limbed, half-smiling man who circled his hips against mine half an hour ago; here's grouchy, uptight Lucas, taking things out on me that aren't my fault.

'Why did we stay so late?' he says, swiping his thumb down to refresh the outgoing trains again. I watch as the red text blinks, the delays lengthening.

'Because we were having fun. Before you switched back to the usual Lucas, who is incapable of fun, and just snaps at me about everything.'

He looks up at me at last, surprised. 'I'm not snapping at you.'

I pull a disbelieving face, spreading my arms out. 'Hello? You literally just yelled at me about it being only a little bit cold.'

'I wasn't yelling *at* you about it being cold. Why would I yell at you about that? It's not your fault, is it?'

He seems genuinely nonplussed. I stare back at him in silence, trying to figure him out.

'Sorry, is this a queue for the toilet?' says a small man in chinos, bobbing up at the top of the stairs.

I wave him through. 'So you were just . . . yelling?'

'This is frustrating,' Lucas says, looking back at his phone to refresh the page. 'I want to be back at the hotel. And I hate . . . this situation. I'm not frustrated with you.'

'Right.' I pause, fiddling with my necklace. 'Actually, no. I don't think that's OK.'

He blinks at me, taking this in.

'You didn't need to raise your voice,' I say. We're in new territory here – I've never called him out on this before, but as I say it, I realise how much it pisses me off. He does it all the time at the hotel. I wonder how often our arguments start because he raises his voice and that in itself just winds me up. 'I'm frustrated too. I'm not yelling.'

'You're just saying unkind things instead,' he says. 'Is that any better?'

'Excuse me?' I'm genuinely staggered by this. I have been

called many things over the years – weird, stupid, ditzy – but I've *never* been called unkind.

'I am *incapable of fun*, you said.'

'Oh, I . . .' I did say that. I guess when it comes to Lucas, I've always just given him shit like that, and he gives it right back to me, so it never occurred to me that it was unkind. I can feel my cheeks getting pink. I press the backs of my hands to my warm skin. 'I thought . . . That's just sort of . . . what we say to each other. It's kind of . . . jokey.'

'Is it?' Lucas resumes pacing. 'Neither of us seems to laugh very much.'

I don't know what to say. I feel quite ashamed of myself.

'You two OK?' Shannon calls up the stairs. 'Our flight's delayed, so everyone is heading home for tonight – can you get back all right?'

We glance at each other.

'I'm sure we'll be fine!' I call. 'Trains are a bit ropey, but we'll get there.'

'Great,' Shannon says, sounding relieved. 'I'd offer you our spare room, but a few friends who live further away need somewhere to crash, so . . .'

'We'll get going, then,' I say, looking at the trains on Lucas's phone screen. Another one cancelled. Yellow exclamation marks in triangles everywhere. 'Thanks so much for having us, Shannon!'

'Safe travels!' she calls, heels already clip-clopping back to the kitchen again.

If this were a Christmas movie, she'd have put us up in her

spare room, and we'd have stayed up all night talking. It would have been cosy and gorgeous. But it's not a Christmas movie, and so Lucas and I end up sitting outside WHSmith at Waterloo, staring morosely at the departure boards, still stewing from our latest argument.

Back there under Shannon's chandelier, I'd come so close to kissing him. He's infuriating and short-tempered and there are a hundred things I don't like about him, but I can't deny that I'm almost *painfully* attracted to him. I kept thinking of Sameera and Grigg saying there's no harm in having a fling with him – nobody can get hurt if you don't even like each other.

But is it normal to want to have sex with someone you hate? Is that something I need to look at? I did a few years of therapy after my parents died, and I learned enough about healthy thoughts to suspect this is a topic my old therapist would probably have wanted to discuss.

I glance at Lucas. He is eating a sandwich angrily, which I didn't know was possible, but he's really managing with aplomb. I roll my eyes. He's so dramatic. So broody and moody and *rude*.

And he thinks I'm unkind. I press my hand to the base of my ribs as the thought hits, accompanied by a quick flash of shame. My parents used to have a sign dangling above the oven in our kitchen that said *No act of kindness is ever wasted* – it was important to them that whatever else I became in life, I'd always be kind, and I'm suddenly terrified that I've let them down. The thought takes the wind out of me.

'There! Platform seven!' Lucas yells, exploding up from his seat.

His sandwich packaging goes flying as we race each other to the snow-topped train. He's a fast runner, but I'm craftier – by the time I jump on, he's still floundering around between two tourists and their luggage.

'Ha!' I say, sticking my tongue out as he eventually hops through the door, breathing hard.

I'm expecting a comeback about how infantile I'm being, but when he looks at me, for a moment his face is unguarded. He's smiling.

'What?' I say, suspicious.

His smile smooths away. 'Nothing,' he says, moving past me, angling – of course – for the only available seat.

Mrs SB texts an update when we get to Woking. *I've given Mrs Rogers no.1 our spare room in Opal Cottage for the night, and invited Mr Graham Rogers and Mrs Rogers no.2 here for brunch and a civil conversation in the morning. Amazing what the promise of a free meal can do.* The message ends with a thumbs-up. Mrs SB only ever uses a thumbs-up without irony, so she must be calmer than she was when Ollie called. Still, I feel awful for causing her all this trouble. It's the last thing she needs right now – and even though she was super nice about us both being off on this trip, I do feel *very* guilty for leaving the hotel on a job that really only needed one of us.

Woking station is packed with pissed-off travellers, all alternating between staring at phones and departure screens. It's too cold; my nose hurts. I just want to go home and crawl into my bed.

'Replacement bus service cancelled,' Lucas growls, not looking up from his phone. He mutters something in Portuguese, and then says, 'What do we do now?'

I'm surprised he's asking me. Lucas usually likes to plough on, making his own decisions and expecting me to trot along after him.

'Cab?' I say, already wincing.

'I *can't*,' Lucas says, and there's real anguish in his voice at the very thought of it.

I get it – I'm not rolling in it either, and a taxi from here would cost us at least £200. I get my phone out and hit up Google. A cheap hotel right by the station has rooms available for £40. I doubt they'll stay at that price for long – other people will have the same idea as me soon enough.

'Look, it sounds like everyone's fine at Forest Manor now, and we can't afford a cab, so . . .' I hold out the screen to him.

He stares at it for a moment. His eyes flick up to mine.

'We can get two rooms,' I say quickly. 'If you want.'

'I would rather . . . Well, it's up to you,' he says.

'One's fine for me. I'll just sleep on the floor.'

He looks irritated. '*I* will sleep on the floor.'

'I don't know if there'll be enough floor for you,' I say, nodding at the size of him.

His lip lifts ever so slightly. 'Book it,' he says decisively. 'Before it's too late. I'll transfer you my share now.'

He's already back on his phone when I open my mouth to say don't worry, it can wait. I swallow it back. I know Lucas is skint, but he's also very proud.

'Thanks,' I say instead.

A few clicks later, and it's done. Unbelievably, incomprehensibly, I am about to spend the night in a hotel room with Lucas da Silva.

The first thing that strikes me about the room is that nobody will be able to sleep on the floor in here. Every spare inch is taken up with a desk, a chair, side tables for the bed, and a footstool that's way too big for the space. Plus that ridiculous thing they put out for your luggage, like a small hammock for your suitcase. Who uses those, and why?

We have no suitcases, obviously. I don't even have a toothbrush. I try to give my teeth a particularly vigorous lick, which achieves nothing other than hurting my tongue, and then I throw myself down on the bed with a long, loud *ugh*.

At least it's warm. There's an air-conditioning unit whirring away over the bathroom door, blasting out hot air. Everything in here is a very washable shade of dark grey. It's completely impersonal – the opposite of Forest Manor Hotel and Spa. This hotel isn't a place where people go the extra mile, it's a place where colleagues go to bed with each other when they shouldn't.

I lift my head to look at Lucas, who is still examining the room with his arms folded. We're not doing that, obviously.

Except a few hours ago I really did want to have sex with Lucas, and that thought hasn't *completely* gone away.

'You did a good thing today,' he says abruptly.

My thoughts immediately go to the dance floor. The sound of Anitta, the feel of Lucas's hand pressing the small of my back . . .

'It's better for both those women to know the truth.'

Oh. Graham. Yes. Graham the bigamist. The other major event of the day.

'That wasn't a good thing for the hotel, though,' I say. 'I've made Mrs SB and Barty's life even more stressful.'

Lucas shrugs. 'Some things are important enough to cause a little drama.'

I raise my eyebrows. It's not like Lucas to be in favour of drama.

'It's early for bed,' Lucas says, checking his watch. 'I think I'll go for a walk.'

'A walk? In central Woking? In a snowstorm?'

Lucas turns his attention to the window, as if remembering the problem.

'We could go to the bar?' I suggest, sitting up on my elbows.

Lucas grimaces. Ah, right – no spending unnecessary money. I reach for the remote control and turn on the telly. It lands on *Love Actually*. I let out a delighted yip and shimmy up the bed so I'm propped up on the pillows.

'You've seen this, right?' I say to him.

He watches for a few moments. 'No.'

'Oh my God. Sit down. That's a crime against Christmas right there. Is this not a thing in Brazil? There's even a super-hot muscly Brazilian guy in it and everything.'

His lip quirks. 'Do you think us super-hot muscly Brazilian guys seek each other out?'

I flush. 'No, that's not – whatever. You have to see it.'

He looks slightly fatigued by this, but perches on the bed beside me, and then after a moment swings his legs around.

'It's *Love Actually*? My sister does tell me I must watch this all the time,' he says. 'What have I missed? Who is that man?'

'Just watch,' I say. Because of course Lucas is one of those assertive males who talks over crucial dialogue.

On screen, David meets Natalie for the first time. Lucas settles in beside me, fingers linked on his chest.

'So he is going to fall in love with that woman?' he asks, as Annie appears on-screen.

'No, that's his chief of staff,' I say, laughing. 'It's Natalie he falls in love with. Your romance radar is terrible.' Then I pause. Is that unkind? 'Sorry,' I say, just as Lucas says,

'So they're colleagues – that means they can't be anything more?'

I keep my eyes on the scene playing out on-screen and give up on actually hearing anything.

'Well, I guess . . . the Prime Minister sleeping with his chief of staff would maybe be a no-no?'

'Hmm,' Lucas says, taking this in.

'What's the deal with office romances in Brazil? Is everyone cool with it?'

'It depends,' Lucas says, 'on how you conduct yourself at work. You have to be appropriate.'

'Yeah, kind of the same here.'

I think of me and Lucas, fully clothed in the swimming pool, splashing each other wildly. Not sure anyone would accuse us of conducting ourselves appropriately.

We watch the film in silence. I wonder why Lucas asked about colleagues being romantically involved. I wonder if it's about me. I wonder if we're about to cross a line that cannot be uncrossed, and whether I care about that, and I already know that I don't.

Lucas turns on to his side, facing me. I shift my head to look at him. I let myself really take him in: the serious brown eyes, the straight brows, the faint hollow beneath his cheekbone. We're close enough that I can feel his breath ghosting over my cheek.

'You have always told me what you think of me,' he says eventually. His voice is low. Behind it, the telly chatters on. 'You've always been honest.'

'That's true.' I shift so I'm lying on my side too. I tuck a hand under my cheek. He echoes the gesture, other hand tapping restlessly at the covers between us.

'Will you tell me what you think of me now?'

I'm not expecting that question. I don't know *what* I think of Lucas these days. I think he's too stern and doesn't know how to laugh at himself; I think he's pedantic and rude. I think last Christmas he behaved like a dickhead. But I also think he's sexy and complex, and that there's a warmth somewhere in there, behind all the scowling.

'I think maybe I don't really know you at all,' I say slowly.

His expression shifts infinitesimally. I wouldn't have noticed it if we hadn't been so close. All of a sudden I'm hit with an urge to just . . . shake him. He's so controlled. I want to make him let go.

I lift one hand to rest against his jaw, framing his face, the heel of my hand against his neck. His stubble is rough under my palm. I feel his jaw clench, but he stays very still, just watching me with dark, liquid eyes. The heat I felt on the dance floor starts up again deep in my belly, a low, wild beat.

The decision I'm making is a bad one – I know it even as I lean towards him, eyes on his parted lips. But I don't care. I don't *care*. I want this, and I'm sick and tired of trying to work out why.

I kiss him. That heat grows tenfold inside me, like I've blown on a flame, and for a second, maybe two, Lucas kisses me back.

Then he's pulling away, spinning to sit with his back to me. I stare at his hunched shoulders, how they rise and fall with each breath. I'm breathing hard too, and my cheeks are hot.

'Shit,' I mutter. 'Sorry. I thought . . .'

'It's fine.' Lucas's voice is sharp. 'I just . . . That wouldn't be a good idea.' He glances over his shoulder for an instant before returning his gaze to the carpet. It's too fast to read anything into his face.

'I'm not looking for a relationship, if that's what you're worried about,' I say, stung. 'I know you're not going to be flying someone like me back to meet your mum.'

He turns at this, shifting to see me properly. *Love Actually* rattles on between us and I reach impatiently for the remote, switching it off.

'What do you mean, *someone like me*?'

'I'm just saying, your type is probably women who work out with you in tiny gymwear and drink green juice. But also like serious films with subtitles. And football. And have really long legs.'

I'm floundering, hot with desire and embarrassment in equal measure. I need to get control of this situation again. At last his expression is one I recognise: he's wearing the faintly exasperated face he uses when he's humouring me. Fine. At least that's not pity.

'You know nothing about my type,' he says. 'Evidently.'

'Well, I know a little bit, don't I?' I sit up and shift to the edge of the bed. 'It doesn't matter. I don't like you, you don't like me, I thought maybe we could just have some fun for a night, you didn't want to, the end. I'm going for a walk.'

'In central Woking? In a snowstorm?'

I glare at him for parroting my words back to me.

'Yes,' I say, lifting my chin as I grab my coat and head to the door. 'See you at bedtime.'

God, that's going to be awkward.

Lucas

It is hard to imagine how that could have gone worse.

Why would she kiss me right after saying she doesn't know me at all? Why then, of all the moments? It was a sentence that simultaneously hurt and gave me hope: she has never *tried* to know me, but perhaps if I could get her to try, she might . . .

I press my hands to my eyes. This has been an unpleasant day. Like a train bearing down on me, a great truth has been rolling in, and as I lie here in this embarrassment of a hotel room, I have no choice but to acknowledge that I want Izzy Jenkins to like me.

Because I like her. I like her stripy hair and the way she plays dirty. I like that she challenges me. I like that she's so much more interesting than she seems at first glance. I want to be the one person who knows every inch of the real Izzy.

My phone beeps: another message from the family WhatsApp, which has turned into a long-running game of let's-annoy-Lucas, with a detour into a series of rapid-fire questions about barbecue marinades from my sister.

Hey Lucas, how's your date going?? Ana asks, with a GIF of a giggling elephant whose significance I couldn't possibly begin to understand.

I hesitate for a moment and then, on impulse, I tap on her name and click *video call*.

She answers after three rings, with her ringlets pinned and enormous fake eyelashes swooping up to her eyebrows.

'Well, hello,' she says, cocking her head.

'It isn't a date,' I say. Whenever I call family, it feels a little strange slipping back into Portuguese again. I am a slightly different man in my mother tongue. Bolder, firmer, louder. I don't think either English Lucas or Brazilian Lucas is the truer one, but the two languages bring out different sides of me, and right now I want to remember the version of myself who breathes through his Rs and goes after what he wants.

'But you wish it was,' Ana says. She's looking at herself in a mirror, adjusting her eyelashes.

'Where are you going?'

'An actual date,' she says, pouting at her reflection. 'He's coming here.'

'Isn't it the middle of the afternoon?'

'It's nap time. I have a two-hour window and a guy who is very open-minded. Don't deflect, you called me for a reason – what's up?'

'Oh, I won't take up your window of—'

'Lucas.'

'Fine. I'll be quick. I think I like her. Izzy. My co-worker. She tried to kiss me and I blew her off because . . . she hates me. I don't want to kiss her like *that*, you know?'

Ana inhales between her teeth. 'And she got upset about it.'

'Mm. Now she hates me more than ever.'

'Her pride is bruised. There's a reason it's harder for women to approach men than the other way around – when the world tells you your worth is about men desiring you, it's hard to take it when they don't, and we're scared to be rejected. You've given her a knock-back. You need to work extra hard to make her feel better again.'

'How do I do that?'

Ana puckers her lips. I'm not sure if this is lipstick-related or something to do with me.

'What's she like? What makes her feel good about herself?'

'She's very independent. And she has a lot of friends. And she likes second-hand things, and pick-and-mix.'

Ana's face suddenly warms into a smile. 'Oh, you are smitten.'

I growl.

'You'll know what to do. If you really like her, it'll come to you, because if you're made for each other, you're made to heal her when she's hurting. I have to go, but I'm glad you called. I'm so proud of you over there, studying, working, going for what you actually want. I miss you.'

'Miss you too. I love you,' I say. Something else that's much easier to say in Portuguese. 'Enjoy your date. I hope—'

The door opens and a pink-nosed, snow-covered Izzy pokes her head in.

'Oh, sorry, are you on the phone?' she says, pausing mid step.

'Is that her?' Ana asks, thankfully in Portuguese.

'Bye,' I say, before she can say anything incriminating and easily translatable. 'Don't worry,' I tell Izzy as I hang up, 'we were finished.'

'Look,' Izzy says, 'it's extremely cold outside and I just got sprayed with slush by a passing bus, so I really need a hot bath. Can we just agree to coexist in silence and forget that . . .' she points at the bed '. . . ever happened?'

I will not be forgetting that kiss. Yes, it came at the wrong moment, and yes, my mind was racing, but the feeling of Izzy's lips against mine – her hand on me, her tongue, that cinnamon-sugar scent . . . My body just *lit* up, as if that kiss was a match thrown on a fire, and it took all of my strength to resist her.

'Fine,' I say, clearing my throat. 'Whatever you want.'

She marches into the bathroom and closes the door. I think about what Ana said: if I'm meant for Izzy, I'll know how to make her feel better. I'm pretty sure that whatever it is she needs, I'm not giving it to her right now. I stare at the ceiling and try to think. She will want to make it clear that she doesn't *need* me. Izzy doesn't like to need anybody. She will want to feel attractive, because I'm an idiot and probably made her feel as though I didn't want her, even though the woman haunts my dreams and has done so for much longer than I'd like to admit.

And she will want to get one up on me again, because that's how we operate.

Maybe that's the answer. Maybe, as painful as this thought is . . . Maybe I need to let Izzy win something.

She comes out of the bathroom in a tantalisingly small towel, her feet bare, her hair wet. The stripes are gone. It never occurred to me that she must take them out when she washes it, but she didn't wear them at the pool either. I had never seen anyone with stripy hair before I met Izzy. It should look tacky, but it doesn't. Izzy has that effect on things.

True to her word, she doesn't speak to me. She just grabs her handbag and then heads back into the bathroom, closing the door with an emphatic *click*. When she re-emerges, she has dressed, dried her hair and pinned the stripes back in. Meanwhile I have finished *Love Actually* and am feeling highly sentimental.

'Listen,' I begin, and she holds up a hand.

'That sounds like the start of a sentence about the incident we agreed not to speak about.' She walks around to sit on the footstool, picking fluff off her jeans.

'I just wanted to say that—'

'Lucas.'

'I don't want you to think that—'

'Have I not made myself clear?'

'It's not that I—'

'Oh my God, are you incapable of listening to me, or—'

'It's not that I don't find you beautiful.'

I almost bellow it in the effort to be heard, but as soon as I've said it, she goes quiet. She looks at me at last. I shift up against the pillows, folding my arms over my chest.

'You are very beautiful,' I say, more quietly. 'And the kiss was . . .'

'Lucas . . .' Her warning is weaker this time.

'It was a beautiful kiss, too. But . . .'

'Yeah. It was stupid. People who don't like each other shouldn't kiss, that's . . . weird and messed up,' she says, looking out of the window beside her. 'I reminded myself of that on my nice scenic walk just now.'

I choose my words carefully. 'My type isn't women in tiny gymwear who watch complicated films. Right now it is a small, irritating Brit with wicked green eyes who is occupying all of my thoughts, even though my brain knows she shouldn't be. Do you understand?'

Her eyes widen.

'But we're not going to kiss.'

'You're being very commanding. You know that annoys me.'

She doesn't precisely *look* annoyed.

'Kissing is off the table,' I say.

She lifts an eyebrow.

'Too dangerous,' I say.

I sit forward, watching how her body responds to my movements – she leans closer a fraction after I do, like I've pulled her in. Like we're still dancing.

'You're right, it would be stupid,' I continue, letting my voice drop lower. 'But – whatever you say – I do know how to have fun. Which is why I would like to propose another game of poker.'

*

166

If I was in any doubt about my feelings for this woman, then every triumphant hand she wins would clear it up for me, because it is agony letting her win at poker. *Agony.*

'You actually suck at this,' she says gleefully, claiming her chips (still raisins). 'You got seriously lucky winning earlier, didn't you?'

'Yes,' I say, through gritted teeth. 'It seems I did.'

'Shirt off, then,' she says, lifting her gaze to me as she deals the cards again. Her eyes are full of mischief.

Strip poker. I am either a genius or an idiot for suggesting this. On the one hand, it has definitely cheered her up, but on the other, I have just committed to fully undressing in a room with Izzy without so much as touching her. This feels like a particularly brutal form of self-torture.

I take my shirt off slowly, sitting up on the bedspread. She's down to her blue strapless top and jeans, and I don't plan on letting her get further than that. As much as I want to undress her, this isn't how that's going to happen. If I ever get to see Izzy naked, it won't be about anything but us.

Her gaze shifts over me. I breathe out, trying not to tense too much. I like how it feels, just watching her watch me. Letting her take without trying to win anything back for once.

'What's with all the muscle, then?' she asks, dealing the cards on the duvet between us.

I'm about to respond with something sharp – *all the muscle* feels so dismissive. But I swallow it back. What she said about me raising my voice struck me hard, because that's how discussions happen at my uncle's house. Everyone is always snapping and shouting. I hadn't realised quite how much of that I had absorbed.

'I get wound up sometimes. The gym is where I go to lose the heat.'

She gives me a quick grin. 'You get wound up sometimes? Who knew!'

I'm glad to see that grin again. I check my cards – ace of diamonds, jack of diamonds. *Ah, cara . . .*

'I started exercising hard when I was a teenager.'

I swallow, wondering how much I can give her. Remembering Camila walking out of my flat saying I didn't have a heart.

'It was about my dad, I think. The fear that I had some fatal disease inside me too. It made me feel safer, knowing I was healthy and looking after my body.'

Her eyes widen. 'I'm sorry, Lucas. That's so horrible. I wish your mum had told you what happened to your dad.'

I shake my head. 'She struggled to talk about it. It wasn't her fault. Anyway, it made me realise how good exercise feels. How it helps you calm down. So – not all bad.'

'Hmm,' Izzy says, still frowning. 'Fold,' she says, setting her cards down. 'That was a rubbish hand.'

'What do you do to cool off when I've wound you up, then?' I ask her. 'No, let me guess. You ring a friend and complain about me?'

She smiles slightly. 'Yeah, sometimes. Or curl up with something wholesome on Netflix if I'm not seeing anyone. Remind myself that the world is full of warmth and fuzziness as well as grumpy Brazilians.'

I let her have that one. She deals the cards again. For a while we just play poker, only speaking when the game requires it. I should fill the silence, but I don't quite know how to talk to her now. Too much has happened today. Everything feels *esquisito*, as if someone's knocked my life askew.

'Is this how it's going to be now?' Izzy says eventually. 'If I'd known all I had to do to make you go quiet was kiss you, then I'd have done it earlier.'

She looks down at her cards, letting her hair shield her face. I want to push it back and lift her chin. Tell her not to hide from me.

'I called you grumpy and you didn't even snap at me,' she says, still looking down at her cards. 'It's weird.'

'It's not the kiss,' I say. 'I am trying to be less ... short-tempered. After what you said about shouting.' I take another deep breath. 'My uncle raises his voice a lot. I don't want to be like that.'

Opening up like this feels as if I'm bending something the wrong way – it's not natural. My body grows more and more tense with the effort. She watches me through her eyelashes, uncharacteristically still.

'He's not *bad*,' I say. I suddenly feel a lot more naked than I did twenty seconds ago. 'He's just ... forceful. He only respects strong people who stand up to him. He was a big part of my childhood, so I got strong.'

'And your mum?' Izzy asks quietly. 'What's she like?'

'She's strong too.' I smile. 'But strong like you. She holds her own but still gives a lot to other people.'

Izzy swallows. I've surprised her, I can tell. Her eyes dropping to my chest for a moment, gaze hovering over my tattoo, the single word just below my heart.

'I didn't expect that,' she says, nodding to it. 'You don't strike me as the tattoo type.'

I'm not, really. But when I made the choice to move to the UK, I suddenly understood the impulse people have to mark something permanently, to say, *this will never change.*

'What does it mean?' Izzy asks. 'Sow . . . da-day?'

'*Saudade*. Sow-da-dee.'

Izzy has another go. She doesn't quite get the final syllable right, but still, I like the sound of Portuguese on her tongue.

'It means . . . missing. Longing. There's no English word like it. I got the tattoo when I knew I would be moving away from my family – my mum, my sister and my grandmother. And my grandfather, too, who passed away not long before. That side of my family are very close, and I knew I would miss them so much. I wanted to mark how important that is to me – how important they are.'

She tilts her head. 'Why did you move?'

It's such a complicated, layered question. The reasons I wanted to live in England as a child are different from the reasons I moved here as an adult; the reasons I've stayed are different from those, too. And I don't want to tell Izzy about the course, which was a huge factor in why I moved to this part of the UK.

The only people who know I'm studying for a degree are my family. Even Pedro doesn't know. He thinks when I am working at the smoothie bar, I am doing hotel business. I always thought

I would feel comfortable talking about it once I got into the course. Then I thought I would feel comfortable once I passed my first term. But the moment I think of telling a friend or colleague about it, I imagine having to confess that I've failed or dropped out or couldn't afford this term's fees, and my mouth just snaps shut.

I know I'm too proud – I shouldn't care so much what others will think if I can't complete the course. But it's hard to shake my uncle's voice, even after all these years, and he has never tolerated failure.

'I've always had a fascination with the UK,' I say. 'And staying at home didn't seem right for me. Working in hospitality, I felt it even more – everyone was travelling from somewhere exciting, and I was just where I'd started. I never felt I was in quite the right place.'

'And now?'

I run my fingers across the backs of my cards. 'I don't know. I think maybe it wasn't a place that I was looking for. But I like it here. I like the job. I like the countryside.' I like that I'm doing my degree at one of the best places in the world to study hotel management, and that I'm doing it for *me*. 'What about you? The tattoo on your spine?'

Her eyes snap to mine, searching my face. 'Umm . . . When have you seen my tattoo?'

I go hot. I've just confessed to looking at her in a bikini when her back was turned.

'When you were . . . When you swam with Louis.'

She raises her eyebrows. 'Oh?'

'You turned around when I was . . . I just . . . saw it. Accidentally.'

She smiles slowly and lifts a hand to her back, tracing the spot in the centre of her spine where I saw the tattoo. 'And how long *were* you "accidentally" checking me out in my swimwear? Did you see anything else of interest? Shall I quiz you on freckle locations?'

'It was a very brief moment,' I say, immediately thinking about the perfect little mole on the curve of her hip.

'Mmhmm. Well. It's a treble clef.'

I wait.

'For my parents. It was always just the three of us. My dad was estranged from his family and my mum was an only child, so we didn't have that big aunts-and-uncles, loads-of-cousins type vibe – it was just us three. Trouble trebled, Dad used to say. Hence . . . treble.' She shrugs. 'It's a stupid play on words. I was twenty-one and thought it was clever.'

'I don't think it's stupid. It's creative.'

She gives me a small smile at that. A different sort of smile from usual.

'I cannot imagine how hard it was for you to lose them.'

'No,' she says simply. 'It changed me completely.'

'What were you like before?'

She pauses as if she wasn't expecting that question. 'Quiet, actually,' she says. 'I held myself back a lot. Now I go full-out because – like I said – life's too short for having regrets.'

I hesitate before answering. I'm not sure Izzy *does* go 'full-out'. She's certainly spontaneous, and she works hard. But her life does not seem to me to be built on taking chances. Just look at the inferior men she dates. The job she's been in for eight years without promotion. The friends she has all over the world, and how rarely she takes time off to visit them.

'Do you feel like you don't hold anything back now? That you *really* go full-out?'

She looks at me shrewdly. After a moment, she snorts. 'Lose the trousers, Lucas. Don't think you can distract me by Mrs Hedgers-ing me.'

Remarkably, for a moment, I had almost forgotten I am sitting here topless.

'Mrs . . .'

'Mrs Hedgers, the career-change coach in Sweet Pea? Has she not got you yet? She did a number on me and Poor Mandy. Told Mandy she's not assertive enough.'

Izzy is breezy and bright again, as though we never spoke about her parents. I'd like to push and ask her more, but I know I'll get nowhere.

'In the time I have known Mandy,' I say, 'she has never once asserted herself.'

'I know, right?'

'What did Mrs Hedgers say about you?'

Izzy shifts so her feet are tucked underneath her on the bed. Her socks are gone, lost when she played a bad hand at the start of the game.

'She said I don't know how to switch off.'

Interesting.

'On Thursday, you'll try some of the ways I unwind and switch off.'

'Oh, will I, now?'

I raise my eyebrows, lying back against the pillows with my hands behind my head.

'Have you forgotten? Thursday is my day. I'm in charge.'

'Oh, shit, yeah.' Something passes across her face. I wonder if it's worry.

'I won't . . . If you want to change your mind about the bet . . .'

'Are you kidding? Please. I'd never have given you that opportunity if I'd won.'

'But it's different. I'm a man. We are always in charge, so . . .' This doesn't come out the way I intended – she's glaring at me. I grope around for the right words, remembering how succinctly Ana put it when she was explaining why it's different for a woman to approach a man than the other way around. 'No, I just mean, it's not the same because of the way society always puts men in control anyway, so me telling you what to do, it just feels like it could be . . .'

'Oh.' Her face clears. 'Yeah. A bit loaded. Well, actually, oddly enough I do trust you to be a gentleman about it. You want to have a safeword or something?' She laughs at my expression. 'If I say, *fuck right off, Lucas*, then you have to back off. Agreed?'

'It is a good safe phrase,' I say solemnly, and I can tell from her face that she doesn't know whether I'm joking.

'Trousers,' she says, pointing at my knees.

'Ah. Yes.' I shift to the end of the bed and stand to take them off.

The atmosphere in the room shifts the moment I start unfastening my belt. Izzy is quiet, watching me as I unbutton my jeans, rolling her bottom lip between her finger and thumb. I thought stripping off would make her feel like she was in charge, but she's not laughing or humiliating me, she's just watching me, and I shiver under her gaze. It's been a while since I've stripped down for a woman, but they're normally touching me by this point. The distance between us should make this less intimate, but somehow it's the opposite.

I lie down on my back again, my head on the pillow. Laid out for her, with the cards and that silly little heap of raisins between us. I hear her breath catch and the sound sends something turning over inside me.

'If I win the next hand, you'll be naked,' Izzy says.

'Mm.'

'I was going to make you run out into the car park in the snow,' she says, 'but now that feels kind of cruel.'

'How were you going to make me do that?' I ask, amused.

She shrugs. 'I'd dare you.'

The room is very small and very quiet. Izzy has her bottom lip between her teeth now, biting down. My breath is catching too.

'But I think maybe dares are a bad idea now too.'

I think we're in one of those sliding-doors moments. Balancing on the edge of a decision we won't be able to unmake. I am struggling to remember why I shouldn't lean across the poker cards and pull her down into a kiss – not the kind of kiss she gave me, sweet and slow, but a fiery, electric-shock of a kiss, the kind that gets you hot in half a second.

'I'm getting ready for bed now, Lucas,' Izzy says. Her voice is low and quiet.

'OK,' I say.

She doesn't move. 'I don't get you,' she says. 'At all.'

I tip my chin, and she sighs out a breath, unmoving.

'You would strip naked for me, but you don't want to kiss me?'

'I never said I didn't want to kiss you.'

Her eyes move over me. 'Kiss me, then.'

I grit my teeth. She's within reach. I could grab her with one arm and have her body against mine before she'd caught her breath. I haven't forgotten how she looked in that bikini at the pool – the soft curve of her breast, the dip at the small of her back. I know how she'd fit against me.

I've got good self-control, but even I have limits. The moment stretches, testing me.

'Right,' Izzy says, moving at last. 'God, I'm a glutton for rejection when it comes to you, aren't I?'

The moment breaks. She slams into the bathroom, and I lie there, breathing hard, reminding myself that what's true in the gym applies here too: holding it a little longer always pays off.

It is perhaps the worst night's sleep I have ever had, and I have slept on airport floors, on many tiny sofas, and, once, at a terrible party I was dragged to by my sister, in the bottom of a closet.

Izzy is a quiet sleeper. She lies curled towards me with her knees tucked up and her hands pillowing her cheek. Even in the darkness, I notice things I have never noticed before. I see how her brows arch to a point, and how a very fine line brackets the corner of her mouth like the blueprint of a smile.

For a dangerous few minutes somewhere between two and three in the morning, I imagine what my life would look like with Izzy in it. I catalogue what she'd think of my flat, wonder which side of my bed she'd claim as hers, imagine how it would feel to lift her against my bedroom wall and wrap her legs around my waist.

And then I spend at least another hour wondering if I've made a terrible mistake by choosing not to kiss her. What if she'll never see me as anything more than the emotionless 'robot-man' who gets in her way all day? Then all I've done is lose my one chance of having any part of her at all. At three in the morning, a kiss with the wrong intentions feels much better than trying and failing to change Izzy's mind, and ending up with no kiss at all.

I manage a few hours of sleep before the winter sun sears through the threadbare curtains and wakes me again. Izzy hasn't moved, but her hair has shifted, laying two strands across her cheek. I get as close as lifting my hand to smooth them back before remembering how inappropriate that would be.

I slide out of the bed quietly and grab my clothes before slipping into the bathroom. I want to get back to Forest Manor. This room feels like a trap – if I spend much more time with Izzy here, I'll kiss her.

She lifts her head as I emerge from the bathroom. 'Oh,' she says, rubbing her face. 'I remember. Woking. Snow. Ugh.'

I straighten my pillow. I don't know where to look. She slept in her top and knickers – her jeans are folded on the footstool.

'We should go. The trains are running again.'

'Yeah? Has it settled?' she asks. 'The snow,' she clarifies when I look blank.

She slides her legs out of the bed and pads over to fetch the rest of her clothes. I turn away with a sharp breath as she bends to pull on her jeans.

'Wow,' she says, opening the curtains.

I step around the bed and look over her shoulder. Outside, the town looks like a different place – it's blanketed in snow, every hard edge softened, every block of flats now capped in white.

'A blank slate,' Izzy says, and the small smile she shoots over her shoulder gives me hope.

Izzy

We travel home in a silence that is only broken twice: once by Lucas saying, 'Please stop kicking the table leg', and once by me objecting to Lucas manspreading, though the moment he moves his knee out of my space, I find to my alarm that I kind of want it back again.

I feel totally panicked by last night. The kiss. The strip poker. Lucas in nothing but boxers. It's hard to even know where to begin with processing it all, so instead I just stare out at the snowy countryside and listen to an upcycling podcast, fully aware that I am forgetting everything the podcaster says in real-time.

When we get back to the hotel, there is a dark-haired woman sitting on the front steps, doubled over, shoulders shaking with sobs. A thin layer of snow dusts the stone around her, but her navy coat is hanging open, as though she hasn't noticed the cold.

Lucas and I exchange a glance and accelerate.

'Madam?' Lucas says. 'Can we help you?'

She looks up at us through blue-rimmed glasses clouded with tears.

'*You*,' she says, with venom. 'You're the ones doing this ring thing, aren't you?'

Shit. Is this Wife 1? Wife 2? Or someone else entirely whose life I have managed to ruin?

'Yes,' Lucas says calmly, ducking down to sit on the step beside her. 'That's us.'

This is kind of him – I think we all know this is *my* pet project. I was quick to remind him of that when it was earning us a fifteen-grand reward.

'You've ruined everything. Graham is – was – he *was* a good husband. We were *happy*.'

Her make-up is scored with tear tracks. She's beautiful, in that classic, statuesque way that always ages so well – I find myself thinking, *How could anyone cheat on someone like her?* As if beautiful people are immune to the damage a screwed-up man can create.

My stomach twists. I feel terrible. I never, ever imagined that The Ring Thing could cause any harm. I just thought about how desperately I would want someone to return the ring my dad gave me if they ever found it. But maybe some things are better off lost.

'Mrs . . .'

'Rogers. Actually, that's his name, so – Ms Ashley, I guess.'

'I see,' Lucas says. 'Ms Ashley, I am very sorry for the pain this has caused you.'

She's sobbing again. I twist my hands together, sitting down on the other side of Ms Ashley, then biting my lip as the freezing cold snow soaks through the backs of my trousers.

'But Graham was *not* a good husband.'

Lucas's voice is firm. I glance at his face, surprised – I thought he would just listen and make some supportive noises, but he's gone in pretty hard there.

'Someone who can lie to you so easily, and give his love to somebody else when he promised it all to you . . . that is not a good husband.'

Ms Ashley drops her face into her hands. 'Oh, God. But Graham is so *nice*. Everyone says it.'

She lifts her gaze to me. I almost recoil at her expression.

'Don't listen to people,' she says. 'You hear me? People are stupid. Listen to your instincts. Yours. Nobody else's. Everyone said I should go out with Graham because he's a good guy and *now fucking look at me!*'

I try not to jump as she starts shouting. I glance up – a car is pulling in to the car park.

Ms Ashley shoots to her feet. 'That's them. *You wanker!*' she screams at the car.

I widen my eyes at Lucas, standing up and brushing the snow off my legs.

'Ah,' comes Mrs SB's voice from behind us, in the hotel doorway. 'Everyone's here very early for brunch! How nice. Mrs Rogers . . .'

'Ms Ashley,' Lucas and I correct her in unison.

'Ms Ashley,' Mrs SB says, not missing a beat. 'I wondered where you'd got to. Won't you come back inside and warm up?'

'I don't think I can do this,' Ms Ashley says, staring at the four-by-four currently parking up, with a serious-faced couple inside: Graham, presumably, and the other Mrs Rogers. 'Look at that car. Is that his car? He would never drive a car like that, but he's driving that car right now. How is that possible?' Ms Ashley fixes her gaze on me again. 'He was always too good to be true,' she whispers, gripping my arm. 'I should have known.'

I grip her hand right back, feeling a bit desperate. I want to give her a hug, but I am pretty sure she doesn't want one from me. 'You couldn't have known. Ms Ashley, it's not your fault.'

'I can't do this,' she says. 'I can't sit in the same room as them. I thought I could yesterday, but I can't do it. Oh, God.'

They're climbing out of the car. The other Mrs Rogers looks as though she is vibrating with rage. She slams the door hard and stalks past her husband. She's younger, curvier, with orange-blonde hair in a crown braid.

'Darling,' says Graham, racing after her. 'Please. Talk to me. I love you.'

He *does* look like a nice guy. A bumbling British type. All tweed and good intentions. He's not seen Ms Ashley yet, I realise – she's hidden behind one of the round box hedges. She steps out now, her arms folded, her whole body trembling.

'Which darling would that be?' she says.

It's extraordinary to watch Graham make his decision. In one second, then two, it all passes over his face: indecision, cunning, deliberation. Not so well-intentioned now. As the other Mrs Rogers falters at the sight of Ms Ashley, Graham picks the life he wants to live.

'The truth is, darling,' he says to the blonde wife he drove here. 'This is all a terrible mix-up. I knew this woman once. I'm sorry to tell you . . . she's quite mad.'

Ms Ashley's mouth drops open. The blonde Mrs Rogers narrows her eyes, keeping her gaze fixed on the woman in front of her.

'Tell me,' she says.

Ms Ashley doesn't hesitate. 'He married me eight years ago in Godalming. We live together in New Milton. He stays away a lot for work. We've had two cats, a miscarriage, eight holidays in Spain, and three days ago he told me he'd never loved me more.'

'All nonsense,' Graham says immediately.

Mrs Rogers nods once. 'In that case – no brunch,' she says, redirecting her attention to Mrs SB. 'We're calling the police instead.'

Ms Ashley tenses. We all wait, wondering exactly which *we* Mrs Rogers means, until she turns slowly and looks at her husband.

'Bigamy is a serious crime, *darling*,' she says.

When the police car pulls up the hotel's sweeping gravel drive, most of the hotel staff, Mr Townsend and even the Jacobs (their cheerfully waving baby included) have come to watch the drama unfold.

The two former Mrs Rogers stand at opposite ends of the crowd, stony-faced, as Mr Rogers gawps in the face of the policeman currently reading him his rights.

'This is ridiculous,' he says, looking back at us all. He is giving off odious these-sorts-of-things-don't-happen-to-men-like-me vibes, which makes me want that policeman to use the handcuffs currently dangling from his belt. 'You're having me *arrested*? Are you quite serious?'

'I think they're pretty serious, mate,' says the policeman. 'I know I certainly am. Get in the car.'

'This is all a terrible misunderstanding,' Graham implores, in the general direction of his wives.

The policeman taps on the roof of the car. 'In. Now.'

'Now, see here,' says Graham, and then – to whoops from the crowd – the policeman places one hand firmly on his head and shoves him in the back seat.

The car door slams shut. Ms Brown flips Graham the bird as the police drive away, and Ms Ashley yells an insult so colourful that Mr and Mrs Hedgers immediately scoop up the children and flee the scene before Ruby asks anyone to repeat it.

'Is it too early to get drunk?' Ms Brown asks Barty and Mrs SB.

'I leave that to your judgement,' Barty says. 'But I will mention that we have a twenty-four-hour licence.'

'Perfect,' says Ms Brown, heading inside. 'Come on,' she says to Ms Ashley, without looking at her. 'I think you and I need to chat.'

As the two of them settle in at our grand, mahogany bar with a Bloody Mary each, I notice my hands are shaking on the menu I'm carrying over to them. It's just . . . I always try to see the best in people. To think that everyone is fundamentally quite nice really. And then someone does something this awful and it makes me wonder how the hell you're meant to know who to trust.

I play with my necklace, the one my mum gave me. It's times like these that I miss my parents the most.

'I really hate you right now,' Ms Ashley is saying as I reach them at the bar.

'Oh, same to you, love,' says Ms Brown. 'Maybe we'll get to the solidarity part later.'

'If we drink enough alcohol,' Ms Ashley says, taking a vicious bite from her stick of celery.

'Can I interest you in some breakfast to go with that . . .?' I ask, my voice a little squeaky.

'You,' Ms Ashley says, zeroing in on me as she sucks up half her cocktail through the straw. 'The ring meddler.'

'I really am so sorry,' I say wretchedly. Today I seem to have done the exact opposite of adding sparkle. I've made everything significantly gloomier.

'Not your fault, love,' says Ms Brown, already waving at Ollie for another drink. 'A lot of men are shits. You do your best to dodge 'em, but . . .'

Ollie shrinks into himself, shaking up the next cocktail as quietly as possible.

'Izzy!' Arjun calls. 'There's something for you at the front desk! Ask me how I know!'

I spin to look at him. His hair is a mess and he's not wearing his apron, which always makes him look a bit weird, as if he's not wearing his shoes.

'How do you know?' I say obligingly.

'Because you are here, and Lucas is off somewhere else, and

Ollie is behind the bar ballsing up that Bloody Mary, and so *I* had to leave the kitchen to answer the reception bell!'

I glance at the two women, but they don't seem to mind someone else doing a bit of shouting.

'No food, love,' Ms Brown says to me. 'Just keep the booze coming.' This is directed at Ollie.

I move to go after Arjun and then remember something. 'Oh! Do you want the ring?' I blurt, patting my pocket.

Ms Brown stares at me, then looks down at her hand, and across at Ms Ashley's. They are both still wearing their wedding rings.

'I think we've got enough rings here, don't you? Just sell it. Keep the money. Looks like this place could use it,' she says, nodding after Arjun. 'Get that man some help, eh, love?'

I mean, I don't think this ring is worth quite enough to employ a sous-chef for Arjun, but I appreciate the intention, and I'm glad we're getting *something* out of this disaster. I thank them and leave the Mrs Rogers to it, heading to the lobby as Arjun flounces back into the kitchen again.

Louis is waiting for me at the front desk. There is a gigantic bunch of red roses beside him. They look unreal – as in, they genuinely look fake, so perfect is every petal and upturned leaf. They're tied with a thick white ribbon and there's an embossed note beside them. My heart sinks. This is really not my sort of thing.

'Open the card,' Louis says, tapping it against the desk.

I flick the envelope open. *Join me for dinner at The Angel's Wing tonight*, it says.

'Louis . . .' I begin.

The Angel's Wing is a super-posh restaurant near Brocken-hurst – it's the sort of place London types go to when they want to be in the countryside but still eat like they're in the city. It's got a dress code and everything.

'Too much?' he says.

I can't precisely say why I don't want to go. I was up for it when we had our swimming date, and there are plenty of reasons to give things a try with Louis: he's good-looking, he's attentive, and he's definitely got the drive and ambition that Sameera thought I should look for in a man.

'The Angel's Wing is really expensive . . .' I say.

'It's on me,' Louis says. 'I should have mentioned that.'

'Izzy!' Lucas barks from the direction of the kitchen. 'Arjun needs you!'

Seriously? I just *saw* Arjun. I don't know where Lucas has emerged from, and it is completely typical that he is now insisting on my presence despite being MIA for at least an hour himself.

Louis nods to the flowers and card. 'I just thought a romantic gesture would be the right thing to go for, given . . .'

'Isabelle!' Lucas shouts.

Isabelle? Excuse me? Only Jem gets to call me Isabelle, and that is because she was my friend when I was eight years old and has earned the right over the last two decades to call me whatever she likes.

Lucas comes marching out of the kitchen. As his eyes move over the bunch of roses, his face flickers.

'Am I interrupting?' he says, in a tone that suggests he knows very well that he is, and feels strongly that there should be no moment for him to interrupt.

'Just give us a minute, would you?' Louis says, with an uncharacteristic touch of irritation.

Lucas's cheek twitches. 'Izzy is needed. She is working. She will be available to discuss personal matters at five p.m. when her shift ends.'

I gawp. Honestly, the cheek of him. Suddenly he's Mr Not In Working Hours after spending yesterday dancing to Anitta in a flat in Little Venice. Part of me is glad he's being his usual self now we're back – it's easier to forget the man I saw laid bare in that hotel room, or dancing with me in Shannon's flat. It's easier to imagine that the last twenty-four hours never happened.

It's also easier to make this decision.

'Thank you, Louis,' I say, turning to him with a smile. 'I'd love to go for dinner tonight. See you at seven thirty.'

I've not lived with a friend since Drew, and this is the first time I've regretted the decision to live alone. I can't decide what to wear, and nobody is replying to my frantic WhatsApp requests for outfit advice. I'm trying to focus on the date ahead, but instead I keep thinking about Lucas's judgemental face as he said, *Am I interrupting?* Eventually, after getting mascara on the bridge of my nose for the third time, I figure out why it's bothering me so much.

I think Lucas was jealous. Not just judging me for being unprofessional – *jealous*.

But what the hell am I supposed to make of that?

As I fasten three of my favourite necklaces, I realise my hands are clammy. I haven't been on a date for a while. It wasn't a conscious decision to stop dating, I just got sick of trawling through Bumble and shaving my legs for men who wouldn't prove worthy of seeing them.

I look at my reflection and the memory shoots up yet again: Lucas's lips against mine, and then that awful, awkward silence as he turned his back on me.

So humiliating.

At least I won at strip poker. Though is it really winning if the consequence is having an image of Lucas looking unspeakably sexy in nothing but his boxers seared to the inside of your eyelids?

When I arrive at The Angel's Wing, Louis is waiting outside in a suit with no tie. He opens the door for me, then the next door, and then he takes my coat and pulls out my chair for me. I say 'thank you' too many times and end up a bit flustered.

The date itself is . . . nice. Louis is fun to talk to – there's nothing not to like. And the food and drink is amazing. Arjun's a fantastic chef, so I'm used to good food, but he doesn't really go in for the cream-laced French stuff they do at The Angel's Wing.

But by the time our desserts arrive, underneath all the wine and dairy in my stomach is a low feeling of dread. I can't stop thinking about what Ms Ashley said. *Listen to your instincts.* And even though Louis is totally the right sort of guy on paper, and even though I'm sure my mum and dad would've loved how much of a gentleman he is . . . there is just something telling me this isn't right.

It *should* be right. But it's not.

'Louis . . .'

'You're not feeling it?'

His voice is light and casual, the same tone he was just using a moment ago to discuss his love of golf.

'I'm so sorry. You're a really lovely guy . . .'

He waves that away. 'I get it, I get why you're hesitant this time around.'

I frown slightly. I told him about my last couple of relationships, but now I wonder if I've overplayed the general rubbishness of Tristan and Dean, because otherwise this comment seems a bit odd.

'I put too much pressure on things with the flowers and all that,' Louis says, reaching to top up my wine as the waitress delivers our chocolate puddings. 'Let's just ease off the gas.'

'I'm not sure we're a good fit,' I try.

He shakes his head. 'Come on, don't shut this down before you've even got to know me, Izzy. Let me take you out again in a few days. We can just go for a walk with a coffee, maybe – something low-key. Let's hang out a bit, see how it feels, see where it goes . . .' He takes a spoonful of pudding and closes his eyes with a moan. 'Try that, oh my God.'

'I mean, we can go out again if you want,' I find myself saying, 'but I need to be honest and say I don't think I'm going to change my mind. Sorry. I don't want you wasting your time with me when . . .'

'My choice what I do with my time. I can handle myself, Izzy,' he says with a wink. 'Just have fun and relax, OK? There's no pressure from me.'

I'm not sure how to argue with that. And this date has been lovely, technically speaking. Was it actually any lovelier than this with Tristan or Dean? I don't remember being particularly swept away by either of their first dates, and both of them became my boyfriends.

So why not Louis?

I text Jem when I'm home to fill her in on how I'm feeling, and she replies with a voice note.

Pigeon, I hear what you're saying, but . . . Your parents wanted you to date a guy who seemed sweet and kind – eight years ago. You were so young when they said that to you, Izz. You're an adult now. You're wiser. I know it hurts so bad that your mum and dad aren't here to give you advice, but for what it's worth, I think they'd tell you that you know best now. If something in your heart says this guy's not quite right for you, they'd want you to listen to that.

It makes me cry. I play it twice more. She's right: it *does* hurt that Mum and Dad aren't here to advise me on what to do. It hurts that I'm having to figure out how to be an adult on my own, and that all the wisdom they've given me is at least eight years out of date. I'll never be able to bring a guy back to the house I grew up in and close the kitchen door to say, *So, guys? What do you think of him? Be honest!*

Louis has messaged me while I've been listening to Jem:

Fancy a stroll around Winchester Christmas market on Friday eve? he's written. *Don't think too hard about it* 😌 *No pressure, just give it a shot!*

Hmm. Now it's an *evening* stroll, and will probably involve food – that seems like a step up from a walk with coffee.

I make a decision then and there: I'll go to the Christmas market with Louis, and if it's still not feeling right, I'll draw a line under things with him. He may say he doesn't mind wasting his time, but life's too short for me to waste mine.

Another message pops up from Jem. *Here for you always*, it says.

I clutch the phone. It's been hard not to feel a little abandoned over the last year, as each of my favourite people have left to another part of the world. I know it's not about me, but I can't help wishing that we could still be here for each other in the way we were before.

But there are different ways of being *here*. I play Jem's voice note one more time and feel so grateful for the friends who still make space for me in their whirlwind lives; the people who know exactly why something will hurt, and who know just what to say to make it better.

Thank you. And you – always, I reply, and then I choose my favourite pyjamas, boil the kettle for my hot-water bottle, and curl up in bed. I've got an unusually quiet few days ahead, and I think I might just spend them on the sofa. It's been such a mad week, even by my standards – I need to re-anchor myself. By the time I'm back at work, I'm sure I'll be full-on Izzy again, ready to face anything.

Even though right now that idea feels kind of exhausting.

Lucas

It's Thursday – my day. Lucas Day. My chance to change Izzy's mind.

I arrive at her flat at six a.m. It takes her quite some time to open the door.

'Oh my God, what is wrong with you,' she says, already walking back inside.

I take this as an invitation to follow, but she turns on her heels and holds out a hand.

'No crossing the threshold,' she says.

'It's Thursday,' I tell her, stopping in the doorway, holding the door open with one arm.

'Yes, I'm aware.'

She's in pyjamas – pink ones with spots. Her hair is pulled up in a topknot and she has the same adorably ruffled look she had that morning in Woking. She fetches herself a bowl of cereal and starts eating, standing in the middle of her flat in a lost sort of way, as if she can't figure out how she's ended up there.

'My day,' I prompt her. 'Because I won.'

'But why are you here so early?' Her tone is slightly plaintive.

'We're going to the gym.'

'The *gym*?' She spins. 'Why?'

'Because I say so.'

Her stare turns into a glare. I suppress a smile.

'Do you have any sportswear?'

'Of course I have sportswear,' she says, looking slightly embarrassed. 'I'm not – I do exercise *sometimes*.'

I think about her comment about my type of woman – their 'tiny gymwear' – and realise I am being an idiot.

'We are going to the gym because it's how I unwind,' I tell her. 'It's not about you. You don't need to exercise. I'm not saying you need to exercise. I'm not trying to say that.'

Her expression warms a little as I squirm in her doorway.

'Stay there,' she says, turning her back on me. 'I'm not inviting you in. I've watched way too many episodes of *The Vampire Diaries* to fall for that.'

I lean against the door frame as she closes the bedroom door. Her flat is the top floor of a converted house. She's styled it in calm pastels: a fluffy cream rug, a pale-blue throw over the back of the mint-coloured sofa. The decor reminds me vaguely of an old-fashioned British sweetshop.

Izzy emerges from the bedroom. She's in gym gear now. Tight grey leggings and a pale-yellow crop top, with red and orange stripes in her hair.

She looks gorgeous. For a moment I wish for the feeling I had before our trip to London – the way I used to be able to look at her and think, *Yes, she's beautiful, but she's a pain in the arse.*

I still think those things, but suddenly I also think about how badly I want to hold her. Sling my arm over her shoulder as we head out the door. Kiss her like it's something we do all the time.

She bends to pull some trainers out from behind the door and hauls an oversized bag over her shoulder. At my enquiring look, she says, 'I've packed for every eventuality. I have a feeling you have some odd activities lined up for me.'

'We're just going to work,' I say, amused. 'This isn't a stag do.'

'Mmhmm,' she says, locking the door to her flat behind her. 'Well, since we've been working together five days a week, I've been dunked in a swimming pool, danced with strangers at a divorce party and fallen on my face in the snow outside a Papa Johns in Woking.'

I raise my eyebrows as we make our way down to the street.

'I didn't know about that.'

'Oh. Right. Well, yeah, my walk in Woking wasn't that fun.'

There is a stocky New Forest pony nibbling at the hedge by the side of the road. Neither of us remark upon it. When I first moved to the New Forest, I was astonished to find myself caught in a traffic jam caused by a gaggle of unfazed ponies, but I'm used to them now. They roam wild around here – it's no stranger than seeing a pigeon.

'God, your car is so shiny,' Izzy says, as we approach it. 'Do you polish it?'

I do, actually, but I know Izzy well enough to realise I'm better off not confessing to that. This car is my pride and joy. She's third-hand and has seventy thousand miles on the clock; I fixed her up myself, painstakingly, with help from a friend who lives on my road. Now she looks as good as new. As a child, I always dreamed of living in England and having a car like this. Back then, it had been because I wanted to be James Bond, and didn't know the difference between a two-hundred-thousand-pound Aston Martin and a fixed-up 55-reg BMW. Now, it's because of what it means: the freedom to live and work in this strange, wet, awkward little country that I have fallen so unexpectedly in love with.

I open the passenger door for Izzy. She looks surprised, and then wary.

'Why are you being nice?' she says.

'It is all part of the grand plan to torture you for a day,' I say, slamming the car door behind her. Her expectations of me are so low. But I can hardly blame her. We have baited each other for months on end – I've been petty, difficult, argumentative.

I've been just like my uncle, in fact. The thought is painful to swallow.

As I drive us to the gym, Izzy looks at something on her phone, biting her bottom lip. I glance across at her.

'Yet another no for the emerald ring,' she says. 'These last two are so tricky.'

'You haven't given up, then? After Graham Rogers?'

'Absolutely not. One bad egg does not make a bad egg box, you know?'

I don't know if this is an odd Britishism or an Izzy-ism, but best to just nod.

'I still believe we're doing something important. Maybe that emerald ring really meant something to somebody.'

I almost say, *And how does that help the hotel, exactly?* But I snatch it back in time. This matters to her. I don't understand why, but I'm trying to be more open-minded, and that means accepting that people aren't always logical. After all, I've not been particularly logical myself lately. For instance, I am currently trying to win over a woman who has spent the last year making my life as miserable as possible, including spending two months trying to persuade Mrs SB and Barty to do 'bagpipe Fridays' in the lobby because I happened to mention a dislike for the instrument.

'The other one looks valuable too, you know,' she says, rubbing her bottom lip between her forefinger and thumb as she stares out of the window. 'There *might* be another reward.'

'I hope so,' I say as I pull in to the car park. 'We need it.'

Izzy nods, saying nothing. She hasn't seen the spreadsheets. She doesn't know how big a hole there is in the centre of the hotel's finances – how the amount we've raised from selling items has sunk into that pit without even touching the sides. But she's not naïve. I can see from her frown that she knows the truth: without a small miracle, there will be no Forest Manor Hotel and Spa by the new year.

When we enter the gym, I get worried. Izzy's shoulders have crept up, and she's fiddling with the bottom of her crop top, shifting on the toes of her trainers. I hadn't expected this. The moment I walk into a gym, I feel comfortable. Even the smell relaxes me – that mix of air freshener, clean sweat and rubber.

It's clear I have work to do here. I steer her towards the gym mats first. No intimidating equipment, and nobody else there at the moment.

'Some stretches, first,' I tell her.

She brightens. 'OK,' she says. 'I can do stretches.'

She is not lying. I watch her touch her toes and try to think pure thoughts.

'Why don't you like the gym?' I ask her as I stretch out my quads. They're tight from yesterday's run, but my arms are feeling good. I skipped upper body on Tuesday so that I would be well rested for today. It is critical that Izzy does not find out about this.

'Everyone here is just very . . .' She looks around, still folded over on herself with her hands on her feet. 'Like you. Like superpeople.'

I realise this is not intended as a compliment, but I can't help feeling a glimmer of pleasure at it anyway.

'They're not,' I say. I look around, seeing what she's seeing, and lift a hand to wave at a few people I know. 'Everyone is welcome at a gym. And if you *talk* to the people who come to the gym a lot, we aren't as bad as we look.'

Her expression is dubious, but I'm no longer worried, because my trump card has arrived.

Kieran, the first friend I made in the New Forest, and the best personal trainer I have come across anywhere. He is a small, scrawny white man with no hair and too many tattoos, and he is that very rare thing: a person I liked straight away.

'Lucas!' he bellows, beaming at me and waving with both

arms, as though he is directing an aeroplane. 'Wow, hi!' he says to Izzy, as she straightens up.

'Hi!' she says, slightly taken aback.

A common response to Kieran's arrival. He treats every day as though he is on set at a children's television show.

'We're going to work out!' Kieran says, already bouncing on the spot. 'But in a fun way! A *really* fun way! Do you like beating Lucas at things?'

'Yeah, I do, actually,' Izzy says.

I may have given Kieran some background before booking this session. It cost more than I could afford, but I can already tell that it'll be worth it.

'I'll never beat him in the gym, though. Look at the man,' Izzy says, waving a hand in my direction.

'Oh-ho-ho,' Kieran says, rubbing his hands together. 'Just you wait and see.'

Izzy

It's undeniable: I feel amazing. Kieran insisted that I take at least fifteen minutes in the shower after our session and now, dried off and dressed in my work uniform, I feel like I'm walking several inches off the ground. I can't remember when I last exercised really hard – did it always leave me feeling like this? It's as if someone's just given me a massage, but like, inside my brain as well as every muscle of my body.

Obviously when the exercise was happening it was largely quite horrible. But Kieran assures me that it gets better as you do it more, and the after effects *are* delightful.

Beating Lucas was pretty great too. Kieran wasn't wrong – there were things I could do better than Lucas. I was better at the skipping rope skills, and I could sprint faster than him on the running machines. And even when we were doing things that were clearly more his ballpark than mine, Kieran never made it feel like losing. Nor did Lucas, to be fair.

It's been interesting seeing him here. He's a different man in this context. Everyone seems to know him – they all come over and hug him, and tell me things like 'couldn't have moved house without this guy', or 'you know what, when my cat died, Lucas was a hero'. I'd like to say I'm shocked to know that there are people who rely on Lucas, but I'm not, actually – I can imagine he'd be a big help if your cat died, or if you needed to move house. If he wasn't your arch-nemesis.

The main issue I've had this morning is Lucas's unrelenting *muscliness*. It's so unavoidable here. The exposed biceps, the impossibly broad shoulders, the sweat. (Why is it that when men sweat, it's sexy, but when I sweat, I look like I've been crossbred with a tomato?) I've never been attracted to big, hench men, and actually, if I look at some of the others in here, it doesn't do it for me at all. It is a Lucas-specific problem. The worst kind.

The only consolation is the fact that I caught Lucas checking me out too. I looked up when we were doing the warm-down and found his eyes on me in the mirror, low-lidded, appreciative. He turned his head away sharply when he saw me looking. No surprise there. After all, he's rejected me three times now. Lucas may want me on some level, but he's got cast-iron control, and his brain's decided he's not interested, so that's that. I mean, my brain has decided the same thing.

But it is quite nice to see that it's not *just* me who's struggling to stick with that decision.

He told me to meet him in the gym lobby, and he's already speaking to the receptionist when I arrive, buttoned up in his work clothes, looking as pristine as usual. Dangerous biceps safely sheathed.

'Let me pay for the session,' I say, coming to join him.

His face takes on the fixed look it gets when he's embarrassed. 'No need,' he says stiffly.

Hmm. This is clearly a lie. As the receptionist holds the card reader out to him, I lean across and tap my card before Lucas can get his wallet out.

'Izzy,' he snaps, exasperated.

I give him my sweetest smile. 'Oops.'

I watch him struggle. He can't *stand* the idea of me doing him a favour, but I can see that deep down, he knows he can't really afford to pay. Something twinges in my chest.

'Thank you,' he says, without meeting my eyes. 'We are having breakfast next,' he tells me, already heading for the door. He forgets to hold it open for me, so I guess the whole chivalric opening-the-car-door thing isn't going to be sticking around.

'No, sorry,' I say, as I clock where we're going for breakfast. 'Juice? That is not food.'

'Smoothies,' he says, and puts a hand on my elbow to steer me firmly inside. I go hot where he's touching me, then every-where else, too. We've very rarely touched – the odd glance of a hand here or there, but that's mostly it. Apart from when we danced. And when I kissed him, obviously.

Ugh. In pops the memory again. Will that ever stop feeling so awful?

'Smoothies are just juices you aren't sure whether to chew or not.'

Lucas looks slightly horrified at this. 'Well, it's free, because Pedro is a friend. So it's what you're getting. He does excellent coffee, too,' he says, nodding to the man behind the bar and gesturing to a seat for me to take. It's actually the exact spot I would have chosen – one of the shiny pink bar stools that looks out of the front window to the street outside.

'A gym friend?' I guess, taking in Pedro, who just *glows* with good health. Sickening, really.

'Yes. He's from Rio too.'

'Oh! That must be nice.'

I give Pedro a tentative smile. He grins back. His dark hair is wavy and carefully styled, and he's wearing a T-shirt that clings to every muscle – he looks like he might be the breakout star of this year's *Love Island*, that one the whole nation falls in love with.

'Hello,' says Pedro, wiping his hands as he emerges from behind the bar. 'Are you Izzy?'

'Yes,' I say, with slight suspicion. 'Why, what's Lucas said?'

'Only how beautiful you are,' says Pedro, beaming as he pulls up a bar stool next to me.

Lucas pulls the stool back again just as Pedro is about to sit on it. Pedro manages to save himself from ending up on the floor by making a wild grab for Lucas, who then almost goes down with him. I burst out laughing, as does Pedro; Lucas brushes himself down and remains expressionless.

'I didn't say that,' Lucas says, sitting down on the stool Pedro had wanted. 'Ignore Pedro. Ignore anything Pedro tells you.'

I look back at Pedro with renewed interest.

'Well, you *are* beautiful,' Pedro says. 'So Lucas should say it. What can I get you? It's on the house. May I recommend the Sweet Peach Party?'

He leans over the menu with me, talking me through it, eyes flicking between me and Lucas. A naughty smile grows on his face as Lucas's expression gets darker and darker – I get the sense I'm part of an attempt to wind Lucas up that I haven't fully understood, but that's fine, I'm on board with it – until eventually Lucas grabs the menu and stalks over to the bar.

'Hey!' I say, turning around. 'I haven't chosen yet.'

'My day,' he reminds me. 'Can I get service here?'

Pedro stands with a chuckle.

'Don't order me one of those protein ones!' I call to Lucas. 'I don't want to get all muscly like you.'

I watch Lucas's grip tighten on the menu as he turns back towards me. 'You don't build muscle just by drinking . . .' He stops as I start laughing. 'Pedro!' he snaps. 'Make her something with broccoli in it, please.'

'Ah, I've found my kindred spirit, I think,' Pedro says to me as he skips back to the bar, pristine trainers bouncing on the polished wood floor. 'Someone who knows how to annoy Lucas almost as well as I do.'

We drink our coffees in the bar, and then have our smoothies on the walk back to the car. In defiance of Lucas, Pedro cheerfully made me something delicious, spiked with fresh ginger and stuffed with tropical fruit. It's admittedly quite refreshing, but I maintain that this is not breakfast. Coco Pops: now *that* is breakfast.

Mrs Muller passes us on her way from the dining room as we enter the hotel. Her hair is in a silk wrap and she has a paintbrush tucked behind her ear.

'Morning, Mrs Muller!' I call.

'Muses striking!' she calls back, with a languid wave. 'Don't talk to me!'

I nod. Fair enough. Mr Townsend smiles up from his armchair, folding his newspaper on his knees as we approach.

'Lucas!' he calls. 'May I call upon you to take me to Budgens tomorrow?'

'Of course.'

This is a fortnightly tradition – Mr Townsend likes very particular snacks in his room, and Lucas likes any excuse to drive his car.

'Coffee afterwards, yes?'

I glance at Lucas in surprise. It's not like him to socialise with a guest, but Mr Townsend said that as though it's become a regular feature.

'I'd like that. Now, if you'll excuse me,' Lucas says, with a nod of his head, 'I must speak to Arjun.'

'How was the night?' I ask Mr Townsend as Lucas disappears into the kitchen. We don't have an overnight receptionist at the moment, but Mr Townsend usually knows exactly what's been going on – he goes to bed late and wakes up early.

'The young 'un slept like a log,' Mr Townsend says, nodding

towards the Jacobs family's room. 'Just one two a.m. feed. Those blackout blinds you ordered have worked like a charm.'

'And you?'

'I got more than enough rest,' he says with a smile. 'Maisie used to say we're better with a little fatigue in our systems. It keeps us fighting.'

I pull a face, scanning the lobby for jobs that need doing. 'She sounds hardcore.'

'She was an actress,' he says. 'Theatre. I think she just wanted an excuse to stay out even later than she already did. That woman could dance the feet off a caterpillar.'

'Sounds like a girl after my own heart,' I say, rearranging the fir branch on the mantlepiece. Though actually it's been ages since I've danced. Except for that day in Shannon's flat, which I am now having to try very hard not to think about.

'So, what's he got planned for you?' Mr Townsend asks, nodding in the direction Lucas went.

'Sorry?'

'It is Lucas Day, isn't it?'

'Who told you that?'

Mr Townsend tries looking mysterious for a moment, and then gives up and says, 'Ollie.'

'Who told *him*? No, don't tell me, it was Arjun. So does everybody know?'

'I don't think Barty does,' Mr Townsend says. 'But Barty never seems to know what's going on around here, does he?'

I manage not to laugh at this, and give myself a rare full marks for professionalism. A family pass on their way to brunch in the dining room, and Mr Townsend and I pause politely before launching back in.

'It may be Lucas Day officially, but I think it's an Izzy day really,' I say. 'After all, you're happy . . .'

'Perfectly,' Mr Townsend says, reaching for his glasses.

'The muses are striking away at Mrs Muller . . .'

'The housekeeping team are no doubt thrilled to hear it.'

'And I got Baby Jacobs to sleep!'

'Certainly an Izzy day,' Mr Townsend says gravely.

I lift my chin, putting the finishing touches on the mantlepiece decorations. Lucas needs to up his game, I'd say.

'Oh my God. No.'

'No?'

'*No!*'

'Is that, *Fuck right off, Lucas, no*?'

I grimace. 'Well, no, it isn't. But I don't want to do this. I thought you'd make me do gross stuff, like scrubbing bathrooms! I didn't think you'd make me' – I wave my hands around the computer screen – '*digitalise*.'

'If you become more familiar with the system, you will learn how useful it can be. Even Poor Mandy likes it now.'

'She likes it if you're asking. When I ask, she says she prefers the booking book.'

'Of course she does. But what happens if there's a fire and the booking book burns? Everything will be lost for ever.'

I do *know* that the online system is more sensible. I'm not a total Luddite. I just love the ritual of the booking book, and guests do too – signing in with the fountain pen, flicking through the thin pages, the heft of that leather cover as it thuds closed on the desk . . . It's all part of the hotel experience, like the gold bell they ding if they need us and we're not there. We could have an intercom-type system for that, but we don't, because dinging is fun.

'I'm updating guest profiles this morning,' Lucas says. 'Which means you are, too. Here,' he says, pushing one of the old booking books my way. 'You can have 2011. Your ring was lost the summer of that year – maybe you'll find something useful.'

Reluctantly, I reach for the book and drag it towards me. Lucas gives a satisfied nod and returns to his computer screen, tapping away.

'How long am I doing this for?' I ask, logging in.

'Until I say so.'

I can *feel* his smile.

He keeps me at the desk like this for an hour and a half. This might actually be the longest I've ever sat still at work, and it's definitely the longest I've sat next to Lucas without one of us speaking to a guest or running off to do something else.

It's oddly companionable. Mostly we don't talk, but occasion-ally Lucas makes an idle remark, and at one point, astonishingly, he makes me a cup of tea. We coexist, basically. I'm quite sur-prised we have it in us.

Infuriatingly, Lucas is right: I *do* find something useful for my ring. As I transfer everything to Lucas's system, I notice that a few of the guests on extended stays were missed when

I made my list of people to contact, because they'd checked in several weeks or months before the time when the ring was found.

I scribble down their names, pen pausing when I hit *Mr and Mrs Townsend*. It's sort of happy and sort of sad to think that Maisie was with him back then. I make a note to speak to him – the ring can't be Maisie's, since she wore hers until the day she died, but he might remember someone losing their engagement ring during one of his stays at the hotel.

Eventually Lucas checks his watch, clicks his pen and declares we're done. He sets Barty's sign on the front desk – *Please ring for assistance and we will be with you in a jiffy!* – and leads me to the store cupboard. It's tidier than when I was last in here – he's sorted the shelves and pulled out all the different paint tins, dusting off their lids.

'That one,' he tells me. 'Can you carry it?'

I give him a withering look and then realise he's teasing me.

'I've seen you in the gym now, remember,' he says, picking up two paint tins of his own. 'You will never be able to pretend you need me to do heavy lifting for you again.'

Damn. I can never be arsed shifting the garden furniture, and guests *always* want it in a different spot. One of the very few upsides of being on shift with Lucas is that I can usually rope him into doing it.

I follow him through the bar to the conservatory at the back of the hotel. It's carpeted and filled with a motley collection of too many armchairs, and it's always been a bit of a wasted space – it's usually where the elderly folk gather at a wedding party to get away from the noise. I've not been back here for a while, and I pause in the entrance, mouth dropping open.

'Lucas!'

'What do you think?'

I look around, taking it all in. He's cleared the room completely and pulled up the carpet, and he's scrubbed the place down too – the windows are sparkling, showing the expanse of frosty gardens outside. It's no longer an old conservatory, it's more like an . . .

'*Orangery*,' I say, clapping my hands. 'We'll call it the orangery! People can eat bar food out here. Or even get married! For small ceremonies, this would actually be beautiful!' I spin on my heels, admiring the space. 'And the paint is for the floorboards?'

Lucas nods. His eyes are warm when they meet mine; he's glad I like it, I think. I look away.

'A thin coat,' I say, tilting the paint tins to check the colour. 'A kind of washed-out white?'

He nods. 'This is your job until lunchtime.'

I roll my sleeves up and start levering open the paint tin. This is *way* better than digitalising. Little does Lucas know, he's just handed me a task that I'd choose over pretty much anything else. I smile as I dip the brush and get to work. Definitely an Izzy day.

Lucas

It is satisfying annoying Izzy. I like getting her to rise to the bait; I like making her eyes flare and narrow, and I like how her humour comes out when she's snapping back at me.

But it turns out that making Izzy happy is a hundred times more satisfying.

'Finished. It looks *great* in there,' she says, bouncing her way back to me across the lobby. 'What's next?'

'Lunch,' I say.

We usually ask for a plate from Arjun for lunch, but today I've requested something special. He regarded me with great suspicion when I said I needed a favour, but when I told him it was for Izzy, he complied without complaint. It was a rare and enjoyable experience.

'We're having it upstairs,' I say, nodding to Irwin, the builder who gave me permission to use the newly reconstructed staircase. *Skip the fourth and eighth step* was his first instruction.

His second was, *And if you fall through the ceiling while flirting upstairs, make sure you're too dead to sue me.*

I take her all the way up to the turret room. This is the second most expensive room in the hotel, after the one Louis is staying in. It is half the size but twice as impressive, in my opinion. It's split over two levels, and one wall is curved. Up on the top level there is a sitting area that looks out over the garden and the forest beyond, and that's where I've set us up for lunch.

'Oh, no,' Izzy says, slowing as she approaches the chairs.

This is not the reaction I had expected to the spread I've set up on the table. We have *moqueca*, rice, *feijão tropeiro*, and *farofa*, of course – there are few meals my mother will serve without *farofa*. It is a beautiful selection of some of my favourite Brazilian foods. As much as Arjun frustrates me, he is an exceptional cook, and he listened to the advice I passed on from my mother when he was preparing all the dishes. They don't smell *exactly* like they do at home, but they're the closest thing I've had since coming to the UK, and my mouth is already watering.

'Fish,' Izzy says grimly. Her gaze shifts slowly to me. 'Well played.'

Merda.

She looks slightly green. Did I know Izzy doesn't like fish? I panic, sifting back through all the times we've raced through a quick plate of food together in the middle of a hectic day.

'God, the smell . . .' she says, covering her nose with her sleeve. 'Do I have to eat it?'

I sit down, swallowing my disappointment. 'No,' I say. I hear the sharpness in my voice and hold still for a moment. It's not

Izzy's fault I've made her a lunch she doesn't like. I didn't ask her if she liked fish stew. *Don't snap*, I tell myself. *You're better than this.* 'But it might surprise you.'

It doesn't surprise her. I watch her try to swallow down the *moqueca* and immediately pour her a fresh glass of water, which she downs in one.

'There,' she says, wiping her mouth. 'I tried it. Can I eat this sausage and bean thing now? Oh my God,' she says, already taking a mouthful. 'Now *that* is delicious.'

Well. That's something.

My phone rings just as we're finishing eating. Ana.

I glance at Izzy, who is scraping up the last of her *farofa*, carefully avoiding the tiny amount of fish stew still sitting untouched on her plate. Is this a good idea? The phone is ringing out – I need to decide now.

'Lucas! It looks like you're eating good food for once!' Ana says in Portuguese when she answers.

Izzy's eyes go wide as she realises what's happening. 'Shall I . . .' she says, gesturing to the door.

A twinge of nerves moves through me as I turn the screen to bring her into shot.

'Oh, hello, who's this?' Ana says, eyes turning as wide as Izzy's.

The mention of another person on-screen brings my mother to the phone at remarkable speed.

'Hi!' Ana says in English. 'You must be Izzy!'

I wonder why I'm doing this. The only answer I can dredge up is that I want Ana and my mother to meet Izzy. And I want

Izzy to realise that my family are good, kind people. Maybe that will make her see me differently.

'Yeah!' Izzy says, sitting up a bit straighter. 'Hi. Nice to meet you.'

'We've heard so much about you,' my mother says, and Ana rolls her eyes beside her. 'I'm Teresa, Lucas's mother. This is Ana.'

'Tell us everything, Izzy,' Ana says. 'What is Lucas like when he's at work? Do all the guests complain because he is so grumpy?'

Izzy laughs. I give thanks for my sister, who can be relied upon to smooth over the trickiest moments. Still looking after her awkward little brother even from five thousand miles away.

'No. They mostly love him, actually. It's me who complains,' Izzy says.

Ana smiles at that. 'I bet the kids love him. Kids always love Lucas.' She pulls a face, pretending to be me. 'Hello, small person, how are you today? Shall we discuss politics? It's like he turns into Uncle Antônio.'

I flinch. Ana clocks it.

'Sorry,' she says. 'That was a stupid joke. You're nothing like him, Lucas.'

'This Izzy is very pretty,' my mother says to Ana in Portuguese, moving the conversation on. The way Izzy's cheeks redden makes it obvious that it was a fairly easy phrase to translate.

'How are you both?' Izzy says, smiling tentatively and glancing sideways at me. 'Are you looking forward to Christmas?'

They both answer at once, in a mix of English and Portuguese, just as Bruno starts crying somewhere very close to the phone. Izzy looks like she is both fascinated and overwhelmed.

'Yes,' I summarise. 'They are. And they're fine. And they miss me.'

'Nobody said that,' Ana says, just as my mother says, 'I miss you so much!'

I smile as I clock Izzy recognising the word *saudade* in there.

'That fish stew looks dry,' my mother adds in Portuguese, peering at the screen. 'Did you make that, Lucas?'

'I should go,' I tell them, keeping to English so Izzy doesn't feel excluded. 'But I'm glad you caught us.'

'It does look dry,' my sister says, scooping Bruno up in her arms. 'You should come home and have Mum's *moqueca* instead.'

My throat aches. 'Soon,' I promise them. '*Em breve.*'

'Oh, who's this!' Izzy says, smiling at Bruno.

Ana introduces him with pride, holding Bruno up to the camera, which he does not particularly enjoy, judging by his indignant expression.

'He's gorgeous,' Izzy says.

The moment I see her face as she looks at my nephew, I know why I answered the phone. This is what I wanted: to bring together these things that matter to me so much.

'Oh, wow,' Izzy says once we've said our goodbyes and hung up. And then, to my horror, her eyes fill with tears.

I'm beside her before I've realised what I'm doing, ducked down, my hand on her shoulder.

'I'm fine!' she says, patting her eyes with her sleeve. 'Sorry, God. This is embarrassing.'

I fetch her the box of tissues from the coffee table, and she dabs at her face, trying not to smudge her make-up.

I crouch beside her and curse myself. I hadn't thought about how throwing Izzy into my family would make her feel. She has no family – not a single person who she knows without question would tell her that they miss her in the same breath they criticise her fish stew.

'I'm sorry,' I say. 'It was thoughtless of me to answer the phone to my family.'

'I don't know why I'm so upset.' She blows her nose. 'Seeing people in super happy families used to always get me, but I've not been like this for ages. It just creeps up on you sometimes, I guess. And . . . I don't know. I'd got a bit complacent. Didn't brace myself.' She smiles ruefully. 'I haven't been looking after myself well enough, maybe? That always has an impact on how I can handle things like this.'

I try to come up with the right thing to say, but all I can think is, *I want to look after you. So that you don't have to do it all, for once.*

'Anyway,' she says, wiping her eyes decisively. 'Today is your day, not mine, isn't it? So I'd better put the self-care on the backburner.'

This lunch has been a disaster. I pause for a moment, wondering if I should just send her home to have a long bath and watch a film. But . . . I think my plan for the afternoon will make her smile. I think I can fix this. So I just straighten up and say, 'Take a few moments. Then I'll meet you downstairs.'

Izzy stands with her hands on her hips and surveys the product of my days off.

216

'If you thought I wouldn't be able to hack this,' she says, eyes sparkling, 'then you seriously underestimated me.'

I had planned to have the adventure playground finished by Christmas, but once Izzy and I settled on Thursday as Lucas Day, I knew I had to get it done sooner. I called in all the favours I had, irritating Pedro more than ever before with my *chatice e perfeccionismo* (fussiness and perfectionism). While it's far from finished, it is certainly serviceable. With Poor Mandy kindly covering the front desk for a couple of hours, we have nothing to do but scale ropes and tackle monkey bars.

I know Izzy. She has the open heart of a child – she loves an adventure. An afternoon of zip wires and climbing trees will surely make her happy. And if she has to jump into my arms during any element of this afternoon, then that will be fine too.

'You are my test case,' I tell her. 'We're doing the full route.' I point at the sketched map I drew up late last night, which shows the order in which each element of the playground should be tackled.

Her grin is infectious. 'Bring it on,' she says.

She brightens with every step she takes up the ladder and along the hanging bridge. I don't get the chance to pull her close, or help her over one of my towers built of pallets, or even squeeze into the treehouse with her, because the moment she steps into it, she's already launching off on the zip wire. But that's OK. Maybe it's better. We know there's chemistry between us. Today is about showing her that we can be *happy* together. We can squabble instead of fight. Sit side-by-side in a comfortable silence instead of a frosty one.

And it's also about showing her I'm not a dickhead. Though this seems to be harder to prove than I had expected.

'Ha! Done! Take that, Lucas da Silva,' she says, throwing down her helmet as she hops off the rope net and on to the grass. 'You thought I'd chicken out, right?'

'No,' I say mildly.

She shoots me a knowing look. 'Confess. You wanted me hanging off the middle of that zip wire like Boris over the Thames.'

This allusion passes me by, but I get the idea.

'This wasn't intended to embarrass you,' I begin, but the last two words are drowned out by the arrival of the Hedgers children, with their father running several metres behind them, his thin grey hair flying.

'Mrs Izzy!' shouts the eldest Hedgers. 'I want a go!'

'Oh, shit,' I mutter. 'This area is not yet open!'

'Sorry, sorry, I did see the sign . . .' Mr Hedgers says, scooping up the youngest of the children and grabbing Ruby by the hand on his way to the eldest one. 'No, Winston, not on the . . . Oh, God. Don't worry, I promise we won't sue you,' he says to me and Izzy as Winston tackles the tower of pallets.

'Thanks,' Izzy says, eyeing Winston and reaching for her helmet again. 'I'll just . . .'

She heads over to help Winston.

'I actually did want to speak to you,' Mr Hedgers says to me, watching Izzy adopt a wary squat beneath his son with her arms upstretched, ready to catch him if he falls.

'Of course.'

I let Ruby transfer herself from Mr Hedgers' hand to my knee, where she hangs, monkey-like, gazing up at me with glee.

'One of the things I love most about my wife is her absolutely unshakeable belief that she can do anything,' Mr Hedgers says. He looks tired. He is a tall, thin man, naturally stooped, but his shoulders are more rounded than usual. 'But she can't. Frankly. And we need help. The insurers said they'd pay to put us up here because of the flooding, but there's a cap on the amount they'll cover. Turns out we'd have to pay ourselves from the twenty-third of December onwards. Annie has been fighting as hard as she can, but even she can't talk them out of it. It was in the contract – we signed it.' He shrugs wearily. 'Pages and pages on those things, of course we only skimmed over it all . . .'

'Somebody should have flagged it to you.'

'I know. But they didn't. And the kids are so excited about spending Christmas here. We don't want to have to move out and go to a budget place just in time for Christmas Day.'

I swallow back a sigh, looking out over the playground. The Hedgers are a lovely family – the children have brought much joy to the hotel in the last couple of months. They deserve a beautiful Christmas, but . . .

'I'll speak to the owners,' I promise. 'But I should tell you that the hotel is struggling at the moment. We may not . . . Well. Let me speak to Mrs Singh-Bartholomew and her husband.'

Mr Hedgers gives me a tired, grey smile. 'Thank you,' he says. 'And if you wouldn't mind not mentioning to Annie that I asked . . . She hates the idea of charity.'

Once we've removed Winston from the playground – a process

that reminds me of levering a barnacle from a rock – I update Izzy on the situation with the insurer. She looks incensed as we make our way to Opal Cottage, her fire-streaked hair bouncing on her shoulders.

'Why are they being such arseholes? It's not like the insurers don't have the money.'

'It's just business to them,' I say, and then swallow back any further insights on this topic in the face of the furious glare she shoots my way.

'Well, it's real people, not just numbers. Those poor kids. This is all so unsettling for them anyway. And we've made the hotel so homely for them!' Izzy tears up slightly. 'I chose Ruby's favourite star to go on the top of the tree!'

How did I ever, ever hate this woman?

'The finance spreadsheets you've been working on,' Izzy says, looking up at me. 'Is it – is it *very* bad?'

It was bad before the ceiling fell in. In an attempt to recover from the losses of the pandemic, we've accumulated debts, we've skipped essential maintenance, and we've cut room prices to try to stimulate demand – a move that hasn't paid off. We have very few bookings, which in turn makes it hard to secure investment. Mrs SB and Barty often say they are not 'numbers people', and it is obvious that the hotel was not run economically even when it made a healthy profit. The result is that now we are in real, serious trouble.

'Yes,' I say quietly. 'It is very, very bad.'

Izzy sighs as she knocks on the door of Opal Cottage, pulling her coat closer around her.

'Oh, perfect!' Mrs SB says.

She is already turning around by the time the door is open, walking back into the cottage. We step into the warmth, shedding our coats and hanging them on the wonky iron hooks beside the door.

'I'm baking!' Mrs SB says.

Izzy and I exchange a glance. We have never known Mrs SB to bake. When we step into the kitchen, it becomes clear what this actually means: Barty is kneading bread in an apron and Mrs SB is reading him instructions from an AGA recipe book.

We explain the Hedgers' financial situation as Barty slaps away at his dough and Mrs SB tells him he's not put enough yeast in. He takes this well. I watch them as Izzy talks. How they just slot together, even when they're quietly annoying one another. I've never looked at other couples like this before, but suddenly – now that I've realised how I feel about Izzy – I'm seeing everyone in a different way. I want to sit them all down and ask them, how did you do it? How did you get from strangers to this, where you're like one person split in two?

None of my relationships have ever been like this. And as much as I think my ex was wrong to tell me I have no heart . . . as I stand here in the warmth of the Singh-Bartholomew kitchen, I do wonder if I ever really gave that heart to Camila.

'Normally I would say yes without even thinking about it,' Mrs SB says sadly. 'You know I'd love to help the Hedgers. But I have to look after all of you, first and foremost. That's my job, and I've not been doing it properly.'

Barty reaches a floury hand across to hold hers for a moment, and then resumes kneading.

'Mrs SB, that's not . . .' Izzy begins, but Mrs SB waves her to silence.

'Don't,' she says. 'You'll make me cry. Let's talk business, please.' She sniffs. 'The Christmas party.'

Izzy and I both freeze.

The Christmas party is a topic we do not discuss.

'What?' Mrs SB says, staring at us both.

'Nothing,' I say, collecting myself first. 'What was it you wanted to say?'

'I'm just wondering how you're getting along with planning it for this year?'

'You want a Christmas party this year?' Izzy says, doing a very poor job of hiding her horror.

'Of course. It might be a last hurrah, after all,' Barty says, dabbing his damp brow.

Mrs SB looks at us expectantly. Last year the party happened in mid December, partly because I had my flights home booked for December seventeenth, and I had led on organising the event. But it's already December fifteenth.

'Since you're both here for Christmas, shall we do it on the twenty-fourth?' Mrs SB asks.

In Brazil, the twenty-fourth is the focus of Christmas celebrations – this will be perfect for me. I have no plans for the day, and a party at the hotel will be an ideal way to stop me missing my family so much.

I glance sideways at Izzy. Her face is set. No doubt she is

remembering that argument on the lawns at the last Christmas party. How I'd snapped at her, how she'd screamed back. How Drew had hovered in the hotel entrance, watching, and then said to Izzy, *You know, you don't actually own either of us, though?*

Which was true. But it had hit Izzy like a slap in the face.

The more I get to know Izzy this winter, the less I understand the way she reacted that night. I always assumed she'd been protecting her friend, but Drew seems to have disappeared from Izzy's life without trace. I'd imagined they were very close, but if they were, there is no way Izzy would have let Drew go – she never seems to let *any* friends go.

So why was she so furious with me for kissing Drew?

I want to believe Pedro's suggestion – that she was jealous. But even if she was ... her reaction was so unreasonable. All year I've told myself that it is classic Izzy – always unreasonable, and nobody else seems to see it. But that doesn't fit with the Izzy standing beside me now.

'Twenty-fourth is great,' Izzy says, voice strangled.

'Oh, I suppose I need to check with the builders about where we'll have got to with renovations by then ...' Mrs SB glances distractedly at her phone.

I pounce. 'If you are looking to delegate the work with the builders and decorators, Izzy would be an excellent choice.'

The look on Izzy's face is one I want to see every single day. I have to look away.

'Izzy?'

'I'd love to. Absolutely. I can handle it from now on, if you just forward me everything you've got in terms of quotes and so on, I can just . . . take that off your plate.'

'Delegating,' Barty says, pointing a doughy finger at his wife. 'See?'

'Well, thank you! Both of you. And how are you getting on with your rings?'

We exchange a glance.

'Oh,' Mrs SB says, smile falling. 'Tell me we aren't due another showdown on the driveway. No more bigamists, please.'

'No, no,' Izzy says hastily. 'Just . . . we've stalled a little. But don't worry. Lucas and I are on it.'

'Good! Now, put your heads together and get to work on the party,' Mrs SB says, waving us off. As we walk out, we hear her scolding, 'Barty! You'll knock *all* the air out of it if you do that!'

Izzy

Lucas tells me to meet him at the car at five fifteen. I'm there at ten past, shivering in my teddy coat and woolly hat.

Lucas arrives at quarter past on the dot. He's changed into his casual clothes again, and under his open coat he's wearing a soft, dark-grey jumper and jeans – he looks like a celebrity caught stepping out for a coffee on a winter morning. He's that kind of handsome, the kind that makes you famous.

'Thanks for the lift home,' I say as we get in the car.

'We aren't going to your flat,' he says.

'What?'

'It is still my day.'

'But it's the end of the *working* day,' I wheedle. Today has been confusingly enjoyable, but it has also involved a *lot* of Lucas – I'm not sure how much more I can take.

'I'm not done with you yet,' he says, with the hint of a smile.

'Where are we going?'

'*My* flat,' he says, pulling out of the car park.

I've never seen where Lucas lives. I imagine it is extremely tidy, and that lots of things are made of very well polished wood. The thought of stepping into his private space makes me a little nervous and *extremely* curious.

We sit in silence for the drive. I hold my rucksack on my lap and cling to it like it's my support animal. Lucas lives about a fifteen-minute drive from the hotel, but it feels like hours.

He fiddles with the radio and 'Last Christmas' sings out through his car speakers. I snort, turning my face to the window. This song always makes me think about him, and not in a good way. I can feel him looking at me, questioning, but I keep my gaze on the grey slush lining the road outside. The song is a useful reminder that no matter how gorgeous he is, no matter if he speaks up for me with Mrs SB, he's still the man who kissed my flatmate on the day I'd confessed my feelings for him and then acted like I was crazy for caring. Red flag after red flag, basically.

His flat isn't like I'd imagined it would be at all. It's surprisingly characterful and homely. The sofa is battered old leather and the wooden coffee table looks handmade. There's an impressive number of books on the shelves, a mix of Brazilian and English titles – I didn't know Lucas read books. Most of them are non-fiction, so I suspect I'm some way away from persuading him to tackle my Sarah J Maas collection, but still, I'm impressed.

'Would you like a beer?' he asks, opening the fridge.

'Oh. Sure. Thanks.' I take the lager he offers me. 'So what are we doing? What brand of torture have you lined up for me next?'

'You're doing my evening,' he says, grabbing a collection of vegetables from the fridge. 'Nothing special. Though I am sure you will find a way to make it torturous.'

He points with a knife to a chopping board hanging on the kitchen wall.

'Ginger root, please. Finely chopped.'

A predictably rubbish job. I get to work peeling the nub of ginger, watching him covertly as he slices a pepper.

'You know, you got a couple of things wrong today. I loved the adventure playground. And the floorboard-painting was right up my alley. As in, just the sort of thing that I like,' I say, as I see his brow furrow, the way it does when he doesn't quite understand something I've said.

'Why do you like painting floorboards?'

'I love making stuff better,' I say, after a moment's thought.

There is something intimate about cooking together like this. It's unsettling. I'm missing the solid, reassuring presence of the front desk, the familiar hum of voices from the restaurant.

'Before my parents died, I was doing an interior design course,' I go on, filling the silence. 'I had this idea of setting up a business that redecorated spaces, only without any new materials. We'd use as much recycled stuff as we could, and where possible we'd use what was already there, just dressed up.'

'Upcycling,' Lucas says.

'Yeah!' I say. 'That's exactly it. Anyway. Obviously it's fallen to the wayside a bit but maybe I'll go back to the course if we lose our jobs.'

I feel him stiffen at that as he reaches for the ginger, combining it with the garlic on his board and adding them to the sizzling oil in the pan. His eyebrows are drawn in a tight frown. He's stressed about the job, I realise – I don't know why this hasn't occurred to me before. I guess it's that I'm sad rather than stressed. Losing the family we have at the hotel is what guts me – I haven't thought much about having to find other work, because I'm relatively confident in my CV, and I know there are a few jobs going around the area. But I guess the stakes are higher for Lucas. I don't know how long he would be able to stay in the UK if he lost his job, and I know money is tight for him.

'It might all just be fine. I think Louis is really considering investing,' I say.

'Hmm,' Lucas says. 'Louis is considering something, certainly.'

I frown. 'What does that mean?'

'He wants the building. I am not so sure he wants the hotel.'

My eyes widen. 'You think he wants to *buy* the place? Take it off the Singh-Bartholomews?'

Now he mentions it, I remember Louis jokingly offering on the hotel last Christmas, and Mrs SB laughing him off. *Could* he? I'd never considered the idea of Forest Manor as anything else, but I guess it would make a beautiful set of flats, or offices, or . . .

'No,' I say, shaking my head. 'Louis would have told me.'

Lucas stiffens at this. 'Food's ready,' he says, shoving a knife and fork at me.

We eat on the sofa. I expect Lucas to turn on the TV, but instead he grabs a pile of yellow cards from the coffee table and sets about reading them while he eats. I snoop over his shoulder – they look like revision cards.

'Are you studying?' I ask, surprised. He's never mentioned it.

He nods, chewing. I wait for him to say more but he doesn't, and he won't meet my eyes, either. I lean forward for the pack of cards that sits on the table and start flicking through. *Modelling consumer decision-making . . . market segmentation . . . perishability vs stock . . . hotel service delivery . . .*

'Hotel management?' I say. 'You're studying hotel management?'

He nods again, flicking to the next card. Like this is no big deal at all.

'Is that your plan, then?' I say, heat rising up my chest. I stab at my stir fry with my fork. 'Take over Forest Manor one day?'

'No. Not at all.'

'Then you'd be able to boss me around and I wouldn't be able to do anything about it.'

'Actually,' he says, 'my degree is not about trying to beat you at something, Izzy. It is something I'm doing for me.'

'Right,' I say. I'm flustered and miserable and I'm not sure why. I wish I hadn't mentioned the interior design course I failed to complete. 'Well, good for you.'

I've always known that Lucas thinks he's better at the job than I am, but I've also always thought he's wrong. Only now he's going to go and make it official, getting a degree and everything. Not that any of this matters – he and I will likely part ways in the new year anyway. He can manage some swanky hotel somewhere and I'll take that waitressing job they're always advertising in the window of Tilly's café in Brockenhurst – which is *fine*. I'd be perfectly content with that.

Lucas stands suddenly, pacing to the French doors opposite us and throwing them open. He's in just a T-shirt and jeans – he took his jumper off while we were cooking – and it's freezing outside. I raise my eyebrows as the cold wind hits me a few seconds later and he says, 'It's too hot in here.'

I can't help it: I think about him in the gym, a bead of sweat running down between his shoulder blades. Christ. How can I find this man so obnoxious *and* so sexy? Even now, as he steps out on to his little balcony and leans his forearms on the glass barrier, I'm noticing the muscles rolling in his shoulders, the bare, pale-brown stretch of his neck.

You'd think all the rejection would make me want him less, but it doesn't. I don't know what that says about me. At least I'm consistent. Not easily swayed by, you know, reality.

He just stays there, saying nothing, so I pull the blanket off the back of the sofa and tug it over my knees – a literal comfort blanket. I need it: I feel so unsteady, like there's a tremor going through the flat, sending everything trembling.

'Izzy,' he says.

That's it. Just *Izzy*. He doesn't even turn around. It's raining now, that faint, drifting rain that sparkles when it catches the light.

'You don't like me, do you?'

The question takes me aback. It's kind of a given, isn't it? Lucas and I hate each other – everyone knows that. He's pig-headed and surly and has a temper; he's deliberately difficult with me at work, and he's rejected me enough times that even if I had no pride, it would be hard not to bear a *bit* of ill feeling towards him. And ultimately, fundamentally, he will always be the man who kissed my flatmate on the day I handed him my heart.

'No,' I say slowly. 'I don't like you.'

'You *used* to like me,' Lucas says, glancing over his shoulder for half a second before returning his gaze to the rain. 'And then I kissed your flatmate.'

I tuck the blanket tighter. We don't talk about that. The one instance when we did talk about that, we ended up screaming at each other across the hotel lawns, and he flew back to Brazil the next morning.

I think of that card all the time. Now that I know Lucas better, I can imagine him cringing at the soppy bits. *My cosy warm heart.* Ugh. Writing that in his Christmas card felt brave and bold, the sort of thing a woman in a rom-com would do. Jem had been so sure it would end in romance, and I'd got caught up imagining our kiss under the mistletoe, the way he would scoop me up against him and tell me he felt the exact same way.

Damn Jem and all her romance novels.

'And that's . . . gone?' Lucas looks down at the beer bottle in his hands.

'Well, you kind of wrecked it, yeah,' I say, feeling it all again: the shock, the embarrassment, that awful conversation with Drew when we got home. She'd *known* how I felt about Lucas, and still kissed him. And maybe mid argument wasn't the time for me to ask her for the overdue rent, but when she walked out she literally threw a Christmas bauble at my head, so I think I win in the game of who-behaved-better.

'I *wrecked* it?' He turns at last. 'What was I supposed to do?'

I stare at him. 'Oh, I don't know, *not* kiss my flatmate under the mistletoe?'

'Izzy, come on. I have never understood why that was such a crime.'

I look away. 'Obviously you are and were entitled to kiss whoever you choose.'

'Thank you.'

That *thank you* sets my teeth on edge. I put my beer down on the table a little too hard.

'Am I still required to be here?' I snap.

He recoils. 'Oh. No. Of course not.'

'Right. Well, I'll leave you to your evening, then. Night, Lucas.'

'Izzy.'

Just *Izzy* again. I move to step away and then breathe in sharply. He's right behind me, his hand on my arm. He moved so fast; the contact is unexpected, and I'm not steeled to it. I'm hot with anger, remembering the way it all felt last year, and the sensation of his skin on mine sends me burning even hotter. He spins me around with a tug of my arm and I look up at him. My breath is cold on my parted lips.

His expression is thunderous. I've seen frustration in Lucas's eyes a hundred times, but there's a new depth to it tonight, and I know – I *know* he wants me.

'You drive me crazy,' he says. His voice is hoarse and his gaze is on my mouth.

I say nothing. We're both breathing heavily, our bodies close, but I'm not letting him lead me into another proposition that he'll knock back. If he wants something tonight, he's going to have to make the first move.

'I've tried,' he says. 'I've really, really tried. And still . . .'

He moves even closer, forcing my chin higher if I want to meet his gaze square-on. He's so huge, all muscle, tightly coiled.

I can't resist. It's something about the way he holds himself back – it tugs at the part of me that can't turn down a challenge. I can feel that he's a breath away from giving in.

I brush my chest against his. He breathes in roughly and that's it, that's *it*. Whatever it was that kept Lucas hemmed in, it snaps. He kisses me.

And it's pure fire. He tilts me back and kisses me so deeply I lose my breath and my footing all at once; he's half lifted me, half thrown me to the sofa cushions, one hand on my thigh as I wrap my legs around him. It's messy and fierce, the way you'd kiss if kissing was fighting. His tongue stokes mine and I dig my nails into his back. I've never felt a tide of desire like this – never gone under so quickly. If he wanted me now, I'd be his.

But he slows the kiss – not breaking away, just easing. Slow, languid kisses instead of hungry ones. I whimper in my throat and then turn my head aside, embarrassed by the need he'll hear in my voice. He turns my head back with one finger and looks me right in the eye.

'If we do this,' he says, voice rough, accent strong. 'Then you don't look away from me.'

I swallow. I'm lying here, breathless, raw, and it's *Lucas* looking down on me. I don't know if it's habit or pride, but I feel a sudden, powerful need to take the upper hand again.

'If we do this,' I counter, 'then we need some rules.'

We're sitting at either end of the sofa, eyeing each other warily. He has a cushion in his lap, like a teenage boy, and I've got my arms looped around my knees so he can't tell they're trembling.

'Why didn't you kiss me before? In the hotel room?' I ask, clearing my throat. 'Why now?'

He looks towards the French doors. They're still open, but I don't think either of us is feeling the cold.

'It's like you said. Two people who hate each other, kissing . . .' He swallows. 'It's weird and messed up.'

'Right.' Did I mean that? Do I think that? Right now all I can think about is how good that felt, and how badly I would like to do it again. 'And what's changed, then?'

He looks down at his cushion. 'What's changed is I have stopped caring about "messed up". I want you.' He looks up. 'You want me. We're adults, we can make our own choices as long as nobody is getting hurt.'

I nod. 'That's what I think. And that's why I think we need some rules. Do this in a sensitive, sensible way, and just get each other out of our systems once and for all.'

He flinches.

'What?' I say, already tense. I do know Lucas wants me – that's fairly undeniable right now – but after putting myself on the line so many times, part of me is waiting for him to walk back out on to the balcony and turn cold again.

'So this happens just once?' he asks.

'Of course,' I say, slightly horrified. 'God, I didn't mean – I'm not asking you to date me or anything, I'm just suggesting one night.'

His face is unreadable. After a moment, he nods. 'Fine.'

'So, first rule,' I say, shifting myself up straighter. 'This doesn't change anything. You don't have to pretend we get along because you've slept with me.'

He stares at me levelly. 'You want us to behave as we always do at work?'

'Exactly.'

'So you will still rearrange the stationery drawer and make me say *booking book* all the time?'

'What, you thought you could kiss me into being nice to you?'

One corner of his mouth lifts. 'No,' he says. 'Not exactly. OK. So what is your next rule?'

'No telling anyone at work.'

His expression darkens. 'Are you so embarrassed of me?'

'No!' I say, frowning. 'It's not that, it's just . . . We're colleagues.'

'Hmm.'

'It won't be good for the hotel if everyone's gossiping about us. You know what people are like.'

His face returns to its habitual stoniness. 'Fine. I wouldn't tell anyone anyway.'

I'm annoying him by trying to take over here, I can tell. This is familiar ground – I don't particularly mind. My body is still thrumming with the force of that kiss, and I *like* this. I like the way we push each other.

235

'Last rule,' I say. 'It's *just* sex. I won't sleep over tonight. There will be no cuddling. That way it's . . .' the word that springs to mind is *safe*, but I say, 'simple.'

His jaw is clenched. 'Simple,' he says.

He stares at me for so long that I start to shift, my confidence waning a little. I've taken so many knocks when it comes to Lucas. I know he doesn't like me. He's made that abundantly clear. I'm just relying on the attraction between us overruling that, and there's always the threat of his brain kicking in at any moment, reminding him of all the reasons we shouldn't do this.

And I can tell he's thinking. Which is not good.

But the moment passes, and quite suddenly, as if a decision has been made, Lucas throws the cushion on to the floor and reaches for my ankle. He circles it with finger and thumb. His expression hasn't changed, but I can see his chest is rising and falling faster than usual.

'Any more rules?' he says, sliding his hand up my calf. 'Or are you finished?'

I can't think of any more rules. I can't think of much at all with him touching me.

'No more.'

'So,' he says, his hand reaching my thigh. 'What happens now?'

His fingers climb slowly, slowly. The tension in my body rises too, spreading like kindling catching light.

The very tip of his finger stops at the seam of my jeans. I am perfectly still, my eyes fixed on his. I have no idea how to do this. I've imagined having sex with Lucas countless times, but I always thought it would start explosively, the way that kiss did a moment ago. I never thought it would begin with eye contact and the slow path of his fingers; I thought we'd fall into one another and I wouldn't have to make the leap.

His gaze shifts across my face. I'm a tumultuous mix of turned-on and terrified. I want Lucas so badly, but I don't trust him at all. Can I do this? Sleep with him without getting attached, without letting my walls down? For all my rule-setting, I've never actually had sex with someone I don't like before.

Lucas's hand slides down my leg again, pausing on my ankle, where he began.

'There is something in consumer rights legislation,' he says, 'called a cooling-off period.'

I blink. 'Oh. Right?' We've gone from hand-on-upper-thigh to consumer rights legislation at breakneck speed; my body is still thrumming with desire.

'Yes. There is a time when you can change your mind. I think that is what we need.'

'What? No,' I say quickly, sitting up. 'I'm good. I've made my mind up.'

I shift closer on the sofa, and he smiles. It is a slow, languid smile I've never seen on him before. It's *extremely* sexy. The smile says, *I know what you want, and I know I can give it to you.*

'Still,' he says, sliding his hand from my leg. 'I think . . . we wait a day or two.'

'What? No. No!'

'One day or two?'

I stare back at him. Is he crazy? He wants me to leave this flat right now?

'We don't need to wait.'

He raises his eyebrows ever so slightly. 'One, or two?'

Oh my God. Why is he so, so annoying?

'Lucas . . .'

'One or two?'

For fuck's sake.

'Do you not want this?' I say, pulling back, drawing my knees up again. 'Because—'

'Izzy,' he says, 'I am trying to be a gentleman. Today is my day, remember? I don't want you to feel any . . . pressure.'

'Well, I don't!' I say. 'I've made it pretty clear what I want.'

'Mm.' He tilts his head. 'Then it will be clear tomorrow too. We can wait one night.'

I swallow, running my hands through my hair, trying to pull myself together. My body feels boneless. All I want to do is melt into him.

'Izzy,' Lucas says, and his voice is gentle now. 'I want you to think about this. I want you to be sure.'

'I *am*,' I begin again, but I trail off in the face of his determined expression. I know that face. Lucas has made up his mind.

'All right,' I say, standing up. 'Tomorrow. After work.'

I feel the traces of the last half-hour everywhere: the warmth of his hand on my ankle, the roughness of his stubble on my cheek, the frustrated ache at my core. Looking down at him on the sofa, I'm struck afresh by how different he is here. At work he's so buttoned-up and serious, but now he's in a crumpled

T-shirt, loose and hazy-eyed. There's something so sexy about seeing him like this. I want to climb into his lap and kiss that insolent slope of his bottom lip.

'Just so you know,' I say, 'if you're really making me wait until tomorrow night, I'm going to make your day as difficult as possible.'

The corners of his mouth turn up just a touch. 'It is an opportunity to torture me,' he says. 'I would expect nothing less.'

Lucas

Izzy assumed the cooling-off period was just for her, and I didn't correct her. But I need this.

'The whole thing is a great idea,' says Pedro in Portuguese, over the noise of the coffee machine. 'Didn't I say you should have slept with her from the start?'

'That's probably why I've come to see you this morning instead of ringing my sister,' I say wryly, glancing at the customers waiting to be served in Smooth Pedro's. I've pulled a bar stool up by the till. I did consider offering to help with the breakfast rush, but last time I helped, Pedro kept whipping me with his dish cloth, so I decided against it. 'I'm hoping you are going to tell me I'm not out of my mind.'

'Absolutely not out of your mind! Oat milk mocha single shot?' he says, switching to English and flashing his most flirtatious smile at the woman at the front of the queue.

She smiles back, flicking her blonde curls over her shoulder. 'Thanks, Pedro,' she says. 'You're actually the best.'

'Damn right,' he says to her and then he winks.

I sigh.

'What?' he says.

'You are making it harder for me to think you're sensible. Sensible men don't wink,' I say, thinking gloomily of Louis, who winks at least once a day, and is definitely an idiot.

'Why the hell would you want to be sensible? You want this girl, don't you?'

I nod into my Yowsa smoothie (ginger, rocket, orange, carrot).

'So take her!'

'Pedro . . .'

'I just mean – she is offering you something. Not everything you want, sure, you want the marriage and babies . . .'

I glare at him. He grins.

'But it's a start.'

'It's a start.'

This is what I told myself last night. Izzy seems programmed to think the worst of me – the reason everything I did yesterday backfired was because she assumed at every point that I was trying to make her as miserable as possible. By the time we got to my flat, I was so defeated, and then she was walking out on me, and I *knew* she'd kiss me back if I kissed her. Resisting any longer just seemed impossible.

'Her rules are a good idea – they'll stop you catching feelings,' Pedro says. He wipes down the coffee machine and throws the cloth over his shoulder.

Those rules. They infuriated me. But I know Pedro is right: I'm developing dangerous feelings already, and if there aren't any boundaries when I spend the night with her, I am at real risk of harm.

'You're a big boy, Lucas,' Pedro says. 'What is it you're afraid of?'

I close my eyes. 'I think I was holding back the only card I had, and now I'm playing it,' I say eventually. 'I have one thing she is interested in and I'm about to give it to her.'

The next woman in the queue is ordering. Pedro ducks his head to listen to her, then spins on his heels to start conjuring up a white chocolate latte.

'You're talking like an American girl about to give up her virginity, *cara*,' Pedro says, and then realises he's speaking English and laughs as the entire queue turns to stare at me.

'Thank you for that.'

'Sorry. I'm just saying, you're not giving anything up. Sex with her means closeness. It means pillow-talk and all those hormones that women get when they have sex with you.'

'Pedro,' I say, rubbing my forehead.

'OK, if you want to be romantic about it, you're showing her how it could be between the two of you if you were together. So many great love stories started in the bedroom. My brother's wife was his one-night-stand rebound girl! And now they have a horrible number of children.'

This is actually quite helpful. 'Thank you, Pedro,' I say.

'No problem! Now remember, be safe, *cara* – condoms are your friend!'

This, of course, is in English. I drink the last of my smoothie, shoot the sniggering Pedro a filthy glance and head for the door.

When I arrive at Forest Manor for my shift, I realise that this feeling in my stomach is actually quite familiar: getting to work and wondering what Izzy will throw at me today. But it's new, too. The excitement, the anticipation for tonight. Thinking about her body, and knowing I *can*, because within a matter of hours – unless she's changed her mind – I'll be holding her.

But it's not Izzy who walks in next, it's Louis. He's wearing an open-necked white shirt under an expensive wool coat, looking every bit the modern Englishman.

'Lucas, hey,' he says, tapping a hand on the front desk. It's strewn with old cigar cases – Mandy was photographing them for 'those little Instagram videos with songs on them' at the end of her shift. 'Izzy about?'

'Not yet. Would you like a table in the bar for a coffee?'

I hate that I have to be polite to this man. I hate that he gets to buy Izzy flowers and I don't.

'No, I can't stop. Just wanted to see if she's still on for this evening.'

I take too long to answer, and he tilts his head, eyebrows raised. Reminding me that he's a customer, and ignoring him isn't an option.

'I don't know,' I say. 'But she didn't mention having plans this evening.'

'I'm taking her to the Winchester Christmas market. Parking's a nightmare but I've got a friend with a space in Fulflood, so we're set,' he says, with a little smile, as if to say, *Aren't I the lucky one?*

She can't be seeing Louis tonight. Tonight is *our* night.

'Would you like me to give her a message?' I snap out.

'No, don't worry,' Louis says, tapping the desk again and pushing away. 'I'll just WhatsApp her.'

All the tension that left me in the gym is surging through me again. My phone rings; I answer too quickly, desperate for the interruption, and the person on the other end of the line says, 'Oh, hi,' taken aback.

Louis gives me a small wave as he heads for the door, and I resist the temptation to return this with a rude gesture.

'It's Gerry,' says the man on the phone. 'My son said a woman rang about a ring?'

I sit up straighter. 'Yes, sir,' I say. 'Can I help you?'

'It was a long, long time ago, but I actually do recall a lady losing an engagement ring while I was staying at your hotel. She asked for my help looking for it. In the end, we never tracked it down. She told me she'd get a replica made so as not to upset her husband, who was a lovely bloke, loved her to distraction. Sorry, I don't remember their names.'

I jot this down. 'Can you tell me which ring it is you're referring to, sir?'

'An emerald one. Izzy Jenkins emailed me?'

'Thank you so much for calling,' I say. 'It's all written down – I'll let her know.'

She walks in just as I tuck the note I've written under her keyboard, beside her to-do list. My whole body tightens at the sight of her, and I smile – I wouldn't be able to stop myself even if I wanted to. She looks beautiful. She's in her uniform, rucksack slung over her arm, gold rings glinting on her fingers and her ears.

'Lucas,' she says, with a quick arch of her brow.

'Izzy.'

I watch her as she comes around behind the desk, slinging her bag under her chair and turning her computer on. She side-eyes me, ponytail bouncing. Her hair is still striped in red and orange, and beside the fine gold necklace she always wears is just one more, with a tiny broken heart pendant. I wonder why she made those choices – the fiery hair, the heart.

She reads my note and frowns.

'What?' I ask.

'Nothing, it's just . . . this makes things more complicated with the emerald ring. If half the couple don't even know it was lost, because the woman kept it a secret . . .' She purses her lips. 'Never mind. I'll get there.' She widens her eyes slightly at her to-do list. 'So much to do today. Chat through the snag list for the bannisters with Irwin, negotiate some deals we can actually afford for staff at the Christmas party, torture you interminably until the evening comes . . .'

She meets my eyes, and her expression is pure wickedness. My heart lifts: she isn't seeing Louis tonight. She's got plans with *me*.

'It's going to be a long day,' she says.

She makes me wait until eleven before she plays her first move. I return from a trip to the post office to find her looking up at me from the desk with a quick, devious smile that hooks something in my chest and pulls it taut. She stands, reaches for my desk chair, and wheels it away towards the lost-property room.

'Am I using your chair today, or . . .?'

'This way, Lucas!' she calls.

I humour her. I'd follow her anywhere these days – maybe I always would have. When I step into the lost-property room, I pause. There's a trestle table set up in here, and an array of face paints on its surface.

'My skills are a little rusty. I need a subject to practise on ahead of the Christmas party,' she says, pointing to my desk chair, now positioned in the centre of the room.

She walks to the door and clicks it shut. The sound sends a shiver across my skin like the trail of a fingertip.

'Sit,' she says, when I don't.

'Did someone make this Izzy Day?' I ask, raising my eyebrows at her.

'Sit, *please*?' she tries, and this time I do as I'm told.

She dips a small, pointed brush into a rectangle of blue paint, moistens it with water and dips again. I watch the way she frowns when she concentrates, how she brushes her hair away from her eyes with the back of her hand. Everything about her is suddenly acutely fascinating.

I wonder when it happened. If there was one single tipping-point moment when I began to fall for her. Did I ever truly hate her? It seems unthinkable now.

Izzy touches the brush to my temple, stepping close enough to skim her thighs against my knees. The paint is cool – I flinch slightly, and she tuts, brush still moving, tickling against my skin. Dab, paint. Dab, paint. Each time she leans in towards me, I have to fight the temptation to look down her shirt.

'So,' I say, as she works her way down the side of my jaw. 'You have me at your mercy. What are you going to do with me?'

'I'm thinking a sort of Jack Frost vibe,' she says, but the quirk in the corner of her mouth tells me she knows what I mean.

The next time she returns to me with the paint, she stands even closer. Heat unfurls along my spine, and on impulse I shift my knees to trap her leg between mine. She breathes in sharply, brush stilling on my cheek. I give in and let my gaze flick to that triangle of pale skin where her shirt falls open at the neck. I can see the edge of a white lace bra, and the soft curve of her breast.

I shouldn't have looked. That has not made this easier.

'Have you changed your mind, then?' she asks, twisting away to reach the paint, but keeping her thigh between my knees. 'About tonight?'

The brush whispers against my cheekbone. Izzy licks her bottom lip. I could have her in my lap in half a second. I want to. She knows I want to.

'No. I've not changed my mind. Have you?'

'I told you my decision was made.'

I incline my head in acknowledgement as she moves away to top up her brush. This time, as she turns back to me, she presses a thumb under my chin and forces my head up, then to the side, baring my throat. She takes the brush to the sensitive skin beneath my ear and I inhale, closing my eyes. She's not even touching me and this is turning my blood to fire.

'You could have had me in your bed last night,' she says. 'One message.'

I knew that. I felt it for every slow minute of the evening.

'You really do have ironclad self-control, don't you?'

She has no idea.

'I want to know what happens when you let go,' she whispers, leaning in. 'I want to make you lose your fucking mind.'

Pelo amor de Deus. My heart is pounding.

'All done,' she says brightly, pulling back, her thigh slipping from between my knees. 'Want to see?'

I open my eyes. She's looking down on me with an infuriatingly familiar expression: the self-satisfied smile she wears when she's beaten me at something.

She holds a small make-up mirror out for me to see myself. I have no idea what I'm going to find – it could be reindeer, or snowmen, or possibly *Lucas is a dick* written on my jawline. But it's amazing. A tumble of white and blue snowflakes running from my right temple to the left side of my neck.

'It's good,' I say. 'Now can I do it for you?'

'You? Paint my face?'

'Mmhmm.'

The reception bell dings. As one, we look towards the door.

'Saved by the bell,' she says, already bouncing away towards the lobby. 'You might want to . . . wait a minute.'

'Yes,' I say, shifting in my seat. 'Perhaps you had better get that one.'

*

We both end up having to wait tables over lunch. Izzy changes into her waitressing uniform in the lost-property room, leaving the door ajar, taunting me, tempting me to follow her inside. When she steps out to see me frozen in my seat, determinedly not looking, she gives me a smug look, as if to say, *Couldn't take the heat, then?*

I imagine I'll be safe waiting tables, but we pass so often, always close enough to brush arms, always locking eyes. I never lose her in that room – I know exactly where she is. At one point, as she moves past me into the kitchen, she whispers, 'Slow day, Lucas? I've never *seen* you check the time so often.'

I am openly staring at her across the dining area when Mr Townsend walks in. By the time I manage to redivert my attention to the specials board, he is regarding me with amused interest. I swallow.

'Can I help you, Mr Townsend?' I ask. 'Has there been a phone call?'

We've come to rely on Mr Townsend this winter: he is the only person ever guaranteed to be in the lobby.

'It's Budgens time,' he says.

Merda. I glance at the Bartholomew clock through the dining-room door, which is propped open so that Izzy and I can see the front desk. After some quick maths, I realise Mr Townsend is right.

'Lunch service ends in half an hour,' I say. 'I am all yours after that.'

'Lovely.' Mr Townsend pauses. 'Why don't you bring Izzy?'

'We can't spare her, I'm afraid.'

'I'd like her to come.'

I eye him with suspicion. He looks back at me with an expression of innocence that brings Izzy herself to mind.

'I might insist upon it, actually,' Mr Townsend says. 'I think stepping out of the hotel together would do us all some good.'

'Excuse me,' says a woman whose toddler is currently drawing shapes on the tablecloth with pea soup. 'Please can I get the bill? Like, as soon as you can? Ideally right now?'

'Half an hour,' I say to Mr Townsend. 'In the lobby.'

'With Izzy.'

The man has more backbone than I'd expected.

'It's up to her,' I say. 'And Mrs SB. And,' I add, as an afterthought, 'Barty.'

Mr Townsend smiles. 'I'll speak to Uma,' he says, planting his stick and setting off into the lobby. 'She can never say no to a guest, that one.'

'Isn't this nice?' Izzy says from the back seat of my car. 'A team trip to Budgens!'

Things have escalated. I'm not sure Mr Townsend is very pleased about this – his aim, I suspect, was to get Izzy and me together outside the hotel, having observed the way I looked at her in the dining room and decided to play matchmaker. But Ollie overheard us talking about the trip during lunch service, and was so determined not to be left manning the front desk again that he made up an obscure ingredient he had to get – himself – for Arjun. And then Barty overheard *him* and said he was coming to get some doughnuts. I believe Mrs SB is managing the front desk, which she hasn't done for approximately forty years. I wonder if she knows how to work the computer.

'Are you all right, Lucas?' Mr Townsend asks me kindly from the passenger seat.

'Absolutely,' I say, though there is sweat prickling between my shoulders.

Right now, in this car with me, I have Izzy, plus one elderly guest, one kitchen porter, and my boss. And yet every time I glance back in the mirror, all I see is *her*. The wicked heat in those palmeira green eyes. The way she seems to know every time I'm looking at her. How her gaze meets mine fast, hard, like we're crossing swords.

She said she'd torture me today, but she's hardly had to – it's the day itself that's torturous. Every slow minute that stands between me and a night with Izzy.

Upon our arrival at Budgens, things go smoothly for an impressive ten minutes. I feel calmer here, away from the hotel. It is easier to think about something other than Izzy Jenkins – even if she is in the same aisle.

We select a box of doughnuts after a long discussion about which of the available flavours is best (all are overrated. Doughnuts are just *bolinhos de chuva* with too much sugar and no personality). Mr Townsend chooses the first of his snacks (shortbread biscuits of a very specific shape). Barty shouts 'Mrs SB likes it rough!' across the chilled aisle (he was referring to puff pastry). And then Izzy opens her rucksack and pulls out the Tupperware of rings, right there by the fridges.

I breathe in sharply.

'Why do you have those here?'

'I wanted to talk to Mr Townsend about the emerald one when we go for coffee after this,' she says, trying to unclip the lid. She presses the box to her stomach, hunching over, nails working at one corner. 'He was staying at the hotel when it was lost, and he might remember something, but I'm just going to check that one's definitely in there, because I did take it out to have it cleaned, and . . . Argh!'

The lid pings off. The two remaining rings go flying.

'Shit. Shit!' Izzy drops to the ground, as though under enemy fire.

'What? What?' Barty yells, looking around wildly.

'Nobody panic!' says Izzy, commando-crawling across the floor of Budgens. 'I've got the silver wedding ring! It's just the emerald . . . one . . .'

She lifts her head slowly. The ring is between Mr Townsend's sensible brogues. He is staring down at it with open astonishment. A member of the Budgens staff pauses behind him, clearly contemplating asking questions about Izzy's position, and then makes the sensible decision to move on and pretend he didn't see anything out of the ordinary.

I am also trying to pretend that there is nothing out of the ordinary about seeing Izzy in this position, mostly by staring fixedly at the ceiling.

'Mr Townsend?' Izzy says.

'That ring,' he says, voice shaking.

Izzy stands and holds it out to him. The bright supermarket lights hit the ring's emerald and it sends green light scattering across the vinyl floor.

'That's Maisie's ring,' Mr Townsend says, almost breathless. 'That's it, right there. She was buried with that ring. What the devil is it doing in your Tupperware box?'

We all make our way to the café, sitting around a circular table, eating our Budgens doughnuts with our café-bought coffees. I feel quite uncomfortable about this, but Barty has no shame, and he was the one who paid for it all.

Izzy explains what Gerry told her over the phone. How the woman who lost that emerald ring had a replica made so as not to upset her husband. How much she'd loved him, and how she hadn't wanted to hurt him by admitting she had lost his precious ring.

'I'm not sad,' Mr Townsend says. His tone is thoughtful. He turns his face to the rain outside, blinking slowly behind his glasses. 'It's very typical of Maisie, actually. She never could stand to upset anybody. It used to drive me up the wall, the lengths she would go to to avoid causing anyone else any bother. And she was always wearing fake jewels onstage, so I suppose she knew how to have something like that made.'

'I think it's romantic,' Izzy says.

'Yeah,' Ollie pipes up. 'She went to *loads* of effort so you wouldn't be upset. That's nice, isn't it?'

'Yes. It is.' Mr Townsend opens his hand, looking down at the ring. It is beautiful. It's Izzy's favourite from the box, I think – she's always fiddling with it. 'Maisie and I were never straightforward. On and off like a light switch, she used to say.'

'You broke up?' I ask.

I don't know whether it's because Mr Townsend is old, or because his wife passed away, but I had always imagined them having a very sweet, sedate relationship. In my head, Mrs Townsend was probably a kind-hearted older lady who wore florals and baked.

But then, I always have idealised the dead. See my father, bitten by a venomous adder while saving a small village, or killed in a high-speed car chase while serving in the Agência Brasileira de Inteligência.

'Oh, all the time,' Mr Townsend says wryly. 'But we always found our way back to each other. That was just our story.' He shrugs. 'Our friends didn't understand. But I've always said that love takes a different shape for everybody. Some of us fall in love the straightforward way, and some of us have a more . . . winding path.'

Mr Townsend is giving me a significant look. I stare down at my Americano as Izzy's phone bursts to life beside her coffee cup.

'Excuse me,' Izzy says, standing. 'Mrs SB's calling. I'm going to guess that . . .' She taps her bottom lip. 'Dinah's bleached something antique.'

'Ruby's climbed something dangerous,' I counter-offer.

She bites back a smile. 'Closest guess wins?'

I nod once as she answers the call.

'Hi, Mrs SB! Ah, Baby Jacobs has peed on that eighteenth-century rug, has he . . .'

Izzy mouths *I win* at me as she heads outside, and I raise my eyebrows. I would say that's debatable.

'Refill?' Ollie asks. He's got himself a bottomless coffee. I am not sure he should be allowed this much caffeine.

'I'll come with you, stretch the legs,' Barty says, getting up.

'It never occurred to me that one of your special rings could be mine,' Mr Townsend says as they make their way to the till. He closes it in his trembling palm. 'All that dashing around and making phone calls. I'm sorry I didn't save you the bother.'

'It's not your fault,' I say. 'And Izzy's enjoying the search, I think. It seems to matter a great deal to her.'

'Well, of course,' Mr Townsend says, eyes still on his closed fist. 'Given the ring she lost.'

He looks up when I say nothing.

'Ah,' he says. 'Was that a secret?'

'She doesn't . . . share personal things with me,' I say, slightly pained. 'She lost a ring?'

'She told me a few years ago, when we were discussing her family. It was a twenty-first birthday present from her father – she lost it while swimming in the sea in Brighton,' Mr Townsend says. 'Very sad.'

I remember how she'd looked in that first conversation we'd had with Mrs SB – how her eyes had shone with tears.

I am struck by an entirely ridiculous urge to trawl the ocean. Perhaps Izzy's ring washed up somewhere? Perhaps I could . . . learn to scuba dive . . .?

'It was years ago,' Mr Townsend says gently. 'It's gone for good, that ring.'

I clear my throat, looking down at my coffee, embarrassed. I had not realised I was quite so transparent.

'So that's why she cares so much,' I say, taking a sip as I try to compose myself.

'Partly, I imagine,' Mr Townsend says. 'But I think Izzy likes anything with a story attached. And rings are objects we give a lot of value to, us humans. Symbols of eternity, dedication, you name it. They were always going to catch her eye.' He looks at me levelly. 'Lucas . . . Do you care for her?'

I am so taken aback, and so overrun with the emotions of the day, that I almost answer him honestly. But then, as I open my mouth, my uncle pops into my head, and I imagine what he'd say if he knew I was spilling my romantic troubles to a guest. And just like that, I clam up. My whole body responds to the thought. Stiff back, chin up, face blank.

'She is a very talented colleague,' I say.

I hate that I'm still like this, even with Antônio so many thousands of miles away. Even with my own car, my own flat, my own job, my own degree – almost. But these traits are so deeply engrained, I don't know how to unlearn them.

In my embarrassment, I almost miss something important that Mr Townsend says: that Izzy likes things with stories behind them. It only comes to me on the drive home, with everyone chatting away in the back seat. Izzy has looked at me – really *looked* at me – just a few times in the last few weeks, and every single time it's been a moment when I've let her see something that I don't necessarily want to show her. Telling her why I exercise. Sharing why I raise my voice sometimes, and why I so badly want to change that. Moments when I showed her there's a story to me.

It's an uncomfortable realisation. I don't like to share personal matters with anybody – it's not how I was raised. But I don't want to be that way. I would like some of Izzy's courage, her openness. I would like to believe that I can let a person see me, and that once they have, they might think more of me, not less.

Izzy

I am so glad Mr Townsend took that well. I'm not sure I could have handled it if The Ring Thing backfired again. I'm frazzled enough today as it is. Torturing Lucas has been fairly torturous for me, too – I *really* hoped he'd cave and follow me into the lost-property room when I was getting changed.

'Never leave again,' Mrs SB says when we return. She gives Mr Townsend a stern look. 'And you, sir, have used up your I'm-a-guest privileges.'

'I only requested two of them,' Mr Townsend points out, making his way over to his armchair. 'Don't blame me for the stowaways.'

'You rascal,' Mrs SB says to Barty as he swoops in to kiss her across the desk. 'You'd better have saved me a doughnut.'

Barty looks guilty. I'm pretty sure he ate at least four.

'Another ring down, then!' Ollie says.

He's crossing the lobby with a specific, bent-kneed dash that means he cannot be seen through the window on the restaurant door. Arjun-dodging has become a habit for anyone who has had to play sous-chef this winter, but Ollie is particularly good at it.

'No reward, though,' he says as he joins us at the desk. 'Yesterday Mrs SB told me we're probably going bust and losing all our jobs. So could you crack on and return a really expensive one, maybe? Save the day a bit?'

'Ollie, that is a very abbreviated version of our sensitive employee–employer chat. But yes,' Mrs SB says, holding out a pile of post to me, then turning it upside-down so the *FINAL NOTICE* is on the bottom instead of the top. 'Just one more reward like the Mattersons gave us could make all the difference now.'

'The last ring does look fancy,' I say, trying not to laugh as Lucas notices that Mrs SB has adjusted his desk chair, and makes a visibly painful effort not to object to this. 'Maybe it'll be fifth time lucky.'

The final ring is a stylish band, beaten silver, slightly askew. I love it. It's not as beautiful as Maisie's ring, but it's clearly designer, and I bet whoever owned it was interesting – you can just tell.

Arjun pops up in the window of the restaurant door. 'Ollie!' he barks.

'Balls,' says Ollie, trying a belated duck.

'I can still see you!'

'He's had me dicing on and off since Tuesday,' Ollie says miserably, dragging his feet as he turns towards the kitchen. 'If you do get a massive reward for that last ring, will you buy me an invisibility cloak?'

'You told me yesterday that you were loving the chance to help prepare the food,' Mrs SB says.

'Yes, but I've got *blisters*,' Ollie says mournfully, as he walks into the kitchen with the air of a man tasked with saving the planet against his will.

'He really dons that chef's hat with a flourish now, doesn't he?' Mrs SB says dryly as we watch him through the door.

'He's doing brilliantly, to be honest,' I say.

'I know. He's a star. You're all stars. This is good for him,' Mrs SB says, with a nod towards the kitchen. 'He likes to be pushed. Whereas *you* two . . . You like a little healthy competition.' She smiles at us, and for a moment I catch a glimpse of the woman she must have been when she and Barty first fell in love: a few years younger than him, and much less conventional. 'I happened to hear that you had a bet running on two of those first rings. Shall we introduce another?'

'Another bet?' I say, as Lucas looks up slowly from the computer screen.

'Yes. You see, this year, I'm giving Poor Mandy a break from being the Christmas elf,' Mrs SB says.

'No!' I say.

Mandy is a *brilliant* Christmas elf. She delivers all the hotel cards and presents – I write every guest a card, and Mrs SB and Barty get everybody a small gift, and Poor Mandy distributes them in this absolutely ridiculous elf costume that must date from about 1965. It is a staple of the Forest Manor Christmas.

'Yes,' Mrs SB says firmly. 'The poor woman never complains,

but that costume simply doesn't fit her any more, and it's not right. I was going to ask one of you to do it.'

Lucas's head turns slowly towards me.

'So perhaps ... Whoever fails to return the ring gets elf duties.'

'Absolutely not,' says Lucas.

'That's a great idea,' I say.

This is perfect. I have no problem with wearing an elf costume and delivering presents, other than the fact that I like my Christmas to be *exactly* like the Christmas before, and I would prefer Poor Mandy to have to do it on those grounds. But Lucas having to dress up as an elf? Yes please.

'The costume won't fit me,' he tries.

Mrs SB is on the customer's side of the desk now. She leans on her forearms, looking slightly gleeful.

'Mandy is an excellent seamstress.'

'But she can't adjust it for herself?'

'Come on, Lucas,' I say. 'What are you, scared?'

'What are you, five?' he says, eyes locking on to mine.

'It'll be fun.'

'This is serious. All of this. I'm not looking for *fun*.'

His tone has shifted; his eyes are dark. I swallow, looking away, conscious of Mrs SB standing on the other side of the desk. We've been like this all day, Lucas and I – even when we're bickering like normal, there's an undercurrent there, the reality of the night ahead never far away. Every time I remember what we're planning to do this evening, my stomach dips like I'm on a plane that's just hit turbulence. Teasing him has been an easy way to feel in control, but the truth is, I have no idea what'll happen the moment the clock strikes five.

'I do know that the situation is serious, OK? I'm aware of the stakes,' I say, keeping my voice light. 'But Mrs SB is right. We work better with a bit of competition.' I pull out one of the waiting lost-property boxes – I need something to do with my hands. 'I think a bet really would be best for the hotel.'

'And you feel the same?' Lucas asks Mrs SB.

'Oh, entirely,' says Mrs SB.

Lucas sighs. 'Fine,' he says. 'I will enjoy seeing you in those elf boots, Izzy.'

That undercurrent again. That edge to his voice, even now, when we're talking about bloody elf costumes.

'I'm not losing this one,' I say. 'Also, I would rock those boots, and you know it.'

Lucas's eyes flick over me.

Mrs SB chortles, drumming her hands on the desk for a moment. 'Excellent,' she says. 'Excellent!'

Lucas's face remains implacable. I imagine him in that elf costume, and discover, quite disturbingly, that Lucas da Silva can make literally *anything* sexy.

Finally, finally, the Bartholomew clock strikes five.

Lucas stops typing instantly. He turns his head to look at me. After a day of teasing Lucas at every opportunity, I have a feeling I'm about to get my comeuppance.

'I'll drive,' he says, picking up his bag and heading for the door.

I scramble to catch him up, wriggling into my rucksack straps as I step outside.

'You're not driving me,' I call, and he slows slightly, not turning around as he crosses the gravel towards the car park.

'Ah. You're seeing Louis tonight instead,' he says.

'What? No. No.' I've caught him up now. 'How do you even know Louis wanted to hang out tonight?'

I only remembered my plans with Louis this morning. I messaged him earlier to cancel, to which he replied, *Tomorrow night instead?*

His persistence is admirable, if slightly exasperating.

'He told me.' Lucas glances at me, eyes dark. 'In detail.'

'I rescheduled him to tomorrow, since we have ... plans tonight. I just meant you can't drive me because I'm not staying over at your place,' I say. 'Afterwards. I can't just leave Smartie here.'

He looks at me properly now. I shiver. I'm excited, nervous, thrilled, and a little bit disbelieving, because that *afterwards* I'm talking about seems like a world I just cannot imagine. What will it be like, seeing him naked? Touching him? Letting him touch me?

'Ah yes,' Lucas says slowly. Almost a drawl. 'That was one of your rules.' He reaches into his pocket for his car keys and begins to walk again. 'I will pick you up at your flat and drive you in tomorrow morning.'

He climbs into the driver's seat, throwing his satchel into the back. I hesitate, glancing towards Smartie.

'Let's just go in two cars,' I say.

'That is ridiculous.'

It *is* ridiculous: petrol is so expensive, the planet is dying, and driving along after Lucas in convoy makes the whole thing feel a bit seedy.

I get into his car, breathing in the smell of clean leather and Lucas. It's *so* tidy in here. My car is filled with bits and bobs: hair bands, CDs (Smartie is old-school), water bottles that roll around under the seats if you take a sharp corner. Lucas's car is pristine.

My legs jitter as he drives, knees bouncing. I meant to get changed before we left – my uniform is extremely unsexy. At least I'm in good underwear. It's been digging in to numerous body parts all day but I'm grateful for it now. I'm hot with anticipation, cold with nerves.

Lucas lays a hand on my knee.

'You can still change your mind, *meu bem*.'

My breath seems louder, everything else quieter.

'I don't want to.'

'But it's always true. You can always change your mind.'

I relax back into the seat. I knew that, of course, but it's calmed me to hear him say it out loud. Something's shifted since that car door closed. Everything's different. For instance, Lucas's hand stays on my knee as he drives. I stare down at it: Lucas da Silva's hand on *my* leg. The mind boggles. How did we get here? And what does *meu bem* mean?

'You have driven me mad today,' he says, taking his hand away to shift gear and then setting it right back there on my knee.

'Don't I drive you mad every day?'

'Yes,' he says, voice almost silken. His eyes stay on the road. 'But not quite like this.'

'No?'

'No. You have been particularly irresistible.'

I've never been called irresistible before. I reach tentatively for his hand on my leg, and trace my fingers over his, listening to the way his breathing changes at the contact. It is so strange to touch him like this. So strange to see him as a man I *can* touch.

'This is weird, isn't it,' I whisper. 'Weird but . . .' *exciting*, I want to say, because there's a giddy, drunken thrill moving through me now, like I'm a teenager again.

'Weird but good,' he says, his voice low and soft.

'Can I . . .' My throat is dry. I swallow, turning my body towards him within the confines of my seat belt. His hand shifts on my thigh, and that tiny movement pulls all of my attention to that one spot, as if suddenly the heat of his palm on my leg is the only thing that could possibly matter.

'Yes,' he says calmly. 'You can. Whatever it is you want.' He turns to look at me for a split second and his eyes are as dark as the sky outside. 'I'm yours.'

'For the night,' I whisper, and his eyes flicker.

'Yes. For the night.'

I want to reach across to touch him, but before I can, the car jerks and I'm thrown forward. His hand grips my thigh tightly then flies to the steering wheel. The engine chokes, chokes again; the car stutters along, and Lucas is steering us to a lay-by on this dark country road and suddenly we're stationary, hand-brake on, both breathing hard.

'Fuck,' I say. 'Is your car . . .'

'I'm not sure,' Lucas says, sounding much calmer than I feel.

'Do you think we should . . .'

He's trying the engine. It makes a sound a bit like a steam train. We both wince. I wonder how long it'll take us to walk back to Smartie from here. We've been driving for almost ten minutes on fast roads. Maybe . . . an hour and a half on foot.

Fucking hell. I'm way too turned on for a hike.

'I'll call my breakdown provider,' he says, pulling his phone out of his pocket. He opens his door as if to step out of the car, realises how freezing it is out there and slams the door shut again with a quiet Portuguese swear word.

The conversation is brief – classic Lucas – and the conclusion is that they'll be here in an hour or two.

'I should wait for them to arrive,' he says. He sounds calm, but his shoulders are tense, and he mutters something else in Portuguese before unclicking his seat belt and turning my way. 'If you . . .'

He trails off. I stare back at him, watching his eyes shift from cool concentration to something slower and hotter. We look at each other for so long that it starts to feel like a dare – like a challenge to the other to glance away first. I draw my bottom lip in between my teeth, just slightly, and it does the trick – his gaze drops to my mouth. I win.

'If I what?' I whisper.

I watch him try to pull himself together.

'If you want to go, you don't have to wait with me,' he says.

'I can wait,' I say, but the truth is, by now, I can't.

He kisses me first, hard, fast. It's exactly like last time – zero to a hundred in seconds, all fierceness and fire, and we're twisted awkwardly and battling to touch each other over the gearbox and the space between us until we break apart in frustration, chests heaving, and he says, 'Come here.'

He pushes his seat as far back as it goes. I climb into his lap. He looks up at me, smoothing my hair back from my face, running his hands down my sides.

'We obviously won't . . .'

'Not here, no,' he says, smiling, and tilts his chin up to invite another kiss.

I've kissed plenty of guys. I know what it feels like to get caught up making out with someone, how the world seems to fade and it's just your bodies and your breath. But this is . . . bigger. Brighter. I didn't know kissing could feel like this – as though it's clearing my mind until there's only sensation.

Lucas kisses with absolute assurance, commanding even when he's trapped beneath me, with one hand urging my body closer to his and the other tangling in my hair, tilting my head so he can kiss me more deeply. I want him so badly it's an aching, desperate urge – I have to get closer, take more of him, give more of myself.

Within ten minutes, we're breathless and beyond reason. *We obviously won't* becomes *we probably shouldn't*, and then after twenty minutes of making out in the driving seat like teenagers, without a single car passing us down this dark country road, it becomes *we could just* and *quero você, I want you* and *God, Lucas* and *please* and *please* and *yes*.

*

'Oh my God. You had sex with him in *his car*?'

I rest my head on Smartie's steering wheel for a moment. I'm held at some lights and Jem is on speakerphone on the passenger seat. 'I actually cannot believe myself,' I say. 'We were on a public road.'

'Izzy! I didn't know you had it in you!'

'Neither did I! But he got me so het up.'

Jem laughs. '*Het up*. You are adorable. Well, I'm happy for you. Assuming it was great? Was it great?'

I swallow, switching into first as the lights change. It *was* great. Dizzyingly, disconcertingly great. We were squashed into a car with the steering wheel digging into my back, still half dressed in our uniforms, but I had never been less aware of my surroundings. I could have been anywhere. And every sensation was amplified, dreamlike. My forehead to his, his hands gripping my waist, the way he shifted underneath me as if he knew precisely what I needed, even if I wouldn't have been able to tell him myself.

'It was intense,' I tell her, exhaling as I speed along to the hotel. I'm early. I'm never this early, but I just couldn't sleep. 'I guess because we hate each other so much, it kind of multiplied everything? That's such an intense feeling, right, and there's always been that fire between us. Maybe angry sex is actually the best sex?'

'Uh-huh,' Jem says slowly.

'You don't think so?'

'Well, no, actually, but it's more that . . . I'm not sure you really hate each other, do you?'

That pulls me up short – I notice I'm going seventy and make a face, braking.

'Course we do. He was such a dick to me last Christmas, don't you remember?'

'I remember,' she says. 'But maybe you've forgiven him for it.'

'What! I have *not*.' I'm quite affronted. 'He's not even apolo-gised – or offered any sort of explanation!'

'OK, well I know you tend to hold a grudge like Gollum with something shiny . . . but have you actually asked him what happened, pigeon? Maybe he didn't get your card.'

I have wishfully considered this option many times in the last year. In the immediate aftermath of the mistletoe incident, I was so sure this was the explanation that I hunted Poor Mandy down at home to ask her again – was she *certain* she gave my card to Lucas? Did he *definitely* read it?

And she'd said yes, he read it. And laughed.

'He got the card,' I say, swallowing. I don't like thinking about it, not when my body is still soft and sore and satisfied from last night. 'Anyway, I've not even told you the worst part. The breakdown cover turned up early . . .'

'Oh, *no*.'

'Not that bad. I was back in my seat.' I'm wincing at the memory of the woman's face, how amused she'd been by my ruffled hair and red cheeks. 'But she offered to give me a lift back to my car as they'd be a while fixing Lucas's, so I just said bye to Lucas and left with her.'

'How did you say bye to him?' Jem asks.

'Oh, weird wave.'

'Little pigeon.' Jem's voice is infused with warmth, and it makes me miss her more than ever. 'You are too cute.'

'Embarrassing, you mean. It was great though: I just went home and had a bath and did my own thing! I think casual one-time sex is the way forward for me.'

'Really?'

'Yes! Why not?'

'Well, maybe I'm not the best person to ask . . .'

'You're always the best person to ask,' I say.

'You are well aware this would never happen to me,' Jem says, amused. 'I cannot even *conceive* of it, Izz.'

Jem is demisexual, as in, she's only attracted to people when she's formed an emotional connection with them first. Great sex with someone you hate is a total contradiction in terms for her, I guess.

'Do you think I've been really stupid?' I say. 'Do you think I shouldn't have had sex with him?'

'Of course not! I'm not judging, not ever, you know that. I'm just not convinced you're getting what you want from a relationship, here. You're . . . *cosy*, Izzy. You've always wanted a partner who wears woolly jumpers and has a nice smile and a lovely family.'

I wish she'd not said *cosy*. It takes me right back to that bloody Christmas card again.

'Well, it's not a relationship anyway, so no need to worry,' I remind her. 'Now . . . speaking of lovely families,' I say, dodging a pothole.

'Don't. I'm actually on the sidewalk outside the house with

270

Piddles, in the very spot where I used to smoke as a teenager and dream of running away. Some things never change.'

'You know, you *can* run. You're a grown-up now. You don't have to spend the holidays with them just because you've ended up back in Washington. They make you miserable, Jem.'

'Oh, but they're my family,' Jem says, and I can hear that she's rubbing her forehead, the way she always does when she's feeling guilty or sad. 'I'm lucky to have them.'

I know what she means. *When you don't have yours.*

'They're lucky to have *you*,' I say. 'I would so love it if you could walk into that house and own the woman I've always known you to be. So what if you're not a doctor or a lawyer or a super-rich businesswoman? You're chasing a different dream, and you're doing brilliantly. They should be proud of you.'

'I'm a backing dancer who's got her first break aged twenty-nine, Izzy,' Jem says dryly. 'I get paid like, twelve dollars a month after tax.'

'Who cares! You have a gift, and the kindest, purest heart, which I personally think matters a hell of a lot more than whether you're a "success". Which you are. So you win on all counts. Not that we subscribe to the idea of it being a competition. God, it's complicated rising above other people's expectations, isn't it?'

'It really is.' Jem sniffs. 'Thanks, Izz. Damn, you've made me cry.'

'I have many rambling pep talks up my sleeve,' I tell her. 'Would you like one every hour, on the hour, just in case you need it?'

'You want me to sob my way through the holidays?'

'Only in a nice way!' I say, turning in to the hotel car park.

Lucas

There was a plan. It involved good red wine and candles. Slow kisses and pillow-talk.

My car in a lay-by was not the plan.

'Isn't this the sort of conversation you should be having with one of your gym buddies?' Ana says in my ear.

I am actually in the gym right now. It is the only place where I feel sane at the moment. I'm on the treadmill, jogging and panicking.

'What about that Pedro guy?' Ana asks.

'Pedro got me into this mess to begin with,' I say, swiping a droplet of sweat from my chin.

There aren't many people here yet, and the morning gym crowd is more serious and subdued. Which suits me just fine.

'Unless you are now using "Pedro" as a codename for your penis, I don't think that's true,' my sister says.

I wince. 'I've messed up, haven't I?'

'Does it feel like you've messed up? Did it not, you know, go well?'

It was the hottest and most intense experience of my life. I have never, ever wanted somebody so badly. Every moment we spent together in that car, I could feel myself drowning in the euphoria of it, even as I begged myself to wait and remember everything, because this was precious.

But I had one shot.

I wanted Izzy to take me seriously. I wanted to tell her my story, to show her that I do have a heart, whatever she's always thought. And instead, I behaved like a thoughtless teenage boy. I should have waited until the breakdown truck arrived. I should have driven her back to my flat for a late dinner, kissed her slowly on the sofa, and told her how beautiful she was.

'It was amazing, but not how it should have gone. I had a plan.'

'Oh, a *plan*. I know how much you love a plan.'

Every time Ana says *plan* it is loaded with sisterly scorn. I scowl, upping the tempo on the running machine.

'It's not that. I just wanted it to be special.'

'Wasn't it?'

It was. But it wasn't *right*. This was my chance to show Izzy there's something real between us – everything had to be perfect. Instead, I'd been almost panicked with desire, desperate for more of her, and then those people had come to fix the car, and . . .

'Hello? Lucas? It is very, very early here, and Bruno has finished his feed, so I'm actually only still awake because I'm being an amazing sister, but if you don't say something soon, I'm going to fall asleep.'

'Sorry. Go back to bed,' I say. 'Love you. Kiss my nephew for me.'

'Love you too. And no chance,' she says. 'I am not waking that baby unless something very big is on fire.'

I smile as I reach for my phone to switch back to my workout playlist. I can't wait to see Bruno again in February. As soon as this thought crosses my mind, I imagine Izzy there with me: charming my sister, tickling a giggle from Bruno, laughing with me as we get the barbecue going in the garden. The image is so potent I lose my footing and have to grab at the treadmill.

I don't want to get Izzy out of my system. That is clearer than ever after last night. I want all of her. Her kindness, her commitment, her technicolour hair and the way she always puts me in my place. I want to take her home and call her mine.

As soon as I arrive at the hotel, it becomes clear that Izzy is still taking her rules extremely seriously.

'Lucas,' she says, giving me a bright smile when I get to the desk. 'I've got a lead on the final ring. Better up your game if you don't want to be dressing as Santa's little helper. Oh, and I've sorted a magician for the party, and Irwin says they'll be done with the staircase just in time.'

She's so ... brisk. Cold, even. But she still smells of cinnamon sugar and I know what the curve of her waist feels like. I've dragged my tongue along the inch of collarbone I can see through the collar of her shirt.

'You OK to cover the desk this morning so I can get on top of all the renovation work?'

'Yes, fine,' I say. 'But, Izzy . . .'

She whizzes away, hair flying.

I spend my morning posting out lost-property items we've sold and trying to decipher Izzy's to-do list. I move mechanically, getting things done, and all the while I'm thinking, *Was that all the Izzy I get?* That thought, the very idea . . . It hollows me out.

And then there's the knowledge that Izzy is going out with Louis tonight. That is making everything considerably worse.

I've never been jealous like this with another woman, but then, I'd never been cheated on before Camila. Izzy is the first woman I've cared about since that relationship ended. Maybe this is what Camila's done to me – for all her protestations that she couldn't change me at all.

I take a pause in the lost-property room, pressing my fingers to my eyelids, trying to gather myself. I *hate* the idea that my relationship with Camila made me weaker. I remember the way I felt when Izzy slipped into the pool with Louis – that feeling I was so convinced shouldn't be called fear – and I wonder whether I *had* been frightened after all. That's what jealousy is, isn't it? Fear of losing someone?

'This is stupid,' I whisper under my breath as I step back through into the lobby. The images play out at the back of my mind: Louis walking Izzy through the crowds of the Christmas market, lacing his fingers through hers, turning to her under the mistletoe . . .

The bell dings.

'Sorry to bother you, Lucas,' Mr Hedgers says when I startle. 'You look like a man with a lot on his mind.'

I was actually imagining Louis slow-dancing with Izzy on an ice rink under the stars, but hopefully Mr Hedgers can't tell how quickly that all spiralled.

'What can I do for you, Mr Hedgers?' I say, settling down in my chair. It's not been quite right ever since Mrs SB sat in it. I shift a little from side to side, but nothing improves matters.

Mr Hedgers gives me a baffled smile. 'I have something of a mystery on my hands, and I'm hoping you can help me with it. Mrs Singh-Bartholomew let us know yesterday that we can stay. That we're covered until the new year. But my wife says the insurer hasn't backed down – in fact, she was just eviscerating them on the phone this morning,' he says, pulling a face. 'I can't understand how Mrs SB made the mistake?'

I frown. It seems unlikely that Mrs SB has changed her mind. I emailed her just yesterday with a summary of my suggestions for budgeting at the hotel, and there is *not* room for random acts of charity, as much as I want to help the Hedgers.

I promise to investigate, and send Mrs SB a quick email, asking to meet her later.

Then I just . . . work.

That's it.

I don't see Izzy all day. She flits in and out of the lobby but is gone before I can speak to her. I can't decide if she is avoiding me on purpose. I hope not. Or perhaps I hope so. What would avoiding me *mean*?

When I do eventually collide with her, it's outside Opal

Cottage, just when I'm due to meet with Mrs SB. The rain is coming down in thick, steady droplets, and she's under a spotty pale-blue umbrella. I'm using my large black one, big enough for two, and it keeps us at a distance, as if we're each walking in our own bubble.

'Hi,' she says, and immediately turns pink.

I relax slightly. Those flushed cheeks tell me she hasn't forgotten about yesterday at all.

'Hello,' I say. I hold her gaze, and her cheeks grow pinker.

Mrs SB opens the door and Izzy flees inside. I follow more slowly, watching her, how fast she's talking, the way her hands keep reaching around as though she needs something to fiddle with. She glances sideways at me, then her gaze slips away again.

'Let me put the kettle on,' she says, voice tipping higher.

I smile as she dashes off. I'm feeling a lot better now. An unsettled Izzy is an Izzy who is feeling things she didn't expect to feel; an unsettled Izzy means *change.*

'Mrs SB, the Hedgers,' I begin, as Izzy clatters around in the kitchen.

Mrs SB's face lights up. 'Wonderful, isn't it?'

'Well, yes, I am glad they are staying, but . . .'

I look at Izzy. She's not going to like this, and while that wouldn't have bothered me a few weeks ago, now I hate the thought of upsetting her.

'We can't afford it.'

Izzy glances over, frowning.

'Oh, I know,' Mrs SB says, sounding puzzled. 'That's why I was so pleased when the donation came through.'

'The donation?'

'On the hotel's Kickstarter page.'

I stare at her.

'Poor Mandy set it up,' she says, laughing at my shocked expression. 'She's been doing all sorts with the internet on her shifts.' She sighs, settling back into her armchair as Izzy returns with cups of tea. 'We're making a little money on there. But it won't be enough. We need real investment. I've seen your email, Lucas, and I've not replied, because frankly it's far too depressing for words. I've tried everything, every loan, everyone. Louis Keele is our last hope.'

I notice that I am grinding my teeth, and hope that it isn't audible. I don't trust Louis' intentions with Forest Manor one bit.

'Izzy, I know you've formed a friendship with Louis – of course I wouldn't want to ask you to do anything you weren't comfortable with . . .'

It's definitely audible now.

'But could you just get a sense of whether there's any hope, there? Whether he *might* . . .'

'Of course,' Izzy says, squeezing Mrs SB's shoulder. 'I'll ask him, OK? I'm seeing him tonight.'

'Perfect,' Mrs SB says, closing her eyes.

No, not perfect. Not perfect at *all.*

As we leave Opal Cottage, Izzy walks ahead of me, and I catch her up in a few strides, putting a hand on her arm. She jumps, turning. The rain has eased a little, and neither of us has put up our umbrellas for the short walk back to the hotel. Izzy folds her arms to pull her coat close around her.

'Yes?' she says. 'What is it?'

'Hello.' I try to hold her gaze, but it slides away from me again. 'So we are not going to talk about it? At all?'

'That's what we decided, wasn't it?'

'We decided to remain professional at work.' I dig the point of my umbrella into the grass, my knuckles tight on the handle. 'I only see you at work. Does that mean we never speak of it again?'

'We can speak about it, if you think we need to.' She glances up at me. 'Do we need to?'

I don't know. I want to apologise to her for not making it more romantic, but she never wanted romance from me. She'll get that from Louis tonight, presumably. I swallow, glancing back towards Opal Cottage. Its chimney is smoking, the Christmas tree visible in the left-hand window. We're standing just outside the front garden, beneath the old oak tree.

'So I'm out of your system now?' I ask, looking back at her. I shift the handle of my umbrella to and fro between my palms, and she watches my hands.

'Mmhmm,' she says. 'Yeah, all sorted. Same for you?'

Something in her voice gives me pause. Carefully, deliberately, I try stepping closer. She stays where she is, eyes flicking to mine. Wary, but also excited, I think. I recall how pink-cheeked and fidgety she was when we first arrived at the cottage, and I let myself wonder if Izzy has been thinking about me as much as I've been thinking about her today.

'No, Izzy. You're not *out of my system*.'

It's raining more heavily again, pattering at the branches

above us. I reach out to brush a raindrop from her cheek with one slow swipe of my thumb.

She inhales at the contact, gaze fixed to mine, but she doesn't move away, so I keep my hand there, framing her face. My heart starts to beat in the low, stubborn, insistent tempo it always hits when I'm close enough to kiss her. I watch for those small shifts that tell me what Izzy's body wants. How she straightens a little, as though pulled towards me, and how her pupils dilate. After just one frantic evening in a car, I can already read Izzy's body better than I've ever read her mind.

'But you're done with me, are you?' I ask.

'What did you think would happen? We'd have sex and I'd suddenly find you irresistible?' she says, but her voice catches in her throat, and my confidence grows. She didn't answer my question.

'You've found me irresistible for some time,' I say, then I smile as her eyes flare with irritation. With me and Izzy, there's always been a fine line between pissed off and turned on. 'That was the problem, wasn't it?'

'I wouldn't say . . .' she begins, and then she trails off.

I've stepped closer, and she's backed up against the bark of the oak tree, her hair sparkling with rainwater, her chest rising and falling fast.

'Lucas,' she whispers.

My heart is thundering now. I lift my hand from her cheek and brace my forearm against the tree above her head to hold a few inches of distance between our bodies. She looks up at me, lips parted. I can see the shift in her eyes, the moment she relaxes. She's letting go. Forgetting about real life, remembering about me. I'd expect it to make me feel triumphant, but instead I feel an unexpected clench of emotion – I love that her body trusts mine.

'Tell me to *Fuck right off, Lucas*, and I'm gone,' I whisper, dipping my mouth to hover above the soft, secret place on her neck that I learned about last night. 'Tell me you're done with me.'

'I'm . . .'

She doesn't finish. I reward the admission with a hot kiss to her cold skin, and she moans.

'What did you think would happen?' I repeat her question back to her, my mouth against her skin. 'That we'd have sex and suddenly we'd be able to resist each other?'

The door to Opal Cottage slams and we move as one: she twists away from me as I push back from the tree, lunging for my umbrella when it slips from my hand.

'You tell Barclays they can shove it up their arses!' Barty shouts as he makes his way up the path. 'Oh, hello, you two,' he says, rounding the corner and finding us hovering guiltily beneath the tree. 'Off back to the hotel?'

'No, I'd better . . . I'll . . .' Izzy's cheeks are as pink as I've ever seen them. 'I'm going that way,' she says, and heads off into the woods.

'Is she all right?' Barty says, as we begin making our way back to the hotel.

I clear my throat, the heat in my body simmering down again. I don't know quite what that was, underneath the oak tree, but there's excitement singing through me now. Because it definitely wasn't nothing. And after a day thinking I'll never kiss Izzy again, not-nothing feels pretty incredible.

'She's fine,' I say. 'We were just arguing again.'

'Oh, you two,' Barty says, shaking his head. 'Always at each other, aren't you?'

I cough again. 'Something like that, yes.'

Izzy

What is wrong with me?

The whole point of last night with Lucas was to stop stuff like this happening. By the time I get back to the hotel – via a cold, unnecessary detour into the woods – I am soaking, and Lucas is at the desk. He looks up at me, heavy eyed, amused. Despite the sobering walk in the forest, I'm warm again the moment his gaze meets mine.

'Shall I fetch you a towel, Izzy?' he asks.

'No,' I say stubbornly, dripping on the lobby carpet. 'I'm fine.'

His lip quirks. He returns his gaze to the computer screen. 'As you wish,' he says, as though he didn't just pin me up against a tree and kiss my neck and make me *melt*.

Infuriating, bewildering robot-man.

I get changed in the spa area and manage to dodge Lucas for the rest of the day, but it does require ingenuity. At one point I have to pretend to get a cramp, and when Ollie asks me to take some tablecloths to Lucas, I end up asking Ruby Hedgers to do it for me. She informs me that this is child labour and tries to extort me for a lot of money; I only avoid a trip to court by giving her a packet of my candy kittens.

At least I'm getting somewhere with my ring. There's one name on the list of guests that jumped out at me this week: Goldilocks. When a celebrity visits the hotel, they usually choose a pseudonym to check in under – only a few key members of staff will be aware of their identity. Goldilocks has pseudonym written all over it. Grilling everyone around the hotel about this takes up most of my afternoon, and is the perfect distraction.

'If I remembered who stayed here in 2019 under the name Goldilocks, Izzy,' Arjun says in exasperation, after I pop into the kitchen to ask for a third time, 'I would tell you purely to shut you up. You are like Izzy-on-crack today. What's got you so wired?'

'Nothing!' I yelp, sliding down off the countertop and wishing my colleagues didn't know me *quite* so well.

Once I'm home and drying my wet uniform on the radiators, everything feels a lot simpler. I had a momentary relapse at Opal Cottage, that's all. It was never going to be a clean-cut thing: find Lucas irresistible one moment, find him repulsive again the next. There was going to be a period of transition. I'm just in that. It's no big deal.

Helloooo, comes a text from Sameera. *We are wondering if you and Sexy Scowly Receptionist are going at it like rabbits now you've 'broken the seal'? Hahaha! x*

I chuck my phone across the room to the sofa and get back to drying clothes. *Breaking the seal* is not the thing here. It's about *getting it out of the system.* Honestly. What's Sameera on about?

As I walk through the Winchester Christmas market with Louis later that night, I take a deep, calming breath and pull myself together. The market is so cute that my cosy heart is about to explode. Warm spiced cider, the smell of dried oranges and eggnog, the sound of children laughing as they race between the stalls . . . It is one hundred per cent, double-shot cosiness. My perfect second date.

So why am I wishing I was somewhere else?

'It's not as simple as whether I have the money to invest,' Louis is saying.

He keeps putting his hand on my back as we move through the crowd. It's not at all gropey or anything, but it's annoying me.

'The money's there, of course, but I have to think about the breadth of my portfolio,' Louis says. 'Think with my head, not my heart.'

'Well, that's not really my forte,' I say brightly. 'But I can tell you that we have so much planned for Forest Manor.'

I try to pep myself up again and focus on the nice things about Louis. How he ticks every box. How I said I'd give this a proper chance. But ever since The Angel's Wing, I've been going off him, and once that process starts, it's so hard to backpedal. Suddenly his slicked-back hair looks greasy rather than stylish, and he winks *way* too often. I'm not even convinced that his gentlemanly listening face is all that genuine, actually.

'Oh, I've been meaning to ask – what's Arjun's deal?' Louis says. 'How long has he been at Forest Manor?'

'Arjun? Oh, for ever. He trained under some super-fancy Michelin-starred chef up north somewhere, though. Why?'

'Just curious. How's his wine knowledge?'

'Amazing, actually. Our wine cellar is legendary. If you want to sample something in particular, you can always just ask me.'

'And why's Arjun stayed at Forest Manor so long, do you think?'

I frown, thinking of what Lucas said about Louis' plans for Forest Manor. I wrap my aching fingers around my gingerbread hot chocolate.

'I think he loves the hotel. Same as me.'

'Right, but . . .' Louis seems to realise that this is more inter-rogation than conversation. He laughs. 'Sorry. Just making sure he'll be sticking around. He's such an asset, and if I'm going to be investing in Forest Manor Hotel . . .'

I relax slightly. If he wants Arjun, he can't be planning to turn the place into flats.

'Why *do* you guys love Forest Manor so much?' Louis asks. 'It's almost certainly going under in the new year. But none of you have left for a new job. What's that about?'

I reach around for the words to capture it. The magic of Forest Manor at its best: sconce lights glowing, live music playing, the warm hubbub of a happy crowd in the dining room. All the weddings: those love stories that found their happily-ever-after against the backdrop of our beautiful sandstone walls. And, for me, the coffees and heart-to-hearts with Arjun after dinner service has ended and neither of us wants to go home; the slow-growing friendships with guests like Mr Townsend who come to the hotel year after year; the sense of being part of something that brings joy in a harsh, frightening world.

'You know when people say somewhere is a home away from home?' I say. 'I think it's that. For all of us. So when we're talking about losing our jobs . . . we're also kind of talking about losing our home.'

'Right, wow. That's cool.'

He doesn't get it, I can tell. Suddenly, I can't be bothered with much more of this. I planned to wait longer, but as we walk slowly between the stalls, I find myself saying, 'Louis, I don't think we should see each other like this any more. I'm just not feeling a spark.'

'This again!' he says, nudging me. 'Izzy, you said you'd relax and give this a proper shot.'

I frown. 'I am. I have.'

'All right, sure,' he says easily. 'I hear you loud and clear. You want a mulled wine?'

'What? No, Louis, I want to head home, OK?'

'You certain?'

'I'm certain,' I say, with emphasis.

'OK.' He smiles. 'Let's head back to my car, then.'

He's just the same all the way home, chatting away. At first I assume it's an act – he was so keen at The Angel's Wing – but he seems genuinely fine. Maybe he was losing interest too, or maybe he just doesn't want me to feel bad about calling things off. Whatever the reason, I'm relieved: I'd worried he might get petty, or even let it affect his potential investment in the hotel, but he asks more questions about Forest Manor as we hang around outside my flat, and then hugs me goodbye like we're friends. It's nice to wave him off with absolutely zero regrets.

Once I get inside, I settle in on my sofa with a bowl of Krave and an episode of *The Vampire Diaries* that I know so well I can reel off half the lines from memory. Everything I could possibly need.

Except I keep checking my phone. Opening WhatsApp, closing it again. If I'm honest with myself, I'm thinking about Lucas. I want to know what he's doing tonight.

For some reason.

Ugh.

I stare at the TV. The trouble is, last night was just so . . . memorable. I feel like every inch of it is traced across my skin – as though instead of getting rid of Lucas, I've tattooed him there. The rasp of his breath, the solid muscle of his shoulders, the words he whispered in low, quick Portuguese . . .

I swallow. Maybe the problem is that it was all so rushed.

Maybe it's not really getting it out of your system if it's a snatched hour in a car. Maybe I just need a bit . . . more.

And then, just as I'm about to cave and open WhatsApp, a new message appears. From Lucas. Who has not messaged me since 2021.

How was the market?

I scrunch up my nose. Since when does Lucas ask me how my evening is going?

It was gorgeous, I reply after a moment. *So festive.*

I pause, and then I do something very bad. I type, *I was kind of preoccupied, though.*

Preoccupied with what?

Thinking. About last night.

His next reply doesn't come for fifteen minutes, and I feel as if I am quite possibly about to die of embarrassment. I fidget on the sofa, trying to concentrate on the television. I'll just quit my job, I think to myself. I'll just never go back to work, so I never have to see him again after sending that message and not getting a reply.

When he finally writes back, the message is infuriating.

How was Louis? is all it says.

I type my reply before I can think better of it.

Are you jealous?

His response is instantaneous this time.

Yes.

I knew it.

Was it a date?

What's it to you? I type.

Can you just tell me that he was respectful?

I roll my eyes. *Lucas.*

Yes?

Is it any of your business what happens between me and Louis?

There's a knock on the door. I slurp the last of the cereal on my way to answer it, sliding the empty bowl on to the kitchen counter.

It's Lucas at my front door, messaging. He must have left his flat the moment I said I was thinking about last night.

He doesn't look up when I open the door; my phone pings in my hand. He's wearing his usual black coat open over loose, low jogging bottoms and a long-sleeved tee, with a duffel bag by his feet. The idea of him right there in my hallway seems as strange and impossible and exciting as the sight of him tipping his head back against the driver's seat, muscles pulling taut in his shoulders, eyes piercing mine.

After a long moment facing each other across the threshold, I glance from Lucas to my phone screen.

No. But can it be my business to check you're OK?

'No,' I say out loud.

'Why not?'

I narrow my eyes at him, but I'm tingling. I've spent all day avoiding that tingle.

'You don't get to be jealous,' I tell him. 'You don't even like me, Lucas. In fact, I'd say this isn't about me at all. It's about another man. It's a stupid macho possessive thing and it's a total red flag for me, if you didn't have enough of those already.'

'I can assure you,' he says, 'I am not thinking about Louis right now. I am thinking about you.' His tone is clipped, and his eyes are all darkness. 'Are you going to let me in?'

'Why would I let you in?'

He doesn't answer that. Not as if he doesn't know, more as if he thinks it's obvious.

'You're being completely obnoxious,' I tell him. 'We had rules. You're breaking them.'

'Tell me to leave, then.'

We face off on either side of the threshold. Slowly, slowly, his gaze shifts. Taking me in. My jumper dress, leggings, the woolly socks I slipped on when I got in the door. Back to the neckline of my dress, the only place where I'm showing skin. As he lifts his eyes to meet mine again, I feel like he's stripped me bare. The tingle is a buzz now, insistent, like the giddy rush of a tequila shot hitting your stomach.

'We said one night,' I say, but even I can hear the lack of conviction in my voice.

'Then I'll leave,' Lucas says, not moving an inch.

I say nothing. He waits.

'Is that what you want, Izzy?'

It absolutely isn't. We made those rules for a reason, though. One night felt safe – I could do that without getting hurt. But to give him more than that, this man who drives me mad all day, who goes out of his way to make my life difficult, who *laughed* when I told him I had feelings for him?

That would be dangerous.

'Tell me to go,' he says, his voice low and rasping as he stands there in my hallway, one step away from coming in.

But I don't. Despite all the reasons I should, that low hot buzz has set in, and no part of me wants to send Lucas away. I know what it feels like between us now. He's not just some abstract fantasy. He's real, and that's even harder to resist.

I cross the threshold between us and kiss him hard, pulling him inside, letting the door close behind us with a short, sharp slam.

*

He doesn't stay over, he just . . . doesn't leave.

We doze for stretches at a time, but the whole night, we're in bed together. From the moment he crosses into my flat and hitches me up against him, he barely says a word in English. He whispers Portuguese against my stomach, my thighs, the back of my neck, but we don't talk.

I wake again at seven, lying flat on top of him, my ear pressed to his chest, my legs falling on either side of his. I can't believe I slept like this – I can't believe *he* did. His body is warm beneath mine, but I'm cold – the duvet is on the floor somewhere. I lift my head, resting my chin on his ribcage, looking up at him. He shifts beneath me, and the feeling of his nakedness sends a ripple through me, tired and distant but there.

He opens his eyes and lifts his head to look at me. We say nothing. I wonder if I should feel embarrassed, or shy, but I don't – I can't muster the energy.

He rubs my arms. 'You're cold,' he says. His voice is throaty and warm.

I twist to the side, rolling off him, reaching over the edge of the bed for my duvet. He pulls it up for me and makes sure my feet are tucked in. I settle on my side, and he does the same, his hand finding its way back to my hip. That casual touch doesn't feel strange, which is strange in itself.

'Sorry,' I say, my voice a little hoarse. 'I didn't mean to fall asleep.'

He regards me steadily, brightly lit under the bedroom light we never turned off last night.

'It doesn't have to be just one night,' he says. 'Or just two.'

I can already feel how much I'll crave him when he's gone. The idea that I could dial down the desire with a night in bed feels so stupid now that I know his body like this. I know the sounds he makes, the way his hands shift over my skin, the casual confidence with which he drives me crazy.

I should shut this down. It's a bad idea on so many levels I've lost count.

Instead, I say, 'We'll piss each other off so much.'

'Maybe.' His eyebrows twitch. 'But we have your rules to help with that.'

'Right, the rules.' I bite my bottom lip. 'Yeah. But . . . I think we'd need one more.'

'More rules,' Lucas says. 'Oh, good.'

'No talking about the past when we're together. If we're fighting, it'll only get toxic.'

His eyes rove over my face, as though he's looking for the answer to a question. I turn over, staring up at the ceiling, my body suddenly too warm under the duvet. I mustn't forget that Lucas has already shown me who he really is. I have to hold on to that.

For an aching moment I wish I could just phone my mum, tell her that I've slept with someone I shouldn't have, and then let her tell me what to do. Let *her* protect me from a broken heart. Just give myself one morning off from always fighting to look after myself.

'All right. But I have a rule too.'

I turn back to him. He's hazier this morning: there's a brush of stubble on his jaw and a tired glaze to his eyes. His hand dropped from my waist when I shifted, but he places it back there, one thumb sliding up and down my bottom rib.

'No seeing other people,' he says.

This doesn't entirely surprise me.

'You mean no Louis?'

He says nothing, just watching me. I am struck by the total bizarreness of having him in my bed, and it sends a shiver through me. He feels it and tightens his grip on my waist for a moment, as if to steady me.

'You are so weird about Louis,' I tell him, trying to gather myself.

'Do you like him?'

I hesitate. I know precisely why I've held back on telling Lucas that there is nothing between me and Louis. For all my talk about red flags, a little, guilty part of me likes that he's jealous.

'No,' I say eventually. 'I've been clear with Louis that there is nothing romantic between us and there never will be. Happy?'

After a long moment, Lucas gives me the ghost of a smile. 'Happy,' he says.

I look away, reaching for my phone to check the time. 'We should go to work,' I say, and another shiver goes through me, because I'm going to have to stand side-by-side with Lucas at the desk, and he's going to be pedantic and rude, and all this – this slow hot dream of a night – will be gone the minute we get out of this bed.

I watch him get ready. How he changes from the man who unravelled me to the man I see every day: shirt perfectly tucked, jaw perfectly shaved, back perfectly straight. As he pulls on his waistcoat, I open Instagram on my phone, looking for distraction, and scroll past a dog video, a book recommendation, and a post from Drew Bancroft.

I pause. Scroll back up again. She's different. Her hair, once long and bouncy, is now cropped short around her ears, and she's changed her big, square glasses for a pair of round ones. *Can you believe this face can't find work rn?!* the caption reads. *If you've got a job going, hit me up please, I promise you I'm fabulous and NEVER late (lol no but really I am working on that).*

Looking at her makes it a *lot* easier to remember the humiliation of that night. Seeing Lucas's hand on her hip as they kissed in the very spot where I'd dreamed of kissing him, screaming at him across the lawn and watching his face turn disdainful . . .

'You'll be late,' Lucas says, looking at me in the mirror.

I switch off my phone screen. 'I won't.'

He glances at his watch. 'You will.'

'I *won't*.'

I pull the duvet up to my chest and try to slow my breathing. I can't believe he stayed here all night. I can't believe I've agreed to doing this again. I can't believe how badly I *want* to.

I'm freaking out a bit. Understandable, maybe, but I'd rather do it when Lucas *isn't* standing right there in front of my bedroom mirror.

His face is blank as he turns to look at me over his shoulder.

'Izzy. It's quarter past. *I* am going to be late. You are still naked under that duvet.'

'Just go, Lucas, OK?'

295

He frowns, reaching for his duffel bag. 'Fine. If that's what you want.'

As he walks out of my bedroom, I tell myself I'm an adult. I can do this, if I want to. And there's no denying I want to.

I just have to keep my walls up, that's all.

Lucas

Every night we spend together, I learn something about her. The small formation of freckles on her ankle; how she's ticklish there. The way her voice lifts when certain people ring her – Sameera, Grigg, Jem – and how it tightens for anyone else. The photograph of her parents on her bedside table, and how she touches it absently sometimes, the way you might stroke a cat.

By the week before Christmas, I am gone. I am out of my own control. Every time we touch, I feel myself tumble a little further, and every time she gives me a bright, professional smile at work it hurts a bit more. I had imagined the danger in this arrangement would be Izzy losing interest in me after we had sex. But it seems the real danger is me falling in love.

We stick to the rules, but as far as I'm concerned, they're no protection at all. We may not fall asleep together – aside from that first extraordinary night at her flat. But we still hold each other, move together, wrap each other up almost every night.

She shows no sign of getting me out of her system, and I'm more addicted to her than ever.

One night she messages me at three in the morning – she's woken and can't get back to sleep. I suggest a change of location. She's outside my flat within twenty minutes, in my bed within another two, and when dawn breaks, she's naked in my arms, dozing, satisfied. I watch the sky lighten in the gap between my curtains and savour the feeling of her body against mine.

'Can we talk?' I say.

I feel her go still. 'What kind of talking?'

'I want to say that I'm sorry for being jealous when you went to the Christmas market with Louis.' My heart quickens. I've wanted to tell her this for days. If I want Izzy to see me as a human being, to take me seriously, then she needs to know my story. 'He makes me . . . You make me . . . I *am*,' I say, correcting myself in frustration, 'I am on edge when you're with him. My last relationship . . .'

She stiffens in my arms. I keep talking, faster now.

'Camila cheated on me.' It is *painful* saying this out loud. 'Then she acted like – like it was my fault, because I didn't give her enough. So she said she went looking for that love elsewhere. I know it's no excuse for my possessiveness. But I wanted to tell you that there's something behind the jealousy other than just, you know, that I am a man with so many red flags, as you called me. I want you to understand that I'm working on this. I want to be better.'

'Lucas, I . . .' Izzy pulls away from me, reaching for the

overnight bag she brought with her last night. 'That's . . . Thank you. For telling me that. But . . .'

This is not going how I hoped it would. She's tense, avoiding my gaze entirely.

'Izzy?' I say.

She looks upset. I reach for her, but she steps away from the bed.

'I'm just conscious of the time,' she says, and I watch as she pulls herself together, pasting on the Izzy that I see at work: bright, smiling, ready for anything. It's amazing. It takes her less than five seconds.

'We have half an hour. You can stay for a coffee if you want,' I say, feeling a little desperate.

She frowns at me as she ducks down to pull on her socks. 'You don't have to do that.'

'I want to. I'd like to.'

I have to choke it out, and the moment I do, I regret it: her eyes flare wide with alarm again. It's the closest I've come to saying *I like you* out loud. Between Izzy and me, that phrase probably feels as significant as *I love you* would to any other couple.

'You want to have coffee with me?'

'Is that so strange?'

'Yes?' Izzy says, frown deepening. 'A, you hate how I make coffee, you always say I get the milk-to-granule ratio wrong—'

'I would make the coffee. This is my apartment, clearly I will make the coffee. And we will use a cafetière.'

'Oh, of course we will,' she says, and I can't tell if she's amused or irritated. 'B, you go to great lengths never to spend more time than necessary with me every single day, so why would you want to keep me in your flat when you could get me out of it?'

'Because – it's not like that now. I don't do that any more. Haven't you noticed?'

'C,' she says, shoulders creeping higher, voice getting louder. 'We have rules about this stuff.'

'Yes,' I say tightly. 'We have rules. Of course.'

'Lucas, I can't do this if you start – if you start being all nice to me and making me coffee and . . .' She swallows. 'There's a reason we have the rules.'

I cannot think of a single good reason for her fucking rules and I wish I could tell her that, but I can see in her panicked eyes that I'll lose the tiny amount of Izzy I get as soon as I say those words out loud.

'You enjoy your coffee,' she says, yanking her jumper on. 'I'm sure it will be very strong and manly with nary a drop of milk.'

I just stare at her. I have no idea what to say to that. She flushes.

'Maybe we should . . . stop this,' she says. 'It's so – we shouldn't . . . I don't think I can do this.'

'What? No. No, Izzy, wait,' I say, scrabbling out of bed, but she's already slipping away towards the door, doing the awkward wave she does when she's feeling flustered.

'I have to go,' she calls. 'I'll see you at work, OK?'

I stare at my bedroom wall as I hear the front door slam. Fuck. I knew this thing between us was fragile, but I didn't realise I could break it with a single cup of coffee.

*

By the afternoon, I have moved through panic, irritation, frustration and despair. Now I have landed on resolution.

I have a plan.

We had been getting somewhere – she'd messaged me in the middle of the night when she couldn't sleep, and I'd held her as she dozed. Those are small acts of trust. But then I opened up about Camila, and it was too much too soon, and she fled.

If I'm going to change Izzy's mind about the sort of man I am, I suspect I need to take a step backwards before I can move forwards again. I need her to feel comfortable, and there is one dynamic that always works between us.

I finally track her down as I'm leaving the spa. She shoots past me in the corridor, avoiding my gaze, and panic rises through me again. I want to do what I did outside Opal Cottage: test her, move closer, seek out those signs that she still wants me. Instead, I let her go, and then, as she reaches the doors to the spa, I call over my shoulder, 'Just so you know, I've almost found the last ring owner.'

This is an exaggeration. But I have spent two hours on the phone to lots of publicists about whether their clients lost a wedding ring, and various people said they would call me back.

Izzy stops short and swivels to stare at me. 'You mean . . .'

'Goldilocks.'

I can understand her surprise: I have given this contest very little of my attention over the last week. But this morning, I got to work. I found the name I suspect Izzy found days ago – or rather, the fake name.

'You can't have almost found her,' Izzy says. 'I've spoken to *everyone* and nobody can tell me who she is.'

'Well, then. I hope you are practising your elf voice,' I say. I fold my arms, leaning against the wall of the corridor, watching her. 'Poor Mandy always does such a good one.'

Izzy's eyes spark. 'Please,' she says, scathing. 'You're bluffing.'

I shrug. 'OK,' I say, pushing off the wall and heading back towards the lobby.

'Wait,' she says. 'Wait.' She glances around as I turn to face her again. 'This morning,' she says tentatively. 'When I . . .'

'Ran off?' I say, keeping my eyebrows raised.

Her eyes narrow. 'I did not run off.'

'Why were you so scared to have a cup of coffee with me?'

'I was not *scared*.'

'Were you afraid you might enjoy it?'

'Oh, come on.' She straightens up. 'I'm *definitely* not afraid of enjoying a morning coffee with you. God. Do I need to remind you that we have coffee behind the desk most mornings, and it usually ends in an argument about whether or not you are a snobby arsehole about my choice of Starbucks syrups? Spoiler: you absolutely are.'

My lip twitches. Her eyes are sparkling again. Izzy can fake a smile, but she can't fake the way her eyes light up when she's really having fun.

'So you called things off this morning because . . .'

She hesitates for just a moment before saying, 'You weren't sticking to the rules.'

'Ah,' I say. '*Not* because you were scared to have coffee with me.'

'I am *not* – ugh,' she says, throwing her hands in the air. 'You are so infuriating.' She points a finger at me. 'And you are not going to see me in that elf costume.'

I give her a slow smile. 'We'll see,' I say, and walk away.

My smile stays in place as I wind my way through the guests beginning to arrive for the early dinner sitting. I dodge a couple gazing up at our Christmas tree, and two of the Hedgers children, who are fencing with Mr Townsend's walking stick and my umbrella, which I am sure I put behind the front desk.

It's handover time. Poor Mandy greets me with a confused frown as I approach her.

'Izzy says I need to get you a bottle of the 2017 Sauvignon?' Mandy says, immediately getting distracted by several loud *dings* from her phone.

'What? Why?' I ask, moving around the desk. Already my mind is racing. What does it mean? Is it an apology for this morning? Would she like us to drink it together? Is it a gift? What for? 'Oh,' I say, as I look over Mandy's shoulder at Izzy's handover notes. 'That says Louis, not Lucas.'

And suddenly I am no longer thinking of all the reasons Izzy wants me to have a bottle of good wine. Instead, I am thinking of why she would give Louis one. Perhaps she would like *them* to drink it together. Perhaps it is a gift for *him*.

Mandy finishes typing frantically on her phone and squints at the page, pulling her glasses up from her chest, where they dangle on a chain. 'Does it?' she says rather plaintively. She is far too loyal to admit to struggling with Izzy's handwriting. 'Are you sure?'

'I'm certain,' I say.

If my voice is short, Poor Mandy doesn't seem to notice. Her eyes are widening.

'*Does* it?' she says. 'That says Louis? Not Lucas?'

I frown at her. 'Is there a problem, Mandy?'

'No!' she squeaks, still staring down at the word *Louis* on Izzy's notes. 'No, no problem at all! Just . . . me . . . being my usual daft self. Off you go, now, it's your home-time.'

She shoos me away from the desk, her phone dinging loudly again. I collect my bag, reluctant to leave. I would like to stay here for the arrival of Louis' wine. But then my phone buzzes in my pocket, and I find a message from Izzy.

Did you actually put a toy elf on my car?

I smile. So she's going home, then. And if I'm fast, I'll catch her in the car park.

Izzy

Honestly, the man is a child.

The elf is sitting on my wing mirror, and it is giving me the finger.

This is a family hotel. Anyone could have seen this elf. As Lucas strides over to me with that smug half-smirk on his face, I fold my arms and glare at him, but the truth is I'm having to fight not to smile. I feel better than I have all day.

That conversation at his flat this morning really freaked me out. As he'd talked about his ex, this weird surge of emotion had come over me, almost like a hormone hit, like PMS. I felt kind of *vulnerable*.

I never give this man anything – that's how we operate. Both of us are stubborn; neither of us budge an inch. But there he was, naked, telling me about his past, and suddenly I was feeling . . . something. I thought of Jem saying I'm too *cosy* for a relationship like this, and I wondered with panic if she might

305

be right. Lucas was starting to look like a flawed, complex, gor-geous man, when it's absolutely imperative for my well-being that he remains an emotionless arsehole.

Because that's who he is. No matter how he touches me, or what his story is, he's still the guy who laughed at my Christmas card, kissed Drew, and spent all year acting like I'm totally unreasonable *all* the time. He's not one of Jem's romantic heroes, misunderstood and just waiting for the right person to unlock his inner nice guy – he's a regular, thoughtless, competitive pedant who happens to be very good in bed.

But now that we're at work, and he's back to himself, I feel better. All is well. Lucas is still impossible, my walls are still firmly up, and I'm still perfectly safe.

'I thought you might want a – what's it called?' Lucas says, nodding to the elf. 'A sidekick.'

'We have a million things to do, the hotel is falling apart, and you have time to buy a toy elf?'

'I am very good at multitasking,' Lucas says gravely. 'It is part of what makes me so excellent at my job.' His eyes glitter in the darkness. 'For instance, I have managed to spend all day looking for Goldilocks, arranging music for the Christmas party, manning the phones, *and* thinking about you naked.'

I swallow. I was so determined never to sleep with him again after the conversation this morning, but now the suggestion sets something alight deep in my belly, and suddenly my evening plans – *The Princess Switch*, spiced tea, mince pies – feels way less interesting than the idea of driving Lucas home.

'Get in,' I tell him. 'And that elf is riding in your lap, not mine.'

*

The next day should be my day off, but I'm in anyway because we've organised a huge jumble sale at the hotel. It's all-hands-on-deck this morning. Poor Mandy is 'live-tweeting the event', apparently; Barty is polishing everything in sight; even Arjun is carrying an old set of chiffon curtains out on to the lawn. I down a second coffee, trying to look like I wasn't up half the night with Lucas. Arjun already knows something is going on – he saw us pulling in together in Smartie, and gave me a look that said, *Do you know what you're doing there, Ms Jenkins?*

Which I don't. At all. Obviously. Last night with Lucas was breathtakingly hot, and this morning I woke up in his arms, which was a) against the rules and b) extremely risky. We barely made it in on time.

I take a deep breath. It's an absolutely stunning winter morning – with the sun just beginning to scorch through the mist, the gardens are glowing.

'Your friend Grigg is trying to get hold of you,' Lucas says, coming up behind me.

His voice is a dangerous shade of conversational. Lucas playing it casual means he's plotting something, generally. I turn away from the crockery I'm arranging on a picnic blanket to find him holding a large coffee table in one hand in the way that I might hold, say, a large coffee.

'Over there,' I tell him, pointing. 'And what do you mean, Grigg's . . .' I check my phone. Three missed calls. 'God, is he OK?'

'He's panicking about your Christmas present,' Lucas says, showing no signs of carrying the table off to the correct area of the lawn. He's wearing a black scarf over his coat – who owns a plain black scarf? 'He rang reception.'

'Oh.' I have a bad feeling growing in my stomach now. I turn back to my crockery. Would it look better if I put all the teacups together, or . . .

'He wants Jem's address, since you're spending Christmas with her.'

'Right,' I say, unstacking saucers as loudly as possible without breaking anything valuable. Maybe I can just drown this conversation out and then I can pretend it's not happening at all.

'When we went to Shannon's divorce party, at Brockenhurst station, Jem said that you were spending Christmas with Grigg and Sameera.'

'Is that what you choose to remember about our trip to London?'

I can feel the steadiness of Lucas's gaze on the back of my neck.

'Izzy,' he says, with great deliberation. 'Where will you be celebrating Christmas this year?'

'I'm working Christmas.'

'Yes. You are. And do your friends know that?'

'Umm.' I squint down at the picnic blanket. I'm concerned that I might cry if he asks me any more about this.

'I know what it feels like to be away from your family at Christmas,' Lucas says.

I glance over my shoulder at him. Very few people really get that my friends are my family now, just like the team at the hotel. Lucas looks back at me, unreadable, and for a frightening moment I find myself wondering whether he might actually know me really, really well.

I turn back to the teacups. 'I would usually be with Grigg and Sameera this year, but they're spending it in the Outer Hebrides with Grigg's parents.'

Grigg's parents have never taken to Sameera – they have this stupid thing about how me and Grigg should have got together, and it's always awkward when the three of us are with them, mainly because I get so irritated I'm at risk of saying something tactless and that makes Sameera nervous. Now that they've got baby Rupe, it's extra important for them to bond as a family.

So I just told them I'd be with Jem for a second year running, as otherwise she'd be solo for Christmas. They knew she'd got a job in Washington for six months, but I was always a bit vague on the when, so it was all very simple.

'Why don't you tell them the truth?' Lucas asks.

'They'll feel sorry for me.' I look out at the activity on the lawns, the racks of old coats backdropped against the misty grey trees, the cars already pulling up in the car park. 'They all have a lot going on right now. I don't like being a burden on them.'

'I very much doubt they see it that way.'

'Coffee tables are in the corner by the holly bush,' I say. 'You can put that one next to the mahogany one.'

He waits so long I sigh in frustration and straighten up, spinning to look at him.

'Don't feel sorry for me,' I say. 'I'm fine.'

He just looks back at me, and for a moment I have to fight not to tear up. This is stupid. I *am* fine. I've known about this

Christmas business for months – it's just a logistical problem, that's all, and it's easier to keep everyone in the dark so they don't worry about me. I've not cried about it once, so I've no idea why I'm feeling so emotional now.

'Would you put that table down?' I say, exasperated. 'It must weigh about twenty kilos.'

Lucas glances at it, uninterested, shifting its weight slightly in his hand. 'Christmas will still be special, even though they're all a long way away,' he says.

'I know. I *know* that.'

'Ooh, are these teacups a set?' asks a woman behind me.

I spin, never so grateful for an obvious question. 'Yes! They all match. Saucers are just here . . .'

I chitchat until I feel Lucas move away. The woman is just the sort of customer I like – an over-sharer in a fabulous bobble hat – and by the time we've finished talking, I've managed to push all the Lucasness of the morning out of my mind. I'm back to bouncy Izzy again. Smiley, sparkly, and firmly in control.

The next day is the 20th of December, which means I'm off work for the day. It's my mum's birthday, and – even in the days when I couldn't bear to be alone for a moment – I've always spent it solo. The year before Mum died, we'd had a girls' day, just the two of us, and I like to do the same now.

I wake up late and have coffee and cereal in front of *Nativity!*, which my mother always staunchly declared was the world's best Christmas film, though my dad was *Die Hard* all the way.

At first, after the accident, I missed my parents with an

awful, gulping pain. The sort of pain that scoops all the breath out of you. It's not like that now – the ache is duller, and I've adjusted to the emptiness, so it rarely catches me off guard. But as I watch the kids of *Nativity!* dance their way across the stage for the finale, I let myself sink back there for the first time in years. I double over, head on my lap, and remember the day when my life tore in two.

Maybe Lucas did have a point when he said nobody can live life to the fullest all the time. Sometimes it's good to curl up under a blanket and wallow. Afterwards, I pick myself up, chuck the tear-and-snot-soaked blanket in the wash and wipe my face. I shrug on my mum's old denim jacket, pin back my hair and head to Southampton for some Christmas shopping.

I'm just browsing through the rails in Zara when I spot Tristan. My ex-boyfriend.

Tristan and I lasted about three months. I ended it with him, but it could have gone either way – in a matter of weeks, he'd gone from writing me lengthy WhatsApps about how much he loved me to the occasional *Hey, sorry, work's so busy!*, despite the fact that his job was reviewing tech products and he hardly ever seemed to be sent any. He was very defensive about the job. He was defensive about a lot of things: his receding hairline, the fact that his parents bought him a flat, the way he sometimes texted his ex-girlfriend when he was sad or drunk.

He has a new woman in tow now, someone petite and pretty. I watch her fetch Tristan the shoes he wants in a different size, and from over here behind the dresses I feel as though I'm watching the scene play out on TV, with Tristan in the role of 'very average man'. He's so *small*, and I don't mean that physi-cally, I just mean he's . . . blah.

Tristan will no doubt continue to flop through life, eventually marrying one of these women and letting her support him as he pursues some far-fetched ambition he'll be very sensitive about. I can't believe I ever wanted this man.

Really, I'm not sure I *did* ever want him much. He was sweet, at first, and I've always gone for sweet guys – they're safe and comforting, like milk chocolate or boots with a two-inch heel. Nothing remarkable, but no risk of breaking an ankle, either.

But there's no *fire* in Tristan. No grit. Tristan would never stand up for me; he'd never dunk me in a swimming pool fully clothed or dirty dance with me in a divorcee's living room. In the entire time I was with Tristan, we never did anything more exciting together than start a new show on Netflix.

I turn away, abandoning the dress I'd considered buying, and head blindly for the car park. I can't start comparing Lucas to my ex-boyfriends. I shouldn't even be *thinking* of him in those terms. The man has already hurt me once, and everything I've seen of him tells me that he's capable of doing it again without so much as blinking. He's an emotionless, uptight perfectionist, and yes, we have great sex, but that's *all* we have. And it's very, very important that it stays that way.

But I can't stop thinking about wishy-washy Tristan. Playing out scenes from our relationship. Imagining those moments with Lucas, and then trying very hard not to notice that if Lucas had been there, they wouldn't have been *blah*, those moments. No single moment with Lucas ever has been.

Lucas

I am stuck. I don't have a clue how to move things forward with Izzy without scaring her off, but I can't go on like this for much longer, having her without having her. I know it's exactly what I agreed to – but it's also torture.

Surprisingly, it's Pedro who finally gives me an idea. He comes over for a beer in the evening and he tells me that if you want to change the way someone sees you, sometimes all you need to do is change the background. This is actually a comment about optimising Smooth Pedro's Instagram page, but wisdom can come from the most unexpected of places.

So on the night of December 21st, I tell Izzy that we aren't going back to my flat, we're going to Pedro's caravan in the woods.

'Pedro lives in a caravan?' she asks.

'A very nice one. He needed someone to look after it while he's away.'

(Staying in my flat.)

'And it's in the middle of the woods?' Izzy asks with suspicion.

'What, do you think I am leading you into these woods to feed you to the ponies?'

'Well, no,' she allows. 'But I'm not really in the right footwear for this.'

I stop and crouch in the middle of the dimly lit woodland path. It's a beautiful, sharp winter evening. I can smell pine and moss: the deep, ancient scent of these English woods.

'Are we doing squats?' Izzy asks.

'No,' I say, as patiently as I can manage. 'You are climbing on my back.'

'Oh!'

She jumps aboard without hesitation, and another fragment of my heart goes tumbling. Her body trusts me now, even if the rest of her doesn't. I shift her slightly so we're both comfortable; she laces her hands around my neck and settles in.

Pedro's caravan really is very nice. He's strung lights around his porch, and they dangle over the bed inside too, tracing tracks across my eyelids as I lie back in the sheets and close my eyes. I wonder if I will ever be able to see a string of fairy lights without thinking of Izzy Jenkins.

'Oof.'

She lands right on top of me. Knees on either side of my hips, and – I open my eyes – no trousers on. She snuggles in, doubling over to lay her head against my chest.

'Mm. Good duvet.'

I close my arms around her and hold her like she's mine, but she's not mine at all. She starts to kiss my neck and my body responds instantly. I put my hands on her upper arms, holding her back.

'The lasagne will be done in ten minutes.'

She pulls back. 'Lasagne?'

'It's just a pre-made one,' I say. 'I thought we should eat.'

We never eat together, usually. But there isn't a specific rule against it.

'Well, I guess . . .' She frowns. 'I *am* hungry.'

'We could wait for it outside on Pedro's porch. You can see the stars.'

Her frown deepens. 'Umm,' she says. '*Or* we could . . .'

She presses a slow kiss to my neck. My breath hitches. I brush my hands up and down her arms, trying to ignore the way she wriggles in my lap, making this plan significantly more difficult.

'Come on,' I say, closing my eyes for a moment and then rolling her over, pressing a kiss to her lips as I shift off the bed. 'There's a heater out there.'

She pulls her trousers back on and follows me slowly. It's beautiful out here. The caravan sits in a carefully mown patch of lawn bordered by the forest on all sides. Pedro has laid some pale wooden decking, with two chairs facing out to the trees. I bend to switch the lights off as Izzy settles in her seat.

I have to walk with my arms out in front of me to find my chair. Slowly, my eyes begin to adjust. The moon is half full, bright white above the trees, and the stars are extraordinary. It's as if someone has sown them like seeds across the sky.

'Oh, wow,' Izzy breathes, looking up. 'I've actually never seen them looking so clear. I guess . . . less light pollution here than at the hotel.'

'It's beautiful, isn't it?'

I can barely see her nod in the darkness. I sit back in the chair, trying to find calmness in the star-soaked sky.

'How was your day?' I try.

She pauses. 'You have literally never asked me that before.'

'No?'

'Nope. Never. Anyway, you know how my day was. You were there.'

It's a rare acknowledgement of real life outside of our evenings together. I pounce on it.

'You seemed irritated with Poor Mandy this afternoon.'

'She said she'd help me find out who Goldilocks is, and then got distracted doing a reel for Instagram. I love that woman, but she gets scattier by the day, and introducing her to social media means she's pulled in even more directions at once.'

I hear Izzy sigh. An owl hoots in the forest and another answers. Through superhuman effort, I manage not to point out that asking for help to find the owner of the last ring could *definitely* be regarded as cheating. The bet was between me and Izzy. But I suppose I should have known she would play dirty.

'We're all stressed, with New Year looming, I do get that,' she continues. 'I feel pretty scatty too, to be fair. The renovation work is just so . . . consuming, but in a really good way, like I feel as though I'm doing something *me* and . . .' She pauses. 'Sorry. I shouldn't be talking about work.'

'I don't mind.'

'No, it's . . . It's better that we keep it separate.' She pulls her knees up underneath her, face upturned, pale in the moonlight.

'I'm glad you're enjoying work on the renovations. Is it what you'd like to do, longer term?'

'Lucas . . .'

I am prepared for this.

'We said no talking about the past. I'm talking about the future.'

I can feel her hesitation. This conversation is making her uneasy. I wish I knew why. She's so determined to keep me out of her life – I can't understand it. What's the risk? Why can't she just try?

'Well . . . yeah. I still have a bit of a yen to do the upcycling business thing. I would never want to leave Forest Manor, though, if it still existed. It's my home.'

'You could work part-time at both.'

'I guess.' She reaches down to pull a blanket out from under the chair, tucking it over her knees, hair swinging across her face so I can't even see what little the moonlight gives of her expression. 'But starting my own business feels so risky. It'd be safer just to get a waitressing job if the hotel goes under.'

I frown. Izzy never particularly enjoys waiting tables at the hotel.

'Time sometimes feels like it's . . . I don't know,' she says. 'It's just streaming by and I'm happy, obviously, I'm so content in my life, but, like, I haven't even *thought* about the upcycling project for months, and it's been years since I first came up with the idea, and I've just . . .' She rubs her face. 'Anyway.'

'Go on.'

'No, it's fine, I'm all good. Ignore me.'

The oven dings.

'And there's the lasagne,' Izzy says, with audible relief.

She flicks the light on as she heads back inside, and the stars blink out, washed away by the artificial glare. I stay where I am, running over what she told me. *Content*, she said. As though it means the same thing as happy. But I don't think it does.

'Oh, you burned it!' she calls from the kitchen.

I sit bolt upright, horrified. 'Did I?'

I hear her snort with surprised laughter. 'Oh my God.'

'What?'

I look over my shoulder as she appears in the doorway, over-baked M&S lasagne on a tray in her hands.

'Sorry, I just had to see your face, Mr Perfectionist.'

She's grinning. Her hair is half tucked into the neck of her jumper. Izzy always seems at home wherever she is, but right now she looks particularly comfortable. This is good. This is pro-gress. When we're in bed together, Izzy relaxes, but when we're not, she's usually wary, as if I'm about to sprout devil horns.

'What?'

'You just cannot handle messing anything up, can you?' she says, teasing.

I eye the lasagne. It is very dry and brown at the edges. Pedro's oven must be more powerful than mine. Izzy starts to laugh.

'You are ridiculous. It's a lasagne! Nobody cares.'

'I care,' I say. 'I want you to have the best things.'

She sobers at that, looking at me, round-eyed.

'Lucas,' she says, softly now. 'You can relax. It's just me.'

It's just me. Like she isn't fucking *everything.*

'After all, what's the point in having a fling with someone you don't care about if you can't let things hang a bit, you know?' she calls over her shoulder as she heads back inside. 'Just enjoy the fact that you give no shits about what I think of you, and try *not* being perfect for once.'

I look back at the sky and then close my eyes as the caravan door swings shut behind her. *Ah, porra.* We're getting absolutely nowhere.

She doesn't stay over at the caravan. I spend the whole next day fearful that I've scared her away, but then, at one minute past five, my phone buzzes, and my heart leaps in response, like Pavlov's dog salivating. A message at this time almost always means the same thing. *Come to mine later?* it says.

I wolf down my dinner at home and check my reflection on my way out, trying not to notice the tension in my jaw. Every time we do this, things get better and worse all at once. There's no way to argue that this is anything other than foolishness – I am clearly going to get hurt. I'm getting hurt already. And still I knock on her door, feeling that double kick in the gut when she opens it dressed in delicate, pale-pink lingerie.

'You look incredible.' My throat is dry.

She blushes at the compliment; it touches her shoulders and throat, and I lift my hand to trace the heat on her skin, feeling her pulse quicken under my touch. She pulls me inside and into the bedroom, on to the covers, under them, into her, and just like every time, I let myself believe that she'll ask me to stay the night.

Her phone rings when she's close, almost there, sweat beading on the skin between her breasts. Her head is tipped back so I can see the full bareness of her throat. These moments are always the ones when I am most hopeful. When she comes apart in my arms, she's absolutely herself, hiding nothing. If she's ever going to really *see* me then I sometimes think it'll be in a moment like this, as we teeter, eyes locking, bodies letting go.

'Look at me,' I whisper.

And she does. The phone rings out, and she gasps against my lips just as I gasp against hers. She grips me so fiercely, and I hold her just as tightly, and for a moment I wonder if she might not want to let me go.

The phone rings again, and this time she groans, loosening her grip and rolling away to answer it.

'Grigg,' she says, reaching for her dressing gown. 'Do you mind if I answer? You can just chill here if you want.' She hesitates. 'Or go, if you'd rather . . .'

'I'll wait,' I say quickly.

She disappears into the living area, then I hear the door to her spare room closing behind her. I look around her bedroom. I've never been in here without her before. The colour scheme matches the living area, and matches Izzy: soft pastels, faint polka dots and fluffiness.

I catch sight of the bath through the bathroom door and wonder. There is no specific rule about baths, but running her one would feel like a step up from leaving the minute we're done, and she did say I could stay here. What was her plan for afterwards?

I head into the bathroom. There is a gold-edged mirror above the basin, and make-up cluttered across the surfaces. I'm just turning on the taps when I hear her voice.

'The sex is *incredible*,' Izzy is saying.

It is almost perfectly clear through the bathroom wall, even with the water running. I retreat to the door after a split second's hesitation, but then she says, 'But I'll never be his girlfriend, will I?'

I freeze. I can't hear Grigg and Sameera's response, just a tinny rattle of voices.

'I mean, the sex doesn't really change anything. He's still . . . Lucas. *That* guy.'

I should leave. I don't. Horror settles quietly in my stomach.

'Who, Louis?' she says.

I bite down on my lip.

'Oh, yeah, I guess so.'

More echoing, indistinct voices.

'Yeah, he's still a contender,' she says. 'Still in the game. That's how he'd put it,' she says, and there's something in her voice I can't identify – a sort of fondness, maybe, or wryness. 'Ugh, it's been such a mad couple of weeks. Anyway, how are you two? How did Rupe manage the journey?'

I withdraw, clicking the bathroom door shut.

I leave her flat, walking blindly to my car. I think about all the ways I've tried to show her the sort of man I am. How I've treasured every moment with her, and tried to make her feel treasured too, and yet still I'm '*that* guy'. Good enough to take to bed but not a *contender*. Not like Louis.

Before this winter, she would just have been proving everything I already felt about myself. But these last few weeks have changed me. *I've* changed me. Now, through the chorus in my head telling me I'm not good enough, there is a small voice saying, *actually . . . I deserve better than this.*

Izzy

What the fuck?

I stare down at the bath, water still glugging down the overflow pipe, and then around at my empty flat.

He just . . . left?

I know I was gone a while chatting to Grigg and Sameera, but surely he'd pop his head in to say bye if he had to shoot off?

I call Grigg back. He looks unperturbed.

'What did you forget?' he says.

'Lucas left.'

'Left?'

'He's . . . gone. Without saying bye. He left the bath running . . .'

Grigg blinks a few times and then says, 'Maybe he's passed out somewhere?'

'God, maybe,' I say, heading out of the bathroom to check for collapsed Lucases behind sofas and doors. My flat is small – this doesn't take long. 'Nope. Just not here.'

'It must have been an emergency. Have you rung him?'

'No,' I say, feeling stupid. 'I rang you.'

'Call him, then call me back, OK?'

He's gone. I flick to my WhatsApp with Lucas. Above our last exchange – *Come to mine later? I'll be there at eight* – is this:

You left your pink socks with fairies on them here.

Are you sure those aren't yours?

. . .

Ha OK bring them next time you come over. Or wear them to work? Good conversation-starter?

I actively avoid starting conversations. Conversations find me more often than I would like as it is.

You are so ridiculously grumpy for a man in hospitality.

I warm up sometimes. For some people.

I swallow. It looks . . . flirty. Coupley, almost. That's exactly what Sameera and Grigg said on the phone, too. *So are you dating, now?* Sameera had asked, nose wrinkled. *When does having non-stop sex become a relationship?*

But it's not a relationship – it can't be. There are rules.

I gnaw the inside of my lip as Lucas's number rings and rings. No answer. I hang up and message Grigg, and then sit down on the edge of the very full bath.

I am more unsettled than I would like to be. Lucas and I are . . . a fling. We're flinging. I shouldn't care if he's acting like a dickhead, walking out without saying goodbye. But I do, and that's scaring me a *lot*, and the overfull bath is making the whole thing feel especially dramatic.

I message him.

Are you OK? Where did you go?

He sees it but doesn't reply. I can't decide whether I'm worried or angry, but I hope it's angry, because if I'm worried, that means I care, and I *mustn't*. I've put my heart on the line for Lucas da Silva before and it was such a disaster. I am not a person who lets someone burn her twice. Life is too short for wasting time with people who don't deserve you.

I'm fine. I just needed some space.

I stare at the message, baffled, until another pops up.

Apologies about the bath.

Ugh. This man. He is *bewildering*. I chuck my phone on to the bathmat and strip off. If I'm going to mope around about Lucas, I might as well make use of this bathwater. I sink into the water, my heart thumping hard, and I tilt my head back as the heat begins to relax my muscles. *You don't care about Lucas*, I remind myself. *He doesn't care and you don't care.* But as I close my eyes, I can still feel my heart thudding in my ears, and it's not slowing down.

'Sweetie, I only have five minutes, max,' Jem whispers into the phone. 'It is *so* cold out here. I may die of frostbite, and Piddles definitely feels the same way. But I have so much I want to say to you. I feel like I'm going to have to be Mean Jem.'

Jem is standing outside her parents' house – if she takes a call inside, she'll wake everybody up. It is so good to hear her voice. It's the middle of the night and I am foraging in my fridge, because after lying awake for hours you really start to realise how long it's been since your last meal. I don't normally go this long without eating when I'm awake, so why start now?

'You know what I think your mum would say to you right now?'

Oof. Jem is one of the few people who will throw my parents into conversation without flinching. She lived on my road when we were at primary school, and was around at our place all the time – my dad used to joke that they'd only wanted one kid but it seemed this extra one came with the house. She's the only person who could guess at what my mum would say and actually have me listen.

'She'd say you're being stubborn as a mule and blind as a bat. How can you not see how much you love this boy?'

I stare wordlessly across my kitchen. I can hear Jem blowing on her hands to warm them up.

'Hello? Can you hear me?' she says.

'Yeah, hi, I can hear you, I just . . . *What?*'

'Izzy . . . I'm pretty sure you've loved him all year.'

'I have not! I hated him until about five minutes ago!'

'OK, so, let's try this,' Jem says. 'Tell me the other people you've really hated in your life. People who give you that icky, skin-crawl, what-an-asshole feeling.'

I think about it. 'Obviously evil dictators and stuff.'

'People you know, I mean.'

'Oh, Mr Figgle!' I say, grabbing a bottle of milk and heading for the freezer. Milkshake. Milkshake is the answer. 'Our old PE teacher, remember? He was so horrible to the kids who didn't play sports, and do you remember he laughed at Chloe when she said it wasn't fair that only the boys got to have a football team?'

'Anyone else?'

'Kyle from my interior design course,' I say. 'He gaslit like, six girls on the course. A total sleaze.'

'Gross. Go on.'

I think I'm already out. Hate is a strong word and generally speaking I quite like most human beings. Except Lucas, obviously.

'So . . . did you want to have sex with either of those people?' Jem asks.

'No, eww,' I say, peeling a banana and splitting it into the blender.

'But *Lucas* . . .'

'Yeah, it's a bit different, he looks like a Brazilian god,' I point out, whirring the blender. 'Sorry, milkshake. Mr Figgle looked like a meerkat.'

'Do you think . . . maybe . . .'

'It's OK,' I assure her. 'You can be Mean Jem.'

'Sometimes you can be a tiny bit stubborn? And sometimes . . . you like to take the easy option.'

I pour out my milkshake in silence.

'Sorry, I love you,' Jem says. 'I love you, I love you.'

'Yes, I love you too,' I say tetchily. 'What do you mean, take the easy option?'

'Well, committing to a relationship with a man who's hurt you before? That's hard. Having sex with him and insisting that you don't want anything serious? Much easier.'

This blows my mind a little. It feels terrifyingly true.

'Shit.'

'Truth-bomb?' Jem says apologetically.

'Yeah, kind of. I felt like doing it this way would be safe,' I say, testing the thought out, chewing my bottom lip. 'But when I realised he'd left the flat I felt . . .'

Jem waits patiently. But I do feel the pressure of her impending frostbite.

'I felt scared.'

'Ooh, OK, now we're getting somewhere!' whispers Jem. 'Scared of what?'

My voice keeps getting smaller and smaller.

'. . . Having lost him.'

'This guy you hate, you mean?'

'Fine, hate is over dramatic, I know that. But we don't get on. We disagree on everything. We argue all the time. He behaved like a twat last Christmas and never apologised!'

But even as I say it, a hundred other things come to mind. How fiercely he stands up for what he thinks, even when it would be easier to back down and agree with me. How his eyes go soft when he talks about his baby nephew. How he pulls me against him when I turn up at his door, like he can't stand another second of distance between us.

'What would happen if you talked to him about last Christmas, little pigeon?'

I recoil at the very thought. My whole body shrinks inwards as though someone's doused me in cold water.

'No,' I say firmly. 'No, we have a rule about talking about the past.'

'Do you think . . . maybe . . .'

'Go on, just say it.'

'Do you think this is why you made that stupid rule in the first place?' Jem says in a rush. 'Like, *why* don't you want to talk to him about last Christmas?'

'Argh. Because – Jem, it's so humiliating.'

'And why's that?'

'Because . . .'

'Without wanting to put the pressure on, I have lost all sensation in my feet.'

'Because it actually *hurt*,' I blurt. 'I didn't think it would. I thought it was fun and brave when I wrote it, but knowing he laughed at that card? Tossed it aside and made out with Drew, of all people? It makes me want to curl up in a ball.'

'And why's that?'

'Because . . . Because . . .'

'Even my *hair* is cold right now.'

'Because I *really liked him*.'

'Yesss,' Jem says. I hear a creak down the line – I suspect she just did a small hop on the porch. 'It wasn't a casual "hey, I fancy you", that card. It was you handing him your heart. And you've never done that with a guy before.'

'I've had loads of boyfriends,' I say. I can hear how defensive I sound. This whole conversation is making me squirm.

'Ye-es,' Jem says. 'But men like Tristan and Dean.'

I scrunch up my nose. 'Yeah?'

'They're sort of, umm . . . nothingy? Like, they're safe options. You're OK when it ends because you never really cared about them in the first place.'

'Can we do you now?' I say, getting a bit desperate. 'Are you having a crisis, at all?'

'We can do me tomorrow, when I can feel my extremities again. Lucas isn't safe and nothingy, right?'

He's not. He's fire and steel and ice. When I'm with him, whether we're in bed or in the hotel, I'm always feeling *something*.

'I have a really horrible feeling about how this conversation is going to end,' I say.

'I think you have to talk to Lucas about last Christmas,' Jem says.

I make a sound somewhere between a wail and a growl. 'No! No, you're wrong, I can just keep that in a box for evermore and keep having lovely sex with my annoying colleague!'

'OK, so, none of that is happening. But I really love you. And I'm sorry. Can you forgive me for being Mean Jem?'

'Don't be ridiculous, you've been a massive help,' I say. 'Thank you for risking frostbite for me.'

'Always!' she says, and then she shrieks. 'Piddles! Oh, shit.'

I wince at the cacophony on the other end of the line. There is definitely a cat yowling over there. And possibly a dustbin falling over.

'Anything I can do?' I say, sipping my milkshake.

'Unless you can catch Piddles remotely, no,' says a breathless Jem. 'Bye, pigeon.'

'Good luck!' I call, just as the barking begins.

Lucas

When Izzy walks into the Forest Manor lobby in the morning, I'm braced. I'm sure my face is wearing the wary expression I've seen so often on hers over the last year.

I was up until three a.m. and still I have no idea what I want to say. I walked out of her flat and left the bath running. That is ridiculous. I don't *do* things like that, but then, around Izzy, I do all sorts of things I thought I would never do.

And I can't stop hearing the words she said. *I'll never be his girlfriend, will I?*

Every time I remember how good it feels between us, I come back to that, and the anger flares up again. The worst part is that I've led myself right here: I went into this situation knowing that she disliked me and wanted nothing more than a physical relationship. She has been extremely clear about that. So I *can't* be angry. Which only makes me feel more furious.

'Hello,' Izzy says. Her tone is perfectly cool. 'As you can see, I have not drowned. No thanks to you.'

If she wants to rile me up, she's done it. *That's* how she wants to start this conversation? Flippancy, finger-pointing, childishness? It's everything we used to be, and I hate it.

I jerk my head towards the lost-property room and spin away from the desk. There's nowhere to sit in here except on a box, so I stand with my arms folded, and after closing the door behind her, she does the same.

'I apologise about the bath . . . situation.' I can hear how stiff I sound. I'm being the Lucas she used to know, the one I've been working so hard to help her forget. *That guy.*

'Thanks. And how about the disappearing act?'

'I heard you on the phone. I had to leave.'

Her eyebrows fly up. 'You were listening to my phone call with my friends?'

'No! No. I went to run you a bath and the wall . . . I just heard it.'

'Right.' Her gaze is level. 'And what exactly did you "just hear"?'

The air crackles between us. It always does. I'm furious and scared, but I still want to walk her back against the wall and kiss her.

'What you really think of me. That's what I heard.'

She frowns. 'I don't remember exactly, but I don't think I said anything about what I *really think of you* except maybe . . .' Her cheeks are turning slowly pink. 'How good it is between us. The sex.'

There's a knock at the door just as she says *sex*. We both jump as if we've been caught half-dressed.

Izzy opens the door. It's Louis Keele. The way my body reacts is shameful. A rush of adrenaline, my fists bunching, muscles flexing. It's pure, animal jealousy and there's no place for it – but the way he looks at Izzy makes me want to hit him.

He's still a contender, she said. *That's how he'd put it.*

É, com certeza . . .

'Can I grab you for a sec, Izzy?' he says. Ignoring me completely.

They walk out into the lobby. I follow. Louis clearly wants to have Izzy to himself. I hover within reach, looking busy, making it obvious I'm in earshot. Louis stays on this side of the desk, crossing that line, because he's just the sort of man who doesn't respect a boundary.

'Listen, I'm still weighing up the investment,' he says. 'My dad suggested getting another tour from someone who really knows the *heart* of the place. And who does heart better than Izzy Jenkins? What do you say – could you spare some time this afternoon?'

'Sure!' Izzy says. 'Whatever you need.'

They chitchat. Izzy pats his arm when he says something about his father, and I remind myself that she is like this: tactile by nature with everyone but me. Even now, she still won't touch me like that at work.

I'm exhausted. I scan over the hotel's Kickstarter page and am unable to register whether the sum has gone up since I last hit the button. Someone drops by to pick up an item they saw for sale on our Facebook page, and says 'Totally love you guys!' on her way out, which strikes me as a sign that Poor Mandy is selling things far too cheaply. Then Arjun leans his head through from the restaurant and calls for Izzy, finally pulling her away from Louis.

'Are you all right, Izz?' I catch Arjun saying as they walk through to the kitchen.

He glances back at me. I wonder how much she's told him.

'I'm fine! It's chopped parsley you want, right?' Izzy says brightly, because of course she already knows exactly what he needs.

'I'm shooting my shot with Izzy today, you know,' Louis says to me. He leans forward on the desk, watching Izzy disappear through the restaurant doors with Arjun. 'Got high hopes.'

'Have you?' I snap, not even bothering to veil the dislike in my voice – I don't have the energy. 'I thought you two were finished.'

He gives a coy smile. 'This thing with Izzy's been slow-building since last December – we've had the odd setback, but . . .'

I grip the back of my desk chair, breathing too fast.

'Last December?'

'Yeah. When I first came to the hotel.' He fiddles idly with the cord on my telephone. 'She told me how she felt about me then.'

My whole body flinches, knuckles turning white on the back of the chair.

'I had a girlfriend at that point, so I didn't act on it, but I kept the card she sent me.' Louis pats the back pocket of his trousers. 'I'm going to whip it out today. Win her round once and for all. Nothing says romance like holding on to a love letter for a whole year, does it?'

I don't know what to say. I am staring at Louis' back pocket, desperate to read this card, playing the words Izzy said over and over as my heart races. *I've been clear with Louis that there is nothing romantic between us and there never will be.*

Louis must be mistaken. He must be.

'What did . . . What did her card say?'

Slowly, with deliberation, Louis pulls out a battered Christmas card from his pocket. He waves it at me with a cheeky grin. This fake heart-to-heart we are having makes my skin crawl.

'Says she's *infatuated*. Gets hot every time we cross paths at the hotel. Wants to kiss me under the mistletoe.' He shrugs. 'I get why she's colder this year – we need to build the trust. I didn't reply to the card, did I? Probably hurt her feelings. But there's been that spark between us once, and that sort of thing doesn't just go away. She's single, she's made that clear, so . . .'

I know why he's telling me this. He's marking out his territory, playing his move so I know there's no use me playing mine. We may be standing here in smart shirts talking politely, but really we're fighting like stags.

'Anyway. Wish me luck, lad,' Louis says with a wink, and then he claps me on the arm.

I twitch. I am one scrap of self-control away from spinning around and punching him in the stomach.

'See ya,' he says, strolling away with a smile.

That's it. It's finished. If there's even anything to finish. I was never hers and she was never mine, so I suppose there's no break-up here. Just me, opening myself up to someone who's chosen someone else.

And why wouldn't she? Despite everything I've done, when she looks at me, she sees a man who's not good enough. And for all the effort I've made to fight those feelings, for all the times I've hung up on my uncle and told myself *you're doing great*, it's really fucking hard to believe I'm worth something when the woman I love thinks a *cuzão* like Louis is a better man than me.

I look up to find Mr Townsend watching me. I turn away sharply, aware of the tears in my eyes.

'Son,' he says, 'are you all right?'

I breathe out slowly, trying to get control of myself. 'No,' I say. 'I'm not. I want to go home.'

Izzy

No. No no no no no no no.

Louis and I are in the turret room, at the window where Lucas gave me Brazilian food and introduced me to his family. The sun is setting above the trees, gorgeous in powder pink.

I have the card in my hands. *The* card. It has two cute penguins on the front, both wearing Christmas hats. I never thought I would see this card again.

It's a lot smaller than I remember. I am holding it with my fingertips, as though at any moment it might explode.

'Louis.'

I open the card and in comes a wave of shame and humiliation as I remember writing it, how brave I'd felt. Putting myself out there. Being bold. Living life to the fullest, just like my parents always wanted.

Dear Lucas, it says. *I have a confession to make.*

'Louis . . . This wasn't your Christmas card.'

For the first time since I've known Louis, he looks unsure of himself.

'Pardon?' he says, ducking his head to look at it with me.

'Lucas.' I press my hand to my forehead. *Oh my God.* 'I wrote this for *Lucas*.'

'Then why does it say . . .' He trails off. 'You have really bad handwriting,' he says after a moment, and there's an edge to his voice now.

'I am so sorry, Louis.'

'So it's Lucas you want, then,' Louis says, stepping back slightly. The sunset bathes us in rosy light; it's a very romantic setting. I suppose that's why he got the card out. The perfect moment. 'It's always been him?'

The question floors me. Because . . . well, yes, it has, really. I've cursed him and crossed him and kissed him, but yeah, it's always been him, hasn't it? Nobody has ever made my cosy warm heart beat the way he does.

I was infatuated then, and if I am entirely honest with myself, I'm infatuated now.

And he never knew. He *never knew*.

'I really am so sorry, Louis. But I need to go, I've got to . . .'

He frowns, interrupting me. 'Your colleague, that sorry-for-herself one, she gave the card to me. She said it was for me.'

I wince. Poor Mandy has never complained about my handwriting, but Lucas always says she gets him to translate half the stuff I write down. I thought he was exaggerating. It's always perfectly clear to *me*.

'I guess she must've read it wrong too. I'm sorry.'

Louis' expression shifts. He seems to go from affable to calculating in a flash.

'Does Mrs SB know you and Lucas have been getting off with each other on company time?'

I stare at him. 'What? No, she . . . But we haven't been . . .'

I trail off. Because, well, we have, a bit.

'What are you going to do?' I ask. 'Dob me in?'

I'm kind of joking, but Louis just looks at me appraisingly for a moment.

'Do you know how many women would kill to have me take them to The Angel's Wing?'

'Excuse me?'

'You think you're really special, Izzy, with your multicoloured hair and your cute "mission" to save this hotel. But the truth is you're just a mousey little nobody in a dead-end job. It's kind of sad.'

My mouth drops open. Louis' nastiness is so sudden and so unexpected that his words don't really land at all – in fact, as he slicks back his hair and adjusts his expensive jacket, I find myself wanting to laugh at him.

'A mousey little nobody? Oh, Louis.' I shake my head, shoving the card into my back pocket. 'You know what's really sad? The fact that you seem to think you're somebody.'

I spin towards the door, already moving. I don't have time for this slimeball – I need to find Lucas. I need to explain. God, what's he been thinking all this time? What was he thinking when we had that screaming match after the Christmas party last year? What was he thinking when I said I hated him, couldn't trust him, never would?

I want to cry. It's as if the last year has shifted like an optical illusion, and suddenly I'm seeing a completely different picture. I just – I just *have* to find Lucas.

Poor Mandy is settling in at the desk, Mr Townsend is in his chair, the motley collection of builders are mostly on ladders, and three restaurant guests are making their way to the door. But no Lucas in sight.

It's half four – I've never known him leave early before. Typical. I hover in front of the desk for a moment, craning my neck to look for his car in the car park, but it's not in his usual spot – he'll have gone home, to the gym, or to Smooth Pedro's. My money is on the gym, and I'm itching to get into Smartie and chase him down, but . . .

'Mandy,' I say, turning to look at her.

'Oh, God, Izzy, I'm so sorry!' she blurts instantly.

She covers her face with her hands. I stare at her.

'You know, don't you?' she says, peeking out between her fingers. 'I promise you, I only figured out what happened the other day when Lucas told me I'd misread Louis' name on your handover notes. I *swear* it was an accident.'

'You knew this had happened and didn't tell me?' I say, voice rising. I clutch the edge of the desk. 'Mandy!'

'I'm so sorry! I just couldn't – I couldn't . . . What good would it do now?'

'A lot, actually,' I say, closing my eyes. All those times I worked so hard to keep my walls up . . . All those times I assumed Lucas was being an arsehole . . .

'If it helps, I've paid for the mistake every day, working with you and Lucas while you're at each other's throats, the two of you kicking me back and forth between you . . . Not that I'm complaining!' she says hurriedly.

I place my palms flat on the desk and look at her, hunched over the keyboard, her glasses trembling on their chain. I remember what Mrs Hedgers said about Mandy, how she struggles to assert herself, and suddenly – despite all of the frustration coursing through me right now – I want to give her a hug.

Poor Mandy. It can't be easy.

'Mandy,' I say, 'you have every right to complain.'

'Oh, no, I . . .'

'No, listen to me. Speak *up*. If Lucas and I drive you nuts, tell us. If you prefer the online system to the booking book, say so. If you realise you've made a mistake handing out my Christmas cards and have given some bellend the card in which I declare my love for someone else entirely, *tell me*. This isn't even your fault, Mandy, it's my stupid handwriting, but you have made things so much worse by sitting on this!'

'Have I? Have I really?' She looks wretched. 'I've thought about this nonstop, you know. That'll be why he didn't mind kissing that friend of yours under the mistletoe, won't it?'

'Yes,' I say, my toes literally curling at the thought of all the times I've told Lucas he was a dickhead for kissing Drew. I scrunch up my eyes, wishing I could take back every time I tried to make Lucas feel small this year in an effort to make myself feel bigger.

'Excuse me, Izzy,' Mr Townsend says, straining to stand.

I shoot over to help him out of his armchair, ignoring the teeny flutter of irritation I feel at the diversion. Mr Townsend has sat here so often we just leave his reading glasses on the side table now, and there's a Mr Townsend-shaped dip in the cushion. If anyone else sits in this armchair, everyone in the lobby tends to look alarmed until the encroacher feels uncomfortable and leaves again.

'I think I may have done something rather unhelpful,' he says, leaning on my arm. 'I couldn't help but overhear . . . As I understand it, the Christmas card that Louis received last year *wasn't* intended for him? And your . . . unique handwriting . . .'

'Yes. The card was meant for Lucas.'

'Ah,' Mr Townsend says, holding his fingers delicately to his lips. 'In that case, you might want to sit down for this, dear.'

I let him transfer his hand from my arm to the back of the armchair, and I take a seat, though sitting down is the last thing I want to do. I'm absolutely buzzing, desperate to find Lucas, desperate to apologise and kiss him and tell him – God. I don't know. Hopefully I'll know when I see him.

'Louis told Lucas,' Mr Townsend says, 'about the card, that is. And . . . Well, Lucas was rather . . .'

'No,' I breathe, gripping the chair's arms. '*No*. Was he really upset?' I stare up at Mr Townsend. This is a *disaster*.

'Devastated, actually. I think he cares for you very deeply, my dear.'

I whimper. When I think of everything I've put Lucas through this year, I can hardly believe he cares about me at all. No wonder he's always snapped back at me when I've given him attitude. He must have thought I was completely unreasonable, hating him without ever offering an explanation. I press the heels of my hands into my eyes, liquid eyeliner forgotten, and curse my stupid pride. Why didn't I just have an adult conversation with him about that Christmas card? Why didn't I just suck up the embarrassment and say, Hey, why *did* you laugh at me for saying I was infatuated with you? And why did you kiss my flatmate under the mistletoe instead of me?

'He said he wanted to go home,' Mr Townsend says.

I glance at the Bartholomew clock above the front desk and do my usual calculations. Lucas will probably be back at his flat by now. At least I know not to waste time going to the gym first.

'Thank you,' I say, moving to stand.

Mr Townsend lays his hand on my shoulder. 'He said he wanted to go *home*,' he says.

I look up at him.

'I explained to Lucas that I am lucky enough to have accumulated a lot of money in my life, and that every Christmas I like to find ways to spend it that bring the world a bit of joy. It's something my wife started with me – we'd sit at our front window and watch the world go by all year, and then by December, we'd have an idea of everyone who needed a helping hand. The little girl who yearned for a bike like her brother's, the lady who wished she could afford to visit her new grandchild . . .'

I reach up and squeeze his hand on the armchair, and he smiles down at me.

'The family whose insurance company won't pay for a few more days at the hotel.'

My eyes widen as the penny drops.

'And the young man who is heartbroken and homesick at Christmas, who can't afford to go back to Brazil.'

Oh. *Oh. Oh, shit.*

I shoot up out of the chair. 'When's his flight, Mr Townsend?'

Mr Townsend looks at the clock. I wait while he does his own calculation – he's been at the hotel long enough to know the drill.

'It departs for Faro from Bournemouth airport in an hour and a half,' he says. 'I'm so sorry, Izzy. I thought it was a good deed.'

I'm already running to the door. 'Don't worry, Mr Townsend! Not your fault!' I yell over my shoulder, and then I stop short at the exit, spinning to look at him. 'When you say lots of money . . . You don't have a spare hundred grand to save the hotel, do you?'

He smiles. 'I'm afraid that is rather too much for me.'

I sag. 'That's OK. It's such a nice thing you do. You've made the Hedgers' Christmas.'

'And ruined yours,' Mr Townsend says wryly.

'Not if I drive very fast!' I call, pushing through the door, wincing at the blast of freezing air. 'And I always drive very fast!'

As far as I can tell from googling while driving (do not recommend, extremely dangerous) – Lucas's flight boards in thirty-eight minutes.

'Move! Move!' I hoot my horn. 'Oh my God, Jem, there's a fucking pony in the way!'

'Ride it?' Jem suggests.

She's on speaker. She rang for entertainment and distraction – she's currently hiding in her parents' spare bedroom with the disgraced Piddles, feeling (as she put it) 'about the size of a frickin Borrower' after a lunch with her overachieving cousins. She was *delighted* when I told her I was actually chasing a man down at an airport, rom-com style.

'Don't be ridiculous, they go at twenty miles an hour, max,' I say, hooting the horn again. 'Oh my God, I'm going to have to get out.'

I yank on the parking brake and tumble out of the car, shooing the horse aside and then running back to Smartie.

'I'm on the move again!' I yell.

Jem gives me a little supportive *whoop*. I slam the brakes on as a pheasant trundles across the road.

'Argh, pheasant! Bloody New Forest wildlife!' I shout. 'These animals have no respect for an epic love story!'

'Maybe that bird is on his way to his one great love,' Jem says. 'Always remember you never know what kind of day someone else is having.'

'Can you not be sickeningly nice, just this one time?'

She laughs. 'You'll make it, little pigeon.'

'I really won't! He'll already be through to departures, I don't know *how* I'm going to find him – how do people do it in films?'

'I dunno, actually,' Jem says thoughtfully, as I climb up the gears, the pheasant having finally reached the other side of the road. 'It involves a lot of running . . . And ducking under things. Or jumping over things.'

'I wish I'd gone to the gym more than once in the last six months,' I say, speeding up. 'He won't answer the phone, so that's out. At least he's tall. He'll be easy to spot in a crowd. I'm just going to have to wing it when I get there. Oh, God, what if he never forgives me for being such a knob?' A wash of fear moves through me. 'What if he doesn't like me any more? What if he's just going to reject me all over again, in front of an airport full of people?'

'Then it'll hurt,' Jem says. 'But you'll handle it.' Her voice softens into its lowest key. 'You can cope with so much more than you think, Izzy. You've coped with the very worst thing in the world.'

I screech around a corner. 'Do you think losing my parents has made me too scared of risking things? I always try to live life to the fullest, you know, but am I not actually doing that at all?'

'You are in so many ways – you're so brave! But letting someone in, loving someone, that's hard for all of us. And you've got the extra challenge of knowing what it feels like to say goodbye to the people you love most. So . . .'

'I'm going to do it, though,' I say, the adrenaline soaring. 'I'm going to tell him I— I'm going to tell him I'm in love with him.'

'Go seize the day, my little pigeon. My romance-loving heart could really do with a happy ending right now.'

I can hear the smile in Jem's voice.

'I'll do my best to deliver,' I promise her, 'and kill as few pheasants as possible in the process.'

'Atta girl.'

In all my wild imaginings of how this airport chase is going to go, I've been envisaging it like *Love Actually* or *Friends*. Sprinting through crowds, shouting Lucas's name, desperate to find him.

I had forgotten what Bournemouth airport is like.

It's basically one room. There's no queue for security – it's all very calm. Slightly wrong-footed, I approach the woman checking tickets and passports.

'Hi! I don't have a ticket! I'm here to tell a man I love him!'

She eyes me. 'Roger,' she calls, without looking away. 'We've got another one!'

Roger appears from somewhere, hitching up his belt. He is very large and looks very bored.

'May I start by saying, do not try to push past me,' Roger says. 'I will catch you immediately and escort you to Bournemouth police station.'

If asking politely doesn't work, pushing past the security guard is my Plan B, so this is a blow.

'Now, which flight is this gentleman on?'

'To Rio de Janeiro!' I say breathlessly.

'Via Faro, then,' Roger says. He checks his watch. 'You're very late,' he says, displeased.

'I know! But – can I just go through and speak to him?'

'No,' says Roger.

'Please?'

This does seem to placate him slightly. Maybe the romantic-declaration types aren't usually big on pleases and thank yous.

'You can't go through without a ticket.'

'Can I buy a ticket to somewhere? Where's cheap?' I say, looking around wildly at the self check-in machines.

'Do you have your passport?' asks the woman at the desk.

'Oh. No.'

'Then no, you can't buy a ticket,' she says.

I shift from foot to foot. 'What can I do?'

They both regard me steadily. They are ruining my momentum here. That flight is boarding right now, and they are talking so *slowly*.

'Look,' I say, pulling the Christmas card out of my back pocket. 'Here. Last year, I wrote this card for the man I love, to tell him how I feel about him. I really put my heart on the line. And then I *thought* he read the card and laughed at it and kissed my flatmate under the mistletoe instead. But he didn't! The card went to the wrong person, because people are really crap at reading handwritten notes, and I've been torturing this lovely man all year because I thought he was a dickhead and he *wasn't*.'

'Your handwriting is awful,' Roger observes. 'Is that supposed to be a C?'

'Aww, *cosy warm heart*,' says the woman. 'That's sweet.'

'Right?' I say desperately. I'll take whatever wins I can get. 'Can I go through? Explain the whole thing to him before he flies off to Brazil and never comes back?'

'No,' Roger says.

I just about refrain from screaming in irritation.

'Do you know what you want to say to him?' the woman asks.

'No,' I say. 'Not at all. But I'll know when I see him.'

The woman sucks her teeth.

'That won't do,' she says.

'What do you mean?'

'Well, there's one way we can put you in touch with this gent,' she says. 'But you'll really need to know what it is you want to say.'

Lucas

'*Attention all passengers for flight 10220 to Faro . . .*'

I try to eat another mouthful of my WHSmith sandwich. It makes me think of Izzy, and our trip to London together, when we had bought food at Waterloo before our train journey to Woking. How I'd realised what she meant to me that day – how obvious it had seemed.

I find it very sad that I am triggered by WHSmith, especially as there is nowhere else to buy a good sandwich right now.

'*We have a message for Lucas da Silva.*'

I freeze, sandwich halfway to my mouth.

'*Dear Lucas.*'

Que porra é essa?

'*I have a confession to make. Last year, I wrote you a Christmas card.*'

Is this some sort of cruel joke?

'*I told you I was infatuated. That every time we crossed paths in the hotel . . .*'

It must be. I set down my sandwich, heat rushing to my face.

'*I felt hot and jittery. I asked you to meet me under the mistletoe at the Christmas party.*'

This is her card to Louis. It's all the parts he quoted to me, with that sly smile on his face. I want to press my hands to my ears, but it won't block out the woman reading the message over the tannoy – it's too loud. There's no escaping it.

'*You were there when I arrived. Under the mistletoe. But you were kissing someone else.*'

The woman beside me tuts. I look around – everyone is doing the same, looking for Lucas da Silva, presumably. I have a creeping sense of strangeness, as though everything I think I know is shifting, but I'm not there yet – I still don't understand.

'*I was heartbroken. Humiliated. And I took it out on you. I thought you were heartless and cruel. I spent a whole year avoiding you, one-upping you, making your life as difficult as possible. But Lucas . . .*'

I jump at the repetition of my name. I was just beginning to think this message must surely be for someone else. Because if it's from Izzy – if that card was meant for me . . .

'*You didn't deserve that. Any of it. Because you never got that card – it went to the wrong person.*'

I drop my head into my hands. It can't be. Surely it can't be.

'*So this time around, I'm going to be completely upfront. I'm still jittery every time I see you. I'm still infatuated – more infatuated than ever. In fact, there are a whole lot of things I want to say to you that I don't think you should hear via Lydia on the tannoy – that's me, by the way.*'

A few people around me laugh. There are smiles, now, and someone is filming this on their phone.

'So meet me under the Airport Security sign right now, Lucas da Silva. It's not quite mistletoe. But it will have to do. Yours, Izzy.'

I'm running. Jumping suitcases, hurdling over people's outstretched legs, dodging my way through duty free. As I sprint back through security, a guard gives me a nod and a smile, but I'm looking for Izzy, Izzy, Izzy, my heart thumping her name.

She's there. A little bedraggled, still in her uniform, her bag at her feet. Something soars in me at the sight of her.

She runs the moment she sees me. We both come to a stop as we hit the belt barriers, dithering; I move to zigzag my way through them but Izzy ducks under, scuttling through, and I laugh, opening my arms to her.

She throws herself at me. I'm almost knocked backwards.

'Lucas, oh my God.'

I hold her, breathe her in.

'I'm so sorry.'

'That card . . . It was meant for me?'

She pulls back for long enough to tug it out of her back pocket and hand it to me.

'Merry Christmas,' she says. 'Sorry it's late.'

I kiss her. Without thought, without question, without wondering how to play this or whether it's the right move – I just scoop her into my arms and press my lips to hers. I can feel her shaking against me, the slight chill of tears on her cheeks. We've kissed so many times, but not once have we kissed like this, with neither of us holding any part of ourselves back.

There's applause around us. We break apart, sheepish, and find a man and woman in uniform watching us like indulgent parents. Lydia and a colleague, I presume. I look back down at Izzy. She's so beautiful, with her hair striped in pink and her make-up all smudged from kissing me.

'Hi,' I whisper to her.

'Hi,' she whispers back. 'There is so much I want to say to you right now.'

'Izzy,' I say. 'There are so many times this winter that I've wanted to tell you I . . .'

I trail off. She is pressing her finger to my lips.

'Me first,' she says, with fierceness. 'I love you. I am completely, helplessly, undeniably in love with you. And I am so sorry about the stupid card. Poor Mandy said you got it and laughed at it. I really thought you didn't give a shit about my feelings. I thought you'd had every opportunity to apologise for the way you'd acted, and you genuinely didn't think you'd done anything wrong. It all just seemed like such a red flag that I . . . I wrote you off completely. I decided you were an arsehole and I didn't want to let anything change my mind, because . . . I think it's because I try to be – I want to be *strong*, and look after myself . . .' She buries her face into my chest and holds me tightly as she cries. 'I am so, so sorry.'

'Izzy, shh, you're OK. It's OK.'

I sit with what she's said as I press my lips to the top of her head, the airport bustle resuming around us. What would I have thought, in her position? I would have trusted Mandy's word too. I would have assumed the worst of Izzy, because it's easy to believe someone would laugh at you. Easier than believing they'd love you back.

And was I all that different? I never gave Izzy the opportunity to explain why she was so upset by my kiss with Drew. I returned from Brazil to find her cold and argumentative; the way she treated me confirmed everything I already thought of myself, so I snapped back when she snapped at me, and suddenly that was all the two of us did. I decided Izzy was unreasonable, difficult, over dramatic. I wrote her off too.

'You thought I chose to kiss Drew under the mistletoe instead of you,' I say slowly, piecing it together.

'Mmhmm,' she says into my coat. Her sobs have calmed, and her shoulders are steady now, but she won't lift her gaze to mine.

'Izzy,' I say, pulling back and raising my spare hand to her cheek, nudging her to look up at me. I don't want her to spend a single second thinking I'd want anyone but her. 'That kiss meant absolutely nothing. We met, we flirted a little, and then she said, *Hey, look, mistletoe*, and I thought, why not? If I had received that card, I would never, ever have kissed her.'

'Well, it doesn't really matter,' Izzy says through her tears. 'Because I fell in love with you anyway. Even though I tried *so* hard not to.'

Someone clears their throat behind us, and we pull apart, turning to look.

'You want that exchanged?' Lydia says, pointing to the ticket I'm still clutching in my right hand. 'Because a . . .' She consults the note in her hand. 'A Mister Townsend just rang and said if you don't take this flight, he'll be one good deed down, so he'd

354

like us to exchange it for an extra ticket for your February trip instead. Made no sense to me, but we'll do it if you want it.'

'An extra ticket for . . .'

I glance down at Izzy. She wipes her cheeks with hands that are red with cold.

'Would you like to come to Niterói in February?' I ask her, ducking so my nose brushes hers, my arms still looped around her.

'You want to take me home to meet your family?' Her hands tighten around my waist.

'Izzy – of course I do.' I swallow, fighting the urge to shut my emotions down. 'I want you to be *part* of my family.'

Her face breaks into a wide smile – a genuine one, a smile that makes her eyes bright.

'Oh my God. I'd love to come.'

I kiss her again. My heart is pounding. For a moment it feels too frightening to say the words I want to say out loud. But then I open my eyes and look at Izzy, tear-stained and windswept, her face upturned to mine. After weeks of holding herself back, she's all here. I want to be the same.

'I love you, Izzy Jenkins.'

'Even my tacky pink trainers?' Izzy asks, through a tearful laugh. She clutches my arms.

'I love your pink trainers.'

'Even my messy little car?'

'I love Smartie. She's yours.'

'Even my handwriting?'

I start laughing, pulling her into my chest again. 'Hmm,' I

say, kissing her forehead, her hair, every part of her I can reach. 'Maybe give me a day or two on that one.'

We can't stop touching each other. Izzy suggests car sex again, and tries to argue that there'd be a 'symmetry' to this. We bicker about whether this is or is not romantic from the airport to the edge of the forest, and I love it. In one dizzy rush – like that moment in Shannon's flat – I realise I want to squabble with Izzy for the rest of my life. Except this time, when that emotion hits me, there's nothing ruining it. She doesn't hate me. She doesn't want Louis. She wants me.

'Wait,' I say, and she brakes slightly. 'No, I mean . . . On the phone. You said Louis is still a contender. Still in the game.'

'Well, he is, I think,' Izzy says, then she pulls a face. 'If I haven't put him off.' She turns to me in the silence that follows this. 'What? Why are you giving me your arch-nemesis face?'

'I thought . . . me and you . . . Are you my girlfriend?' I blurt. My heart is pounding again, those old feelings never far away.

'Yes! Aren't I? After the unbelievably romantic airport I-love-you thing?' She looks panicked. 'Have I misunderstood?'

'Have I?'

'Hang on,' Izzy says. 'This is always where we go off the rails. Tell me what you think is going on. I'll tell you what I think is going on. We will continue to talk about it until we are both on the same page and everything is sorted out. This is how we do things now, OK?'

'OK,' I say, loosening my clenched fists and taking a breath. 'What did you mean when you said Louis is still a contender?'

'I meant he's still thinking of investing in the hotel. Grigg and Sameera had asked for an update on the job, so . . .'

Oh.

Understanding dawns on Izzy's face.

'No, you didn't! Lucas! This is why you shouldn't listen in on phone conversations. God!'

'Noted,' I say, clinging to the door handle as Izzy pulls in for a car coming the other way.

She's not an *unsafe* driver, but she does go very, very fast. Her phone buzzes, screen lighting up.

'Would you mind checking that for me?' she says, nodding to her phone. 'It might be Jem. She'll be wanting her happy-ending update.'

I can't help a smile at the gesture of trust – yesterday, Izzy would never have let me look at her phone. I take it from the cup holder between us. There's one message, from Louis.

Hi Izzy. I've just let Mrs SB know that another investment opportunity has come up and my dad and I think it's a better fit for us. Good luck, no hard feelings. Cheers, Louis.

I read it out to Izzy.

'No hard feelings?' she says. '*What a—*'

'*Merda.*' I clap a hand to my mouth. Thinking about the hotel has reminded me of something important. '*Eu pedi demissão.* I resigned!'

'What?' Izzy stares over at me in horror. 'From the hotel?'

'Yes! I emailed Mrs SB my letter of resignation at the airport.'

'Well, unresign!' Izzy says. 'How am I meant to do my job without you getting in my way all the time? Call her! Call her!'

She points at her phone in my hand. I dial Mrs SB's number and switch to loudspeaker.

'Izzy!' Mrs SB shouts. 'Are you with Lucas?'

We exchange a glance.

'Yes, actually,' Izzy says. 'How did you—'

'Louis told me you're a couple!'

Both our eyes narrow in unison.

'Louis?' I say, incredulous.

'That can wait!' Mrs SB yells. 'Lucas! Barty and I are racing to the airport to stop you. You can't leave, Lucas, you mustn't. If I could offer you a pay rise, I would, or some job security of longer than two weeks, frankly, but – please! It's not over yet!'

'You're racing to the airport?' I repeat, checking the time on the dashboard. 'My flight departed forty minutes ago.'

'What? Did it? Barty!'

'It's the time difference!' Barty protests in the background. 'It's very confusing!'

'He's not leaving, Mrs SB,' Izzy says, with a smile in her voice. 'I'm bringing him home.'

'Izzy, you *angel*. If there's a Forest Manor Hotel in the world, it needs you two in it, do you hear me?'

Both our smiles waver at the reminder of reality. The likelihood is there will be no job to return to within a matter of days.

'Stop thinking negative thoughts!' Mrs SB says. 'I can hear them from here. We still have *days* left to save the hotel. It's not too late. We've not sold some of the larger antiques yet, and there's your last ring, too . . .'

Izzy pulls a face. Clearly she's doing no better than me at finding the mysterious Goldilocks.

'Forest Manor Hotel is a survivor,' Mrs SB says. 'She sheltered sixty children from the Blitz in her day. She's weathered storms and pandemics and more expensive structural damage than this, let me tell you. We *will* be open in the new year.'

'What was it you said about Louis, Mrs SB?' Izzy asks.

'Oh, yes. He came in and told me you were romantically involved. He seemed to be under the impression that I'd fire you both,' Mrs SB says. 'He was most disappointed when Barty and I cheered loudly enough to bring the ceiling down all over again. I don't know *what* that young man thinks he's up to, but since this afternoon, he's also contacted the local press with a story about our front desk going unmanned and sent the food safety inspector around.'

'What?' Izzy says, startled. 'That vindictive little . . . *weasel!*'

'Don't worry,' Barty shouts. 'Even *The Forest Local News* didn't think that story was worth printing. And you know the inspector has a soft spot for Arjun's truffles. He's been installed on table sixteen for hours.'

I can't resist. 'I told you Louis was a dickhead,' I say.

'Brace yourself, Lucas, because I'm only going to say this once,' Izzy tells me. 'You were *absolutely* right.'

Izzy

Lucas's flat is so familiar now – the creak of the leather sofa, the smell of his shower gel from the morning, the hum of the electric heater he puts on for me because I feel the cold more than he does. But as we turn to face each other on the sofa, so much is different. Now that I know the truth about last Christmas, I can see how tightly it was always holding me back. I'd never given myself over to him the way I am now – I've never *relaxed* like this, guard fully down.

'Do you think it will be different now?' I ask quietly, taking one of his hands and pulling it to my lap. I run my fingers over his, tracing his knuckles, then the lines of his palm. 'Between us?'

'Maybe. More intense.'

I flick my gaze up to his. *More* intense?

'Mm,' he says, with a small, slow smile. 'I know.'

'Can I ask you about something?' I run my nails lightly back and forth across his forearm.

He watches my hand. 'Of course. Anything.'

'Your ex. Camila.'

He stays still. I slide my hand back to lace my fingers through his.

'I'm listening now. Will you tell me about what happened with her?'

'It's nothing big,' he says, and his eyes flick up to my face as I shake my head.

'I think maybe it is.'

'She just . . . It was my fault, really. I found it difficult to open up to her. She read it as lack of feeling.' He shrugs. 'Lots of people see me that way.'

Including me, for the last year. I swallow, my throat suddenly dry.

'But actually, you feel *big*,' I say, lifting my hand to his chest. 'But it's all stuck in there. Right?'

He snorts lightly but doesn't deny it.

'And she cheated on you?'

'Yes. That's how it ended. She said, *You don't have a heart, so don't tell me I broke it.*'

I inhale sharply. Not because it's cruel – though it is – but because I could imagine myself having said it once. Lucas *can* seem heartless: he's so logical, and so inscrutable, and so bloody *muscly*, and for some reason all those things in combination read as a certain kind of guy. The uptight robot-man. The guy you sleep with but nothing more, because that's all he's got to give you.

But Lucas is the man who makes Ruby Hedgers laugh until

she snorts. He's the man who heard my Christmas plans and said, *I know how it feels to be away from your family at Christmas*, because he understood that my friends *are* my family now. He's made my blood boil, and my body burn, but he's also made me laugh and challenge myself and have real fun. He is a hell of a lot more than he looks.

'Deep down, I think you're *all* heart,' I whisper, shifting closer.

He gives me a small smile at that.

'And I get that it's made you a little prickly about cheating. But I do need you to trust me. Even if I'm chatting with a guy.' I laugh as he winces. 'Lucas.'

'Yes, I know. I do trust you. I do. I'm sorry.'

'And I know I've jumped to conclusions more times than I can count in the last year – I've always assumed the worst of you,' I say, looking down at our twined hands. 'I was horrible when you told me about your hotel management course, and then when you tried to open up about Camila . . . I just couldn't fit it together with the guy I was so sure you were. It freaked me out that you were . . . I don't know. I needed you to be a dickhead, so that I could stop myself from falling in love with you. But you kept being lovely and interesting.'

He squeezes my hand for a moment and then lets go, letting me explore him, my fingers tracing up to his elbow, his bicep.

'I promise to think the best of you from this moment on. To ask you if I think you've done something hurtful. I promise never to be unkind.' I smile slightly. 'Though I kind of like that you've seen that side of me. The worst of me. People tend to think I'm super nice, and I do try to be, obviously, but . . .

Sometimes everyone's a bit of a bitch, aren't they? I get a bit exhausted trying to keep it up nonstop without ever slipping up and swearing at bad drivers or complaining about guests, you know?'

'Ah, yes,' Lucas says, and his bicep flexes under my palm. 'Angelic Izzy. I never thought you were that, by the way. Not even when you were nice to me.'

I laugh. 'No?'

'No. You have . . .' He reaches for my other hand, the one that isn't working its way over the muscles of his arm, and pulls me closer, until one of his knees crosses over mine. 'You have too much bite to be an angel. Too much sting.'

I take the invitation and lean forward to press my teeth to his neck, then suck – not hard enough to leave a mark, but hard enough to make him chuckle and pull me against him until I climb up into his lap. He wraps his arms around me, and I feel something new. He's held me like this before – my legs framing his, his face buried in my neck – but this time having his arms around me settles something that I didn't know needed settling. I feel safe.

'*Meu amor*,' he whispers, his lips against my ear. 'My love.'

I close my eyes and move against him. It still feels frightening to tell him I love him, even with his arms locked around me, holding me tight, urging me forward, back. But I've made my mind up. No more easy options – I want this, the bright, explosive joy of it. I want to say those words every day.

'I love you,' I whisper.

'*Eu te amo*,' he whispers back, and then he lifts his mouth to

363

mine, and I have to still my hips for a moment, because the kiss is almost too much with the taste of those words on his tongue.

He's right. It is more intense. He takes me to his bedroom and we whisper it all night: *eu te amo. I love you.* By the morning I feel changed. Lucas has always shaken me up, leaving me furious, frenzied, weak with wanting, whatever it might be. But now it's different. Now he holds me steady, too.

As much as I wish that card hadn't gone astray, I can't regret the last year. We know each other so well now. This isn't the culmination of a few stolen glances at work, it's a relationship that's been twisting and turning for over a year, and I know it'll be stronger for it.

He makes me coffee and brings it to me in bed, naked, slow, letting me look. I pull him to me, and he settles his head against my chest, watching the rain come down through the window.

'We have so much to do,' he says, without particular intent. His fingers find mine, lacing over my stomach. 'Christmas party tomorrow.'

'And just over a week until it's all over. New Year's.'

He sighs. 'I don't know what I'll do. I've applied for some receptionist roles nearby, but . . .'

I sit up, looking down at him. 'You and I pretty much run Forest Manor. You can't go back to receptionist work now – you deserve something in management.'

'Then I would have to look further away.' His hand tightens on mine. 'And I don't want to. I like it here.'

I squeeze his hand back.

'And you're right: you and I *do* pretty much run Forest Manor,' he says, looking serious. 'And you hate waitressing.' He raises his eyebrows.

'Yeah, I've thought about that a lot.' I bite my lip. 'Honestly, I don't want to take a waitressing job. But I don't want to move either. I just *wish* we could find a way to keep the hotel going. Maybe if we find Goldilocks . . .'

His stubble rasps against my bare skin as he lifts his head to look at me. 'We will keep trying,' he says. 'Maybe we can do it together.'

'Excuse me?' I say, pulling back in outrage. 'You may be my boyfriend now, but that bet is still on.'

He winces. 'Really?'

'You want to concede and wear the elf outfit?'

'. . . No.'

'Well then.' I kiss him on the nose. 'In that case, I'm still planning to kick your arse at this.'

Lucas

It's Christmas Eve: party day, and my second day as Izzy Jenkins' boyfriend.

I am the sort of happy I would have previously considered unobtainable – and I am very close to making today absolutely perfect.

'If you could just try to remember ...' I say, glancing up towards the hotel's main entrance.

'Are you actually calling me at eight in the morning on Christmas Eve to ask me if I remember a celebrity staying on my floor at your hotel in 2019?' says the woman on the other end of the line.

It is a refreshing and necessary reminder that I might be trying a *bit* too hard.

'My apologies,' I say. 'If anything comes to mind, please do get in touch by email.'

'Right,' the woman says, and I wince at the *click* as she hangs up.

'No luck?' Poor Mandy says sympathetically, popping up from the front of the desk, where she is doing what Izzy refers to as 'festooning'. Everyone is either festooning for Izzy or chopping vegetables for Arjun right now.

'No luck,' I say.

Poor Mandy pats my arm. She has been patting me a lot since the Christmas-card debacle was cleared up. I think she feels responsible for Izzy and me torturing one another for a year. Which she is, a bit.

'Do you know what, dear?' Mandy says, beginning the arduous process of checking her phone: glasses coming down from her head, hand going into her pocket, a lot of wriggling and bouncing up and down in her chair as she eases the phone out from her jeans, the case flipping open, her glasses dropping down her nose and up again . . . 'I may be able to help you.'

I appreciate Poor Mandy – she is always reliable, she's very popular with the guests, and she works all the worst shifts. But I am almost certain that her idea will involve tweeting to our 112 followers, and I simply cannot see that helping.

'Thank you,' I say. 'Feel free to try.'

'Any luck?' Ollie calls as he dashes past with a tray of jellies.

'Not yet,' I call after him. 'Do you know if Izzy is having—'

'I'm Switzerland!' Ollie yells over his shoulder. 'You're getting nothing out of me!'

'Anything on the ring?' Barty calls down the newly functioning stairs as he dashes along the landing. Everyone is dashing today. It is giving the hotel a faint buzz, as though someone has dialled all the appliances up at once.

'Not yet,' I call. Everyone's support is appreciated, but also, when I have no updates, slightly irritating.

'Lucas! Anything on the—'

'Not yet!' I snap, and then look up to find the cool gaze of my girlfriend.

'—Christmas party menu that's vegan?'

'Oh.'

I soften instantly. Izzy looks amused.

'Yes. Here.'

I show her Arjun's latest scribbled version of the menu. She scans over it and I watch, hungry for the sight of her. All that time I spent thinking I could do without Izzy Jenkins in my day, and now I truly cannot have too much of her.

'Have we—'

'Yes. They're set up in the orangery.'

She taps her bottom lip, still scanning the menu.

'Does Arjun know about the—'

'Yes. He swore a lot, but we got through it.'

Izzy nods. She looks up at me.

'And—'

'Yes.'

'I didn't actually—'

'I am confident that it is already done.'

'It's not, because—'

'Have a cup of tea. Stop thinking so hard.'

'I was going to say, have I told you that I love you today?'

'Oh. No. You haven't.'

'See?' She looks smug as she turns away. 'Told you it wasn't all done yet. Mr Townsend! How can I help you?'

Mr Townsend is making his way over from his armchair. He is doing a remarkably good job of dodging various members of the housekeeping team, as well as a small chihuahua that arrived with Dinah today. 'Doggy daycare problems,' she announced as she walked in with it on a lead. 'Do not give me shit about this.'

'It's Lucas I need, actually,' Mr Townsend says. 'Will you join me in the orangery? I'd like to try out those new sofas.'

He smiles as he takes my arm.

'Oh, fine!' Izzy says, shooting me an arch look, as if to say, *So you're the favourite now!*

I raise my eyebrows back at her – *Of course I am.* Then my phone buzzes in my hand, and I look down to see *Antônio calling.* My breath hitches. It's Saturday. I didn't phone him on Thursday. I didn't forget – I just didn't want to.

And I don't want to speak to him now, either. I have noticed that the more I value myself, the less grateful I feel to my uncle, and the more I wonder why I put myself through these conversations at all. For now, for a while, he will have to wait until I feel ready to talk to him.

The call rings out as Mr Townsend and I make our way through to the orangery. I exhale slowly.

'I have something for you,' Mr Townsend says, as I settle him on a sofa.

Izzy found this sofa on Gumtree, being sold . . . by us. It's an old one from Opal Cottage – once a bold shade of red, it is now russet and faded, but somehow it has come to life again under the patterned cushion covers that Izzy created from an old set of hotel curtains. She has such a gift for this: bringing out the best in things.

'Here.' Mr Townsend opens his palm. The emerald ring sits in the folds of his hand, circling the point where his lifeline splits. 'It's for you. Or rather, it's for her.'

Ai, meu Deus.

'Mr Townsend . . .'

'I've been carrying it around since we went to Budgens, not knowing what to do with it. The fact is, it doesn't quite belong to me any more. That's how it feels. Because Maisie lost it and replaced it. The ring she wore on the day she died was hers, and this one . . . It was lying in wait for someone else to find it, perhaps.'

'I can't possibly . . . And it's far too soon . . .'

Mr Townsend looks up at me shrewdly. 'Is it? I only met my Maisie a dozen times before we were married.'

'But these days . . .'

'Oh, yes, these days, these days.' Mr Townsend waves his other hand. 'Some things change, but love doesn't. When you know . . .'

You know. I understand why people say that about love now: there's no quantifying this. It is too enormous – too dizzyingly deep.

And it's true that I've thought of marrying her. If I could, if this world were perfect, I'd dredge the ocean for that ring from her father, the one she lost, and I'd get down on one knee and hand it to her. But this world isn't perfect, and neither am I.

Sometimes things are lost, and you grieve for them, and they change you, and that's OK.

It might not be perfect to propose with the emerald ring, but it *would* be beautiful. It has a story – a legacy. It's part of the family she found here at the hotel.

'I can't possibly accept this from you,' I say, but even I can hear that my voice is a little less convincing now.

'Keep it in your pocket until you need it,' Mr Townsend says, just as Mrs Hedgers enters the room, trailing tinsel behind her.

'Sorry to interrupt,' she says as she leans to tape one end of the tinsel to the edge of the window frame. 'Izzy's orders.'

Mr Townsend presses the ring into my hand and cups it in his own. I shake in his grasp, and we stay like this, both holding that ring; for a moment it holds two messy love stories inside its loop. Then Mr Townsend removes his hands, and it's just one love story. Mine, for a while. Until I give it to Izzy, and it becomes hers.

For an unpleasant half-hour, it seems nobody will come to the Christmas party. Our invitations suggested a start time of 2 p.m. – Izzy wanted the children to be part of the celebration. The plan was that people would come and go when it suited them.

But it doesn't seem to be suiting them to come at all.

'They'll turn up,' Izzy says, adjusting yet another candle.

She has done a beautiful job in here. We've made the lobby the centre point of the party – it's where the face painting and the magician are set up, along with the live band, a collection of jazz musicians who once played a wedding here and have been kind enough to help us out with a cut-price performance. The buffet is through in the restaurant, and our bar is filled with comfortable seating. Ollie is in charge of cocktails in the orangery, a role that he accepted with much grumbling and thinly disguised delight.

I doubt Izzy can tell, but I am even more nervous about this party than she is. My Christmas present for her will be revealed tonight, and I am having sudden terrors that I didn't get it right. After all, I planned it before the two of us got together. And I've taken a bit of a risk.

'Rather quiet, isn't it?' Mr Townsend says, shuffling over.

Izzy looks irritated, then melts when she realises it's Mr Townsend speaking.

'They'll come,' she says. 'Where are the Hedgers? They always bring the fun. Lucas, will you give them a knock?' On seeing my expression, she adds, 'It's not intrusive, it's helpful! I promise they won't mind.'

I shoot her an unconvinced look and get a tongue-out face in return. I head to Sweet Pea. Mrs Hedgers opens the door: she looks completely different from the woman I saw just a couple of hours ago, in the orangery. Her hair is loose around her shoulders for the first time since I've known her, and there are tear tracks on her cheeks.

'Oh, I'm so sorry,' I say, already backing away, but she beckons me in and wheels herself back inside. I have no choice but to catch the door and follow her or let it shut behind her.

I step inside, feeling uneasy. I don't enter rooms while guests are present, generally – it feels like I am doing the same thing Louis did when he stepped behind the front desk.

'Lucas,' she says, reaching up to the dresser for the tissues and neatly blowing her nose. 'I was hoping to catch you, actually. The children are in the gardens with my husband, burning off some energy before they're expected to socialise with people who may not appreciate the degree of barging that takes place on a regular Hedgers-family Saturday.'

'I don't want to intrude,' I say, already backing towards the door.

'Stay,' Mrs Hedgers says.

It's more command than request. I do as I'm told, holding my hands behind my back, hovering in front of the door.

'My husband finally told me what Mr Townsend did for us. And do you know what I felt? I felt irritated. Irritated that we'd had to accept charity and irritated that I hadn't *won*. I hadn't beaten the insurance company. It hadn't gone my way.'

'I'm sorry,' I say. 'I can understand that.'

She smiles, sniffing. 'I know you can. You like to get things done and you like perfection.'

I incline my head. 'Thank you.'

'It wasn't precisely a compliment,' she says, patting at the cushions on the settee until they're lined up just right. 'I'm the same. And I'm brilliant at what I do. But I'm not brilliant at everything, and I find that very hard. Is this ringing any bells?'

I believe I am being Mrs Hedgers-ed.

'Yes,' I admit. 'I'm ... I can be ... uncompromising.'

This time her smile is smaller. 'The perfection you're always

373

chasing, Mr da Silva – no amount of hard work will get you what you want. Trust me. I've worked very, very hard.'

She wheels towards the mirror, beginning to fix her make-up. It's a surprisingly intimate gesture for a woman I see as so put-together, and I'm sure it's very deliberate.

Mrs Hedgers catches my eye in the mirror. 'The ring Mr Townsend gave you. May I give you some advice about it?'

I watch my own expression shift ever so slightly in the mirror: eyes a fraction wider, eyebrows flinching. Today has been the strangest day. The hotel has been a meaningful part of my life since my very first shift here, but this winter it seems to have woven itself through every element of me – I am hardly surprised to find yet another guest involving themselves in my personal life. Perhaps because I've spent all winter involving myself in theirs.

'A ring can make a good thing stronger and a bad thing weaker. You need to be as whole as you can be before you put one on your finger. So all I'd say is ... don't ask the question until you feel sure of her answer.'

This is precisely how I described my ideal proposal when I first spoke about marriage with Izzy all those weeks ago, under the fairy lights: I thought I would ask the love of my life to marry me, and I'd know she would say yes. But Mrs Hedgers is right to suspect that I'm running away with myself. Since yesterday, my mind has been playing out the future, already thinking of all the ways I could lose her, and suddenly the idea of securing Izzy Jenkins in marriage is extremely appealing. I want her to be *mine* before she realises she's far too good to be.

I'd considered this February, when we go to Brazil together. Or summer at the latest.

'When you know she loves you, and you trust it – ask her then. That's my opinion,' Mrs Hedgers says, flashing me a freshly lipsticked smile. 'For what it's worth. Which, by the way, is a lot. Hard work doesn't get you everything, but it does help with the pay cheques, I find. Now, I must go and find my better half, and then I must thank the man who has saved my Christmas.' She swallows. 'Please remind me that there is no shame in accepting help.'

'There is no shame in accepting help.'

She nods, pulling her hair up and clipping it in place. 'Sometimes you do need someone else to say it,' she says. 'I don't know why, but you do. Right. Shall we?' She gestures towards the door.

Izzy

I'm dotted in face paint. The band is playing Harper Armwright's 'December Kisses', and a group of tipsy ladies are dancing an unrelated Scottish reel by the front desk; Charlie and Hiro are here, our very first success story of The Ring Thing, enjoying a glass of mulled wine by the fire with Mr Townsend. Arjun has finally stopped laughing about the fact that I'm now Lucas's girlfriend ('I am never going to let you live this down, Jenkins, you know that, right?') and has even taken a short break from the kitchen to enjoy the festivities.

I am full to the brim with happiness. For a bright, freedom-filled moment the future of the hotel doesn't seem to matter, because right now we're at our very best. Forest Manor Hotel is glowing with festive joy, and if you squint a bit, the sleet coming down outside the windows might even pass for snow.

And it's almost time for Lucas's Christmas present. Planned and pulled together late last night, in whispered phone calls taken while hiding in his bathroom, because until yesterday I was genuinely planning to buy him a lump of coal.

I just have one last thing to do before the clock strikes six, and it's going to be unpleasant, no matter how joyful the mood in here.

Last week, I decided that unfinished business is bad for the soul, so I offered Drew Bancroft a job.

Well, only three hours' work, making cocktails with Ollie. I'm not *that* nice. But I thought an olive branch was overdue, and I kept thinking of her Instagram post about how she couldn't find work. Before I knew it, I'd DMed her.

And now she's here, filling a punch bowl with eggnog in the orangery. She's rocking a serious-New-York-journalist kind of look which I can't help admiring. It's so weird seeing her in the hotel again. I hope this wasn't a terrible idea. I was feeling very secure and loved-up when I reached out, but now I'm remembering seeing Drew at the *last* Christmas party. Which was . . . awful.

I'm briefly waylaid greeting guests – the Jacobs, and Lucas's friend Pedro, and a couple of the temps I've worked with this year – so by the time I get to her, she's fully prepared to face me.

'Oh my God, *hi*,' she says, as if she had forgotten my existence until this very moment but is delighted to have been reminded. She reaches a long-nailed hand out to touch my arm across the bar. 'I appreciated you reaching out.'

And finding me some work, I wait for her to say. She doesn't.

'Hello, Drew,' I say, trying to sound olive-branchy. 'How are things?'

'Listen, I've been thinking,' she says, entirely ignoring the question. Drew has always worked to her own script. 'I want to tell you . . .' she pauses dramatically, 'that I forgive you.'

I stare at her. Beside her, Ollie freezes midway through zesting an orange, his eyes going wide.

'*You've* forgiven *me*?'

'For kicking me out the way you did.'

'For . . . Drew. I did not kick you out.' My heart is *pounding*. I think of all the times I bit my tongue with Drew and tried to be a 'good friend', and I think of all the times I snapped at Lucas about something meaningless, and I can't believe I got this so twisted. 'Let's recap: you knew how I felt about Lucas. You knew I wrote him that card. You kissed him under the mistletoe. I got upset. I asked you to give me the month's rent you owed me and move out by the end of January. And then you threw a bauble at my head and stropped off.'

She rolls her eyes, and suddenly she looks exactly like the woman I lived with last year, despite the new hair and glasses.

'Izzy, please. The bauble thing was an accident.'

'How?' I ask, genuinely bewildered.

'I think you need to let stuff go?'

'Right,' I say, because there is definitely some truth in this. I am a grudge-holder. I can be petty. I know this. It has caused me some bother this year. 'Well, if you say sorry, I am happy to let it go.'

'Say sorry?'

Ollie has stopped even pretending to make cocktails. He is just watching this unfold, half of a squished orange segment in his palm, a drop of juice trickling down to his elbow. Around us, the crowd mills and hums, and beyond them, the garden stretches out in frosty whites and greens through the orangery windows.

'Why would I say sorry when you were such a bitch about it?'

I take a deep breath, and I smile. My favourite smile, the one I reserve for the very worst guests.

There are times for olive branches, and then there are times for the sort of childish pettiness that a year of baiting Lucas has really helped me hone.

'Drew . . . you're fired,' I say.

Her mouth drops open. 'Excuse me?'

'Yes. You're fired. I am firing you. You need to leave now.'

Ollie's expression turns aghast, but he'll manage solo. He's good under pressure. He's also sensible enough not to object.

'This is three hours of bar work, cash in hand. You can't *fire* me. It's not a job.' She looks around, suddenly aware of the interest of the crowd around us.

My smile stays in place. 'If I could have fired you from being my friend, Drew, I'd have done it, but that's not a thing, so I'm taking what I can get.'

Then I catch the time on her watch: three minutes to six.

'Argh!' I jump.

Drew looks at me as though I am unhinged.

'Bye, Drew! Off you go! Have a nice life!' I say, spinning on my heels and sprinting away. I will not be wasting one more minute on Drew Bancroft – especially when I barely have one minute to spare.

I get to the lobby just in time. Dinah is wheeling the old projector in from the lost-property room, and up on the landing Kaz, Reese, Raheem and Helen throw white sheets over the bannisters so that when the projector starts up, the video should line up *just* right.

Well, we're out by about a metre. But it'll do!

'Surprise!' shout Lucas's family, their image projected on the sheets, just as I spin around to hear a different chorus of voices yell, 'Surprise!'

Lucas is standing in the doorway to the hotel, framed by Grigg, Sameera and Jem.

I can't compute it. They don't quite look real. But then they descend on me, burying me in one big hug, and behind us on the makeshift bedsheet screen the da Silvas are yelling *Feliz Natal!*

'Oh my God!' I say, emerging from the middle of the huddle and swiping my hair out of my face. 'How are you all here?'

'Lucas,' Jem says, wearing her widest, warmest smile.

Sameera tucks my hair behind my ears and kisses me on the forehead as my eyes fill with tears.

'You! You!' she says. 'Lying to all of us about where you were spending Christmas! This is not the time or place, but as soon as the festivities are over, I am going to have a right go at you. Oh, God, it's so good to see you!'

'Lucas told on me?' I say, wiping my eyes as Grigg pulls me in for another hug. 'You guys! You should be in the Outer Hebrides! And *you* should be in America!' I say to Jem.

'We fly back tonight,' Sameera tells me, grinning at Grigg. 'His mum would kill us if we missed Christmas lunch, and I can't be away from Rupe any longer or I will literally explode. But Jem is staying, right?'

'Absolutely,' Jem says. 'As soon as Lucas messaged me, I thought . . . What am I doing here, being told it's not too late for me to turn my life around, when I could be with people who love me *and* the life I've chosen? So Piddles and I jumped on the next flight.'

I squeeze her arm. I know that will have been a lot harder than she's making it sound. Behind her, Lucas's sister is yelling at him in fast Portuguese; Grigg and Sameera move aside so I can see Lucas's expression, and it's like going back in time and seeing what Lucas would have looked like as a little boy. His face has just *lit* up. Pure, stripped-back, childlike delight.

'Izzy!' Lucas's mum calls. 'Izzy, thank you for having us!'

'Oh my gosh, thank you for being here!' I shout up at the giant image hanging above the crowd, all of whom are staring at these goings-on with delight and/or bewilderment. 'With *very* little notice! I know the twenty-fourth is the big day over there, and you're right in the thick of Christmas, so thank you for taking the time.'

'Always, for Lucas,' she says, looking down at her son. 'Love you. Miss you.'

'*Saudade*,' Lucas says, and he holds his hand to his heart, where the word is tattooed on his skin. '*Tô com muita saudade.*'

'Tell them about the flights,' I say, coming to stand beside him.

'*Feliz Natal!*' shouts a little girl, popping up in the corner of the screen. One of the cousins, presumably, and totally adorable.

Lucas laughs. 'Helena! *Feliz Natal!*'

'What flights?' says Ana. She was the one who set this up for me – I found her on Instagram last night. She loved the idea. It was Ana who came up with using the bedsheets.

'We're coming home in February,' Lucas says, face breaking into another boyish grin.

'*We!*' Lucas's mother shrieks in delight.

Lucas laughs and takes my hand. 'Yes, both of us,' he says.

'That is, if you'll have me,' I add.

'We've wanted you since that first photo, *amiga*,' Ana says. 'Anyone who annoys Lucas that much belongs in this family.'

They stay for almost an hour. Helena and her brother learn how to say 'I want more sweeties' in English, thanks to the potentially quite dangerous influence of Ruby Hedgers, and Ruby learns how to say 'I want to go to Rio de Janeiro!' in Brazilian Portuguese, which might be a problem for Mr and Mrs Hedgers, given the cost of flights. But having the da Silvas hanging out over the party takes everything up a notch. By the time Arjun declares the evening buffet open, complete with an array of desserts in the orangery, everyone is very loud, very happy and – for the most part – very drunk.

'Your friend, she's so beautiful!' Pedro shouts at me as we dance.

He's here as a guest, but spent at least an hour helping Arjun in the kitchen, and doubled up as a magician for a while when our actual magician had to take a phone call. We are not afraid to call in a favour here at Forest Manor Hotel, and it turns out Lucas's friend is way too generous for his own good.

'Jem, you mean?'

I look back at her – she's dancing with a few of the women from housekeeping, eyes closed, hips swaying. She's in her favourite dress, the red velvet one with a sweetheart neckline, and her dark-brown skin is sprayed with fine gold glitter. All her piercings are gold today too, shining under the Christmas lights. She *does* look gorgeous.

Pedro is already angling to dance her way.

'Pedro sleeps with women and never calls them back,' Lucas says in my ear, dancing behind me. 'I'm sorry. I thought I should say.'

I laugh, turning to wind my arms around his neck so we can dance the way we did on that strange, snowy day in London.

'That won't work with Jem,' I say, half to Lucas, half to Pedro. 'She's demisexual. She has to form an emotional connection first – she would never sleep with a guy she's only just met.'

Pedro stares at me, abruptly abandoning his dance moves. 'Demi . . . sexual?'

'Uh-huh.'

'So she won't want to sleep with me?'

'Not unless you've built an emotional relationship, no.'

'*Emotional*?' Pedro says, looking positively panicked.

'It's nice, Pedro.' I'm trying not to laugh. 'You should try it some time.'

A tap on the shoulder distracts me from Pedro's wide, anxious eyes.

Ugh.

Louis Keele. I tighten my arm around Lucas's waist as we

both turn to look at him. Louis is wearing a casual smile, a crisp shirt, and a little too much cologne. I glance up at Lucas. *He's* wearing a familiar glower.

'Hey, you two, I was hoping to catch you,' Louis says. Very relaxed and friendly. No suggestion that last time he saw me he was viciously unpleasant, but I suspected he'd play it this way after his 'no hard feelings' text. 'I thought I should give you a heads up about my new investment,' he continues, his smile beginning to look more like a smirk. 'Only fair. An old schoolhouse in Fordingbridge came on to the market and I just . . . Well. I couldn't resist. It's going to make a beautiful hotel.'

'You . . . are opening a hotel?' Lucas says.

'Oh my God,' I say, before Louis can answer. 'Is that why you were asking so many questions about Forest Manor?' My voice rises. 'Were you *ever* considering actually investing? Or were you just trying to steal all our best ideas?'

'I was considering investing,' Louis says, extremely insincerely.

'You wanted to poach Arjun, didn't you?' I say, advancing on Louis with a pointing finger.

Lucas tightens his grip on me. 'Easy,' he says, but I can hear the smile in his voice.

'Who wouldn't want to poach Arjun?' Louis says. 'He's the best chef in the New Forest. He wouldn't budge, though. You lot really have your claws in him.'

'And what insults did you have for Arjun when you failed to seduce him?' Lucas asks politely. 'Is *he* a small, mousey nobody, too?'

Louis' eyes flick to mine. I smile, as if to say, *Yes, of course I told him everything. Yes, we are mutually deciding not to destroy you. No, I am not confident I can prevent him from breaking rank and beating you to a pulp if he so chooses.*

Louis swallows. 'Look, like I say, I just wanted to give you the heads up. There's a bit of competition on the horizon.'

I pull myself up as tall as I can, and only wobble slightly in the process – not bad three cocktails down.

'Well,' I say, in my sweetest voice. 'That won't be a problem. Lucas and I love a bit of competition.'

Lucas

'The thing about true love, right, is that sometimes you have to really push yourself out of your comfort zone to find it?' Ruby Hedgers tells me, from the top of the frame of a four-poster bed in one of the newly refurbished upstairs bedrooms (closed off to party guests, discovered by Ruby when the clock hit bedtime). 'Like, Hamza from my class at school fancied Sophie, and everyone said she was sooo out of his league, but then he gave her the cake his mum made him for his lunch and she said he could be her boyfriend.'

'Ruby,' I say, 'aren't you six?'

'Yes,' she says, with great solemnity. 'Yes I am.'

'Isn't that a bit young for boyfriends?'

'Totally,' she says, in the same tone. 'But Sophie doesn't know that. Which is lucky for Hamza.'

'There you are,' Mrs Hedgers says, entering the room behind me. 'Lovely to have your lifts back in order, Lucas. I particularly

386

enjoyed the slow jazz and gold-embossed wallpaper – hello, Ruby, I bet you can't climb down that post like a fireman's pole, can you?'

Ruby promptly begins climbing down to prove her mother wrong. I give Mrs Hedgers an impressed look, which she takes with the nod of a woman who knows her own talents.

'Lucas,' she says. 'There is a young couple trying to—'

'*There* you are,' says Izzy's friend Grigg, bursting into the room behind Mrs Hedgers. His wife Sameera runs in behind him, coming up short, slightly out of breath.

'Oh, look. Everyone has been looking for us,' Ruby says with delight, pausing mid descent.

'Lucas,' Grigg says.

I have never seen a man with such bulging bags under his eyes – but the eyes themselves are steady and kind. Grigg is one of those people who would manage to make something look crumpled even if it were very recently ironed, while his wife is just the opposite: she exudes the sort of effortless glamour that makes her stained white T-shirt look vaguely iconic.

'We don't want to bother Izzy, because she's talking to the project manager of the building team about a local property looking for someone to coordinate a redesign for them . . .'

He smiles as my eyebrows shoot up.

'But I think one of your colleagues may be having a minor panic attack in the swimming pool,' he finishes, and my eyebrows drop into a frown again.

Merda.

'Have you . . .'

'Go. I'll take it from here,' Mrs Hedgers says, as Ruby clings to the post of the bed like a koala, contemplating her path down.

I don't run, of course – that's against hotel policy. But I do walk very, very fast.

The swimming pool should be locked to guests today – much like the upstairs bedrooms. But when we get there, the door is ajar. Poor Mandy is sitting on the edge of the pool, trousers rolled up to the knees, feet dangling in, with Pedro and Jem on either side of her and a mobile phone in each of her hands.

'I just wonder if keeping all these expensive phones *directly* over a body of water might not be the smartest move, sweetie?' Jem is saying, reaching tentatively for the phone nearest her.

'Mandy?' I say.

Her head snaps up. Her eyes remind me of a horse that has been startled and is likely to stand on your foot.

'Lucas,' she breathes. 'There's just . . . so much to do. So many people.'

I look around. The spa area is an oasis of calm, the noise from the party a low background hum behind the sound of the water.

'Mandy . . . why do you have two phones?' I ask, approaching.

I catch Pedro's eye. He mouths *No sudden movements* at me in Portuguese.

'What? Oh.' Mandy looks from one to the other. 'I thought if I put Twitter on this one and Instagram on this one then all the notifications wouldn't be quite so overwhelming. But then I couldn't get Twitter *off* this one and Facebook wouldn't update on this one so now I've got everything everywhere and . . . it's just . . . so . . . *much*.'

'I'm thinking maybe you've had enough screen time . . . Mandy?' Jem says, looking at me for confirmation.

She eases the nearest phone from Mandy's hand and tosses it to me. I catch it. Thankfully. That was a very confident throw, and while I'm quite pleased that Jem rates my catching skills, I would also prefer her to never do that again, particularly this close to a swimming pool.

'Oh, wow,' Pedro says. He's bent over Poor Mandy's other phone while Mandy stares listlessly at the garden through the window opposite, eyes glazed. 'You guys have ninety thousand Instagram followers?'

'*What?*' I say, starting forward and crouching down beside him.

'Hashtag The Ring Thing,' Jem says, looking over Pedro's other shoulder.

I watch Pedro breathe in at her proximity and try not to smile. It looks like Pedro decided to introduce himself to Jem, then. Fascinating. I wonder if he has *ever* formed an emotional connection with a woman before. I am very much looking forward to my next morning coffee at Smooth Pedro's – there is almost too much to tease him about.

'Hashtag save Forest Manor Hotel. *Both* trending,' Jem says.

'You need to use hashtags,' Mandy says faintly. 'They're good for engagement.'

'This photo of you and Izzy arguing over a Tupperware box has two hundred thousand likes,' Pedro says, mouth hanging open.

'You need to add a personal touch,' Mandy says, in the same vacant tone. 'It makes your brand much more relatable.'

The last time I checked our social media profiles, they did not look like this.

'Mandy,' I say, 'when did this happen?'

'Oh, sort of all the time, really, over the last few weeks,' she says. 'The more pictures I posted about Izzy's Ring Thing, the bigger it got.'

Pedro swears. 'You have a direct message from someone with fifteen million followers here. And . . .'

'*There* you are,' Arjun says, barging into the spa with his chef's hat in hand and some tapenade on his forehead. 'There's a Harper Armwright outside the hotel with a six-piece band. What the fuck?'

'Oh, yes, Harper,' Poor Mandy says dreamily. 'She'll be here to collect her wedding ring.'

I've heard of Harper Armwright. She did a duet with Michael Bublé; Izzy has one of her old CDs in her box o'bits. But I'm not a fan, particularly – I would choose Los Hermanos over Harper Armwright any day.

And yet even I feel somewhat starstruck when I see her outside the hotel. She carries herself like she's special. It's in her every move: the slow turn of her head, the set of her shoulders, the thoughtlessness with which she leaves the car door for somebody else to close. And it's in the warm, well-practised smile she gives us, with an extra special moment of eye contact for

Sameera, who is hopping on the spot and whining *Oh my God it's Harper actual Armwright* under her breath.

'You must be Lucas,' Harper says to me, with a voice like honey. She holds out her hand for me to shake. 'One half of my Christmas miracle.'

We manage to smuggle her in under Izzy's woolly hat and a pair of sunglasses I keep in my glove box. It's her security team who draw attention. I glower at them when they refuse to look less conspicuous, and they glower right back. I have the vague sense that I may have found my people.

'I must have lost it when the paparazzi turned up – we left this place in such a hurry,' Harper says, sliding the ring slowly on to her finger and breathing out. 'All those years it was just sitting here? It's like . . . Wow.'

We're in the lost-property room. It seems to pale around Harper's glow. This woman belongs on stadium stages and in penthouse suites – as much as I am proud of Forest Manor Hotel, this is not the part of it I would most like her to see. Izzy shifts a couple of steps to her left, covering the sun-bleached section of wall where a large box sat for many years.

'My wife was gutted. She made it herself, did you know that? It's *completely* unique, and it slots perfectly beside hers.' She smiles down at the ring on her hand. 'When a friend sent her your Instagram post about this cute mission you're on? To return all those lost rings? And then you put up a pic of this one earlier today and I just thought, *No way*. But there it was.' She shakes her head in wonder. 'It's literally priceless, this ring.'

We all wait with bated breath. Mrs SB is gripping Barty's arm; Izzy has her bottom lip between her finger and thumb. Poor Mandy is staring at a fixed point on the wall, fingers tapping at her sides as though she is still subconsciously responding to direct messages.

Nobody has said the word *reward* yet. But everyone is thinking it.

We wait. Harper keeps smiling. One of her security guys checks his watch.

'Now, since I'm here,' Harper says, looking between us and dialling her smile up a notch, 'how about a little set?'

'A set! Right!' Mrs SB says brightly. 'Lovely.'

Izzy and I exchange a glance. *No* reward? But Harper Armwright must be worth about half a billion pounds.

Ollie!' Mrs SB calls suddenly.

I turn to see Ollie standing open-mouthed in the doorway.

'Is that . . .' he begins, voice hoarse.

'Yes, dear, Harper Armwright,' Mrs SB says briskly. 'I'm going to need you to help her get set up for a performance.'

'Per . . . formance . . .' Ollie whispers, clutching at the door frame, as though perhaps he might otherwise not be able to remain standing.

'My fans will be so excited – we'll do a reel, yeah?' Harper says to one of the members of her team, who nods enthusiastically, whipping her phone out. 'I've already told them how super-cute this place is. It'll be perfect. *So* Christmas.'

Barty's phone sings out the old Nokia theme tune. Harper

jumps slightly and then stares in fascination as he pulls out his 1990s mobile phone.

'Sorry,' Poor Mandy says, coming to life and snagging her glasses down from the top of her head. 'You told your fifteen million followers that our hotel is super-cute?'

'Yuh-huh,' Harper says, as she waits for her security guy to declare she's safe to leave our lost-property room. 'Can I get one of those?' she asks a member of her team, pointing to Barty's phone.

'Apparently our website has stopped working,' Barty says, phone still at his ear as the security guard looks left, right, left again, and then gestures Harper through after Ollie, who seems to have remembered how to be a functional human being.

We all turn to stare at Barty.

'It says there is "too much traffic". Apparently, we've had one hundred bookings in the last six minutes.'

Mrs SB lowers herself slowly on to a box. Harper beams around at us from the doorway.

'Oh, that's so nice!' she says, then waves goodbye over her shoulder, her hand just about visible behind the gigantic bald man in sunglasses who follows close behind her.

Slowly, as one, we turn to look at Poor Mandy. The lights on the tree shine through the door from the lobby, alternating red and green, flashing in Mandy's glasses.

'Sorry,' she says. 'You said do the social media. Did I go too far?'

'Mandy,' Mrs SB says, voice choked. 'Dearest Mandy. I am so sorry.'

Poor Mandy looks baffled as Mrs SB pulls her into a hug, and then Barty and Izzy join them, and then, because it's Christmas, and because Izzy loves me back, and because Mandy has just saved my job, I pile in too.

'What are you sorry for?' Mandy asks, from inside the hug.

'When someone doesn't value themselves, dear,' Mrs SB says, pulling back and wiping her face, 'it's far too easy to take their word for it. But you're absolutely *brilliant*. So brilliant, in fact, that you've saved Forest Manor Hotel from oblivion.'

'Oh, I'm *so* glad to have helped,' Mandy says, looking over-come. 'I did wonder . . . but I didn't want to get anyone's hopes up, and . . .' She breathes on her glasses and then wipes them on her reindeer jumper. 'Anyway, it was all Izzy and Lucas, really. It was all The Ring Thing. I just spread the word. I have to say, I'll be very glad to delete Twitter now,' she says, just as Mrs SB cuts in to say, 'I'll be promoting you to Head of Social Media Marketing with immediate effect!'

'Oh,' Poor Mandy says, looking stricken. 'Really?'

'Well, you have such a knack for this!' Mrs SB says, waving her phone.

'Right,' Poor Mandy says forlornly. Then, after a deep breath, she lifts her chin and says, 'Actually, I'd rather stay on reception, if I may.'

'Oh!' Mrs SB looks at Mandy with surprise. 'Yes! Of *course*.'

Mandy draws herself up. 'But I am very happy to train who-ever you recruit to work on our social media,' she says, voice wobbling slightly. 'And I look forward to the pay rise that will be forthcoming once the hotel is back on its feet in the new year.'

There is a shocked, admiring silence, and then, behind us, the lobby fills with cheers as Harper hits the opening notes of an acoustic 'December Kisses'. It feels like an appropriate response.

I don't think Mandy will be called *Poor Mandy* any longer. That name doesn't suit her at all.

Izzy snuggles into me, shifting up the bench. It's four in the morning, and we're in the pergola, lit by the fairy lights. The trees reach above us, their branches criss-crossing the star-sprayed sky. My muscles ache from hours of dancing on the lobby rug with Izzy in my arms.

'So, I guess ... Mandy won the bet,' Izzy says, resting her head against my shoulder. 'She found Harper.'

'Does that mean we both have to dress up as elves tomorrow?' I ask, kissing the top of Izzy's head.

'Yep,' Izzy says. 'Looks like it. Good old Mandy. I'm so proud of her.'

'We have not made Mandy's year easy,' I say.

'God, we were a nightmare, weren't we? Do you remember that week back in January when we refused to communicate directly, and she ended up as the go-between?'

I snort. 'Do you remember the time you moved the location of every single icon on my computer home screen and pretended the temp did it?'

'It *could* have been the temp.'

'Was it the temp?'

Izzy waves a hand, as if this is beside the point. 'Do you

remember the time you told Arjun that I thought his mousse was too floofy?'

'You did say that,' I point out.

'Not *to Arjun.*'

'Do you remember the time you glued my mouse to the desk?'

'That was actually an accident,' Izzy says, grinning.

'Do you remember the time we almost kissed in the pool?' I say, my voice quieter now.

'Do you remember the time I chased you down at the airport?' she says, her voice dropping too, her fingers winding between mine.

'Do you remember the time I let you win at poker?' I whisper.

She gasps, spinning in my arms to look at me. 'You did *not.*'

I'm laughing now.

'Lucas! That is honestly the worst thing you've ever done to me. Worse than pushing me into the swimming pool.'

'I did not push you into the swimming pool,' I say.

Then she gasps suddenly, raising a hand to her mouth. 'Oh, my God. I've just remembered.' She grips my arm. 'I put Christmas cracker jokes in all the guests' cards last year, didn't I?'

I smile. 'You did.'

'So the Christmas card you got from me . . . the one I wrote for Louis, the one you laughed at . . .' She covers her face with her hands.

'It said, *Why does Santa have three gardens? So he can "hoe hoe hoe"!*'

'Fucking hell,' she says between her fingers. 'I can't believe you even laughed at that, to be honest.'

'Well, I thought it was cute,' I say as she settles back against me. 'Remember, I liked you back then.'

I hold her as she laughs, looking up at the stars between the leaves. After a few moments, I start to smile. My eyes are adjusting to the darkness, and I can see what's growing in the branches above us.

'Izzy,' I whisper, and she lifts her face to mine. 'Look up.'

It takes her a moment too. She laughs.

'Shall I go get Drew, or . . .'

'Shut up, Izzy.'

She's still laughing when I lay her back across my lap and kiss her under the mistletoe.

December 2023

Izzy

'Good morning, Ms Jenkins. This is your four forty-five wake-up call.'

I squint at the time blinking on the hotel clock, shoving my new fringe out of my eyes and feeling blindly behind me. Nothing, just empty sheets. What the hell? Is he pranking me? This would not be the first time, but a wake-up call pre five a.m. is particularly cruel, even by our standards.

'Thanks,' I manage. '*Obrigada*. Did I . . . request this wake-up call? Like, did I ask you to call me?'

'I'm sorry,' the receptionist says, sounding a little stressed. 'I'm not sure I understand.'

'Don't worry about it,' I say, rubbing my eyes hard with my free hand and rolling over. 'Thanks. And happy New Year.'

I press the button by the side of the bed to lift the blinds, and there he is, being predictably ridiculous: my boyfriend. Doing push-ups on the hotel balcony before the sun is even up.

'What exactly am I doing out of bed at this hour?' I ask him as I slide the balcony door open.

Lucas looks up at me, a faint sheen of sweat on his forehead and chest. His gaze shifts up my bare legs to the sight of me in his white shirt from the night before, and his eyes smoulder. Even after twelve months, he just *melts* me when he looks at me like that. I scowl at him, like, *Don't distract me*, and he smirks, like, *I make no promises*.

'We're going swimming,' he says, standing up. He is already in his swim shorts.

'*Now*? No. That's disgusting,' I say, turning back towards the bed. 'Goodnight.'

I flop forwards on to the cool sheets of our king-size bed. He grabs me by the ankle and I shriek as he tugs me back.

'Come on,' he says. 'You will love it.'

'It's night time.'

'It is about to be daytime.'

I turn my head to look outside. With all the lights in our room turned off, I can see the sky turning from black to deep indigo; the sea is a shade paler, the sands ghostly white. The majestic Pão de Açúcar – Sugarloaf Mountain – is already visible, rising dark above the horizon. Excitement flutters in my stomach.

'Swimming like, in the sea? At sunrise?'

'Precisely,' Lucas says.

I spin just in time to catch my bikini when he throws it my way.

OK. Maybe I don't mind getting up early. We've splashed out on three nights at this luxury hotel in Rio de Janeiro for

New Year's, at the end of our Christmas with Lucas's mum in Niterói. Do I really want to spend any more of my hours here unconscious than absolutely necessary?

Once we're down in the lobby – with a wave for the receptionist – it's only a few steps from the hotel to the beach. The air is already warm with promise, as if the sun barely left last night, and as Lucas and I run to the water's edge the sand shifts feather-soft beneath my bare feet. Lucas goes under first. I swim hard to reach him, the seawater cool enough to make me suck in a breath. I lunge for Lucas just as he spins to lunge for me. We pull each other under, laughing, snorting, spluttering, and end up tangled up with my legs around his hips just as the sun begins to draw a single bright line on the horizon.

He kisses me hard. I realise he's shaking a little around me, his hands balled in fists – it must be cooler than I realised. I wrap my arms around the familiar solidity of his shoulders and kiss him back just as hard, my fingers in the short stubble of his hair, my knees tightening at his sides. We're kissing as if we're saying something we don't have words for. And that's what gives me the idea.

Because lately, when I feel like this – that there's no way to show him how much I love him, that there just aren't words or kisses fierce enough for this – a question pops into my head. And with the vast, beautiful sky turning pink around us, it suddenly feels like the perfect moment to ask it.

'Lucas,' I say, pulling back from him. 'Will you marry me?'

For a long moment, he just stares at me, the droplets on his skin catching silver-pink in the sunrise.

'Lucas?' I say after a moment, gripping his shoulders tighter. 'Should I not . . . Do you not . . .' I glance at the skyline. It's an artwork of pink and purple and orange. 'This just seemed like a totally perfect moment to propose.'

'I know,' Lucas says, voice catching slightly in his throat.

He shifts, one arm letting go of me in the water as he moves to show me something in his closed hand.

A ring.

I know that ring. It's Maisie Townsend's ring. My hand flies to my mouth.

I saw Mr Townsend just a couple of weeks ago, before we left for Brazil; I'm still working part-time at Forest Manor while I launch my business. We'd caught up over Arjun's new afternoon tea, and as I'd walked him back to his room, Mr Townsend had said something that now makes a lot more sense. *Have a good Christmas*, he'd said, and then, as the door was closing behind him, he'd added: *And happy New Year from Maisie and me.*

My knees go loose with shock, and I almost go under. I grab Lucas, spluttering, as he says, 'Why do you think you're in the sea for the sunrise?'

'Oh my God,' I say, clinging to him, reaching for the ring.

He closes his hand again.

'Izzy Jenkins,' he says, 'have you really just one-upped my proposal?'

I throw my head back and laugh.

'Do you know how much planning went into this? There is a picnic breakfast waiting for us on that beach. I had to bribe the receptionist to do a wake-up call – in English – because the hotel doesn't even offer them. I had to get this ring out of the hotel safe while you were brushing your teeth, and you *kept* wandering out of the bathroom.'

'Give me that ring!' I say, reaching for his hand.

'Do you even have a ring for me?' he asks, a smile tugging at the corner of his mouth as I try to peel back his fingers.

'Well, no,' I admit. 'It was kind of a spontaneous thing.'

'So . . . no ring,' he says, counting off on his other hand. 'No picnic breakfast waiting.'

'Great setting though,' I say, gesturing to the dramatic sky. 'You have to give me that.'

'One-all on setting,' he agrees.

'And a point to me for actually asking the question,' I add, still trying to open his hand. Even the man's fingers are ridiculously muscular – there's no budging him. 'You haven't technically asked me anything yet.'

'My apologies,' Lucas says, and he stills my hand with his, catching my gaze. 'Izzy,' he says, and now I'm not laughing. 'Izzy Jenkins. My love for you grows stronger every day. I want for ever with you. I want to find out how big and bright this love will be when we're old and grey.'

His bottom lip trembles ever so slightly. I've long since learned that I was wrong to think of Lucas's expression as implacable: the emotion is always there if you look closely enough.

'I've known I'll ask you to marry me since that moment at the airport last Christmas, but I wanted to wait until I truly believed enough of myself to trust that you would say yes. I still think this isn't a question you should ask because you need to know the answer.'

'Oh my God,' I say, beginning to cry.

Lucas's hand tightens over mine, and then he extracts his fist, unfolding his fingers and holding the ring out to me over the water.

'Mr Townsend gave me this ring to give to you when the time was right. He knew you had lost a ring that mattered to you, and he wanted to start a new story for you with this one. I wish I could have found the ring your father gave you. But I think this one holds its spirit, maybe.' He smiles. 'There's something I would have never said before I met you.'

I'm all tears and seawater. I swipe at my cheeks with trembling hands.

'Izzy, will you accept this ring, and do me the honour of becoming my wife?'

'Yes. Yes.' I sob as he slides the ring on to my finger. 'Oh, my God. I can't believe . . .' I clench my fist. 'Let's get out of the sea. I am *not* losing this one.'

Lucas laughs. I love that laugh – it's his lightest one, unselfconscious and full. I want to make him laugh like that a hundred times a day for ever.

'OK, so now I have asked the question . . .' he says.

I grab his hand as we find our footing on the sand and begin to walk to the shore. Rio de Janeiro stretches before us, waking up, if it ever truly slept. Apartment windows blink bright in the sunlight, and the fierce blue mountains rise behind it all, just waiting for us to explore them.

'Yes,' I say, looking over at the man I hated, the man I love, the man who makes me burn my brightest.

'I win? At proposing? I win this one?'

I laugh. 'You win this one,' I say, and he scoops me up in his arms, whooping, dancing up the beach.

I feel the ring pressing into my palm, carrying so much within it. I'm crying, laughing, clinging to Lucas as the December sky lightens above us. What an honour to wear this ring. And what an honour to call this difficult, wonderful, obstinate, generous man mine.

Acknowledgements

This is a book I wasn't supposed to write – I had no publication scheduled for 2023. Essentially, *The Wake-Up Call* was created through the sheer stubbornness of Izzy and Lucas, who refused to shut up even when I told them to. Now that you've read the book, this probably won't surprise you.

A lot of brilliant people came together to bring this story out into the world, people who said, *sure, that wasn't the plan, but let's do it anyway*. I'm grateful to be surrounded by such innovative and creative talents.

Tanera Simons, my partner in crime (or should that be partner in rom-com?): thank you, as always, for your patience, care and clear-headedness. You're a wonder. Cassie Browne, Emma Capron, Kat Burdon, Cindy Hwang, my super-creative editors: thank you for giving me the nudge I needed to let this book fly, and for all your help shaping the story. Helena Mayrink: thank you so much for your brilliant insights, ideas and support on the Brazilian aspects of this novel, as well as all the Portuguese translations, and thanks also to Pedro Staite for your help – and for letting me borrow your name!

Jon Butler, Stef Bierwerth, Hannah Winter, Ellie Nightingale, Ella Patel, Hannah Robinson, Angela Kim, Hannah Engler, Lauren Burnstein, Tina Joell, Chelsea Pascoe and everyone at Quercus and Berkley: thank you for all your creativity, passion and hard work. To Georgia Fuller, Mary Darby, Salma Zarugh, Kira Walker, Sheila David and all at Darley Anderson Agency: thank you so much for continuing to share my books with people around the world.

Thank you to my parents for all the sage advice while I navigated writing this book. Thank you to Gilly McAllister for too many things to name, but primarily for being the other (better) half of my brain. Thank you to Caroline Hulse and Lia Louis for listening to many rants and providing much wisdom. To my sister, Ellen: thank you for being my rock.

Sam, my love. Thank you for treating these stories of mine with such respect – so much so that you took a pause in your career so that I could tend to mine. You are a rare, extraordinary man, and the most wonderful father. To my little bug: thank you for filling my life with the purest, brightest, most profound joy.

Lisa, Lucy, Beth, Hannah, Rhianna, Kate, Carly, Alison, and all the amazing team at my son's nursery: thank you for looking after my little boy with such love and care while I am writing these stories. Without you, this book would not exist.

Finally, dearest, dearest readers . . . I dedicated this book to you, which perhaps feels a bit redundant (I mean, of course the book is for my readers) – but I felt it needed saying for this one. I will never stop feeling lucky to do this job, and I only get to do it because you read the stories I write. Thank you for the faith you put in me every time you pick up one of my books. I mean it – I truly treasure you.